22/12/16

12/2/16

KT-430-782

This book should be returned/renewed by the latest date shown above. Overdue items incur charges which prevent self-service renewals. Please contact the library.

Wandsworth Libraries
24 hour Renewal Hotline
01159 293388
www.wandsworth.gov.uk

Wandsworth

GRAHAM MASTERTON trained as a newspaper
reporter before beginning a career as an author.
After twenty-five years writing horror and thrillers,
Graham turned his talent to crimewriting. The first
book in the Katie Maguire Series, *White Bones*, was
published by Head of Zeus in 2012 and became
a top-ten bestseller. The series was inspired by
Graham's five-year stay in County Cork.

THE KATIE MAGUIRE SERIES

White Bones

Broken Angels

Red Light

Taken For Dead

Blood Sisters

Buried

GRAHAM
MASTERTON

BLOOD
SISTERS

HEAD
of ZEUS

First published in the UK in 2015 by Head of Zeus Ltd
This paperback edition first published in 2016 by Head of Zeus Ltd

9 7 5 3 1 2 4 6 8

A catalogue record for this book is available
from the British Library.

Paperback ISBN 9781784081355
Ebook ISBN 9781784081324

Typeset by Ben Cracknell Studios, Norwich.

Printed in the UK by Clays Ltd, St Ives Plc

Head of Zeus Ltd
Clerkenwell House
45–47 Clerkenwell Green
London EC1R 0HT

WWW.HEADOFZEUS.COM

For my mother, Mary, without whom
this child would not have been born

Is minic a rinne bromach gioblach capall
Irish saying: 'A raggy colt often made a powerful horse'

One

'Did you hear that?' said Cliodhna.

'What?' said Brian. He was turning around and around in circles, trying to see where their Irish wolfhound Christy had gone. They were high on the cliffs near Nohaval Cove. A strong blustery breeze was blowing and granite-grey clouds were tumbling in towards them from the south-west, trailing sheets of rain beneath them.

'I'm sure I can hear someone screaming,' said Cliodhna. She pushed back the hood of her red waterproof jacket so that her blonde hair flew up. 'It sounds like it's coming from down there, on the beach.'

Brian stopped circling and listened. 'Nah,' he said, after a while. 'I don't hear nothing.'

'I could have sworn it was someone screaming.'

'*Christy*!' Brian shouted. 'Where the feck are you, you stupid gobdaw!'

'You shouldn't talk to him like that, Brian,' Cliodhna protested.

'Why? He's not going to start talking like that himself, is he?'

'No, but it's disrespectful. He's one of God's creations, just like us.'

Brian was just about to shout '*Christy*!' again when the wind dropped for a moment and he heard a hoarse, high-pitched shriek from somewhere below them. It reminded him of the appalling cry that a fellow bus driver had made when he had been crushed against the wall of Capwell Bus Depot by a reversing 214. It was a cry of agony and spiritual hopelessness, the cry of somebody who knows they are so severely injured that they are inevitably going to die.

'Mother of God,' he said. He ventured to the edge of the cliff, as near to the edge as he dared, with the long grass lashing against his legs. There was a small beach below, but the cliff overhung it so much that it was out of sight. All he could see were the jagged black rocks and the sea foaming between them as the tide came in. The sea itself was a dark, poisonous green.

'That's never Christy, is it?' said Cliodhna. 'Don't tell me he fell off the cliff.'

Brian came away from the edge, shaking his head. 'No. No, I wouldn't say so. It doesn't sound like Christy at all. More like a man, I'd say. I'd better go down and take a look.'

'Maybe we should call for an ambulance. I mean it sounds like he's hurt, doesn't it?'

'Well, just let me take a sconce first. I doubt you'll be getting a signal out here, anyway.'

Brian made his way back until he reached a narrow gully between two massive serrated rocks. It had been a few years since he had climbed down there himself, but it looked as if people were still using the same steep path to reach the beach. There was even an empty Sanor bottle wedged in a cleft in one of the rocks.

As he started to slither downwards, clinging on to gorse bushes and clumps of grass to stop himself from losing his footing, he heard the scream again – harsh and throaty and filled with despair. He turned and looked back at Cliodhna. She had her hand pressed over her mouth, as if she wanted to call him back but knew that he had to go on.

The clouds had rolled over now and blotted out the sun, and the first few spots of rain began to fall. Brian edged his way around an overhanging rock, but then the path dropped so steeply that he was forced to face the cliff and climb down backwards, as if he were going down a ladder.

When the path levelled out more, he was able to turn around, and for the first time he could see the beach. It was a V-shaped cove, no more than sixty or seventy metres across. Its sharply pointed rocks looked as if they had been deliberately embedded in the sand to repel invaders.

Now, however, only the tips of the rocks were visible, because the whole beach was heaped with the bodies of dead horses. Brian couldn't even count how many. Most of them were brown and bloated, though others had rotted until they were no more than sacks of hairy skin with bones protruding from them. He could see hooves and manes and tangled tails. There was surprisingly little smell, but then it was winter and the cold sea must have washed over them with every tide.

He didn't climb down any further, but took his iPhone out of the pocket of his windcheater and took six or seven pictures.

'Brian!' called Cliodhna. 'Brian, are you all right? Christy's not down there, is he?'

'No. No, he's not. I'm coming back up!'

Brian had just started to climb back up to the top of the cliff when there was yet another scream, so loud and so close that he jerked back in shock, his boots scrabbling on the rock as he tried to stop himself from sliding all the way down to the beach.

He turned around again and saw that one of the horses had lifted its head, and was staring at him with one bloodshot eye. It let out a low squeal like deflating bagpipes, and then its head dropped back down again. *Jesus*, thought Brian. *The poor creature's still alive. What in the name of all that's holy am I going to do now?*

He struggled his way back up. By the time he reached the top of the cliff it was raining hard. Cliodhna was standing with her hood up and her shoulders hunched.

'What's wrong?' she said, when she saw the look on Brian's face. 'What's down there?'

'Horses,' he told her. He took out his iPhone again to see if there was a signal, but he knew it was hopeless. They would have to drive to the nearest house and phone the emergency services from there.

3

'Horses?' said Cliodhna. 'What do you mean, horses?'

'Horses. A whole hape of horses. All of them dead, of course, except the one that's screaming like that.'

'What are you going to do?'

'Call for a vet, of course. They'll have to put it down, won't they? I can't give a fecking horse the kiss of life.'

He looked around, one hand raised to shield his eyes from the rain. 'Where's that Christy? I could take a stick to that fecking dog sometimes!'

'I'll stay here if you want to go and make a phone call,' said Cliodhna, and as if to emphasize the urgency of their situation the horse screamed yet again. Perhaps it was the echo from the cliffs, but it sounded the same as when Brian had first heard it, like a man screaming.

'Okay,' he said. 'But stay here, all right, and don't go too close to the edge there. You won't be able to see anything and I don't want you ending up with all of them horses.'

He started walking towards the corner of the brown ploughed fields where he had left his Volvo estate. As he came closer to it, he saw that Christy was sitting next to it, grey and bedraggled and soaking wet, with his tongue hanging out. When he saw Brian, he stood up and shook himself, but stayed where he was, as if he all he wanted to do was get into the car and go home.

Brian stopped and stuck two fingers in his mouth to give Cliodhna a piercing whistle, and beckoned her to come and join him.

He turned back to Christy, who made a strange, creaking noise in the back of his throat. Brian thought, *You don't like this place, do you, boy? You know that something fierce terrible has happened here. Seems like you're not at all the gobdaw I thought you were.*

4

Two

When Katie came out of the small toilet at the side of her office she found Detective Inspector O'Rourke standing beside her desk, holding a blue manila folder.

'Oh, Francis,' she said. 'I'm sorry if I've kept you waiting.'

'Not a bother, ma'am,' said Detective Inspector O'Rourke. Then, 'Are you all right, ma'am? You're looking a little shook, if you don't mind my saying so.'

Katie did her best to tidy her hair with her fingers and tug her jacket straight. 'I'm grand altogether, Francis, thanks. We went for a curry last night and I think I must have eaten a bad prawn.'

'Look, I won't tell you about the last time *I* had a curry,' smiled Detective Inspector O'Rourke. 'My friends and family didn't have sight of me for a day or three, that's all I can say.'

Katie sat down and said, 'What do you have there?'

'These? Oh, these are the figures you asked for on immigrant convictions. Sorry they took so long. But we've just had a call in from the Mount Hill Nursing Home in Montenotte. One of their residents has been found deceased and the doctor who examined her says there could be suspicious circumstances.'

Katie felt her stomach tighten again. She closed her eyes and pressed her hand over her mouth and wondered if she needed to go back to the toilet, but after a few moments the nausea subsided, although she felt both chilly and sweaty.

'You're *sure* you're okay, ma'am?' said Detective Inspector O'Rourke, cocking his head sympathetically to one side.

'Yes, I'm fine. I'll get over it. Who's the deceased?'

'Female, aged eighty-three. Found in her bed this morning by nursing staff. They assumed at first it was natural causes. Well, it's a retirement home, like, so of course their residents are deceasing on a pretty regular basis.'

'So what led the doctor to think her death might be suspicious?'

'Well, he was called to certify that she had passed away. But when he gave her a brief examination he discovered that a foreign object had been inserted into her.'

'A foreign object? What kind of a foreign object?'

Detective Inspector O'Rourke ran his finger around his shirt collar, as if he were finding this difficult to say.

'It was a figurine, like,' said Detective Inspector O'Rourke. 'The Blessed Virgin, as a matter of fact. The doctor extricated it, out of respect, but apart from that he hasn't touched the victim in any way at all.'

'She had a figurine of the Virgin Mary inside her?'

'Somewhat sacrilegious, like, but yes. Detective Sergeant Ni Nuallán and Detective O'Donovan will be on their way up there to talk to the manager and the nursing staff, and I've advised the Technical Bureau, too. Sergeant Ni Nuallán has notified the coroner's office, of course.'

'Do we know who she was, the deceased?' asked Katie.

'She hasn't been formally identified yet, but apparently she was Sister Bridget Healy, late of the Bon Sauveur Convent at Saint Luke's Cross.'

'That name rings a bell,' said Katie. 'Why does that name ring a bell?'

'I have no idea at all, ma'am,' said Detective Inspector O'Rourke. 'I don't generally have much to do with nuns.'

Katie stood up. 'I think I'll go up there myself, just to get a sense of this. Why don't you come with me?'

'Of course,' said Detective Inspector O'Rourke. Then, 'There's something about this that's making your nostrils twitch, isn't there, ma'am?'

'Whenever I hear "suspicious death" and "convent" in the same sentence, Francis, I always catch the reek of something rotten. Maybe I'm wrong in this case, but I'd like to go up there and have a sniff around.'

'Whatever you say, ma'am. Here.' Detective Inspector O'Rourke handed her the folder that he had brought in. He had been appointed here to Anglesea Street Garda station only seven weeks ago, and Katie was beginning to trust him and rely on him. He was short and stocky, with chestnut hair that was shaved short at the sides, so that his crimson ears stuck out, but wavy on top. His face was round, with a blob of a nose, and he had very pale-green eyes, with eyebrows that appeared to be permanently raised, as if he were pleasantly surprised at something that he had just found out. He looked more like somebody's good-natured uncle than a Garda inspector, but Katie had soon come to realize that he was astute, and a good judge of character, and extremely tough-minded.

She had met his wife, Maeve, too, and she seemed to be equally tough-minded. Katie would have found it difficult to pick the odds between them if it came to a domestic fight.

He tapped the folder with his finger. 'Eight per cent less immigrants were successfully prosecuted over the last six months,' he told her. 'Thirteen per cent less illegal immigrants were deported. Just thought you'd like to have confirmation that we're fighting a losing battle.'

'Don't I know it,' said Katie. 'Anyway, we're having a meeting with Nasc tomorrow afternoon about immigrant crime and we can discuss it then. There's still too many saintly do-gooders who think that expelling an immigrant for rape or robbery is the same as transportation to Australia back in the famine days. 'The Fields of Athenry' and all that.'

Detective Inspector O'Rourke pulled a face. 'Myself, I can't see much of a parallel between Michael stealing Trevelyan's corn to feed his starving children and Bootaan stabbing a pregnant woman in broad daylight because she wouldn't hand over her moby.'

Katie went over to the coat stand and took down her dark-maroon duffel coat. She wondered for a moment if she ought to go back to the toilet, but her stomach seemed to have settled now. She had been taking vitamin B6 capsules and drinking ginger tea, and she certainly wasn't suffering as much sickness as she had with Seamus, God rest his tiny soul.

* * *

Montenotte was on the steep north side of the city and on clear days the Mount Hill Nursing Home enjoyed a panoramic view of the River Lee below and the city centre and the hazy green hills beyond it. This morning was foggy and cold as a graveyard, but the fog was gilded with sunlight and Katie expected that it would soon evaporate.

The nursing home had been converted from a convent built in the 1880s for the care of the poor and the elderly. Its grey-painted frontage was over eighty metres long and three storeys high, with dormer windows in its dark slate roof. Two Garda patrol cars were parked outside, as well as a white van from the Technical Bureau and an ambulance.

As they turned into the car park from the Middle Glanmire Road, Katie was relieved to see no TV vans and no reporters' vehicles that she recognized. She wasn't in the mood for fielding questions about the suspicious death of an elderly sister from the Bon Sauveur.

Detective Sergeant Ni Nuallán was waiting for Katie and Detective Inspector O'Rourke on the front steps. She had grown her blonde hair longer and pinned it up into a pleat, and she was wearing a short-belted navy-blue cashmere overcoat. She was puffy-eyed and wearing no make-up, but she still looked pretty.

'There's not much to see here, ma'am,' she said. 'Just an old dead woman and a whole lot of other old folks who'll soon be going upstairs after her.'

'Your coat's only massive, Kyna,' said Katie, laying a hand on her shoulder. 'I could do with a coat like that myself.'

'Oh, thanks. It's only Marks and Spencer's but they were knocking off thirty-five euros and how could I say no to that, like?'

'Have you talked to the staff yet?'

Detective Sergeant Ni Nuallán took out her notebook. 'I've had a word with the manager, Noel Pardoe, and Nevina Cormack, who's the director of nursing. Also Dr McNally, who was first called when Sister Bridget was found, but he's had to leave to see a patient. He's given me his mobile number, though, in case.'

She pushed open the heavy, varnished oak doors that led into the care home's vestibule and Katie and Detective Inspector O'Rourke followed her inside. A flustered-looking man in a sagging brown tweed jacket was standing by the reception desk, talking to the iron-haired receptionist. He was bulky and untidy, with his tie crooked and his white shirt gaping to show his belly. His hair was the colour and texture of Shredded Wheat and his skin was still faintly orange from a summer holiday suntan.

'Mr Pardoe, this is Detective Superintendent Maguire and this is Detective Inspector O'Rourke,' said Kyna.

Noel Pardoe held out a pudgy hand with a gold signet ring. 'Well, well. Detective Superintendent, is it? I wouldn't have thought that Sister Bridget's passing was sufficiently mysterious to bring out the top brass.'

Katie ignored his hand and gave him the briefest of smiles. 'Every suspicious death merits my attention, Mr Pardoe, even if I don't always show up in person.'

'Of course. I didn't mean to suggest that you wouldn't be giving this matter your fullest attention. I'm quite sure you will. But in spite of the one unusual aspect of Sister Bridget's demise . . .'

'You mean the figurine?'

'Well, yes, the figurine,' said Noel Pardoe, licking his lips as if the word "figurine" actually tasted unpleasant. 'Regardless of that, you have to understand that our nursing staff give our guests the most meticulous care and attention, and it would surprise me hugely to discover that Sister Bridget passed away from anything other than natural causes. She had a weak heart,

9

and liver problems, as I explained to your sergeant here, and none of us expected her to be with us on this Earth for very much longer, God bless her.'

Katie said, 'Let's leave the cause of death to the coroner, shall we? I'd like to see her now, if I may.'

'Of course. Not a problem. Your technical people are up there now.'

'I'd also like a word with your director of nursing after.'

'Yes, of course. I'll tell Nevina that you're here.'

He led them across the vestibule to the lift. The four of them crowded into it and stood facing each other in awkward silence as it took them up to the third storey. They walked in single file along the corridor and Noel Pardoe's left shoe creaked on the parquet flooring like a duck quacking.

'I'll leave you to it, then,' he said, as if he couldn't get away fast enough. 'I'll see you downstairs after, when you're finished.'

Sister Bridget's room overlooked the gardens at the back of the nursing home, with a view of rusty-coloured trees and a rockery where a painted statue of the Virgin stood with the Infant Jesus in her arms. Katie thought she looked as if she were waiting for a bus.

Bill Phinner, the chief forensic officer, was standing beside the high, hospital-type bed, while a young female technician was down on her hands and knees with a small hand-held vacuum cleaner, taking samples from the mottled-green carpet. Another technician was dusting the bedside cabinet for fingerprints. Bill Phinner was lean, with swept-back grey hair, and was almost as hollow-cheeked and cadaverous as the victims he was called to examine.

'Good morning to you, ma'am,' he said to Katie, without looking at her.

'What's the story, Bill?' said Katie. The room was uncomfortably hot and she unfastened the toggles of her duffel coat.

Against the left-hand wall stood a tall mahogany cabinet crowded with books, most of them Bibles or lives of the saints, as well as a variety of religious ornaments and statuettes. The most outstanding was a monstrance – a stand supporting a gilded metal sunburst with a circular crystal in the middle to display a communion wafer, the body of Christ. There was also a purple crystal rosary and a plaster figure of Saint Francis with his arms outspread, surrounded by birds and rabbits. One of the rabbits had its head broken off.

On top of the folded-up blankets at the foot of the bed, sealed in a vinyl evidence bag, lay the pale-blue figurine of the Virgin that the doctor had removed from Sister Bridget. She was staring up through the plastic with a serene expression on her medicine-pink face.

Katie approached the bed and looked down at Sister Bridget. She was a hawk-like woman with a large curved nose, a sharply pointed chin and a tightly pinched-in mouth. Her hooded eyes were half-open, as if she were still dozing, but Katie could see that the whites of her eyes were spotted with lesions that looked like tiny red tadpoles.

'Petechial haemorrhages of the conjunctiva,' Bill intoned in his dry, abrasive voice. 'I'd say that she was smothered with her own pillow.'

'So, not natural causes?'

'Oh, not a chance. Asphyxiation, no doubt of it.'

'And what about the figurine?'

'It's the Immaculate Heart of Mary. A good-quality resin and stone statuette, hand-painted, twenty-five point five centimetres high, suitable for use both indoors and out. It has a maker's mark on the base – Pilgrim Fine Editions – so we may be able to trace where it was purchased. I'd say it easily cost close to three hundred euros, maybe more.'

'Any prints on it?'

'A few smudgy partials, but when we take it back to the lab there's a good chance that we can enhance them.'

'And when was it inserted?' asked Katie. 'Before or after she was suffocated?'

Bill lifted up Sister Bridget's ankle-length brushed-cotton nightgown. She was skeletally thin, with patches of dry skin and purple blotches that were consistent with liver disease. Her left breast was smudged with a large crimson bruise, half-moon shaped, as if her assailant had forced her down on to the bed with the heel of a hand. There were even more bruises on her stomach and the insides of her skinny thighs. Her grey-haired vagina was gaping and between her legs her nightgown was stained with a wide brown patch of dried blood.

The technician who had been collecting particles from the carpet switched off her vacuum cleaner and stood up, so that apart from the crinkly sound of her oversized Tyvek suit, the bedroom was silent. Bill continued to hold up Sister Bridget's nightgown for a few moments and then carefully and respectfully covered her up again. He didn't have to say anything. Katie knew that if Sister Bridget had bled when she was assaulted, her heart had still been beating.

Three

They went back down to the vestibule, where Noel Pardoe was waiting with Nevina Cormack. The director of nursing was a short woman with thick-rimmed spectacles and a severe black bob with streaks of grey in it, cut high at the back of her neck. She was wearing a nubbly grey cardigan which looked as if she had knitted it herself, and as she came forward to introduce herself, Katie could smell a strong musky perfume that didn't seem to sit with her skin type at all.

'I'm sorry to confirm that Sister Bridget was deliberately suffocated,' said Katie.

'Oh. So she *didn't* pass from natural causes?' asked Nevina. 'She wasn't at all well, you know.'

'No, I'm afraid not. She was physically assaulted and then asphyxiated with her pillow.'

Nevina crossed herself. 'That's awful!. I can't imagine who might have done such a thing! I told your sergeant here that she had no visitors this morning and we saw nobody suspicious at all around the premises.'

'Was Sister Bridget well liked here?' Katie asked her.

'Oh yes. Absolutely. She had her ways, of course. Most elderly people do. But she wasn't *dis*liked, let me say that.'

'Please, she's gone now,' said Katie. 'No matter what you say about her, you can't hurt her, and if we're going to find out who killed her, it's very important that you tell me the truth.'

Nevina glanced across at Noel. He made a face at her and shrugged, as if to say that she ought to be candid.

'To be honest with you,' she said, 'she *was* inclined to be a little *haughty*.'

'Haughty?'

'Well, a lot of the time she forgot that she wasn't running the Bon Sauveur Convent any more, and she seemed to believe that she was in charge of the whole nursing home. Our nurses were very patient with her, but she expected them to wait on her hand and foot, like, and never gave them a single word of thanks. There was one of our gentleman residents, too, and they were always arguing because she kept sitting in his chair in the TV room.'

'We'll have to have a word this gentleman,' said Katie. 'But it doesn't sound as if anyone here bore enough of a grudge against Sister Bridget to suffocate her.'

'We try to encourage a family atmosphere here,' said Nevina. 'Like I say, many of the residents do have their ways, and some of them are not aware of where they are, or even *who* they are, God protect them. But I certainly can't see any of them doing what was done to Sister Bridget.'

She stood there twitchily for a moment, squeezing and unsqueezing her fists. 'If that's all, then?' she said. 'It'll be lunchtime soon and I have so much to be getting on with.'

'Oh yes, please, carry on,' Katie told her. 'We may need to talk to you again, but that'll do for the moment. We'll be removing Sister Bridget's body in a short while and taking her to the University Hospital for an autopsy. We'll keep in touch with you so that you can inform any relatives or friends she may have had.'

'Not that I know of,' said Nevina. 'She told me once that all of her brothers and sisters and cousins had died and she was alone in the world.'

Katie and Detective Inspector O'Rourke and Detective Sergeant Ni Nuallán went outside, and Detective O'Donovan came out to join them. The fog had lifted now and the wet car park was dazzling, so Katie put on her round-lensed sunglasses.

'I've questioned almost all of the residents now, ma'am,' said Detective O'Donovan. 'About a third of them make some sort of sense, but like Nevina said, the rest of them don't know one end of a knife from the other.'

'Maybe one of them could have suffered some kind of psychotic episode?' Katie suggested.

'Theoretically, like, I suppose it's possible. But none of them that I've interviewed so far would have had the physical strength to hold Sister Bridget down and spifflicate her, even though she was so old and feeble. Most of them couldn't wave their arms to swat a wazzer.'

'What about visitors, or intruders?' asked Detective Inspector O'Rourke.

'Nobody saw anybody coming to see Sister Bridget this morning,' said Detective Sergeant Ni Nuallan. 'In any case, they don't usually allow visitors until the residents have had their lunch, which is about twelve. If they get too excited or upset it puts them off their food. There's a CCTV recording from the reception area, though, and we'll be running through that. The only other access into the building is through the garden gate, and that's always kept locked to stop the residents from wandering off.'

'Do you think the motive was sexual?' said Katie, as she walked back towards her car.

Detective Inspector O'Rourke shook his head. 'I wouldn't have thought so. I mean, I've come across a few cases where sexual predators have a taste for ladies of a certain age, and more than a few cases where priests have taken advantage of elderly nuns. It could be a bit of both, admittedly, but that figurine – that definitely leads me to think that the motive was more religious than sexual.'

'I agree,' said Detective Sergeant Ni Nuallán. 'It's like a deliberate blasphemy. Like, your religion hurt me so I'm going to use your religion to hurt you back.'

'You might be on the right track,' said Katie. 'It's conceivable, of course, that the offender could have been nothing more than a header. On the other hand, it does seem more likely that somebody wanted to take their revenge on Sister Bridget, for some grievance or other.'

She paused. 'Maybe they weren't looking for revenge on Sister Bridget herself – not personally, like – but on the nuns of Bon Sauveur, or nuns in general. When you think of those priests who were murdered in revenge for abusing young boys – '

She opened her car door and said, 'Kyna, why don't you go up to the Bon Sauveur Convent and ask a few questions about Sister Bridget? I doubt if there's anybody still there who knew her, but she might still have a reputation. There might be stories about her, and there must be records.'

'Okay,' said Detective Sergeant Ni Nuallán. 'I'll get up there directly. It'll only take us another half-hour to finish off our interviews with all of the residents here. Especially the chair fellow. I can remember how my grandpa used to get pure tick if anybody sat in his favourite seat.'

'Fair play,' said Katie. 'People have been killed for less than that, after all.'

* * *

She returned to the station and put on the electric kettle in her office to brew herself a mug of ginger tea. As she poured the boiling water into it, her iPhone pinged. It was a text message from John, asking her if she would be finished early enough for them to have supper that evening at the Eastern Tandoori.

She hadn't yet told him that she was pregnant. She hadn't been able to think how she was going to explain it to him. He had come all the way back from San Francisco to be with her and mend their relationship, and he had sworn that he hadn't been unfaithful to her with any other woman while he had been away. Sooner or later she would have to tell him, though, and she would also have to tell him that the baby's father had been her next-door neighbour, and that he had eventually turned out to be a wife-beater.

So far she had managed to conceal her morning sickness, too, just as she had pretended to Detective Inspector O'Rourke that she was feeling unwell because had she eaten a bad prawn at an Indian restaurant. It had been the most nauseating thing she had been able to think of, but now John wanted to go for a curry. The Eastern Tandoori had been one of her favourite restaurants, on the first floor on Emmet Place overlooking the river, but now the very thought of it made her feel queasy. In her imagination, she could even smell fenugreek.

She sat down at her desk and texted back: *Might be held up. Sorry. Major case just come up. Prob. have to make do w. takeaway. XXX.*

She was still texting when Chief Superintendent Denis MacCostagáin came in, as tall and round-shouldered and mournful as ever. Detective Horgan called him 'Chief Superintendent Aingesoir' behind his back, which meant 'Anguished' because he always appeared to be so sad. Since he had been promoted, though, he had taken to his new position very comfortably. He was mournful, but he was highly organized and so methodical that sometimes he could make Katie itch with impatience. However, he was not at all misogynistic. He talked to Katie in the same dreary drawn-out tones as he talked to all of his other officers, and showed her no prejudice – although he showed her no favours, either.

He came up to her desk with a torn-off sheet of notepaper in his hand and studied it for a few moments before he said anything, as if he wasn't at all sure where he had found it.

'There's been some dead horses found,' he said at last.

'Dead horses?' Katie asked him. 'Where exactly?'

'Down at the foot of the cliffs at Nohaval Cove. Twenty-three of them, according to Kenneth Kearney. A member of the public reported it and Kenneth sent one of his ISPCA officers to investigate. The officer found one animal still alive but in a very poor condition with three of its legs broken, so he put it down.'

'Nohaval Cove?' said Katie. 'Those are fierce steep, those cliffs there. How did the horses get down there? They weren't driven over, were they?'

'Kenneth seems to think so. Either driven over or thrown over bodily. It's near on eighty-five metres from the cliff top down to the beach, so it's a miracle that even one of them survived it.

Chief Superintendent MacCostagáin checked his wristwatch, even though there was a clock on Katie's office wall. 'How are you fixed?' he asked her. 'The thing of it is the media are all gathering there and I know how good you are with the media. It'll show how concerned we are, too, if we send out a senior officer. You know that the public get much more upset about cruelty to animals than they do about women and children being mistreated.'

'You're not wrong about that, sir,' said Katie. She stood up and said, 'Okay, then, I'll take Horgan and Dooley with me. I imagine you've sent out a patrol car already?'

'Three altogether. Two from here and one from Carrigaline. And Bill Phinner's sending out a technical team. I want to get those cliffs cordoned off as soon as possible. When word of this gets around there's going to be the usual crowd of rubberneckers and we don't want any of *them* taking the high dive off the top.'

When Chief Superintendent MacCostagáin had left, Katie tried to sip her ginger tea, but it was scalding hot and she had to leave it. She hadn't eaten this morning because she had been so sick, so she was pleased that she had at least made herself a cold chicken and soda bread sandwich, the leftovers from last night's supper. She took the foil packet out of her desk drawer and put it into her satchel.

Four

The rain had passed over by the time Katie reached Nohaval Cove, although the wind was still strong, and she tugged up the hood of her duffel coat as she climbed towards the grassy edge of the cliffs. Detectives Horgan and Dooley followed close behind her, their raincoats noisily flapping.

Three gardaí were knocking metal stakes into the ground and unrolling blue and white crime scene tape, while five more were standing around talking to an ISPCA officer and two technicians in white Tyvek suits. They were all stamping their feet and jigging up and down to keep warm, so that they looked as if they were performing an old-style step dance.

Two officers had managed to drive their Land Cruiser close to the path that led down to the beach, but everybody else had parked in a line along the muddy farm track – two patrol cars, a blue animal rescue ambulance, an estate car and a van from the Technical Bureau, and three cars which Katie recognized as belonging to news reporters. There was no sign yet of a TV outside broadcast van.

As she approached, the guards all stopped jigging and respectfully stepped back, while Sergeant Kevin O'Farrell came forward to greet her. He was a big, blocky man, with bright sandy hair and a red face that always seemed to be close to bursting.

'Glad you could make it out here, ma'am,' he told her. 'The press over there, they've been coming at me with all kinds of awkward questions, like do I think that Travellers were responsible for tossing these horses off the cliff.'

19

'Okay, and what did you say?' Katie asked him.

'I've told them no comment just at the moment. The last time I talked to the press about Travellers was when they ran that sulky race up the main Mallow Road, and I got myself corped for what I said about that.'

'Oh yes, I remember,' said Katie. 'You must never forget, sergeant, that everything the Travellers do is traditional. Traditional fighting, traditional shoplifting, traditional trespass. I don't know if throwing horses off the top of cliffs is traditional, but I expect we'll find out soon enough. Is this the inspector from the ISPCA?'

'Yes, ma'am,' said Sergeant O'Farrell. He beckoned the inspector to come forward – a small, neat man with a dark-brown beard. He had the gentlest brown eyes that Katie had ever seen, almost Jesus-like, and she could easily imagine him gathering abandoned puppies in his arms or leading broken-down donkeys into peaceful fields.

'Tadhg Meaney,' he said, taking off his glove and holding out his hand. 'Normally I'm based at the Victor Dowling Equine Rescue Centre at Dromsligo. Kenneth Kearney called me this morning and asked me to come down here. It's appalling – totally shocking. I've never seen anything like this in my entire nine years of working for the ISPCA. Never.'

'I was told one horse was still alive,' said Katie.

'Barely. I doubt if it would have survived another twelve hours. I shot it. Quickest way.'

'Do you want to take us down to the beach so that we can have a look?'

'Of course. But be careful. It's very steep and slippy and I nearly took a hopper myself. It's better if I go first.'

Tadhg Meaney led Katie and Detectives Horgan and Dooley to the deep cleft in the rocks where the path down to the beach began. Then the four of them made their way down to the cove, clinging to the rocks and gorse bushes to stop themselves from losing their footing. Detective Horgan had bought himself a new pair of tan brogues only the day before yesterday and he swore under his breath all the way down.

'Less of the effing and blinding if you don't mind, Horgan,' said Katie, as they came to the most precipitous part of the climb. 'You can indent for a new pair when you get back to the station.'

'Sorry, ma'am. They were in the sale in Schuh and they only had the one pair my size.'

Once she had managed to climb down to the beach, Katie turned around and looked at the tangled heaps of dead horses. The tide was out now, almost as far as it would go, and their bodies were draped with stinking strands of dark-green seaweed. Gulls were screaming overhead, angry at being disturbed from their pickings.

Without moving them, it was almost impossible to count exactly how many horses were lying there because their legs and their heads and their ribcages were so intertwined, and some of them had rotted and collapsed into the carcasses of the horses lying underneath them. Closer to the foot of the cliff, though, the bodies were not so seriously decomposed and three or four of them looked almost as if they might suddenly stir and clamber on to their feet at any moment.

Two technicians were carefully high-stepping between them, taking photographs, and the intermittent flashes seemed to make them twitch, even those grinning skeletons that looked like horses out of a nightmare.

Those that had still had eyes were staring at Katie balefully. *What am I doing here, lying on this beach, stiff and dead and broken-legged?*

'That's one thing they always get wrong in the films,' said Tadhg Meaney looking down sadly at a large bay gelding with a hugely bloated stomach. 'When a horse dies in the films, its eyes close. They only do that because it's sentimental. When a real horse dies, it carries on looking at you. And as you know yourself, superintendent, quite a few humans do that, too.'

'Do you think that the horses were still alive when they were thrown off the cliff?' asked Katie.

'The one I had to put down was still alive, of course. About the rest of them I can't really tell you for sure – not until I've carried out a full autopsy. Even then it might be difficult, except if they were euthanized beforehand or if they'd already fallen from some sickness or other. Equine flu, maybe, or encephalopathy, or Cushing's disease. Or if they've eaten something poisonous, like foxgloves, or buttercups.'

'How old are they? Is it possible that they're past their best and somebody just wanted to get rid of them without having to pay for a licensed knacker's?'

'Yes, that's perfectly possible. I don't know how much Fitzgerald's are charging these days, but it must be close to a hundred and fifty euros. Multiply that by all of these carcasses and that comes to a fair expense.'

Detective Dooley said, 'Maybe somebody is charging horse owners the knackery fee but simply dumping the animals here and pocketing the proceeds.'

'I'll lay money it was knackers,' Detective Horgan put in. 'I think we should take a trip up to Knackeragua and ask them a few pertinent questions in Gammon.'

'*Travellers*,' Katie corrected him, sharply. Secretly, though, she couldn't totally dismiss his suggestion that these horses might have been illegally disposed of by somebody from the Pavee community. Prejudiced or not, it had been almost the first thought that had come into her head.

'I'm surprised they didn't sell them for horsemeat,' said Detective Dooley. 'They could have made a fair bit of grade by doing that, couldn't they? How much does an edible horse go for these days?'

'Not these animals,' said Tadhg. 'Even if they were healthy and not pumped full of pentobarbitone. Whoever disposed of them would have had to show their passports to the meat processors, to prove that they weren't officially excluded from the human food chain. Apart from that, there's hardly any meat on them. So far as I can make out, they were all race-fit thoroughbreds.'

'You're *codding*,' said Detective Horgan. 'These are all racehorses?'

Tadhg bent down and grasped the rigid fetlock of the gelding that was lying beside him so that he could lever up its hoof and show them its shoe. 'See that? That's a level-grip racing plate. It's made of aluminium to save weight. And look at this one over here.' He held up the hoof of a horse that was so decayed that its tan-coloured hide tore like rotten sacking when he twisted its leg. 'This one's a front jar calk plate, aluminium again, for lightness, but with a steel toe grab inserted in it so that it gives the horse better grip in very soggy going.'

'So these are not just unwanted animals from riding stables?' Katie asked him. 'Or sulky trotters that have run out of trot?'

'Not at all,' said Tadhg. 'Every year in County Cork we collect over two hundred stray or injured or unwanted horses, and there's no doubt at all that the problem's getting worse. Ordinary middle-class folks can't afford to keep horses for their kids any more, like they used to, and often they just drive them out to a field somewhere and abandon them. Then there's the Travellers, like you say. They claim to love their horses but they don't have the first idea how to look after them properly. We were trying to start a horse-training course for them but the funding was pulled.'

'It's not all down to Travellers, though, is it?' said Katie. 'It's a massacre in the racing business – even for horses that don't get thrown off cliffs.'

'Well, you're absolutely right. The sheer inhumanity of it. Too many Irish stables are still breeding a ridiculous surfeit of horses every year. I mean, they do that so that these multimillionaire owners have more of a choice of the bestest and the fastest. But that still means that hundreds of unwanted thoroughbreds are being put down. And the older horses are sent to the knacker's, too. They might have had their moment of glory, but these days nobody can afford the expense of looking after them once they're past it. It's off to France to make salami.'

23

He pointed to three chestnut foals, lying almost on top of each other, as if they had huddled together for protection in the last seconds of their lives.

'There's the young ones, too. Look at them. If they don't survive forty-eight hours after they're born, a breeder doesn't have to pay the stud fee for having their mares covered, and some of the fees are extortionate.'

'What's the average stud fee these days?' asked Katie.

'Some studs used to be asking a quarter of a million euros as a nomination fee, but that was when things were booming. They can't demand so much now, after the recession, but it can still be tens of thousands, and if the price of bloodstock drops sharply enough during the eleven months that it takes a foal to gestate, then that foal is pretty much doomed. It will either be aborted or else it will meet with an "accident" shortly after birth.

'These days a breeder will be lucky to get a few hundred for a foal at auction, and if they can't cover their costs, some breeders simply abandon them at the auction house. So what else are you supposed to do with them then? After one auction recently eighteen foals were sent off for slaughter. Eighteen!'

He paused, surveying the beach with its piles of dead horses. Some of their manes and tails were waving in the wind, like the tattered flags and torn uniforms at the end of a bloody battle.

'I just can't understand why the people who threw these horses over the cliff didn't contact us first,' he said. 'They could have done it anonymously. I think it's well enough known that we only put down horses as a last resort and that we do everything we can to find them a shelter. So why this? You have it absolutely, superintendent. This is nothing short of a massacre.'

'But I assume they've all been microchipped – apart from the foals. You should be able to tell who their owners were.'

'Hopefully. I was talking to your technical fellow and we'll arrange to have the bodies transported to Dromsligo. We have an empty shed there, where we can lay them out decent-like and carry out a proper post-mortem.'

They all climbed back up the cliff. By the time she reached the top, Katie was panting for breath and her stomach muscles felt tight. Detective Horgan gave her his hand to help her up the last few feet between the rocks.

'Thanks a million,' she gasped. 'I didn't think I was going to make that.'

Another two patrol cars had arrived and she could see four reporters standing around the Land Cruiser smoking and talking to the gardaí, including Dan Keane from the *Examiner* and Jean Mulligan from the *Echo*, although the RTÉ van still hadn't showed up and neither had Fionnuala Sweeney from the *Nine o'Clock News*. Before she went to talk to the press, however, Katie walked back to her car. She climbed into the passenger seat and reached over to switch on the engine to warm herself up. Then she took her chicken sandwich out of the glovebox and sat there steadily chewing it, even though she was sure she could still taste seaweed and rotting horse in the back of her throat.

She opened the bottle of apple and blackcurrant Jafsun she had brought with her and took a swallow, and then for no reason at all that she could think of she started to cry. She glanced over towards the small crowd of officers and technicians and reporters gathered by the edge of the cliff and was relieved that none of them were looking in her direction. She wiped her eyes with a tissue, but she still felt a lump in her throat and she couldn't eat any more of her sandwich. She crinkled it up in its kitchen-foil wrapper and put it back into the glovebox.

* * *

Dan Keane from the *Examiner* was the first one to approach her as she walked back towards the cliff edge. He took a quick last puff at his cigarette and then nipped it out and tucked it behind his ear. Jean Mulligan came close behind. She was a fiftyish woman with pouchy cheeks and wiry grey hair, an experienced journalist who had recently returned to write for the *Echo* after her husband had died.

'Morning, superintendent!' Dan called out. He had to shout because of the buffeting noise of the wind and the thin, high whistling of the grass – like a thousand schoolboys all around them whistling between their teeth. He yanked his notebook out of his raincoat pocket, but then he quickly had to clamp his hand on to his brown trilby hat to stop it from blowing away. Jean Mulligan produced a digital voice recorder, but she, too, had to hold down the left-hand lapel of her coat so that it wouldn't keep slapping her in her face.

'Your man from the ISPCA said he's counted twenty-three dead horses down on the beach there.'

'There may be more,' said Katie. 'We'll only know for sure when we've separated them and lifted them all up to the cliff top. Some of them are very badly decomposed, so it's not easy to give you a final body count, not just yet.'

'They weren't *washed* ashore, were they, superintendent?' asked Jean. 'I mean, they weren't driven into the water from a beach further along the coast? Or deliberately thrown into the sea from a ship? Or being ferried on a boat that sank? Perhaps the tide brought them here.'

'No, Jean, the ISPCA officer was quite sure from the state of their injuries that they were either thrown or driven off the top of the cliff. Almost all their legs are shattered and some of them have broken necks. Not only that, they weren't all thrown or driven over at the same time. Judging by their varying states of decomposition, some of them must have been lying there for some considerable time, possibly as long as two months. Others are comparatively recent.'

'One of them was still alive, right, when they were discovered?' asked Kenny Byrne. He was a young freelance who supplied news stories to the *Corkman* in Mallow and the *Southern Star* in Skibbereen, as well as Cork's 96 and Red FM. He had tight blond curls and acne, and Katie always thought that he was far too young to be a reporter – although two or three times he had given tips to the Garda that had helped them locate runaway teenagers and arrest ecstasy dealers in local clubs.

'Yes, Kenny, one horse was still alive, although it was gravely injured and the officer had to put it down.'

'Can you tell us who found the horses in the first place?' asked Jean.

'I can't, no. All I can say is that they were two innocent people out walking. They prefer not to have their names published, and we can fully understand their concern. The way these poor creatures have been disposed of is clearly a criminal act, although it's far too early for me to say what its full implications are.'

'You'll allow our photographer down on the beach to take a few pictures?' said Dan Keane, although it was more of a statement than a question.

'Of course, yes. The more coverage you can give this, the better. Even if it wasn't done all at once, throwing nearly two dozen horses off an eighty-metre cliff top is not exactly what you'd call an inconspicuous activity. Somebody must have seen something that can give us a useful lead.'

'Do you have any idea at all where the horses might have come from?' asked Jean.

Katie knew that it was no use trying to hold back the information that the horses were all thoroughbreds. Dan Keane was a racing man and would recognize them for at once for what they were, even though many of them were so decomposed, and in any case their shoes would give the game away immediately.

'We don't yet know if they came from one particular stable, or several different stables, but as far as we can ascertain they're all race-trained thoroughbreds.'

'Racehorses? All twenty-three of them?' asked Johnny Byrne.

'Look, as I told you, we haven't had the opportunity yet to examine them all, but every one that we've seen so far appears to fit into that category.'

'But who's going to throw twenty-three racehorses off a cliff? Like, what for, like?'

'Somebody who doesn't want to pay for their legitimate disposal, I would say,' Dan Keane put in. 'Or somebody who doesn't want it known that those particular animals are dead.'

'Well – those are both possibilities that we'll be looking into,' said Katie. 'They should all have been microchipped, of course, so that should help us to trace their owners.'

'Oh, this is going to be an interesting one all right,' said Dan Keane. 'Think of all the reasons why you wouldn't want it known that a racehorse was dead. Whatever it is, you can bet one hundred to one that there's money behind it, and *big* money, too.'

'It's much too soon to say,' Katie told him. 'I'm not going to start making accusations of any kind, not until we have some credible evidence about where they came from and who might have disposed of them, and why. Obviously, though, we'd like to hear from anyone who has any information that might lead us to understand what happened here. Did anybody see dead horses being carried on the back of a pick-up truck? Or horseboxes being driven along the farm tracks towards Nohaval Cove? It's the usual Garda confidential number – 1800 666 111 – and you can rest assured that nobody will know that you called us.'

'How are you going to get the horses off the beach?' asked Johnny.

'As of now, I have absolutely no idea at all,' said Katie. 'I expect we'll have to call in a crane or something like that. We're going to transport the bodies to the equine centre at Dromsligo for a full post-mortem. Once I have more information, I'll be discussing it with the ISPCA and Weatherbys and the Department of Agriculture, as well as the Department of Transport, Tourism, and Sports, and also with the county council.'

'What about Horse Racing Ireland?'

'Well, of course, them too. But there's nothing more I can tell you just yet – not only for operational reasons but simply because I don't know any more.'

'Well, I'll say one thing for you, superintendent,' said Dan Keane, tucking away his notebook and then snatching at his hat as it flew off his head. 'You're never afraid to tell the truth, are you?'

Five

Detective Sergeant Ni Nuallán turned into the gates of the Bon Sauveur Convent and drove up between the high stone walls to the steeply angled car park. It was starting to rain again as she walked up to the arched front porch and tugged the wrought-iron bell-handle.

The convent was grey and gothic, and it looked even drearier in the drizzle. There was a hexagonal chapel at the far end, with a fan-shaped stained-glass window, and a three-storey dormitory wing with a sloping slate roof. The gardens were dark with dripping yew bushes, like a crowd of hunchbacks.

A minute passed and nobody came to answer the door so Detective Sergeant Ni Nuallán tugged the handle again. She couldn't hear a bell ringing so there was no way for her to tell if anybody had heard her or not.

She was about to tug the handle a third time when she heard the quick scuffling of soft-soled shoes and the door was unbolted and opened just wide enough for a pale young woman's face to appear. She was wearing a white nun's habit with a white veil and a white scapular, so that in the gloomy interior of the convent hallway she appeared almost ghostly.

'How are you doing there?' said Detective Sergeant Ni Nuallán, holding up her ID. 'I'm from the Garda and I'd like to have a few words with your superior, if I could.'

'I'm sorry,' said the young nun, with a lisp. 'It's our meditation hour.'

'Well, I hate to interrupt her, like, but this is quite urgent. Do you think you can call her for me?'

'Oh no, I couldn't disturb her.' The young nun glanced behind her as if she was already worried that her superior was coming up behind her to give her the seven shows of Cork for opening the door and chatting to strangers when she was supposed to be silently communing with God.

'Tell her that a former member of your order has been murdered. Sister Bridget Healy. She was resident at the Mount Hill Nursing Home.'

'No? Serious?' The young nun pressed her hand to her mouth and her brown eyes widened. She wore no make-up, of course, and her eyebrows were unplucked, but Detective Sergeant Ni Nuallán thought she was still quite attractive. Too pretty to be a nun, anyway.

'*Please*, sister,' she said. 'It's critical that we find out who killed her. If it was somebody who has a grudge against your particular congregation, or nuns in general, it could very well be that other sisters are at risk. It could very well be that *you're* at risk.'

'You'd better come in,' said the young nun. 'I'll take you through to Mother O'Dwyer's office and then I'll see if I can catch her attention.'

She opened the door wider so that Detective Sergeant Ni Nuallán could step inside and then she led her along a long panelled corridor with arched gothic windows on one side and framed engravings of biblical scenes on the other. Halfway along the corridor, in an alcove, stood a life-size bronze figure of a woman in a long robe, polished to a high shine. Her arms were extended and her eyes raised to heaven.

'Saint Margaret,' said the young nun, bowing her head as she passed the statue, almost as if it were alive.

The convent smelled of boiled cabbage and stale incense. Detective Sergeant Ni Nuallán was wearing high-heeled boots and her footsteps made a loud clacking sound on the parquet flooring, so that she felt even more intrusive.

31

'And what's your name?' she asked the young nun.

'Oh, me? I'm Sister Rose – Sister Rose O'Sullivan.'

'You're wearing the white, so I suppose you're a novice?'

'That's right. I have another five months to go before I take my temporary vows.'

As Sister Rose showed her into the waiting room outside the mother superior's office, Detective Sergeant Ni Nuallán was tempted to ask her what had led her to take up holy orders. She could understand a sense of duty to the community. She felt that herself, and strongly. But it was possible to serve the community without devoting yourself completely to God, and remaining single, and chaste.

'If you'd like to take a seat, I'll go and find Mother O'Dwyer for you,' said Sister Rose.

'Thanks,' said Detective Sergeant Ni Nuallán. When Sister Rose had left, though, she didn't sit down, but went to the window and looked out at the convent's vegetable garden, where knobbly yellow stalks stood, stripped of their sprouts. Then she slowly circled around the room to examine the photographs hanging on the walls.

All of them showed groups of young women, every one them cradling babies in their arms or holding small children by the hand. On either side of these groups stood sisters of the congregation of the Bon Sauveur in their black cowls and habits. Each of the photographs was labelled 'Saint Margaret's Mother and Baby Home', and dated. The earliest was March 1927, the latest April 1975.

What caught Detective Sergeant Ni Nuallán's attention more than anything else was that nobody in the photographs was smiling, neither the nuns nor any of the young women, nor even the little children. Their expressions were all strained and anxious, as if they had just received distressing news and their whole world was about to fall apart.

Walking slowly around from one photograph to the next, she felt unexpectedly saddened. What made her sadness even keener was that she could do nothing to help any of the young women who were staring out at her so worriedly. Even if they hadn't passed away long ago, they would be elderly now and their children would be grown up, or gone, or passed away, too.

'I understand that you have tragic news,' said a thin, sharp voice.

Detective Sergeant Ni Nuallán turned around to see Mother O'Dwyer standing in the doorway, as if she had been watching her.

'Yes,' she said. 'I'm afraid that I have.'

'And you are—?'

'Detective Sergeant Ni Nuallán, from Anglesea Street Garda station.'

Mother O'Dwyer was a tiny woman, almost like a religious figurine herself. She was wearing the same black habit and black scapular as the nuns in the photographs, although she was also wearing an oval silver medallion hung around her neck, with the image of a sad-faced female saint on it. She wore rimless glasses that reflected the wintry light from the window so that she looked as if she were blind. Her face was round and pale, but her nose was triangular and up-tilted, like the gnomon of a sundial, and there was a large wart close to her right nostril.

'Sister Rose said that Sister Bridget Healy has been found murdered.'

'Yes. I'm very sorry to have to bring you that news. You have our condolences.'

'You had best come into my office,' said Mother O'Dwyer. She looked suspiciously around at the photographs on the walls, as if she didn't want the young women and children in them to overhear what they were going to say.

She opened her office door and gestured that Detective Sergeant Ni Nuallán should go inside. She then followed her and closed the door very quietly and tightly.

The office was small and stuffy and smelled of leather and faded potpourri. One wall was filled floor to ceiling with books, mostly religious. On the facing wall there was a framed print of a saintly looking woman with her arms outspread, staring up at the sky with an ecstatic expression on her face. Beside her, a naked cherub was holding up a wooden cross, his modesty covered by a coil of blue cloth that conveniently happened to be floating past.

'Please, Sergeant, sit down,' said Mother O'Dwyer, and seated herself behind her own leather-covered desk. Detective Sergeant Ni Nuallán sat in a low but high-sided chair, which made her feel that she was sitting in a bucket.

Mother O'Dwyer fussily and precisely closed a prayer book on her desk and moved an empty teacup to one side, tutting as if she expected that one of the novices would have come to collect it by now.

'Perhaps you can apprise me of the circumstances of Sister Bridget's passing,' she said.

'She was found dead in her own bed this morning at about seven-fifteen,' said Detective Sergeant Ni Nuallán. 'Our chief technical officer thinks that she was suffocated, probably with her own pillow. There will, of course, be a full post-mortem.'

Mother O'Dwyer crossed herself, twice. 'That's dreadful. Just dreadful. Do you have any notion who might have done such a terrible thing?'

'It's far too early to say yet. We don't have any immediate suspects. But there was something unusual about her murder and we think that it might give us some kind of a lead. That's the reason I've come to see you.'

'What do you mean, "unusual"? The deliberate taking of a sacred life can never be considered to be "usual", can it?'

'Well, no, of course not. But this was unusual whichever way you look at it. If I can ask you first, though, Mother O'Dwyer, how long were you and Sister Bridget contemporaries here?'

'Let me see . . .' said Mother O'Dwyer. 'I became a candidate here when I was twenty-six, in 1973. Sister Bridget left in 1994, when she was sixty-two years old, because of her health. So that's, what? Twenty-one years.'

'And how did you and she get along together?'

'That's a very strange question, sergeant. All of the sisters in this community "get along together", as you put it. We were called by God and we have to "get along together" in order to fulfil our holy duty.'

'How many sisters do you have here now?' asked Detective Sergeant Ni Nuallán.

'Thirteen now, altogether. There used to be more when Sister Bridget was here – twenty-one when I joined. But since we no longer provide residential care for single mothers and their infants, there's not the need for sisters that we used to have, and sadly fewer young women these days are feeling that they're called by Jesus. We're living now in extremely amoral times, I'm sorry to say. I blame the interweb myself. Twitter, it's Satan's own notice board. Well, that and lower-class behaviour. Drinking in the streets. Promiscuity. Girls don't have the decorum any more.'

'Would you say that you and Sister Bridget were close?'

Mother O'Dwyer took off her spectacles. She had a slight cast in her left eye, so that it was difficult for Detective Sergeant Ni Nuallán to tell if she were looking at her directly or not. '"Close" is not the word I'd use,' she said. 'Of course, Sister Bridget was older than me, but she was also a very private individual. Her closest relationship was with God. She liked to see things done after a certain fashion, though, especially when our assistant superior, Mother Kelly, was unwell and Sister Bridget temporarily took over her duties. She was extremely what you might call "meticulous".'

'Did that irritate anybody? I don't necessarily mean you. but was there anybody else you can think of who found her annoying?'

'Like I say, sergeant, in this congregation we all "get along" together. It's our vocation.'

'That's not really what I asked you, Mother O'Dwyer. Getting along with people means that you tolerate them and keep your mouth shut even when they give you ire. You had a very closed environment here – twenty-one women of varying ages living in each other's pockets. If I'm correct, you weren't allowed out at night, either, in those days – you had all to be back here in the convent by the time it fell dark. Not only that, you also had the stress of taking care of unmarried mothers and their children. You can't make me believe that you never got on each other's nerves, ever. You may have been called by God, but you were still human, and more than that, you were women.'

Mother O'Dwyer replaced her spectacles on her pointy nose and pursed her lips to show that she wasn't going to comment any further, but that lack of response was enough to suggest to Detective Sergeant Ni Nuallán that at least some of the sisters in the convent had found Sister Bridget overbearing – 'haughty', as Nevina Cormack had put it.

'You said that there was something unusual about her death,' said Mother O'Dwyer.

'Yes. She was sexually assaulted.'

Mother O'Dwyer crossed herself again. 'She was *raped*? Oh, dear Mary Mother of God! After eighty-three years of keeping herself chaste for the Lord!'

'We don't know for sure yet. We'll have to wait for the autopsy. But she was sexually assaulted with a religious figurine, and that religious figurine was left inside her.'

'A religious figurine? Of what?'

'The Immaculate Heart of Mary.' Detective Sergeant Ni Nuallán held out her hands about a foot apart. 'It was approximately this big.'

'Oh dear God, you're making me feel quite faint,' said Mother O'Dwyer. 'The Immaculate Heart of Mary was the figurine that Sister Bridget kept on her window sill in her room and always used for prayer and meditation. She was devoted to the inner life of Our Lady, her virtues and her hidden imperfections, and to Our Lady's faultless love for her Son Jesus Christ.'

'So this particular figurine was important to her?'

'Important? It was everything. In spite of all the wounds that Our Lady's poor heart sustained, her love never wavered. It was Our Lady's inner strength that helped Sister Bridget to understand how she, too, could give *her* love wholeheartedly to God. That's if you follow what I'm saying.'

'Of course,' nodded Detective Sergeant Ni Nuallán. She had caught the gist of what Mother O'Dwyer was trying to explain to her, although she had never been very bright when it came to catechism. When she was six years old, her first attempt at answering 'Who made me?' had been 'Mummy and Daddy'. But it wasn't Sister Bridget's devotion to the Immaculate Heart of Mary that interested her. It was the likelihood that her murderer had known her well enough to violate her body with the one figurine that she had held to be most sacred.

'I don't like to harp on about it,' she said. 'But are you totally sure there was nobody at the convent when Sister Bridget was here who actively didn't like her? Maybe it wasn't another sister, but a visiting priest, or a member of the public that she was tending to? Or maybe one of the unmarried mothers?'

Mother O'Dwyer stood up and walked around her desk. She went up to the engraving of the ecstatic woman and the cherub with the cross and said, 'Do you know who this is, sergeant? This is Saint Margaret of Cortona, in one of her frequent communications with Jesus. She is the patron saint of single mothers and protector of illegitimate children, both born and unborn, and she still shields them from harm, even today. That is because she herself was a single mother and succumbed many times in her early life to the temptations of the flesh.

'However, she became penitent, and when her father refused to have her back in his house she went to Cortona to take care of fallen young women like herself, for no remuneration, living on bread and water. Her selfless service to those who had wandered astray morally was beyond reproach, which was why she was canonized, and Sister Bridget was the same. If Sister Bridget's words were ever sharp, it was only because she was speaking in a young woman's best interests, and those of her child.

'I find it impossible to believe that any member of our congregation would have harmed Sister Bridget, nor any of the young women that Sister Bridget looked after. And that's all I can say to you.'

'There must be some other sisters here who knew Sister Bridget,' said Detective Sergeant Ni Nuallán. 'Is it possible that I can have a word with them, too?'

'They're all meditating at the moment, I'm afraid – as indeed I was, and shall have to return to it. Perhaps you'd like to call back later this evening, after our supper. Seven-thirty would be the most convenient time.'

'All right, then,' said Detective Sergeant Ni Nuallán. She stood up and straightened her skirt. 'I'll probably bring another officer with me, if that's all right, just to get through things quicker.'

'No bother at all,' said Mother O'Dwyer. 'I'm absolutely certain, though, that you'll be wasting your time. You'll hear the same story from every single one of them. We're a community of women who have given their lives to God and to helping those unfortunate individuals who, for one reason or another, are incapable of helping themselves. We get along very well, thank you. That's one of the reasons they call us "sisters". Sisters of Jesus Christ, sisters to each other.'

Mother O'Dwyer opened the door and Detective Sergeant Ni Nuallán stepped out into the waiting room and took a deep breath. It had been so leathery and stuffy inside Mother O'Dwyer's office that she had been close to suffering an attack of claustrophobia.

Sister Rose was sitting outside, in her white novice's habit. She stood up immediately and Mother O'Dwyer said, 'I hope I've answered all of your questions, sergeant, and put your mind at rest, at least as far as this congregation is concerned. Sister Rose will show you out. God be with you.'

'Thank you, and with you,' said Detective Sergeant Ni Nuallán, and followed Sister Rose along the corridor towards the front door.

When they were out on the porch, though, Sister Rose nervously looked back and then closed the door behind her until it was only an inch ajar.

'I don't know if I should be showing you this,' she lisped.

'Sorry, what?'

'*This*,' said Sister Rose. She reached underneath her scapular and took out a pale-blue handkerchief, folded into a pyramid. She glanced behind her again and then looked left and right across the glistening wet asphalt car park. When she seemed satisfied that nobody was watching them, she held up the handkerchief in the palm of her hand and carefully unfolded it.

Inside it was a small curved piece of bone, only a little more than three centimetres long. One end was slightly stained, as if it had been soaked in tea. At the other end there were three tiny teeth.

'Where did you get this?' asked Detective Sergeant Ni Nuallán. She took a pair of crumpled latex gloves out of her coat pocket and tugged one of them onto her right hand. Then she reached across and carefully picked up the bone up between finger and thumb.

'In the garden, at the back,' said Sister Rose. 'I was weeding and I just found it there, sticking out of the flower bed.'

'When was this?'

'About six weeks ago. I didn't know who to tell. I showed it to Sister Brenda and I asked her if I should take it to Mother O'Dwyer, but she said best not to. She said best to throw it in the bin and forget I ever found it. There would be all kinds of trouble and they might even close down the convent.'

Detective Sergeant Ni Nuallán turned the bone this way and that. 'Why *didn't* you throw it in the bin?' she asked.

'Because it's part of a small child's jawbone, isn't it? Sister Brenda said it might be a dog's, but I did biology at school and I know it's not a dog's.'

'Well, I'd say you're right,' said Detective Sergeant Ni Nuallán. 'It is a child's jawbone, and these are its milk teeth. If you were going to show it to anybody at all, you should have showed it to us.'

They heard the sound of footsteps inside the convent hallway and Sister Rose turned around in panic, wringing her hands together.

'Please don't tell Mother O'Dwyer I gave it to you! Please! This is what I've wanted ever since I was at school, to join the convent!

If she finds out what I've done, she'll throw me out! She'll probably have me excommunicated!'

Detective Sergeant Ni Nuallán dropped the piece of bone into the left-hand latex glove and tied a knot in it to make it secure. Then she laid a reassuring hand on Sister Rose's shoulder and said, 'Look, don't worry. We don't have to say where it came from. But we'll have to investigate. If there was a jawbone in the garden, there could be more bones, too, the rest of the child's skeleton; and if there's one child's skeleton there, there could be more.'

'I know,' said Sister Rose, and there were tears sparkling on her eyelashes. 'That's why I kept it. It's a sacred part of that poor child's body. I prayed for its little soul. I don't know who it was or how it died but I prayed that it didn't suffer, and I commended its spirit to God, and to the Virgin Mary, so that She could be its mother and take care of it now.'

'Well, it's taken you some time, but you've done the right thing now,' said Detective Sergeant Ni Nuallán. 'What I need to know is exactly *where* in the garden you discovered it. I don't want you to show me now because we'd be seen and soon as we send a technical team to search the convent grounds the sisters would realize it was you who tipped us off. Do you have access to a computer?'

'Yes, in the secretary's office.'

'Then draw me a sketch map of the garden, with a cross to mark the spot where you found the jawbone, scan it and send it to me. Here's my card with my email address. Do it as soon as you can, please, Sister Rose. Meanwhile, I'll be taking this jawbone to have it examined and a DNA sample taken. With any luck at all it *will* be possible to find out how it died, this child, and who it is. And hopefully we can find the rest of its remains and give it the decent burial it deserves.'

'Thank you,' said Sister Rose. 'Thank you so much and God bless you.'

Unexpectedly, she gave Detective Sergeant Ni Nuallán a quick hug. Then she smeared the tears from her eyes with her fingers, pushed open the convent door, and went back inside.

Detective Sergeant Ni Nuallán stood in the porch for a few moments, looking at the door and listening to the rain crackling in the yew bushes. Then she went down the steps and walked back down the slope to her car.

She believed in God, and in Jesus Christ, and in the perfect love of the Virgin Mary. But ever since she was at school she had instinctively distrusted those who claimed to be their representatives on earth – cardinals, bishops, priests and nuns.

On this wet afternoon, though, she suspected that she was carrying in her pocket a small fragment of a lost child – and that small fragment had the potential to bring down whole cathedrals, and whole religious hierarchies, in an avalanche of stone and stained glass and silk and gilded mitres.

As she drove out of the convent gates on to Gardiner's Hill, a nun walked past her carrying a large black umbrella.

The nun smiled at her.

'You're going to need that umbrella, sister,' said Detective Sergeant Ni Nuallán to herself, out loud. 'It's a hard rain's a-gonna fall.'

Six

Katie didn't return home until half past eight. It was a comfort to see that the lights were on and the curtains were drawn, and when she let herself into the hallway she could smell chicken and vegetables cooking. Barney came pit-pattering out of the kitchen to jump at her, closely followed by John.

'Home is the detective superintendent, home from the crime scene,' John misquoted, and came forward and took her in his arms.

It was nearly three weeks now since he had come back and she adored having him here, in spite of the pain she had suffered when he had left her. With one sleeve of her coat half off, she let him hold her tight against him. He was wearing a long striped butcher's apron which smelled of cooking, but underneath the smell of cooking she could smell *him*, that spicy oaky smell that she could breathe in when he got out of bed in the morning and she moved over to rest her head on his pillow.

He had cut his black hair shorter and brushed it up higher, to look more business-like, but she still thought he had that god-like look about him – those dark-sapphire eyes and that long, straight nose. After all, many of the Irish were supposed to be descended from the Iberians, or even from Éber Donn, the Dark One, the god of the underworld.

'I couldn't stand the thought of another Chinese takeaway,' he told her as she hung up her coat and went through to the living room. 'I've made us my legendary smoked chicken stew.'

'Oh, you shouldn't have bothered. I'm not that hungry. But thank you, anyway.'

'Did you eat at work?' he asked her.

'I had a turkey salad sandwich and an iced slice.'

'I thought you *hated* turkey. Remember when I said we should start breeding turkeys at Knocknadeenly? You told me they tasted even more disgusting than they looked.'

'Well, I don't know. I just have a thing for turkey at the moment.'

'Supper will be ready in about twenty minutes, if you want any. If you don't, don't worry, we can always heat it up tomorrow. How about a drink?'

He went over to the drinks table and picked up the bottle of Smirnoff Black Label, but Katie said, 'No – no, thanks. I'll just have a glass of Tanora.'

'Are you sure you're feeling okay?' John asked her. 'You're not coming down with the flu, are you?'

'No, no. I'm grand altogether. Just tired, that's all. It's been a long day. Have you watched the news at all yet?'

'Unh-hunh. I was working on my laptop till six, then I started cooking.'

'Oh, well. Somebody's been throwing horses off the cliffs at Nohaval Cove, twenty-three of them. I had to go down there and check them out myself. It was carnage, I'll tell you.'

'*Horses*? Jesus. What did they do that for?'

'That's what we have to find out. They were racehorses, so that may well give us an answer.'

'Jesus. Were they dead when they were thrown off, or were they still alive?'

'I don't know. We have to find that out, too. And we had a murder to deal with, at an old folks' nursing home in Montenotte. Some poor old nun.'

'You make my day sound utterly boring. The most exciting thing I did was sell a shipment of PfSPZ malaria vaccine to the Jajo Hospital in Lagos.'

Katie reached up and took hold of his hand. 'Don't say that's not exciting. That's that new vaccine you were telling me about the other day, isn't it? The one that gives you the same resistance as if you've been bitten by a thousand mosquitoes.'

'That's right. Without actually *looking* like you've been bitten by a thousand mosquitoes.'

'Don't you have a drink?' she asked him.

'Sure. I have a beer in the kitchen. I'll get you that Tanora, too.'

'It's just that I need to talk to you.'

John kept hold of her hand but raised one eyebrow. 'Okay . . . what about?'

'Get your beer and I'll tell you.'

He went into the kitchen and Katie could hear him opening the oven and checking his stew. He came back with a bottle of beer and a glass of Tanora for her.

'Okay, then,' he said, sitting on the couch next to her. 'What do you need to talk about? You think I should start paying you rent, is that it?'

She leaned across and kissed him on the lips. 'No,' she said. 'You don't have to pay me rent. Having you back, that's all the payment I need. I thought I was never going to see or hear from you, ever again.'

John shrugged. 'I was an asshole. I couldn't see the bigger picture for my daily sales targets. I guess that's the default mentality of people in online sales.'

'Oh, come on, John. You had to think of your own career. You didn't want to be stuck here in Cork if it meant you couldn't develop your own business potential.'

'Well, I know that, and I guess that it's still partly true. Cork isn't exactly the sales centre of the universe. But that very first morning, I sat down at my desk in San Francisco and my pal Nathan came over and said, 'I'll bet you don't miss Ireland one iota, do you? All that rain. All that economic austerity.' And do you know something? I realized that I *did* miss Ireland. I missed Ireland so much that it physically hurt. I missed Ireland because nobody else in the world understands us Irish, and never will. But most of all, I missed Ireland because I missed you.'

Katie touched his cheek very gently with her fingertips, as if she needed to reassure herself that he was really here. But he *was* here, and he was just the same John. He still had that small scar on his forehead. He still looked away when he was talking to her and then immediately looked back again as if he didn't ever want to take his eyes off her.

She wanted him so much, but she needed to tell him that she was pregnant. He had already noticed that her tastes in food and drink had changed dramatically, and how tired she was at the end of the day. Fortunately, he hadn't yet heard her being sick in the mornings, but it was only a matter of time before he realized what was happening.

The trouble was, how was she going to explain why she had taken her next-door neighbour to bed? Because she was lonely, after John had left her? That would sound as if she were blaming *him* for her falling pregnant. Because she felt sorry for herself and needed to be reassured that men still found her sexually attractive? That would sound so selfish and small-minded. Out of anger? Out of lust?

David Kane had been a charmer, but he had also turned out to be a liar and an arrogant wife-beater. She hadn't realized what a bully he was before they had sex, although she had to admit to herself that she may have suspected it. She kept on seeing him in her mind's eye, when he was on top of her, so detached and self-absorbed, as if he didn't care who she was, as long as she was a woman and bringing him to a climax. In spite of that, though, he hadn't forced himself on her.

In the end, too, he had sacrificed his own life to protect her by shielding her from a gangster's bullet. But had that redeemed him? He had assured her that he had had a vasectomy and didn't need a condom, but now there was another life involved.

'So, what did you need to tell me?' asked John, swigging his beer.

'I needed to tell you that I'm scared.'

'What are you scared of? Is it something at work? It's not that assistant commissioner is it, that goddamned what's-his-face?'

'Jimmy O'Reilly.'

'That's him, Jimmy O'Reilly. Come on, Katie, you don't have to worry about him. You told me yourself that your dad gave you enough dope on him and his scams to keep you safe for ever. All you have to say to him is "High Kings of Erin" out of the corner of your mouth and he'll be buffing up your shoes with the grease from his nose.'

Katie shook her head. 'It's nothing at all to do with Jimmy O'Reilly. In any case it would be practically impossible for me to prove that he took bribes from criminals in return for dropping charges against them, *and* he knows it, so these days we're just frosty to each other. Polite, but frosty. In fact, we're so frosty that Kyna Ni Nuallán wondered if we were having an affair.'

'If you are, I'll give him a beating.'

'Of course I'm not. I'm allergic to the man.'

'All right. So what is it you're scared of?'

Katie took hold of his hand and squeezed it. 'I'm scared of history repeating itself. You came back because you missed me, but what's going to happen after a few months when you realize that Cork is still as small and narrow-minded as it ever was and that it's still raining and it's still a struggle for you to make yourself a decent living?'

'Katie, I've thought about that, believe me. But like I told you, Nils and Nathan and me had a long discussion about it, and for the time being they're happy for me to run their European and Middle-Eastern and African sales from here. I can also set up my own freelance sales business on the side.'

'And you really won't miss San Francisco?' she asked him. *Tell him you're pregnant.*

'Of course I will. I'd be lying to you if I told you I won't. I'd also be deceiving you if I said that I won't have another shot at persuading you to come out and live there. You'd love it. But in the meantime, if the condition for living with you is living in Cork, then I choose to live in Cork.'

Katie closed her eyes for a moment. *Tell him you're pregnant.*

'Okay,' she said. 'I only hope you feel the same way in the middle of February, when it's really damp and cold and you haven't seen the sun for so long that you've forgotten what it looks like.'

'Don't you worry, sweetheart. I was a prick before, resenting the way you arranged that job for me at ErinChem. But it's surprising how distance makes you look at your life in perspective. From six thousand miles away, I could see that you loved me and that you'd only been trying to make it easier for me to stay here. I could see that there was no way that you were going to quit the Garda – not *then*, anyhow, and maybe not yet. But I can wait for you, Katie. Maybe it does rain a whole lot. But I have an umbrella and I can put it up and stand underneath it and wait for you for as long as it takes.'

Tell him you're pregnant.

The clock in the hallway chimed nine. Katie said, 'Oh – nine o'clock – I want to see the news. I'm wondering if the TV people managed to get down to Nohaval to film those horses. Horgan told me their van got bogged down on some farm track somewhere.'

'Why don't you sit there and watch the news and I'll bring you some of my amazing stew?'

'All right,' agreed Katie, tucking her feet up under her. 'But just a dooshie bit, okay?'

John stood up, but then he leaned over her and lifted her face in both hands and kissed her. God, she loved that blue-black colour of his irises. Looking so intently into his eyes was like staring into deepest outer space, glittering and mysterious.

'I love you, Katie Maguire,' he told her, so close that she felt his breath against her lips.

Tell him you're pregnant. That was what you needed to tell him, so tell him.

I can't. Not now. The moment's passed.

47

The moment is never going to pass, girl. You have to tell him.
I can't.

So what are you going to do? Get rid of it and never tell him?
I can't do that. Wherever it came from, it's a human life. It's a baby.

That depends on whose life is more important. Do you seriously mean to tell me that you're going to give up this one chance of happiness for a child you never asked for, and never wanted, and was conceived because you were lied to?

The nine o'clock news came on and Katie reached over for the remote and turned up the sound.

'Good evening and welcome. Tonight's main headline . . . twenty-three racehorses are found dead on the beach at Nohaval Cove. Gardaí say they were thrown from the eighty-five-metre-high cliff top. When they were discovered by a local couple walking their dog, one at least was still alive.'

'Jesus, that's loud!' called John, from the kitchen. 'Are you sure they can hear you in Sligo?'

Katie folded her arms and stared at the screen, although she wasn't really listening to the news bulletin. All she needed was the volume. Anything to drown out the argument inside her head.

* * *

In bed that night, John turned over and held Katie very close. She could feel the bone-like hardness of his penis through her nightgown, against the small of her back. He stroked her shoulder and ran his fingers into her hair. God, she was aching to have him inside her.

But, 'John,' she murmured, reaching over her shoulder and clasping his fingers. 'I'm really, really tired. Maybe in the morning.'

'You really don't have anything to be scared of,' he told her. 'I'm not going to leave you again, Katie. I've learned my lesson. I'm not going to leave Ireland, either. This is where I was born,

48

this is where I was brought up. My cousins are still here. My mom and dad are buried here. In fact, I'm going to go to Ballyhooly this weekend and lay some flowers on their graves.'

Katie twisted herself around and kissed him. 'I'll say one thing for you, John Meagher. You really know what to say to turn a woman on, don't you?'

Seven

They had been fishing all morning in the shallows of the Glashaboy River, trying to catch trout. The trout season was closed until 1 February, but they had hopped off from school for a day and they were bored and they were too well known in Dunne's Stores to try and hobble a few bars of chocolate.

After yesterday's rain it was a dry, fresh day and the surface of the Glashaboy was glittering. They had caught nothing so far, although they had seen six or seven small speckly fish among the weeds. Bradan blamed Tommy for the bait he had brought, which was small cubes of toasted cheese, the remains of his family's breakfast.

'For feck's sake, you can only catch trout with things that they eat in their natural habitat,' Bradan had told Tommy, when Tommy had first opened the grease-stained bag of toasted cheese to show him what he had brought. 'Trout don't eat cheese and in any case where would they get a toaster from?'

'Well, yeah, I suppose you're right,' said Tommy with a frown. He looked around at the wide, wind-rippled river. 'And, you know, like, even if they *did* manage to get hold of a toaster, they're in water, aren't they? They'd all be electromacuted.'

Bradan was thirteen and he had learned the word 'habitat' from attending at least three natural science lessons at school. Tommy, his friend, was eleven and still had difficulty reading any words at all. They lived two streets away from each other in Mayfield, but they could have been brothers. They were both tall and gangly-legged for their age, with wiry flax-coloured hair and pasty faces and buck teeth. Their long-suffering history teacher, Mr Coughlan, said that they could have been street urchins from a photograph taken in the 1930s, come to life.

'What we need is worms,' said Bradan.

'Mind you, if they *was* electromacuted,' mused Tommy, 'they would all float to the top, wouldn't they, and then we could catch them easy.'

'For feck's sake, Tommy, stop talking *buinneach*, would you? They don't have a fecking toaster and even if they did, where would they plug it in?'

Tommy looked around again, as if he half-expected to see an extension lead lying on the grass next to the water's edge.

'We'll have to dig for some,' said Bradan.

'What?'

'Worms, you daw! What have you got that we could dig with?'

'I have this,' said Tommy, unbuttoning one of the pockets of his baggy cargo pants and taking out a stainless-steel dessert spoon.

'That's a fecking *spoon*! What the feck are you carrying a fecking spoon around for? Don't tell me – your mam wouldn't allow you to have a knife!'

'No, my grandpa said I should always carry a spoon with me. Much more useful than a knife. You can do all sorts things with it like getting flies out of your drinks, or taking a few crafty mouthfuls out of a peanut-butter jar in the supermarket.'

'Oh yeah, and I can just imagine the security guard coming up to you and saying, 'Did I just see you taking a few crafty mouthfuls out of that peanut-butter jar with your spoon? And you're going, "Mmmff? Mmmmm-mmh! Me? *Mmmwwoh!*"'

'Ah, g'way.' Tommy knelt down on the river bank and started to dig with his spoon into the mud. Bradan searched around for a stick so that he could dig, too. He was still looking when three large silvery-grey balloons soundlessly appeared over Glanmire Wood on the opposite side of the river. They were all tethered together, and as he watched them they rose higher into the air, clearing the treetops, and then they came floating across the river towards them.

Each balloon must have been about the size of a Zorb ball. They floated in complete silence, dipping and swaying slightly in the wind. But one of the reasons they were dipping and swaying was because they were carrying a weight. A figure was hanging beneath them, and although they were sixty or seventy metres distant, Bradan could see that the figure was suspended by a rope around its neck.

It was dressed in a long black habit, like a nun, and when it spun around on the end of its rope to face him, Bradan realized that it *was* a nun. He could see her waxy-white face, staring at him.

'*Tommy*!' he screamed.

Tommy had found a pale-pink wriggling worm and he was tugging it out of the peaty soil between finger and thumb. 'It's all right, Brade,' he laughed. 'It's only a fecking worm! It won't bite you!'

'No, Tommy! Look, Tommy! Up there! *Look*!'

Tommy turned around and looked and immediately dropped his spoon and stood up, cupping his hands over his eyes.

'It's only a fecking *nun*!' said Bradan.

Tommy stared up at the balloons as they came nearer and nearer. They floated almost right over their heads, and they could see the nun's black button-up shoes dangling from beneath her habit. As she passed over, they heard a light pattering sound in the grass, and then on the stony path, as if it were starting to rain. Bradan held out his hand and a bright-red drop splashed into his palm.

'Holy Jesus!' he screamed, showing his hand to Tommy. 'It's only blood! She's only fecking bleeding!'

He wiped his hand furiously on the grass and then knelt down beside the river and washed it completely clean.

The balloons bobbed and jostled and turned in the wind and the dangling nun swayed from side to side. Then they began to float slowly upriver. About a half-mile further upstream, the Glashaboy narrowed into the Butlerstown River, which ran up beside the main road to the village of Glanmire. The trees were taller there and the balloons were floating so low that there was every chance they would get caught in the branches.

'It's a joke,' said Tommy, at last, still staring at them.

'What do you mean, it's a joke?' Bradan retorted. His voice was still shrill. 'Some fecking joke!'

'It's a *joke*, Brade. You know, like them zombie walks where everybody dresses up like they're dead.'

'If that's supposed to be a joke, I don't see what's so fecking funny about it! Scared the shite out of me.'

'So what are you going to do about it? Call the shades? We're on the hop from school, Brade. That's nothing but a joke and the only people who will get themselves into any kind o' bother is us. "Why weren't you in class today?" "Oh, we heard there was a dead nun floating down the Glashaboy on some balloons, bleeding like a pig, and we thought we'd better check that she wasn't real."'

Bradan kept on watching as the balloons drifted out of sight behind the trees, with the figure still slowly rotating beneath them.

'I think we ought to call the shades. We can do it anonymous, like. They won't ask who we are.'

'It's a joke, Brade. Forget it, would you? Look, my worm's gone and disappeared now. I'll have to dig it out again.'

'But what if it wasn't a joke? What if it was real?'

'It's none of our beeswax, is it?'

'No,' said Bradan. 'I'm going to ring them anyway.'

'Well, ring them. But if we get into trouble for hopping off school, then you have to lend me a borrow of your Xbox for two weeks solid, *and* your Wolfenstein game, and two Mars bars. And a backer on your bike to school every day.'

Bradan stepped into the river, as far as he could go before the water started pouring into the top of his rushers. For a few moments he could still see the tops of the balloons above the treetops, but then they vanished. He waded back to the bank and took out his mobile phone.

'I still say it's a joke,' said Tommy. 'Oh no, shite, look, I'm only after spooning the fecking worm in half!'

Eight

When she came out of her office toilet the next morning, Katie found that a beige manila folder had been left on her desk.

A sheet of headed paper from the Cork City Office of the Director of Public Prosecutions was attached with a paper clip. On it, the state solicitor Finola McFerren had scrawled, *With any luck, five years imprisonment!*

She sat down and poured herself a glassful of sparkling Ballygowan mineral water. She hadn't been able to stomach coffee lately, but she felt much better this morning and she had managed to keep her muesli down.

She opened the file. It contained the prosecution's papers on the arrest of Michael Gerrety for sex with an underage girl and reckless endangerment of a minor. Gerrety had successfully avoided prosecution for years, even though the girls advertised on his Cork Fantasy website as 'masseuses' were nothing more than prostitutes, and he owned and ran more than seven brothels in the centre of Cork.

He had always been careful not to pimp girls under the age of seventeen, even though he regularly farmed them out to other, less-scrupulous pimps. But he had been caught out when Roisin Begley, the sixteen-year-old daughter of local property developer Jim Begley, had run away from home thinking that life as a 'fantasy girl' was going to be glamorous and earn her a pile of money.

Roisin had lied to Michael Gerrety that she was already seventeen and he had slept with her himself before setting her up in business as a prostitute. But she had rapidly become disillusioned with the squalor of the sex trade and the depraved demands of the men who paid for her services. She had been rescued from her brothel by Detective Dooley, who had eventually tracked her down by posing as a punter.

Now the Book of Evidence was ready for Michael Gerrety to be tried at the next session of the circuit criminal court. Finola McFerren had attached a note for Katie pointing out that his only feasible defence would be to claim that it had been reasonable for him to assume that Roisin was old enough. In the eyes of the law, it would be no excuse for him to say that she had consented to sex, or even initiated it.

Katie was still reading when Chief Superintendent Denis MacCostagáin knocked at her office door.

'Katie, would you have a moment?' he asked, lugubriously.

'Of course, sir. Nothing wrong, is there?'

He came into the office and made a point of closing the door behind him. He sat down, unfolded a handkerchief and wiped his nose.

Then he said, 'Would you believe that Bryan Molloy has made a reappearance?'

'*Molloy*? Serious? I thought he'd maybe skipped abroad or hung himself from the nearest lamp post.'

'No, not at all. He's turned up at the Garda Ombudsman's office in Dublin, complete with some heavyweight lawyers in tow. I haven't been sent the full details yet, but it appears that he's lodging a formal complaint against you and several other officers here at Anglesea Street.'

'What for?' Katie demanded. 'If anybody should be lodging a formal complaint against anybody, it should be *me* against *him*.'

'Well, he says that he was the victim of constant harassment and insubordination from your junior officers, which was actively encouraged by you, and that you personally made a number of false and slanderous accusations against him. This led to him suffering from a nervous collapse and having to quit his position as Acting Chief Superintendent.'

'*False and slanderous accusations*?' said Katie, in utter disbelief. 'Bryan Molloy paid a gunman to kill one of the most high-profile gang leaders in Limerick so that he wouldn't have to go to the bother of arresting him! He accepted hundreds of thousands of euros in bribes to let some of the worst criminals in the district escape prosecution!'

She was so angry that she had to stand up and pace up and down her office. 'It's pure *incredible*! I only have in my possession the actual gun that he supplied to Donie Quaid to shoot Niall Duggan! And witnesses, too! And as for persecuting him, Mother of God! He only spent every minute of every day trying to belittle me and undermine me. He had me suspended!'

'Well, I know all that, Katie,' said Chief Superintendent MacCostagáin, with a sniff and a mournful sigh. 'I came only to warn you. I think he wants to get his own back on you, and damages. But more than anything else, I'd say he wants his pension restored, and I think he'll do anything and say anything for that.'

'Have you told Jimmy O'Reilly yet?'

'I have, yes. I don't think he was all that surprised, to tell you the truth.'

'Of course he wasn't surprised. Jimmy O'Reilly and Bryan Molloy are as thick as thieves. He's probably known where Molloy was hiding himself ever since he went missing. They've probably been texting each other twenty times a day like a couple of giggly teenagers.'

'Now, then, Katie,' Chief Superintendent MacCostagáin cautioned her. 'Careful what you're saying. You need to be doggie wide with this one. I know that certain accusations were made against Bryan Molloy and Jimmy O'Reilly. But you know as well as I do that you need cast-iron proof of what they were accused of, especially when it comes to those two. They have friends in high places. They have friends in low places, too, who are even more dangerous.'

'Nervous collapse!' said Katie scornfully, shaking her head. 'That man doesn't have a single nerve in his entire body!'

Chief Superintendent MacCostagáin stood up. 'I'll let you know if and when I receive any further information,' he told her. 'It may very well be that the GSOC turn him down. He's no fool, that Simon O'Brien. But all the same, Bryan Molloy can be very convincing, and you can't question his record against the gangs in Limerick. Well, I know *you* do, but everybody else still believes that he was the boy.'

When he had gone, Katie sat down again. *Bryan Molloy.* She could hardly believe it. She had assumed that she had seen and heard the last of him. Still, she knew what a bully he was, and how vengeful, and it must have really rankled that his corruption had been uncovered by a woman officer. He had probably felt like a jihadist who discovers that he has been bombed by a female pilot.

She was making notes on her tablet about the Gerrety prosecution when her phone rang. It was Detective Horgan, sounding weary.

'Just to let you know that all the horses have been hoisted off the beach, ma'am. They've been shipped to an old tractor shed near the Equine Rescue Centre at Dromsligo. That fellow from the ISPCA will be starting tests on them in the morning, along with another vet from Horse Racing Ireland, and some fellow from the Department of Agriculture.'

'All right, Horgan, good. I'll try to get up there myself this afternoon. As soon as we check the horses' identities and find out how they died, we can start asking questions around the training stables and the racetrack. I don't want to go rushing into this, though. Racing's a fierce tight business and it's not going to be easy to persuade anybody to talk about this.'

'Tell me about it. My cousin Tierney works for Jim Culloty at Churchtown and the only tip he's ever given me is not to waste my money betting on the horses.'

* * *

She finished reading through the Book of Evidence against Michael Gerrety and then stood up and went across her office to take her coat from its hook. She could see that the lights were on in Michael Gerrety's apartment at the top of the Elysian, and she wondered how he was feeling now that she had at last managed to take him to court, with a very fair chance of conviction. Irritated, probably, but contemptuous. Michael Gerrety was another of those men who thought that women had been put on this earth simply to serve them.

She was walking along the corridor when Detective Sergeant Ni Nuallán stepped out of the lift and came briskly towards her.

'Ma'am? Are you heading off somewhere?'

'Dromsligo. They've taken all of those dead horses up there for a post-mortem. There's going to be media there, too, so I'll have to be saying a few well-chosen words.'

'I talked to Mother O'Dwyer at the Bon Sauveur Convent.'

'And?'

'And I got the *strongest* feeling that Sister Bridget was not at all popular. The trouble is, Mother O'Dwyer wouldn't say so directly, and there's no possible way of proving it.'

'She didn't give you any names? Anybody who might have borne a grudge against her for any reason?'

Detective Sergeant Ni Nuallán shook her head. 'They're all sisters in Christ, she said, and they get along with each other like sisters.'

Katie said, '*Pff*! If *my* relationship with *my* sisters is anything to go by, there's more fighting in that convent than the Battle of the Boyne.'

'There was something, though,' said Detective Sergeant Ni Nuallán. She took the twisted latex glove out of her coat pocket and held it up so that Katie could see the fragment of jawbone inside it. 'The young nun who answered the door gave me this – Sister Rose O'Sullivan. She said she found it in the convent garden when she was weeding the flower beds.'

Katie took it and examined it carefully. 'It has teeth in it. A child's first teeth, by the look of it. When did she find it?'

'About six weeks ago, that's what she said. She showed it to one of the other sisters but she told her to throw it away and forget about it. She's only a novice, so she was scared to show it to Mother O'Dwyer.'

'What's a child's jawbone doing in a convent flower bed? The Bon Sauveur used to be a home for unmarried mothers and their babies, that's what I find disturbing. I hope to God we're not going to find it's another Tuam.'

'I asked Sister Rose to draw me a sketch map, showing exactly where she found it. She's going to email it to me.'

Katie handed the jawbone back to her. 'Take it to Bill Phinner, would you? See what he has to say. We may have to send it to the path lab in Dublin. Oh, Jesus. This is just what we need. They found the bones of seven hundred and ninety-six children buried at Tuam, didn't they? Let's pray that there was only one little soul buried at the Bon Sauveur.'

Just then her iPhone warbled. She took it out of her pocket and said, 'Detective Superintendent Maguire.'

'Oh, glad I caught you, ma'am. It's O'Donovan. I've just had a call from Sergeant Finlay at Glanmire. You're not going to believe this. It's another dead nun.'

'Please tell me you're joking,' said Katie, looking at Detective Sergeant Ni Nuallán with her eyes wide. Detective Sergeant Ni Nuallán frowned, and mouthed, 'What?'

'He says she's about the same age as Sister Bridget. Late seventies, early eighties, something like that.'

'Where was she found?'

'She came down in the Butlerstown River, that's what he said, right by the Glanmire Bridge.'

'I don't follow you. What did he mean "she came down"?'

'It seems like she was hanging from three gas balloons, ma'am. Hanging by a cord around her neck.'

'*What*? I can hardly believe this.'

60

'Sergeant Finlay says he's closed off the road. He's been down to inspect the body to make sure that life was extinct but otherwise nothing has been touched.'

'Okay, Patrick. I was supposed to be going to Dromsligo to look at all of those dead horses, but I think the horses will have to wait. I'll be down directly. Have you notified the Technical Bureau yet?'

'Not yet, ma'am, but I will.'

Katie pushed her iPhone back into her pocket.

'Another elderly nun,' she told Detective Sergeant Ni Nuallán. 'This one was floating through the air, apparently, hung from three gas balloons. She's landed in the Butlerstown River.'

'Holy Mary. No wonder you couldn't believe it.'

'Come on,' said Katie. 'I'm beginning to think that we're being plagued by nuns.'

Nine

She climbed over the low limestone wall at the side of the bridge and made her way cautiously down the precipitous slope that led to the water's edge, pushing some of the bushes aside and grabbing at others to stop herself losing her footing.

Detective O'Donovan was already there, along with Sergeant Finlay and three other gardaí from the Glanmire Garda station, which was only a few metres down the road. Tangled in the trees beside them were the silvery-grey balloons. Two of them were almost completely deflated now, but one was still bulging and bumping in the breeze. The nun was lying face-down in the bushes, with her feet in the river. The cord with which she had been suspended was still knotted around her neck.

'So what happened?' asked Katie, holding out her hand so that Detective O'Donovan could help her take the last few steps down to the river bank.

'Two young mums were pushing their kids across the bridge and they just looked up and saw these three balloons coming down and getting themselves all snagged up in the trees,' said Sergeant Finlay. He was a short, round man with a bristly grey moustache and two double chins. He looked as if he were close to retirement, if he didn't explode first. 'They came rushing down to the station, "There's all these balloons, there's all these balloons, with a nun hanging off of them!" I thought they were messing to begin with, but you never saw anybody in such a panic.'

'And by the time you got here, she was definitely dead?'

'Oh, no question,' said Sergeant Finlay, shaking his head from side to side as if he needed to convince Katie beyond any doubt at all that there was nothing he could have done to save her. 'Her eyes was wide open but she didn't blink when I waved my hand in front of her face and her lips was blue. I felt for a pulse, but nothing. Apart from that I haven't interfered with her at all. This is exactly how she landed.'

Katie looked around. The river here was only about twenty metres wide, and shallow, and the peaty soil had stained it to the colour of weak tea. It ran very slowly, so that further away from the bridge there was an archipelago of green weed. The breeze was rustling in the trees, but apart from the swishing of passing cars, and the gardaí talking to each other, the afternoon was strangely quiet, as if God had said, *Hush, one of My servants is sleeping her very last sleep.*

She approached the nun's body, with Detective Sergeant Ni Nuallán close behind her. The nun lay on her stomach with her head turned to the left, so that most of her face was visible. She was pale, with wrinkles around her eyes and mouth, and wisps of white hair showing from underneath her coif. As Sergeant Finlay had said, her eyes were wide open, the palest duck-egg blue, but spotted with tiny red petechial haemorrhages.

'Think there's any connection to Sister Bridget?' asked Katie.

'She's a nun, and she's elderly, and from the looks of her eyes she died of strangulation, but who knows? Maybe there's no connection at all. What's the date? Maybe it's just open season on nuns.'

They waited around for another twenty minutes until the Technical Bureau van arrived, as well as the chief technical officer, Bill Phinner, in his bronze estate car. Three technicians suited up on the bridge and were then helped to climb down to the river bank by the gardaí.

'Well, well,' said Bill Phinner. 'I thought I'd seen everything. But a crash-landed nun? Jesus.'

'The wind's blowing from the south-south-west,' said Detective O'Donovan. 'That means she must have floated up the Glashaboy

63

from Lota. Or it could have been even further. She could have come all the way across the river from the south side, Blackrock even.'

'Kieran! I want at least three samples of gas before that fat feller totally deflates!' Bill Phinner shouted out. One of his technicians gave him the thumbs up and clambered around to the other side of the bulging balloon, carrying a Gresham gas-sampling kit in a small black case. Sergeant Finlay looked up sharply, as if he had thought for a moment that Bill Phinner was referring to him.

An ambulance arrived, but it took another hour before the technicians had finished photographing and measuring the nun's body *in situ*. It was beginning to grow dark now, and a chilly evening wind was ruffling the surface of the river, so Katie raised the hood of her duffel coat and pulled on her thick brown woollen gloves.

Two of the gardaí went to the Cafe Chino in the Glanmire bus park and came back with burgers and chips and buttered scones, and Tayto chocolate bars with bits of cheese and onion crisps in them, as well as polystyrene cups of coffee and tea and cans of soft drinks. Detective Sergeant Ni Nuallán and Detective O'Donovan both hounded their burgers as if they hadn't eaten for a week, and O'Donovan ate a Tayto bar, too, but all Katie could manage was a raisin scone and half a can of Coke Zero. She was beginning to feel very cold and tired.

At last, one of the technicians climbed back up to the bridge and said, 'She's all ready to be moved now, sir. Do you want me to call the paramedics?'

'Let's go down first and take a look at the poor soul,' said Bill Phinner, draining the last of his tea and perching his empty cup on the wall.

He went down first, turning around now and again to give Katie a hand, with Detective Sergeant Ni Nuallán and Detective O'Donovan following behind them. They gathered around the nun's body, which was still lying face-down as she had landed. The last balloon was almost completely deflated now and hung drooping in the trees, like an elephant's skin.

Two of the technicians knelt down beside the nun and very carefully turned her over on to her back. They had already closed her eyelids, so that at least she wasn't staring at the sky. Twenty or thirty horse chestnut leaves were stuck to her habit, yellow and brown and shiny red. One of the technicians shone a bright LED forensic flashlight on to them, and it was only than that they saw that the red leaves weren't naturally red but bloodstained. The intense white light showed that her habit was soaked in blood, too.

'Would you look at this?' said Bill Phinner. He tugged on a pair of white latex gloves and crouched down beside the body. He took hold of her habit between finger and thumb and lifted it up, heavy and wet. They realized now that it had been cut apart all the way down the front, from the coif to the hem. As Bill Phinner folded the two sides apart, Katie could see the nun's thin, pale legs, with squiggly blue varicose veins. There were drips and runnels of blood down her shins and her grey socks were soaked with blood.

Without a word, Bill Phinner opened up the nun's habit even further, right up to her collarbone, exposing her naked body in its entirety. Her breasts lay flat on either side of her chest, but from just below her breastbone her abdomen had been sliced wide open. Her intestines were bulging out and hanging halfway down her thighs in beige and bloody coils, and Katie could smell the sharp tang of bile and excrement.

She stared at the nun with her hand pressed over her mouth. She had seen worse, but this was making her stomach muscles clench and unclench. She had seen a woman in Knocka whose husband had pressed her face against an electric hotplate for over half a minute. She had seen a man in Barnavara who had fallen up to his waist in a feed-mincing machine, and had been virtually chopped in half, but was still able to talk to the firefighters who were trying to extricate him with crowbars.

But the sight of this disembowelled nun made her feel hot and sweaty and breathless, and she began to gag.

'Holy Mary, Mother of God,' said Detective Sergeant Ni Nuallán. 'What on earth kind of a devil did this?'

Katie thought that she might be able to control her gagging, but she couldn't. With her hand still pressed against her mouth, she stared at Detective Sergeant Ni Nuallán with watering eyes. Then she turned around and bent over the water's edge and splashed out a torrent of half-chewed scone and raisins and warm brown cola.

Detective O'Donovan grasped her left arm to stop her from teetering forward into the river, while Detective Sergeant Ni Nuallán put her arm around her shoulders. She waited, breathing deeply, until the spasms subsided.

'Are you all right now?' Detective Sergeant Ni Nuallán asked her, and she nodded and stood up straight. Almost at once, though, her stomach convulsed again and she had to lean back over the river. This time she brought up nothing but saliva, but she still felt as if her insides had been twisted into a complicated knot.

She stayed where she was for a minute or so, but at last she began to feel better. She took out a tissue to wipe her eyes and her mouth and blow her nose, and then she said, 'Thanks. I'm fine now. Thanks a million.'

'Let's get one of these officers to drive you home,' said Detective O'Donovan. 'You've probably been overdoing it lately, the caseload you've got. Either that or you've eaten one of them salmon sandwiches from the station canteen.'

'No, no, I'm grand altogether. I have to stay here and see this through.'

Detective Sergeant Ni Nuallán said, 'No, ma'am. I know it sounds insubordinate, like, but I really think you should go home and take it easy for the rest of the day. I mean it.'

She was holding Katie's right hand with her left and looking directly into her eyes. Did she realize that Katie was pregnant? There was something in her tone of voice that suggested she had sensed a change in her lately – a change that wasn't connected to dead horses, or suffocated nuns, or her relationship with John. Maybe it was just female intuition.

'No, you're all right,' Katie told her. 'And don't worry about insubordination. I appreciate the thought.'

'You're sure? You needn't go back to the station, I could have somebody come to your house tomorrow morning to pick you up.'

'No, thanks a million. I didn't have time for any lunch and it was just an attack of the gawks, that's all.'

They climbed back up to the bridge while the technicians took more photographs. Katie was still feeling nauseous and she made sure that she didn't look back down at the nun's body. Her mouth kept flooding with saliva, but she managed to suppress any more spasms.

After another half-hour, the nun was zipped into a black vinyl body bag. She was then lifted up to the road, laid on a trolley, and wheeled over to the ambulance. Earlier in the day Dr O'Brien had come down to Cork from the State Pathologist's Office in Dublin so that he could carry out a post-mortem on Sister Bridget. Once he had finished with her, he would be able to turn his attention to this nun, too.

Detective O'Donovan came over. 'What about the horses, ma'am?' he asked her. 'I could drive over to Dromsligo now if you like and see what kind of progress they're making.'

Katie checked her watch, 'Let me call that fellow from the ISPCA first. It's getting a bit late now and they're probably wrapping up for the day. I'll probably be going over there myself tomorrow morning, unless something else comes up. It's not a very nice thing to say, but dead humans have to take precedence over dead horses.'

She took out her iPhone and called the number that Tadhg Meaney had given her. He took a long time to answer and she thought she would have to leave him a message, but she rang him a second time and this time he picked up immediately and said, 'Hallo? Hallo? Tadhg Meaney here!' He sounded out of breath.

'Oh, Tadhg, how are you doing? It's Detective Superintendent Maguire. I'm sorry I couldn't get out to see you this afternoon. I had a bit of an incident to deal with.'

'That's all right, superintendent. We've only just finished disentangling all the bodies and laying them out. Some of them are in a fierce terrible state, I can tell you.'

Katie swallowed and hoped he wouldn't try to tell her exactly how badly the horses had decomposed. 'You still don't know how they died, then? If they were alive when they were pitched off the top of the cliff, or already dead?'

'Not yet,' Tadhg Meaney told her. 'To be honest with you, we may never know, not unless they died of some disease or other, or they were put down. And there is one thing that's got us scratching our heads already.'

'Oh yes?'

'We've scanned three of the horses already, three that were still in fairly good condition. We found the microchips all right in all three of them, but here's the puzzle. None of the microchip numbers corresponded with any numbers registered at Weatherbys.'

'Now, that *is* a puzzle,' said Katie. Weatherbys was the keeper of the Irish Stud Book and the passport details and microchip numbers of every horse and donkey had to be lodged with them by law.

Tadhg Meaney said, 'The mystery is, superintendent, why would you bother to microchip a horse at all if you weren't going to register it? As far as we can work out, these horses aren't just dead. Legally, they never existed in the first place.'

The next morning was so dark and thundery that Katie had to switch the lights on in her office. She had managed to eat some of John's smoked chicken stew the previous night and this morning she hadn't suffered morning sickness at all. She had slept well, too, and if she had dreamed about the disembowelled nun, she didn't remember it.

She read all of the messages that had been left on her desk, and signed all her letters, and she was ready to leave for Dromsligo when Detective Sergeant Ni Nuallán came into her office, holding up a sheet of paper.

'Sister Rose just emailed me a plan of the convent garden,' she said. 'She must have had to wait until all the other sisters were meditating.'

She laid the plan down on Katie's desk. The convent garden was a large rhomboid, just under a third of a hectare, with walls on the east and south sides separating the convent from the housing estate next to it. Under the east wall there was a vegetable garden, and under the south wall a wide herbaceous border. In the middle of the herbaceous border, about twenty-five metres from where it met the east wall, Sister Rose had drawn a cross. She hadn't written anything on the plan, not even *I found the jawbone here*, and there was no message attached to it.

'She's absolutely petrified of being found out,' said Detective Sergeant Ni Nuallán.

Katie studied the plan for a while and then she said, 'It's

bound to come out sooner or later that it was her. We'll have to apply for a search warrant and the judge is going to want to know what grounds we have for digging up the convent garden.'

If the search had been urgent, Katie could have issued the warrant herself, but Sister Rose had waited six weeks to report that she had found a jawbone and it didn't appear as if anybody's life was in immediate jeopardy. Not only that, it was unlikely that Mother O'Dwyer and the congregation of the Bon Sauveur were likely to try and leave the country in a hurry, so Katie would have to make an application to the district court.

'I'll go and raise the warrant now,' said Detective Sergeant Ni Nuallán. 'It should be ready by the time you get back from Dromsligo.'

'All right, grand. But God alone knows what we're going to find in that garden. Hopefully, nothing but poppies.'

* * *

Detective Horgan drove her in the station's unmarked Toyota Prius. It started to rain as they made their way northwards to Mallow on the N20 – rain that clattered against the windscreen so hard that the wipers could barely cope.

Katie thought that Detective Horgan was unusually quiet. Most of the time he was cracking jokes and telling tall stories and playing ridiculous tricks on his fellow officers, like having his girlfriend call up and complain that she had been 'graped'. When they said, 'Don't you mean "raped"?' she said, 'No, there was a whole bunch of them.'

This morning, though, he had been driving for over twenty minutes and hadn't said a word. He was frowning, too, as if he had something on his mind.

'Everything all right?' Katie asked him.

'Oh. What? No. Everything's grand, thanks.'

'Well, something's bothering you. You're not having problems with any of your cases, are you?'

70

'No, no. I need to be leaning on a couple of witnesses a little harder, do you know what I mean? But that's all.'

They drove for another few miles in silence. The rain began to ease off and the clouds began to drift apart, so that the morning was suddenly brighter.

'Then what is it?' Katie persisted.

'It's nothing,' said Detective Horgan. 'It's personal.'

'Look, if it's affecting your morale, whatever it is, I need to know about it. DI Fennessy had problems at home, without going into too much detail, and look what happened to him. Well, we still don't know what's happened to him. He could be dead for all we've heard.'

They had nearly reached Mallow now. The Victor Dowling Equine Rescue Centre was on the north-west side of the town. It had been almost eight years since Katie had last come out here, soon after the centre had opened. There had been a desperate need in Cork for a shelter for abandoned horses – old barren mares, broken-down racehorses, ponies with laminitis, and badly abused sulky trotters. Katie had visited the centre because they also took care of horses that were being held pending Garda prosecutions, either for theft or mistreatment.

Before they reached the turn-off for Dromsligo, Detective Horgan slowed down and drew the Toyota into the side of the road. He switched off the engine and then he turned to Katie and said, 'It's my girlfriend, Muireann. The fact is, I've knocked her up. It wasn't intentional, but now I don't know what I'm going to do.'

'How far gone is she?'

'I don't know exactly. Well, I think I do. Two months at least. It was that time we went to Dingle and stayed at the Skellig. It did nothing but piss with rain the whole time so we stayed in our hotel room and, you know. There was nothing worth watching on TV.'

'Is she going to get rid of it?'

Detective Horgan shook his head. 'I suggested it, like, and said that I'd pay for her to go to England if she had to. But she won't hear of having an abortion. She's told her ma already, and the whole family's dead religious, do you know what I mean?'

'So what are you going to do? Marry her?'

Detective Horgan's face was a picture of misery. 'I *like* her, like. She's great for a laugh and she likes to go clubbing and all that. She used to, anyway. Now she's being all serious and careful and she won't touch drink. But *marry* her – Jesus, I couldn't imagine spending more than a couple of days with her – not consecutive, like – let alone my whole fecking life.'

'Does she *think* that you're going to marry her?'

Detective Horgan nodded. 'We were walking through French Church Street the other day, and she stopped outside that bridal shop and stared in the window. She didn't say nothing, but she couldn't stop smiling and squeezing my hand, do you know what I mean, like?'

'If you don't want to marry her, you'd better tell her. The sooner the better.'

'Jesus, she's going to lose the head with me if I do that!'

'I'm sorry, Horgan,' said Katie, 'you don't have a choice. You can tell her that you'll look after the baby financially once it's born, and take an interest in it. But don't think about marrying her if you don't really love her. It wouldn't be fair to either of you, or the wain.'

Detective Horgan puffed out his cheeks in resignation. 'You're right, ma'am, I know it. My ma and da got married because of me and they *hated* each other. Like, intensely. My ma always used to say that God gave us the light of love but the Devil gave us children to snuff it out.'

Katie unconsciously laid a hand on her own stomach and thought of what John was going to say when she told him that she was pregnant.

'Come on,' she said. 'Let's take a look at these horses. I made sure I didn't eat anything this morning before I came out here and I'm starved.'

Detective Horgan started up the Toyota again and drove them up the narrow hedge-lined road to Dromsligo.

* * *

They parked outside the Victor Dowling Equine Rescue Centre, a sandy-coloured building covered with ivy, with white-painted stables all around it. As Katie climbed out of the car, Tadhg Meaney came out to meet her, wearing a tweed cap and a noisy brown oilskin raincoat.

'Good timing, superintendent,' he said. 'I'm just on my way to the tractor shed myself.'

'How's progress?' she asked him. 'And for goodness' sake call me Katie, or Kathleen if you want to be formal.'

They walked together across the yard and then around to the back of the stables where there was a huge dilapidated wooden building, more like a barn than a shed, with a sagging Killaloe slate roof. Katie could smell the horses before she saw them. They were giving off a ripe, cloying stench that she could actually taste on her tongue. She always thought that decomposing humans smelled *green*. This smell was darker – greenish-mahogany. She took out the perfume-soaked hand-kerchief that she always carried in her coat pocket and held it up to her nose. Tadhg Meaney saw what she was doing and gave her a wry smile.

'Don't blame you,' he said. 'I always dab some Vicks up my nose, myself, and suck a Fisherman's Friend.'

The large double doors at the front of the shed were wide open. Tarpaulins had been spread out all over the concrete floor and on top of them lay the bodies of the twenty-three horses and foals, in three rows, with the most badly decomposed nearest the front. Some of them were little more than skeletons draped with hairy skin, like horses out of a nightmare, their eye sockets empty because the seagulls had pecked out their eyes. Towards the back of the shed they were mostly intact, except that their stomachs had ballooned out enormously.

'Holy Mary,' said Detective Horgan, flapping his hand in front of his face. 'That's some peggy dell of benjy coming off of this lot.'

The shed was brightly lit by portable halogen lamps on tripods, so that it looked like a film set. Two ISPCA vets in white protective suits and face masks were crouched down beside one of the horses in the second row. One of them was taking blood samples with a large hypodermic syringe, while the other was slowly waving a Detect-a-Chip scanner from side to side between its shoulder blades.

'With any luck, we'll have them all checked out by the end of the day,' said Tadhg. 'There are three four-year-olds, seven three-year-olds, nine two-year-olds, and four foals. None of the foals has been microchipped.' He paused, and then he said, 'I just thank God that the salt water helped to preserve them and that the weather's been as cold as it has. Otherwise, you couldn't have seen past the tip of your nose for the flies.'

Katie took the handkerchief away from her face and tried not to breathe in too deeply. 'You said that the microchips of the first three horses you tested didn't tally with any numbers registered at Weatherbys.'

'That's right. And like I said, that's the whole mystery of it. We've scanned another nine horses since those three, and they're all the same, microchipped but unregistered. They all have standard ISO transponders and out of the fifteen numbers on each of them the first eight numbers are correct, starting with 372 which is the country code for Ireland. But their personal identification numbers have never been officially recorded. The problem is that we don't have the poor creatures' passports to see if the numbers match, or if they've been tampered with at all. That's if they ever *did* have passports.'

'Sounds like one of your good old racing scams to me,' said Detective Horgan.

'It does, yes,' said Katie. 'But the usual reason for forging a passport is to get a sick horse accepted by a slaughterhouse, isn't it? You can get six or seven hundred euros these days for a horse that's fit for human consumption. But these are racehorses. You couldn't get enough meat off the whole lot of them to make a pound of sausages. In fact, you'd have to pay a knackery to dispose of them.'

'I'm thinking that they could well have been ringers,' said Tadhg. 'It's been much harder for racehorse trainers to substitute one horse for another since microchips became compulsory. But there are still ways and means of forging passports and changing microchips, as you well know. The whole racing business is even more chaotic than ever these days, Katie, to say the least. Not to mention corrupt. And don't get me started on the cruelty.'

'How long is it going to take you to analyse the blood samples?' asked Katie.

'We'll be testing for just about everything, although mainly for bute, but I should have some early results for you tomorrow or the day after.'

Katie pressed her handkerchief against her face again but the Chloé perfume did little to mask the overwhelming smell of dead horse, and in a way the strong floral scent made it even more sickening. Her stomach made a gurgling noise and she hoped that Tadhg hadn't heard it.

'Thanks, Tadhg,' she told him. 'I'll wait to hear from you so.'

Tadhg stared at the horses and said nothing. He looked so defeated and sorrowful that Katie wished she could think of something to say to console him, even if it was only, 'Tadhg . . . this wasn't your fault.'

She turned away and left him standing there, and it was only when she and Detective Horgan were about to round the corner by the stables that he called out, 'Thanks for coming by, Katie! I'll be in touch as soon as I can!'

* * *

'So, what do you think?' Katie asked Detective Horgan as they drove back down the narrow country road to rejoin the N20.

'Well, it stinks all right, and not only of dead horses. Like we said, it must be some kind of a racing scam. But what I can't understand is, if you're cute enough to pull off a racket involving twenty-three thoroughbred horses, why throw them off a cliff where somebody's bound to stumble across them sooner or later? Why not cremate them, or bury them in a bog, or fill them full of rocks and take them out to sea where nobody's going to find them?'

'Maybe they thought the tide would carry them away.'

'That's possible, but tides turn, don't they? And even if the tide had taken them out, it might well have washed them back in again. Whoever threw them off that cliff either did it for some fiendishly clever reason, or else they're incredibly thick.'

Katie couldn't help shaking her head and smiling. 'This is Cork, Horgan. I think the chances of it being done for some fiendishly clever reason are pretty remote. I'd go for thick.'

They reached the N20. The only other vehicle in sight was a silver Mercedes parked in a lay-by about thirty metres to the north, on the left-hand side of the road but facing towards them. Detective Horgan was about to pull out when the Mercedes swerved out of the lay-by and came speeding in their direction.

Katie instinctively grabbed his arm and said, 'Back up!'

'What?'

'*Back up!*'

Detective Horgan tugged the gear lever into reverse, but as he did so there was an ear-splitting crack! and his head jerked backwards. The Toyota slewed to the left and thumped into the high grass verge behind them. Katie's head banged hard against the headrest but she immediately ducked down sideways so that she was hidden from view.

A few seconds passed. The Toyota's engine had stopped and there was silence.

'Horgan?' said Katie, with her head still resting against his thigh. 'Hoggy, are you all right?'

She felt a warm, wet drop on her ear and quickly sat up. The silver Mercedes had gone and the main road was deserted. There was a circular hole in the windscreen about two centimetres in diameter and when she looked at Detective Horgan she saw that his head was slumped forward on his chest and that blood was dripping from his forehead. The back of his head was a tangle of hair and blood, with a large lump of pinkish-grey brain matter drooping down on to his shirt collar.

She touched her earlobe with her fingertips and they came away red. She took out her handkerchief and wiped them, and then wiped her ear, and then she reached over for the car's radio microphone to call Detective Inspector O'Rourke.

'Francis?' she heard herself saying. 'Yes, this is Detective Superintendent Maguire. We've been shot at and Detective Horgan is down. Yes. I'm at the junction of the N20 with the Dromsligo road, about a kilometre north of Mallow. Can you ask Superintendent McCarthy to send some local back-up, and can you get up here yourself, as soon as you can. Bring O'Donovan with you. I need a technical team, too, and a white van.'

She climbed out of the car and stood beside it with the cold wind ruffling her hair. 'The shot came from a silver Mercedes saloon,' she said. 'Put out a bulletin to stop every car of that description within a thirty-five mile radius of Mallow. Be warned that the occupants could be armed and dangerous.'

'Consider it done,' said Detective Inspector O'Rourke. 'You're not hurt yourself, are you?'

'No, no. Not at all. They might have been trying to hit me, but they took out poor Horgan instead.'

She lowered the microphone and then stood and waited, using the half-open car door to shield herself from the wind. She couldn't stop herself from shaking, partly with cold and partly with shock, but she didn't want to get back into the passenger seat. She couldn't even bring herself to look at Detective Horgan, sitting behind the wheel with his head bowed, although she could see his blood-spotted hand resting in his lap. Her gorge rose and it was as much as she could do to stop herself from retching. She could still taste those dead horses, and Chloé perfume, and there was a strong smell of slurry on the wind, too, from the fields around her.

It took the first patrol car only seven minutes to reach her, followed less than a minute later by another. Their blue lights were flashing, but the road was empty of traffic so they weren't sounding their sirens. Four gardaí climbed out and approached her cautiously.

'Jesus,' said one of them, bending down to peer into the Toyota's offside window. He crossed himself and added, 'Right between the eyes.'

A young female garda said, '*You* didn't get hit, ma'am?'

'No, thank God,' said Katie. 'I was haunted they just took the one shot.'

'Do you have any idea who they were?' asked another garda.

'No idea at all. And I can't think how they knew who *we* were, or how they knew that we were here in Dromsligo.'

'Couldn't have been mistaken identity, I suppose?' the garda suggested. 'We've had some trouble between a couple of the less-desirable families in the area lately.'

'It's possible, but I don't think it's very likely. We don't exactly fit the profile, do we?'

'How about we drive you back to Cork, ma'am?' asked another garda. 'That must have been a fierce shock, like, seeing your man shot right next to you.'

'That's appreciated, but I'll stay for a while,' said Katie. 'Detective Inspector O'Rourke is on his way here from Anglesea Street and I want to talk to the technical team, too, when they arrive.'

'Why don't you come and sit in our car then, ma'am?' said the female garda. She was plump, with china-blue eyes. 'You're looking fair foundered there and at least it'll keep you warm.'

Katie was about to decline that offer, too. Detective Horgan had been shot dead, but she was almost sure that the shooter had been aiming for her, and she didn't want to walk away and leave him sitting there. God, he had celebrated his twenty-seventh birthday only two weeks ago. But she was trembling now, and she was beginning to feel as if the Tarmac was tilting underneath her feet, so she smiled and nodded and said, 'Yes, thanks, I think I will.'

'I have some hot tea in the car, too, if you'd like some,' said the garda as she led her over to the patrol car.

Katie sat in the back seat and took out her iPhone so that she could check on Detective Inspector O'Rourke and see how long it was going to take him to get to Dromsligo. She had a message from John. *Hope ur not 2 busy 2nite. Ive booked us a table @ Hayfield 2 celebr8 amazing flu vaccine sale!*

She started to send him a text in reply, telling him that Detective Horgan had been killed while she was in the car with him, but after only a few words she deleted it. How could she use Horgan's death as an excuse not to go out to dinner?

Far worse than that, she was going to have to break the news to his girlfriend, Muireann.

Eleven

She stayed at the scene until Detective Inspector O'Rourke and Detective O'Donovan arrived, followed ten minutes later by a team of four technicians. The Mallow gardaí had closed the N20 for nearly two hours now and three more officers and seven Garda reserves had arrived to help search the road surface on their hands and knees for any possible evidence.

There were tyre tracks in the lay-by where the silver Mercedes had been waiting for them and the technical experts would take photographs and casts of those, but the shot had almost certainly come from a rifle, so it was highly unlikely that they would find a spent cartridge. Katie was feeling warmer now, and her stomach had settled, so she climbed out of the patrol car to watch the technicians at work and to talk to Detective Inspector O'Rourke.

'Was there any case that Horgan was working on that might have put him at risk of his life?' asked Detective Inspector O'Rourke.

'He arrested Jurgis Walunis last week,' said Katie. 'He's the younger brother of Algis Walunis, that Lithuanian drug-dealer we were talking about the other day. Walunis can be very violent to anybody who crosses him. We've arrested him God knows how many times for assault, but can we ever find a witness to stand up in court?'

'You think Walunis might have done this?'

Katie thought about it, and then shook her head. 'It's not really his style. He likes to hear his victims begging for mercy, and he usually uses a knife or a broken bottle, or a baseball bat.'

'Anybody else?'

'I know that Horgan was checking on two male suspects in Togher because he had information that they were members of the Real IRA and were both in possession of firearms. I'm not sure what the latest story was with that, but he told me yesterday morning that he was hoping to make an arrest this weekend.'

'But what if it wasn't Horgan they were after? What if it was *you*?'

'Well, that was my first thought,' said Katie. 'Just at the moment there's any number of serial scumbags who would breathe a deep sigh of relief if I could be disposed of.'

Technical expert Denis McBride came waddling up to them in his Tyvek suit, holding up a bullet in a pair of tweezers. He was bespectacled and neatly bearded and deeply serious, and one of the best ballistics experts in the country.

'I found this buried in the back seat upholstery,' he said. 'It's a very powerful round indeed – 7.62 × 54 millimetre R – often used for sniper rifles, especially in Russia and Eastern European countries.'

'Well, we know that a large proportion of the guns we find in Cork are smuggled in from the Baltic States and the Czech Republic,' said Katie. 'So, yes – I suppose it could have been Walunis, or one of his gang, but I still don't think that Walunis would have been so clinical. This was a calculated hit. From what I've heard, Walunis has to work himself up into a frenzy first.'

'Obviously I'll have to examine this round more closely, back in the lab,' said Denis McBride. 'At a guess, though, I'd say it came from a Mosin-Nagant or Dragunov rifle, or a derivative thereof. They were manufactured under licence in many different countries – Finland, Poland, Norway – and usually they're not too expensive, about six or seven hundred euros on the black market.'

'Thanks, Denis,' said Katie. She looked back at the Toyota. The interior was fitfully lit up by camera flashes, so that she could see Detective Horgan sitting behind the wheel and the blood that had sprayed all over the seat behind him. She turned to Detective

Inspector O'Rourke and said, 'I think I'll be getting back to the station now, Francis, if you don't mind driving me.'

'Not at all,' said Detective Inspector O'Rourke. 'I should think you've had enough for one day. If I was you, and my missus was me, I'd give you a goody and send you to bed.'

If the circumstances had been different, Katie could have smiled. She hadn't been given a goody since she was off school with the chickenpox – white bread soaked in hot milk with a spoonful of honey stirred in. But then again, it made her think of her mother, and that unexpectedly gave her a lump in her throat.

* * *

They had almost reached the city when Katie's iPhone warbled. It was Detective Dooley ringing her.

'I was wondering if you were still up in Dromsligo, ma'am.'

'No, no, I'm on my way back,' Katie told him. 'I won't be more than a couple of minutes. We're in Blackpool, just passing the brewery.'

'Jesus, that was an awful land about Horgan. None of us can believe it.'

'I know, Dooley, I know. We can all get together later and talk about it. I think we'll need to.'

'You're all right yourself, though?'

'Shocked, like you are. But I wasn't hurt.'

'Thank God for that. I'll see you when you get in so.'

There was something in his tone of voice that made Katie think that he wanted to say more, but was hesitant.

'Was there something else?' she asked him.

'No, no, it'll keep. You'll be back here directly.'

'Go on, tell me.'

'Well – that was why I wanted to know where you were. We've had a response to that appeal you put out on the television.'

'About the dead horses, you mean?'

'That's right. I think it might have given us a really good lead. In fact, better than good.'

'Okay, that's sounds encouraging. Tell me when I get in. I won't be long now.'

They crossed over the Christy Ring bridge and drove along Merchants Quay. It was growing dark now and the street lights along the river were coming on. Katie never liked this time of year. It always reminded her of the happy times that would never come back, and all the people she had lost.

Detective Inspector O'Rourke turned into the station car park and tugged on the handbrake. 'You'll forgive me for saying this to you, ma'am, no disrespect meant, but you won't be overdoing it?'

'No, Francis, I promise. And thank you.'

Detective Dooley was waiting for her in her office. With one shirt tail hanging out and his red tie crooked, he looked like a schoolboy who had come out second-best in a playground scatter.

'Horgan, of all people,' he said, as she hung up her coat. 'He was such a messer, always making us laugh. I mean, Jesus and Mary and holy Saint Joseph tonight, why would anybody want to shoot *him*? It was on the TV news only about half an hour ago, although they didn't name him. I saw you there, too.'

'I'll tell you all about it after,' said Katie. 'Right now, I'd rather get back to business.'

'You don't even have a breeze who the shooter was?'

'Not really, no. Denis McBride said the bullet was probably came from some Russian or Eastern European sniper rifle, but at the moment it's anybody's guess who fired it, or why, or even who they were aiming at. It might not have been Horgan.'

'You mean it might have been you?'

'As I said, let's talk about it later,' Katie told him, sitting down at her desk. 'Tell me about this really great lead we've been given.'

'Oh, right,' said Detective Dooley. 'This young couple came into the station about an hour ago. They're downstairs now, in the visitors' room. They didn't see your appeal for themselves but a friend of theirs did and told them about it and they put two and two together, like.'

Detective Dooley prodded at a white mobile phone and then handed it to her. There was a selfie on the screen of a boy and a girl, both about eighteen years old, their hair tousled by the wind, both grinning and making thumbs-up signs. Behind them rose a grassy slope and on the slope three horses were grazing, two chestnuts and a bay. The horses were at least thirty metres away, and partly obscured by the boy's head and right shoulder, but their coats were shining in the sunlight and as far as Katie could tell they were all in a fair condition, not swaybacked or moth-eaten. In the background she could see the thin blue strip of the sea, so they were clearly standing on a cliff top.

She peered at the selfie even closer. 'How about this,' she said, shaking her head, because there was more in the background than horses. On the right-hand side, half of the rear end of a large dark-green horsebox was visible. Two men were standing next to it, smoking. One wore a red tartan shirt and a pale-brown cap, the other a plain white collarless shirt and a black waistcoat. They had their backs turned away, so their faces were hidden, but Katie could make out the first six digits of the horsebox's number plate, 131-C-74.

'*That* is the cliff top at Nohaval Cove,' said Detective Dooley. 'And *that* is an Annard Renault Midlum 7.5 tonne horsebox. I've checked it out with the RSA and it was registered in March 2013 to one Paddy Fearon of Spring Lane Halting Site.'

Katie studied the picture closely. 'This was taken in the summer, by the look of it.'

'July the eighteenth. They'd been dating each other exactly a month. Between you and me, I think they'd been looking for somewhere to have it in the open air. But then this horsebox and these two rough-looking fellers showed up and threatened them, so they did a legger.'

'I'd like to ask them a few questions,' said Katie. 'Does this phone belong to them?'

'Yes, but I've already sent a copy of that selfie to my own laptop.'

'Good,' said Katie, standing up. 'I don't want to start counting any chickens, but I think you may be right. This could be just the break we need.'

Detective Dooley accompanied her to the doorway, but just as she was walking through it he said, 'Ma'am?'

'What is it?'

He touched his left cheek with his fingertips. 'Sorry – but I think you have some blood on your face.'

* * *

When Katie and Detective Dooley walked into the visitors' room, the young couple were holding hands and looking anxious.

'We won't have to stay here much longer, will we?' asked the boy. 'I should have been back at work an hour ago.'

'No, we won't keep you,' said Katie. 'I just wanted to have a quick word with you before you left. I'm Detective Superintendent Maguire, and you are?'

'Michael – Michael Calvey, and this is Shelagh McGee.'

Katie handed Michael the mobile phone. 'I really appreciate you both coming in to show us your picture,' she said. 'We don't know for sure yet, until we've made further enquiries, but you could have given us some very important evidence.'

'One of our pals saw it on the telly, about them horses being slung off the cliff at Nohaval Cove, and he remembered us talking about it and them two fellers chasing us off.'

'Detective Dooley said this happened in July.'

'That's right. We was only trying to spend a bit of time together, like. We're both of us still living at home with our families and it's a nightmare. Always my younger brothers knocking at my bedroom door and saying are you shifting her?'

'Same in my house,' said Shelagh, blushing. 'With me it's usually me mam knocking and asking us if we want a cup of tea or a piece of cake, but you know she's only checking on us.'

'So you went to the cliff top at Nohaval Cove to get some privacy?'

'Well, that's right, like,' said Michael. 'It was a grand warm day and all but usually there's nobody up there because it's hard to get to, you know? I had my bike then, my Yamaha 125, so there wasn't any problem.'

'What time of day was this?' asked Katie.

'About three in the afternoon. We'd had burgers at McDonald's and then we decided to get out of the city and take a walk by the sea.'

'When did the horsebox arrive?'

'Not so long after we did. Maybe ten or fifteen minutes later, something like that. We could see it coming along the track beside the field and we was thinking to ourselves what in the name of Jesus is somebody bringing a horsebox out here for? Well, you saw it in the photo, it was a big one, too.'

'It parked right up close to where we was sitting,' put in Shelagh. 'Then these two fellers got out and they stared at us like what do you think *you're* doing here? If a look could kill you, like. But Mikey said don't pay them any mind, this is a free country and we're just as entitled to be here as they are, and maybe they won't stay very long.'

'But then they let out the horses?' said Katie.

'They did, yeah, and the horses was just wandering around chewing the grass, like, and the two fellers had a smoke, and that was when we took the selfie. I don't think they saw us taking it, though, they was too busy having some kind of a discussion. We'd already decided to mosey off anyway, because the whole point of us going there was to be on our own.'

'Did they say anything to you?'

'Oh, did they!' said Michael. 'Your man in the red shirt finished his fag and then he came over to where we was sitting and said, "Eff off, the pair of ye!" Just like that. Just, "Eff off!" So I said, "Oh yeah, boy, and supposing we don't?" So he said, "Are ye looking to get yourself mangled, because you're going the right way about it?"'

Shelagh took hold of Michael's left hand between both of hers. 'I think Mikey was ready to claim the feller, but I knew he wouldn't stand a chance and that's not saying that he can't stand up for himself. So I said, "Let's go, Mikey," and so we did.'

'Did you look back when you were leaving to see what those two were up to?'

'I turned around the once,' said Shelagh. 'They was still standing there glaring at us.'

'And you could still see the horses?'

She nodded. 'Yes. But I just wanted to get away from there as quick as we could. I was really freaked, I tell you.'

Katie stood up. 'Michael – Shelagh – thank you both for coming forward. You've been really helpful. We can contact you again if we need to?'

'You won't be putting our names in the papers or nothing?' asked Michael.

'No, we won't be doing that. And I doubt if we'll be asking you to appear in court as witnesses, either. Your selfie is the most important evidence you've given us. At least we have somewhere to start looking.'

Detective Dooley escorted the young couple along the corridor to the reception area and saw them out of the building. Katie was waiting for him outside the visitors' room when he came back.

'We're going to have to play this one very, very careful,' she said. 'You know what Spring Lane is like. Even if we manage to find this Paddy Fearon, he'll probably say that he's never owned a horsebox in his life, or that he's not really Paddy Fearon at all but somebody else altogether, and *that's* if we can manage to interview him without having rockers and bottles thrown at us or some saintly social worker from Pavee Point accusing us of racism.'

'Well, of course,' said Detective Dooley. 'I wasn't planning to rush around to Spring Lane mob-handed. I'll start to ask some discreet questions among the Travellers first. There's a couple of young girls I know from the halting site who think I'm a DJ. And I'll also see if I can't locate this horsebox. With any luck it won't have been resprayed or scrapped or burned out on some farm somewhere.'

'DI O'Rourke has some good contacts in the Traveller community,' she said. 'I'll have a word with him.'

She looked at her watch. 'I'm going to talk to Chief Superintendent MacCostagáin about Horgan and then I think we'll probably have a station meeting. I expect we'll be holding a media conference, too, once Horgan's next of kin have been informed.'

Detective Dooley shrugged and nodded, but said nothing. Katie went up to him and straightened his tie. 'Come on, Dooley,' she said gently. 'There's always a risk involved in this job. That's part of the reason we do it. Tuck your shirt in, take a deep breath, and try to remember the last time Horgan made you laugh.'

'He always used to say that if he got killed, he'd throw a mickey fit.'

'Oh, I doubt if he's doing that,' said Katie. 'I'll bet he's sitting outside the pearly gates right now, itching to tell Saint Peter one of his terrible knock-knock jokes.'

* * *

Chief Superintendent MacCostagáin was sitting at his desk looking glummer than ever. Detective Inspector O'Rourke was in his office, too, as well as Superintendent Pearse and Sergeant O'Farrell and the keen new press officer, Mathew McElvey.

'Well, Katie, this is a fair shock and no mistake,' said Chief Superintendent MacCostagáin. 'Francis here tells me that you weren't hurt at all, and that's a blessing.'

'I've been wracking my brains trying to think who might have done it, though,' said Katie. 'Like, the list of possible suspects is almost endless, but why now, and why there?'

Superintendent Pearse finished making an elaborate performance of blowing his nose and then he said, 'You're right. The timing is a puzzler. On top of that, how the devil did they know you were up at Dromsligo at that particular time and what car you were in?'

'I have no idea,' Katie admitted. 'Not unless we have another mole in the station.'

'They could have been waiting for you outside the station here and followed you,' said Superintendent Pearse. 'That would have been risky, though, with all the parking restrictions around here. There's that loading bay in Eglinton Street, right opposite the car park entrance, but even if they hadn't been moved on or given a ticket, they would have been picked up on CCTV. In fact, I have Sergeant Byrnes going back through all of today's footage right now.'

Detective Inspector O'Rourke held up a torn-off sheet of notepad and said, 'I have all the details of Horgan's next of kin here, ma'am. I don't know if you feel up to informing them yourself, or if you'd prefer me to do it. Apparently his girlfriend's rung the station already asking for him, but she was told that he was unavailable.'

'Where do they live?' asked Katie.

'Old Youghal Road, Mayfield.'

'That's all right. I'll go up there myself. I'll take Kyna Ni Nuallán with me. She's good at breaking bad news.'

Chief Superintendent MacCostagáin peered at his watch and said, 'If you can be back by seven, Katie, we'll be having a station meeting in the conference room. I've already been in touch with the Cork Counselling Centre and they can send a therapist around if anybody feels the need for one. After that we'll be holding a short media briefing.'

'That'll be at eight, in time for the nine o'clock news and the newspaper deadlines,' added Mathew McElvey. Katie thought he looked more like a junior sales assistant in the Bedding Department at Brown Thomas than a Garda press officer, and she was convinced that he plucked his eyebrows. All the same, he was very clever at keeping the media happy without giving away too many operational details.

She was turning to leave when Chief Superintendent MacCostagáin said, 'Katie, one more thing,' and got up from his desk. He took her out into the corridor and along to the glass-enclosed staircase at the back of the building, where they wouldn't be overheard.

'Don't tell me,' she said, 'you've had an update from the Ombudsman's office.'

'That's right,' he told her. 'They'll be sending two of their people down on Thursday morning to ask you some questions about Bryan Molloy. He's not only alleging that you bullied and harassed him. He's also accusing you of concocting false evidence against him. He says that you bribed one or more criminal informants in Limerick and he claims that he can produce witnesses to prove it.'

Katie stood with her mouth open, barely able to believe what Chief Superintendent MacCostagáin had just said to her. 'That man is a living outrage. I really mean it. You know yourself what a gowl he is.'

'No comment, Katie. He really turned things around in Limerick, fair bows, and he's always been straight with me.'

'Yes, but you're a man and you played golf with him.'

'True. But I think he quite fancied you if the truth be known.'

'Well – I'm not going to start worrying about him now,' said Katie. 'I have much more important things to be doing. Like, I have to tell Mr and Mrs Horgan that they've lost their only son, and I have to tell his girlfriend that the baby she's carrying is going to be born an orphan.'

'Oh no, is that true?' said Chief Superintendent MacCostagáin. 'That's tragic.'

'He told me on the way to Dromsligo. He said he didn't know what he was going to do about it. He liked the girl but he didn't want to marry her.'

'Lord lantern of Jesus, it's enough to make the angels weep. And talking of that, what's the story with the flying nun? Do you think there's any link at all with that sister who was killed at the Mount Hill Nursing Home?'

'I won't get a post-mortem report from Dr O'Brien until late tomorrow at the earliest,' Katie told him. 'We haven't even been able to identify her yet, as far as I know. She might have belonged to a different order altogether. I'm hoping that Kyna Ni Nuallán will be able to give me an update. I sent her off to apply for a search warrant for the gardens at Bon Sauveur Convent before I left for Dromsligo. She should have it by now.'

'Oh yes, the child's jawbone,' said Chief Superintendent MacCostagáin. 'Come and have a word with me as soon as you know that you have your warrant. It's going to take us a day or two at least to set up a search team. Of course, if we find anything at all we'll have to be calling in RMR Engineering to carry out a ground-radar survey, and if *they* find anything at all we'll have to be calling in the forensic archaeologists.'

He waited while a female garda came clattering down the stairs, smiling at her briefly and then returning to his default gloomy expression.

'There goes my annual budget, in other words,' he added.

Twelve

Detective Sergeant Ni Nuallán was waiting for her in her office, holding a blue plastic folder and staring out of the window. Katie came in and closed the door behind her, then she walked over to the window and stood facing her. Neither of them spoke, but they looked intently into each other's eyes, trying to interpret what they were feeling.

It had started raining again and the rain made a soft pattering sound against the glass.

Without a word, Katie took Kyna into her arms and held her close. Kyna dropped her folder on to the carpet and held Katie, too. They kissed, tenderly but chastely, both with their eyes open, as if they needed to see one another as close as possible.

'Thank God you're safe,' said Kyna, touching Katie's cheek and then stroking her hair.

For a moment they pressed their foreheads together and then Katie gave Kyna's hand a quick squeeze and walked across to her desk. Kyna bobbed down to pick up her folder and followed her.

'You managed to get the search warrant?' asked Katie.

'Here you are. All signed and stamped. His Honour Judge Monaghan took a little persuading, on account of us wanting to dig up the grounds of a convent, which has only ever been tended by nuns. But I think he was persuaded when I mentioned all of the children's skeletons that were found at Tuam. If he'd refused to grant the warrant, he would have had to explain *why* he hadn't granted it and His Honour Judge Monaghan doesn't like having to explain himself to anybody. Even more than that, he doesn't like scandal.'

'Good,' said Katie. She took the folder, opened it up and quickly scanned the search warrant. 'In fact, this is more than good. He's not only given us the authority to search the convent gardens, but the convent building, too. How did you manage to persuade him to do that?'

'I convinced him that we might find some very important supporting evidence if we could search the entire premises. Maybe there's still some left-over clothing that belonged to the children who were taken in there. Or maybe we can find ledgers that list all of their names and tell us what happened to them. Like, you know, which children were adopted, and which children died, and what did they die of, and what happened to their remains?'

'Excellent work, Kyna. Good. And have you managed to get in touch with Dr O'Brien?'

'Only briefly. He was up the walls when I called him, especially with that second nun being brought in for an autopsy. He confirmed that the cause of Sister Bridget's death was asphyxiation, most likely with a goose-down pillow because he found a goose feather stuck to the back of her oesophagus. Immediately prior to death she had been forcibly penetrated with a blue-painted resin figurine, both vaginally and anally. The anal penetration had caused perforation of the rectum, which accounts for the blood we saw on her sheet.'

'I don't suppose he's had a chance yet to look at the other nun.'

'Not yet, no. Not in any detail, like. But he did say that it looked as if she had died from loss of blood. In other words, she was hanging by her neck from those balloons but the rope wasn't tight enough to strangle her. It wasn't likely that she would have been conscious, in his opinion, but while she was floating over the Glashaboy she was probably still alive.'

'Mother of God. I'll be very surprised if these two killings aren't connected in some way. Whoever the offender is, you can't accuse him of lacking imagination. Or *her*.'

'I don't think we're looking for a woman, ma'am,' said Kyna. 'I can't see a woman treating another woman like that. Especially with the figurine. That was *rape*.'

The emphatic way she said *rape* made Katie look up at her. But she had turned away now, so she couldn't see the expression on her face. She was momentarily tempted to ask her about it, but then she decided to leave it. This wasn't the time for psychoanalysis. They had to drive up to Mayfield and tell Detective Horgan's parents that their son had been killed.

* * *

The Horgans lived in a small orange-painted house in the middle of a terrace of four houses opposite the Cotton Ball pub. The houses on either side of them were dank, with unpainted pebble-dash and litter in their driveways, but the Horgans obviously took a pride in their property. There was a low pierced-concrete wall around the front yard and two privet bushes in wooden tubs. A three-year-old Hyundai hatchback was parked outside, with a cardboard pine tree hanging from the rear-view mirror.

As soon as Detective Sergeant Ni Nuallán pressed the doorbell, the door was opened up by a short, dark-haired girl in a blue wool dress. She had a pale oval face and wore no make-up except for two spots of purple eye-shadow. Behind her in the narrow corridor stood a bespectacled, middle-aged woman in an oatmeal-coloured cardigan. As soon she saw Katie and Kyna she let out a loud honk of dismay.

'Oh, sacred heart of Jesus, I knew it was him! Please don't tell me it was him!'

Tears began to roll down the dark-haired girl's cheeks, streaked with purple. 'You'd best come in,' she said, standing aside.

Mrs Horgan ushered them through to the small, gloomy front parlour, which smelled as if normally nobody was allowed to sit in it. All of the side tables were covered in lace tablecloths, and there was even a row of lace doilies along the mantelpiece underneath a collection of china dogs. Over the fireplace hung a large reproduction of Jack Butler Yeats's painting of a galloping horse, *The Whistle of a Jacket*.

'My neighbour came in and said she'd heard on the news that a Cork detective was murdered,' said Mrs Horgan, miserably twisting the sleeve of her cardigan. 'I don't know why I should have been so sure that it was Kenny. I just felt it in my water. I had Muireann ring him at the station but they said he wasn't there and that's when I knew for certain. I've been sitting here waiting all day for you to come and tell me that it was him and here you are.'

'Did he – did he suffer at all?' asked Muireann.

'No,' said Katie gently. 'I was with him when it happened and it was instantaneous. He wouldn't have felt anything.'

'Oh God, oh God, I don't know what his father's going to say,' sobbed Mrs Horgan. 'Kenny was always his bar of gold. He's going to be devastated.'

As simply and as briefly as she could, Katie explained how Detective Horgan had been shot.

'Do you know who did it, like?' asked Muireann. She kept one hand pressed against her stomach.

Katie shook her head. 'No, we don't. In this job, if you're any good at it, you can't help but make some very dangerous enemies, but we have no idea yet who might have wanted to end Kenny's life. We'll find out sooner or later, though, I can promise you that, and they'll pay for what they did.'

'I can't tell you how much we're going to miss him,' said Kyna. 'He was one of the funniest, warmest people I've ever worked with. You could never tell, could you, if he was joking or not?'

Mrs Horgan pressed her hand to her mouth and nodded, and Muireann tried to smile through her tears.

'He was such a good detective, though,' added Kyna. 'He'd be ribbing people so much that they'd tell him anything. He's not just a terrible sad loss to his family, Mrs Horgan, and to his friends, but to the Garda, too.'

Katie said, 'There has to be a post-mortem, I'm afraid. That's routine after an incident like this. But if you contact Jerh

O'Connor the undertaker's in Coburg Street they'll tell you what arrangements can be made for you to see him once that's done, and they'll help you with the funeral. A Garda Síochána will cover all your expenses.'

Mrs Horgan went into the kitchen to make them all a cup of tea. They were pushed for time now, but they could hardly refuse. While she was gone, Muireann dabbed her eyes with a tissue and then Kyna said, 'Here,' and took the tissue from her and wiped away the rest of her tear-blotched eye-shadow.

Katie said, 'Kenny had a private word with me this morning, Muireann. He told me that you were expecting his baby.'

'He told *you*?' she said, in a whisper. She glanced towards the door to make sure that Mrs Horgan couldn't overhear them. 'He hasn't even told his own parents yet. Well, his dad's in the Mercy at the moment, for his heart, and he didn't want to tell him in case it gave him a seizure. Why did he tell you? He hadn't changed his mind about it, had he? He wanted me to get rid of it at first, but then he said he was okay about it after all. We were going to get married.'

Katie reached out and held Muireann's hand. Muireann blinked at her, so grief-stricken and yet so hopeful that, for the first time in a long time, Katie told a lie. 'He was over the moon about it, Muireann. He said he loved you and he was looking forward so much to marrying you and bringing up your child together. The reason he told me was because he was so happy and he wanted to share it with someone.'

Muireann's eyes filled with tears again and her lower lip trembled. 'It's so sad,' she said. 'I was worried that he didn't want to marry me. Whenever I said that we needed to decide on a date he'd turn all moody and wouldn't discuss it. My dad said that if he didn't marry me, he'd kill him.'

'Your dad said that?' asked Katie.

'Oh, he didn't actually mean it, not for real, like.'

'You're sure about that?'

'Of course.'

Katie looked across at Kyna and Kyna raised one eyebrow,

as if to acknowledge that they should do a quick background check on Muireann's father. Angry and drunk and disillusioned people were always threatening to kill whoever it was that had upset them. Most of the time it was nothing but bluster, but now and again they actually went out and did it. Not only that, it was often the least likely people who carried out their threats. A former Garda inspector himself, Katie's father always used to quote Sir John Pentland Mahaffy: 'In Ireland the inevitable never happens and the unexpected constantly occurs.'

Mrs Horgan brought in a tea tray. They sat drinking their tea and giving each other sad, rueful smiles, although none of them ate the ginger biscuits that she had laid out.

Mrs Horgan said, 'He was always joking, Kenny, even as a small boy. He'd say "Knock! Knock!" and we'd say, "Who is it?" and he'd say, "Canoe!" and we'd say, "Canoe who?" and he'd say, "Canoe help me with my homework?"'

She took a deep, agonized breath and put down her teacup, spilling tea into her saucer. Then she wept, and wept, with her head bowed and her hands covering her face and there was nothing that any of them could do to console her.

* * *

Katie didn't get home until half past midnight. When she turned into her driveway she saw that a shiny black Ford C-Max was parked there already. She climbed stiffly out of her car and as she did so the front door opened and John came out, with Barney snuffling and whuffling at his heels.

'How are you, darling?' said John. He took her briefcase from her and gave her a hug and kissed her. 'God almighty, what a terrible day you've had.'

Katie pressed her head against his dark-green cable-knit sweater for a moment, just for the reassurance of feeling him and smelling him. Then she looked up at him and said, 'I'm okay. I'm just racked, that's all. I could do with a shower and a mug of hot chocolate and a nice warm bed.'

She nodded towards the C-Max. 'You haven't rented that, have you? I know the manager of the Ford Centre at Forge Hill. He would have lent you a borrow of one for nothing.'

'No, I've bought it. I can't live way out here in Cobh without a car, can I?'

He put his arm around her and together they went into the house.

Katie hung up her coat and went into the living room. The television was still on although the volume was turned right down. It was showing a programme about body donation at Trinity College, Dublin, *Parting Gift*, which she had seen before. *That's grimly appropriate*, she thought.

'I saw you on the news this evening,' said John. 'I was really impressed the way you held it together.'

'What else could I do?' she said. 'Horgan's dead and all the weeping in the world isn't going to bring him back. It was the shock, though. We were just about to turn on to the N20 and this Mercedes pulled out in front of us and *crack*.'

John said, 'I'll make you a drink. Are you hungry at all? Have you eaten?'

'No, but I've gone past being hungry. Don't worry about making me a drink yet. Just hold me, would you? That's all I need right now. Holding.'

John sat beside her on the couch and held her close, stroking the back of her neck and running his fingers up into her hair.

'I'm determined to make this work, Katie,' he told her. 'I wouldn't have bought a car if I wasn't going to stay. I've accepted that there's always going to be days like this, when I have to put things off because you're dealing with some crisis at work.'

'Thank you,' said Katie. 'I'm so sorry about the Hayfield Manor. We can go some other evening, can't we? What was it we were supposed to be celebrating?'

'I pulled off a big sale of flu vaccine to the Netherlands, that's all. MediBio have given me a contract and things have started to go pretty well. But for Christ's sake, Horgan's dead and *you* could have been killed, too. Selling a few flu shots doesn't count for squat against something like that.'

'I'm really proud of you, John,' said Katie. 'You know that.'

John kissed her, first on the forehead and then on the lips, and then again. 'So you still don't know who shot at you?'

'No. And we haven't located the silver Mercedes either. Traffic patrols stopped seven cars answering that description within an eighty-kilometre radius from Dromsligo but all of the occupants checked out.'

'It's tragic,' said John. 'I only met Horgan a couple of times, when I came to the station to pick you up, but he seemed like a really great guy. And so goddamn *young*.'

'We held a station meeting,' said Katie. 'Brother O'Leary came in from the Holy Trinity Church and led some prayers. There were a lot of tears, but I think it did everybody good.'

'Any progress with those nuns?'

Katie sat up straight and shook her head. 'No . . . and I'd rather not talk about them just now, thank you. It gives me the gawks just thinking about them.'

'You should eat something, for Christ's sake.'

'No, no. Just a mug of hot chocolate. That will be grand. A mug of hot chocolate and a good night's sleep.'

'Katie?'

'What?'

'We are all right, aren't we? Like, you really are pleased that I came back?'

'Do you really need to ask me that?'

John kissed her again, and then stood up and went into the kitchen. Barney was standing in the living-room doorway, staring at her as if he, too, was thinking, *You have to tell him. You can't keep this a secret for very much longer.*

Thirteen

They served breakfast early at the Greendale Rest Home. By seven o'clock, eighteen of the twenty-five residents were sitting in a semicircle in their Parker Knoll armchairs in the conservatory at the front of the building, with woven blankets to keep their knees warm, dozing or watching *Ireland AM*. The remainder were bedridden, in their rooms.

Eileen O'Shea, the person-in-charge, came out of her office at half past seven to say good morning to all of them, accompanied by her charge nurse, Mary McConnell. Eileen O'Shea was a tall, handsome woman with heavy eyebrows and short brunette hair that looked as if it had been dyed a shade darker than her natural colour. She was wearing a lavender tweed suit and tan lace-up shoes. Mary McConnell was short and plump, with a chaotic attempt at a French pleat. She wore a long vinyl apron that crackled as she walked and she carried a clipboard.

Eileen went over to an elderly woman with glasses that enormously magnified her eyes. 'How are you today, Breda?' she said, almost shouting because she knew that Breda habitually forgot her hearing aids.

'It's Tuesday, isn't it?' said Breda, noisily licking her lips. 'I ought to be going to the market to get the messages.'

'No, Breda, it's Wednesday. You don't have to go today. You can leave it till next week now.'

Breda stared up at her with those huge fishbowl eyes. 'Who are you?' she demanded. 'Who let you in? It wasn't Patrick, was it? I keep telling that boy. Don't answer the door until you know who it is who's calling. That's what happened to your Uncle Paul, God rest his soul.'

'Is she still on donepezil?' Eileen asked Mary. 'Maybe we should ask Dr Murphy to reassess her.'

'Some days she's worse than others, but on the whole she hasn't been doing too bad,' said Mary, checking her clipboard. 'She complains about the side effects, but for her it's a straight choice, diarrhoea or dementia. She can't have it both ways.'

'Who let you in?' Breda repeated, growing increasingly agitated. 'It wasn't Patrick, was it?'

'No,' said Eileen. 'It wasn't Patrick. You don't have to get yourself upset. I'm only here to see how you are.'

Next to Breda sat a tiny, sadly smiling woman with a maroon shawl around her shoulders. She looked more like a little woodland animal than a woman. Eileen was just about to move on to talk to her when the front doorbell chimed. She looked around to see who it was, because the front porch was right next to the conservatory. A nun was standing outside in a long black cape and a black ankle-length habit. She had her back turned, so Eileen couldn't see her face.

'Lucy, would you get that, please?' Eileen called out. But her young, gingery-haired assistant was already bustling out of the office and heading for the door. She opened it and Eileen could hear her talking to the nun, although she couldn't make out what they were saying. After a few moments Lucy came over and said, 'It's Sister Margaret Rooney, from the Bon Sauveur Convent. She says she's come here to visit Sister Barbara.'

'Oh. *Oh*. Well, this isn't visiting time, is it? But I suppose we could make an exception, if she's come from the Bon Sauveur. This is the first visit that Sister Barbara's had from her convent in years. She'll be so delighted. Please, yes – ask her to come in.'

While Lucy returned to the front door, Eileen went over to the opposite side of the conservatory. As usual, Sister Barbara was sitting apart from the other residents, facing the window and the little concrete yard outside, where there was an alcove with a painted figurine of Padre Pio. Sister Barbara never watched the television. She sat there all day with her rosary in her hand, mumbling endless prayers to Saint Anastasia to appear outside the fire door and take her away. *Veni, Santa Anastasia, et salva me*, over and over.

Eileen thought that Sister Barbara must have been lovely when she was young, with that heart-shaped face that was favoured in the 1950s. Her hair was now wild and grey and thinning so that her white scalp showed through, and her cheeks were withered like the last apple in the bowl that nobody wanted. As Eileen approached her, she looked up and gave her a wistful smile, as if to say, is this all my life is ever going to be, until I die, looking at this little concrete yard and praying to be taken to heaven?

'I have a surprise for you, Sister Barbara,' said Eileen. 'You have a visitor. A sister has come to see you from the Bon Sauveur Convent.'

'A visitor? Who is it? Not Mother Kelly? No, that's impossible! What am I thinking of? Mother Kelly must have died years ago.'

'She says her name is Sister Margaret Rooney. Look, here she comes now.'

Sister Barbara twisted herself around in her chair so that she could see the nun and Eileen's assistant coming across the conservatory.

'Sister Barbara!' said the nun and held out both hands. 'It's so good to meet you!'

'Well, I'm amazed,' said Sister Barbara. 'Thanks a million for taking the trouble to pay me a visit. Is there any special reason for it?'

Eileen's assistant brought over a plywood chair and Sister Margaret took off her cape and sat down close to Sister Barbara. 'We were talking about you after our meditation last week and when I heard all about you, and everything that you did during your years at the convent, I just *had* to come and talk to you in person.'

From the creases at the corners of Sister Margaret's eyes, Eileen would have guessed that she was in her early to mid-fifties. She still had the looks of a much younger woman, though, with blue feline eyes and high cheekbones and slightly sulky lips, and Eileen found it hard to imagine why somebody so attractive should have taken holy orders.

In spite of that, she couldn't have been completely unaware of how attractive she was. Eileen noticed that her eyebrows were shaped and her fingernails manicured and varnished, even though the varnish was clear. Perhaps nuns these days were allowed a little modest grooming.

'Would you care for a cup of tea, Sister?' she asked her. 'Sister Barbara, would you like a cup?'

'I'm fine, thank you,' said Sister Margaret. 'I'm just after having one.'

'Yes, please, I'd like one,' said Sister Barbara. Then she reached across to take hold of Sister Margaret's hand. 'You don't know what this means to me, your coming to see me like this. I truly thought that I'd been forgotten.'

'Get away with you,' smiled Sister Margaret. 'You know what you did at the Bon Sauveur, you and your sisters? How could anybody ever forget that?'

'Tell me, then, what were they saying about me? No, I shouldn't ask, should I? That's too much like vanity. But I'm surprised that any of them remember me.'

'Oh, not many of the *sisters* remember you, I shouldn't think. Most of them are far too old now, or passed away. But quite a few of the *girls* you took in, those girls who had fallen from grace, *they* remember you. Them and their children, too. They remember you like it was yesterday. They have dreams about you, some of them. They see your face in front of them as clear as I can see it now.'

Sister Barbara slowly released her hold on Sister Margaret's hand. She picked up the red jasper rosary that she had left in her lap and wound it around her fingers. She was frowning now, staring at Sister Margaret as if she had spoken to her in a foreign language that she could only half understand.

'And those girls? And their children?' she asked. 'What do *they* say about me?'

'They say all kinds of things. How you read the Bible to them, how you taught them to sew, and how to wash clothes, and do the ironing, and sweep the floors, and polish the windows. How you made them realize what sluts they had been, and what whores, and how they would never be fit to mix with pious people ever again.'

Sister Barbara was about to say something when Eileen's assistant came back with a cup of tea, with two shortbread biscuits in the saucer. She set it down on the small table beside her and then gave both women a smile.

'You're all right?' she asked.

'Oh, we're grand altogether, thanks,' said Sister Margaret. 'Sister Barbara and me, we've just been reminiscing about our days at the convent, weren't we, Sister?'

Sister Barbara didn't answer, but continued to stare at Sister Margaret with deep suspicion.

'Tell me something,' she said, when Eileen's assistant had gone back to the office. 'Who sent you here today?'

'God,' said Sister Margaret. She reached over and picked up one of the shortbread biscuits and bit into it. 'God sent me.'

She chewed for a while and then she said, 'I'm on a sacred mission, Sister Barbara. I'm surprised you haven't been sitting here all these years wondering with some trepidation when this moment would arrive.'

'I don't understand what you're talking about,' said Sister Barbara. 'What moment? All I do is pray to Saint Anastasia. I would much rather be in heaven with her instead of here, with every day empty and every day the same.'

'Yes. Saint Anastasia. What a martyr she was. How she suffered for her faith. What a shining light.'

Sister Barbara was silent for a while, watching Sister Margaret

104

finish her biscuit. Then she said, 'Who are you, really? What do you want from me?'

* * *

'Eileen!' called out Breda, in a quavery voice. 'Eileen, it's fierce cold in here!'

Eileen appeared at her office door with her phone in her hand. 'The heating's on full, Breda, what are you cribbing about? I'm right in the middle of a conversation with the HSE.'

'I know the heating's on, but there's a draught.'

'What draught? What are you talking about?'

'Come here and feel it for yourself. As if I don't feel enough twinges.'

Eileen came out into the conservatory and almost immediately she realized that Breda was right and that there was a sharp, stone-cold draft blowing from the opposite side of the room. Most of the other old women had nodded off, but Breda was sitting up straight with her blanket pulled right up to her neck.

Over the canned laughter coming from the television Eileen heard a distinctive knocking sound, irregular but repetitive. *Knock – knock-knock – knock – knock.* She realized then that the conservatory's fire door was open, the door that gave out on to the yard at the back. It could only be opened from the inside, with a panic bar, and it couldn't be closed from the outside.

As she crossed the room towards it, she saw that Sister Barbara's chair was empty and that her blanket was lying on the floor, with her rosary next to it. Her teacup was empty, although there was a single shortbread biscuit left in the saucer.

Eileen stepped outside into the yard. It was a bright, grey morning, not raining but damp and very cold. She hurried around the front of the rest home, past the porch. On the far side of the building there was a parking space for three cars and a high wooden gate to the back garden. The only car parked there was her own Peugeot 206, and when she tried the gate she found that it was firmly bolted, as it should have been.

She went out on to the pavement and looked up and down Carrigaline Road. It was deserted. There was no traffic and no other cars parked within a hundred metres.

She went back inside, closing the fire door behind her but taking care not to touch the panic bar. Then she hurried to her office and said to Lucy, 'Call the guards for me, would you, Lucy? Right now. I think Sister Barbara has been kidnapped.'

'What?'

'She's gone, and there's no sign of her. She had a visitor, a sister from the Bon Sauveurs. They were sitting there chatting away, but now she's gone and the fire door was left open.'

'Are you sure she's not in her room?' asked Lucy. 'She could have taken her visitor to see that shrine of hers.'

'But why would they open the fire door?'

'Maybe she took her out to show her that statue of Padre Pio but didn't close it properly.'

Eileen said, 'Wait there.' She hurried along the corridor that led to the residents' rooms, turning sharp right and then almost running along the last fifty metres to Sister Barbara's room. She fumbled with her bunch of master keys and then opened it. There was nobody there – only Sister Barbara's neatly made bed, with its dark-brown coverlet, and the shrine that she had created for Saint Anastasia with candles and artificial flowers and a mournful picture of the martyred saint herself.

She hurried back to the office. 'She's not there,' she said. 'Call 112. That nun has taken her, I'm sure of it.'

'Maybe she took her back to the convent with her. You know, a trip down memory lane, like.'

'Lucy, will you stop theorizing, for the love of God, and do like I asked you!'

Lucy shrugged and pressed 112. 'Can't see why a nun would want to kidnap another nun, though. I mean, what's the point, like? I could understand if it was a feller.'

Fourteen

By nine o'clock, when Katie and Detective O'Donovan arrived at Cork University Hospital, Dr O'Brien was already at work in the morgue.

He didn't say anything when they came through the double swing doors because he was wearing a surgical mask, but he lifted one hand, like Columbo, to acknowledge that he had seen them.

Katie and Detective O'Donovan waited for him to invite them over to the stainless-steel autopsy table. He was leaning over the pale, naked body of the nun who had been hung from the balloons over Glanmire, watching closely as a young assistant pathologist sutured up her stomach. Katie hadn't been sick that morning, but she was more than willing to wait until they had finished before she came any closer.

There were four other trolleys in the morgue, all of them covered in dark-green sheets. She guessed that under one of them lay the body of Detective Horgan, brought in from Dromsligo.

It was chilly in the morgue and the silvery-grey light that filtered down from the clerestory windows made Katie feel as if they were standing in a black-and-white photograph, and that all of this had happened a long time ago. In a way, it might have done, because so many of the crimes that she investigated in Cork had their root cause in long-standing grudges and family feuds, and the Corkonian's inability ever to forget the slightest of slights. She knew people who would turn their backs on British tourists because the Black and Tans had burned down the centre of the city in 1920.

Eventually the assistant pathologist knotted up the last suture.

Dr O'Brien tugged down his mask and said, 'That's first-class work there, Aoife. I'll be asking you to sew some new shirts for me next.'

He beckoned Katie and Detective O'Donovan to come over. He was short and rotund, with heavy-rimmed spectacles, and he seemed to have put on some weight since he had last come down to Cork, and developed a bulging double chin.

'Hallo, Ailbe,' said Katie.

'Good to see you again, Detective Superintendent,' said Dr O'Brien. 'It's a pity we always have to meet under such tragic circumstances. Good to see you, too, Detective.'

Katie looked down at the nun's body and the Frankenstein stitches that had closed up her abdomen. Apart from that terrible injury, though, and the blotchy purple bruising where the cord had been tied around her neck, she looked as if she had been in fairly good physical condition before she was killed. Her skin was finely wrinkled but she appeared to be well fed, and her fingernails and toenails had been recently cut. Her hair was neatly styled and her eyebrows plucked.

Her eyes were closed now, but she looked like a woman who was dreaming rather than dead. She had a long, oval face, and a long, thin nose, and a small, rather petulant mouth.

'She looks well cared for,' said Katie. 'How old would you say she was? Late seventies?'

'Older than that, I'd say. Mid-eighties. But as you say, she's been well looked after. It's pure amazing the difference in appearance I've seen according to somebody's lifestyle. I've had fellows on this table you would have sworn were in their late sixties and then you find out they're only forty-five. Alcohol and cigarettes and chips, they're the main culprits.'

He reached across and pulled down the dead nun's jaw so that Katie could see her teeth. 'Look at that. Only two crowns. The rest of the teeth are all her own, with the exception of her wisdom teeth and one missing premolar.'

Detective O'Donovan peered over Katie's shoulder. 'That might help to confirm that she's a genuine nun. A fair number of women of her age had all their teeth taken out as a wedding present, didn't they?'

'I haven't been able to establish conclusively if she's a virgin or not,' said Dr O'Brien. 'I can tell you, though, that she's never given birth. So that might be another factor in establishing that she's a real nun. But your technicians have taken scores of photographs, so I imagine you'll be able to identify her soon. If she's been so well fed and taken care of, somebody must have been looking after her on a daily basis, and whoever they are they'll be missing her, won't they?'

'What was used to cut her open?' asked Katie. 'Can you tell?'

'Probably a craft knife, I'd say, judging by the angle it first went in, just below the sternum. Also, there are two or three places where the blade didn't quite slice all the way through the muscle to the abdominal cavity – see here? Because of that, her assailant had to repeat the cut more than once. This leads me to think that the blade was very short, even though it was extremely sharp.'

'Was she alive when this was done?'

Dr O'Brien took off his glasses, breathed on the lenses and then polished them on the tail of his apron. 'No question of that. I'd say she was probably still alive even when she came down to earth, although by then she would have been suffering from irreversible brain damage from oxygen deprivation and loss of blood.'

'I assume you've tested her for drugs,' said Katie.

'Of course. And this will interest you. She was taking propranolol, which is a treatment for heart irregularities, which isn't unexpected for a woman of her age. But I also found traces of flunitrazepam.'

'That's Rohypnol,' said Katie. 'You mean somebody might have given her a date rape drug?'

'Well, she could have taken it to cure insomnia. Whatever the media say about it, that's by far the most common use for it.'

'Somebody slipping a nun a roofie,' said Detective O'Donovan, shaking his head. 'You hear something new every day in this job, don't you?'

Katie stared at the dead nun for a long time without speaking, almost as if she expected her to sit up and explain what had happened to her. The nun remained still and silent, her hair shining silver in the silvery grey daylight.

Detective O'Donovan asked, 'Is there any bruising on her that might give us an idea if she was beaten with anything, or if she was being held down, like, or maybe the size of a handprint?'

'Nothing at all,' said Dr O'Brien. 'Again, that's not conclusive evidence of anything, although it could be an indication that her attacker dosed her with Rohypnol. If he did, he wouldn't have needed to hit her or restrain her, because she would have been dead to the world, so to speak.'

'What we need to do first is find out who she is and where she came from,' said Katie. 'Patrick, would you arrange to have her picture taken out to every convent and every hospital and every school and charity shop where nuns might be working? I'll talk to Mathew McElvey and have him email her picture to the press. Check with the social media, too – Twitter and Facebook and all the rest of them. See if anybody's been posting threats against any religious order, and against nuns in particular.'

'Gollun, there'll be *thousands* of them!' said Detective O'Donovan. '*Millions*, I shouldn't wonder! We'll be sorting through them for *weeks*!'

'I know. But that's our job, isn't it?'

'Yes. Right. Okay. Maybe I can ask them to leave out any tweets about Cardinal Seán Brady and then there won't be so many.'

Katie turned back to Dr O'Brien. 'Is that Detective Horgan you have there?' she asked, nodding towards the three trolleys covered in sheets.

'Yes. He's next on my list. Do you want to see him?'

'No, I don't think that'll be necessary. What about the other two?'

'Floaters found in the river this morning. A man and a teenage girl. Nothing to arouse any suspicions about the demise of either of them. I'll be certifying the cause of death since I'm here, but I don't think there'll be any need for me to be carrying out a full post-mortem.'

'Do we know who they are?'

'I don't think they've been identified yet, either of them. But gardaí were called when they were fished out, so your lot know all about it. A drunk and a suicide, that's my first assessment.'

'That's the story of Cork,' said Detective O'Donovan. 'I sometimes wonder what the Almighty was thinking when he built a city full of boozers and brothels with a river running through it.'

'He was giving you the opportunity for self-retribution,' said Dr O'Brien. 'It saves Him a fortune on lightning bolts.'

* * *

As they were about to leave the mortuary, Katie hesitated and turned around. She looked at the three trolleys draped with sheets and wondered if she ought to ask Dr O'Brien to show her the bodies that were lying on them, after all.

'What?' said Detective O'Donovan, holding the swing door half open.

'Oh, nothing,' said Katie. 'Let's go. I just had a funny feeling about those two floaters, that's all.'

'What kind of a funny feeling? Do you want to take a sconce at them?'

'No, you're all right,' Katie told him. 'Dr O'Brien said there was nothing suspicious about them drowning, didn't he?'

'Well, we know the statistics,' said Detective O'Donovan. 'Thirty-six per cent of all the people who drown in the Lee are suicides, and thirty per cent of *them* are langered. The rest are accidents, but less than one per cent are pushed in deliberate.'

'It's not that – it's just that—' Katie began, but then her phone warbled. It was Detective Sergeant Ni Nuallán.

'Ma'am? We've just had a report that an elderly nun has gone missing. It seems like she was taken from a rest home in Douglas by another nun who came to visit her.'

'Mother of God, Kyna. I don't believe this.'

Detective O'Donovan pushed the door open wider and they both left the mortuary and walked out into the car park. It was chilly out there, and while she talked to Detective Sergeant Ni Nuallán Katie used her left hand to fasten the toggles of her duffel coat.

'Do we know where this other nun came from?' she asked.

'Not really. I've just been talking on the phone with the person in charge at the rest home, a woman called Eileen O'Shea. She told me that the nun arrived about seven-fifteen, saying she wanted to see Sister Barbara Flynn. She gave her own name as Sister Margaret Rooney and said that she had come from the Bon Sauveur Convent, which is where Sister Barbara used to live before she was taken into care.

'Ms O'Shea left them talking together, but about ten minutes later she had to take a phone call in her office and when she came out they were gone, the both of them. She went looking for them outside but there was no sign of them at all.'

'Have you contacted the Bon Sauveur?'

'Yes, of course. I spoke to Mother O'Dwyer herself. She confirmed that Sister Barbara was once a member of the congregation there, but there was never a Sister Margaret Rooney.'

'Never?'

'She even checked the records for me. They had a *Mary* Rooney once, but that was back in 1931, and according to Ms O'Shea this nun only looked about forty-something.'

'You've put out a description?'

'I have, yes. Sergeant O'Farrell has told all of his patrols to keep an eye out for them. Hard to miss an eighty-five-year-old woman in a long mustard-coloured cardigan accompanied by a nun in a long black cape. That's if she really *was* a nun. Ms O'Shea noticed that her eyebrows were plucked and her nails were varnished.'

'Ms O'Shea should have been a detective, by the sound of it, instead of running a rest home. Sherlock O'Shea. Listen, I'm just leaving the hospital now, I'll be back at the station in ten.'

They climbed into their car and O'Donovan started the engine.

'More nun trouble,' said Katie.

'I gathered that. What's happened now?'

Katie told him as they drove back towards the centre of the city. 'I'm just praying to God that we don't find this one dead, like the other two.'

'You think there's a connection?'

'You know me. I make it a firm rule never to jump to conclusions. But three nuns in three days. I can't help thinking that there must be some link between Sister Bridget being murdered and this flying nun and now this other nun going missing.'

'And that link is?'

'The Bon Sauveur Convent.'

'You could be right,' said O'Donovan. 'We'll be going round there tomorrow morning to start digging up their gardens, won't we, if the search team's ready? Those nuns are really going to start thinking we've got it in for them.'

'Well, I hope they understand that we're just looking for the truth, that's all. Somebody may have it in for them, but it isn't us.'

Fifteen

Detective Dooley parked his Ford Focus outside the entrance to the Spring Lane Halting Site, close behind an abandoned caravan with its door missing and weeds growing out of its windows. He folded down the sun visor so that he could brush up his Jedward-style hair in the mirror, then he climbed out and tugged on the shiny black quilted nylon jacket he had bought that morning at Penney's.

He looked around. He could hear children screaming and loud music playing. Apart from that, this was a very desolate place, north of the city behind the Ballyvolane Business Park, next to a semi-private housing estate and some scrubby uncultivated fields. The clouds hung low overhead, grey and pillowy, and there was scarcely any wind.

He walked down the hill towards the halting site, jumping now and then over water-filled potholes. The site itself was a ramshackle collection of static caravans and prefabricated houses which were little more than sheds. To the north and the east, the site was overlooked by steep slopes of sand and gravel, over twenty metres high. The eastern slope was almost vertical, with a spiked fence along the top to separate it from the housing estate. On the opposite side of the site there was a wide lagoon of tan-coloured water where the recent rain had flooded the septic tanks from the outside toilets, and two small boys were cycling through it on their bicycles, around and around in circles, so that it rippled.

A group of six or seven women were standing outside one of the mobile homes, smoking and chatting to each other. They all turned around and stared as Detective Dooley approached. He gave them a wave, although he thought they were probably the most formidable collection of women that he had ever encountered in his life. At least three of them had bare upper arms that looked like the hams that hung up on Tom Durcan's stall in the English Market, except that they were decorated with tattoos. Most of them wore huge hoop earrings and had their hair scraped back from their foreheads in that style commonly known as a 'knacker's facelift'.

Not far away, three young men were standing around a motorbike, while another was bouncing up and down in the saddle, trying to get it started. Every now and then it would roar into life and they would all cheer, but then it would immediately cut out again, to a loud disparaging chorus of 'Jeez, feck it, Michael!'

'*Slum hawrum*,' said Detective Dooley, as he came up to the women. 'What's the craic?'

'What do you want, boy?' asked an older woman, blowing out smoke. She had long, greasy grey hair streaked ginger and black, and a fading black eye.

'Looking for Paddy Fearon,' he said. 'Is he here at all?'

'Maybe he is and maybe he isn't. What would you be wanting him for?'

'Got a little job for him, like, if he's interested. He said I could find him here if anything ever came up.'

'Oh yeah, and where do you know him from?'

'Here and there. Waxy's, the last time I saw him.'

One of the younger women said, 'Oh yeah? And what makes you think that a feller like Paddy Fearon would be living in a shit-hole like this?'

Detective Dooley shrugged. 'It's where he said to look for him, like, that's all.'

The woman flipped her cigarette butt across the concrete and then she said, 'Come on, then, feen, I'll show you.'

She started to walk away, with her hips undulating, and so Detective Dooley followed her. She had soot-black hair, with a ponytail, and if she hadn't been wearing double false eyelashes and thick orange foundation she might have looked quite attractive. She was overweight, though, with huge breasts underneath her leopard-skin bolero and bulging black leggings that only emphasized the size of her buttocks and her thighs.

'What's your name, then?' she asked him. They walked past the young men trying to get the motorbike started and they all turned around to stare at them.

'Declan. What's yours?'

'Tauna.'

'Been living here at Spring Lane long, Tauna?'

'I was born and reared here, wasn't I? Nineteen ninety-two. Sagittarius. And my kids was born here, too.'

'You just said that it was a shit-hole. Why do you stay here, if it's all that bad?'

'Where else would I go?'

'I don't know. Won't they give you a council house?'

'Ah, no! I wouldn't want it any road. I tried living in a house once, but I never want to get caught up in a house again. Jesus, it was so depressing. It was like being trapped, like, so that I couldn't scarcely breathe, and so fecking lonely without all my family and my friends around me.'

'But this place?' asked Detective Dooley. They were walking past the breeze-block shed that housed the communal toilets, with a single washing machine out in the open.

'It's terrible, like. The kids are always getting sick with the gastric flu and there's no bathrooms and no showers and the water tastes of chlorine so strong you wouldn't want to be drinking it. The local people look at us as if they have dirt in their eyes. They want to build a wall instead of that fence so they can forget that we exist.'

'But?'

'But, like I said, Declan, I was born here and reared here and where else would I go?'

They reached a beige-painted Willerby caravan at the far end of the site, close to the foot of the eastern slope. It was larger than

116

most of the others on the site, and in better condition, although it was surrounded by a whole variety of junk, including a rusty diesel compressor, and a kitchen cabinet with no drawers, and a bicycle with no front wheel, and a sofa with no seat cushions, and an ironing board. A brindled pony was tethered outside, eating oats from a yellow plastic bucket tied to its nose.

Not far away, a military-green horsebox was parked on a rectangular patch of concrete next to a dark-blue Opel Insignia, which was splattered with mud but looked reasonably new.

Tauna climbed the steps to the caravan's front door and knocked on it loudly. Then she climbed back down because the door opened outwards.

A middle-aged man appeared wearing a pale-brown corduroy cap and a yellow and black chequered shirt. He had small squinchy eyes and a broken nose and his cheeks and neck were pitted with acne scars.

'What do you want, Tauna?' he said, although he was staring at Detective Dooley. 'I'm up to me bollocks.'

'Declan says he might have a job for you, Paddy. That's right, isn't it, Declan?'

'That's right,' said Detective Dooley. 'How's it going, Paddy? Long time no see.'

'What do you mean, "long time no see"? I never saw you before in the whole of me fecking life.'

'Ah, you're laughed at,' said Detective Dooley. 'Six months ago, not even that, in Waxy's.'

'Well, I must have been langered because I don't remember seeing you there, boy.'

'That was the night that Danny Perrott brought his pit bull into the bar and it shat on your shoe. Don't tell me you don't remember that.'

Tauna let out a hoarse, cigarette-smoker's laugh. 'You never told me about that, Paddy! Shat on your shoe? That's hilarious!'

'Danny didn't think so after I gave him a slap and kicked his fecking dog up the arse,' Paddy retorted. But then he squinted even more intently at Detective Dooley and said, 'Yeah, maybe I do remember you. What was we talking about, like?'

'Horses, of course,' said Detective Dooley. 'What else?'

'Horses, yeah,' said Paddy. He nodded, and kept on nodding as if he were gradually beginning to recall their conversation after all.

'You told me all about what you'd been up to with the horses, like, so I said that I might have a job for you now and then. And now I do.'

'Yeah? Oh – yeah. That's right. So, ah – what is it, this job?'

Detective Dooley looked at Tauna and said, 'Maybe we should talk about it in private. No offence meant, Tauna.'

Tauna pulled a face and said, 'It doesn't bother me, boy. I have to go and feed the kids any road.'

'Thanks. I appreciate it. How many kids do you have?'

'Only the four of them. There was a fifth one on the way but the Lord decided to take him back when I was five months gone. He'll be up there somewhere, in a much better place than this, I can tell you. Along with me brother.'

Detective Dooley watched her walk back past the toilet block to join her friends. Halfway there, she turned around and gave him a wink and a little finger wave.

'You're in there, boy,' said Paddy, with a phlegmy cackle. 'That's if you like skangers.'

'Yeah, well,' said Detective Dooley.

'Come inside, any road,' said Paddy and beckoned him up the steps.

Inside, the caravan's living area was so crammed with furniture and ornaments that there was hardly any room to move around. There were gold velvet curtains at the windows, with brown tassels and tie-backs, and the huge brown Dralon-covered sofa was piled with brown and gold cushions. Every shelf was crowded with floral vases and religious statuettes and onyx boxes and china animals, although there wasn't a single book in sight.

A shaven-headed man about the same age as Paddy was sitting on the sofa in a white sleeveless body warmer and black tracksuit trousers, smoking a cigarette. Sitting close to him was a girl in shocking-pink leggings with a nest of backcombed blonde hair. She was painfully thin, so that her eyes looked huge, like a Disney character.

'What did you say your name was?' Paddy asked Detective Dooley.

'Declan. Declan O'Leary.'

Paddy turned to the shaven-headed man and said, 'Declan was there at Waxy's that night when Danny Perrott's dog did the dirty on me.'

The shaven-headed man gave a gap-toothed grin, with smoke leaking out of the gaps. 'Jesus, that was one night I'll never forget, if I could only fecking remember it.' He held out a horny hand encrusted with gold signet rings and said, 'Beval. And this skinny malink is Patia.'

'Will you stop calling me that?' Patia protested in a nasal whine.

'Why the feck should I? It's fecking true, isn't it? There's more fecking meat on a butcher's pencil than there is on you.'

'Declan says he has a job for us,' said Paddy. 'Would you care for a drink, Declan?'

'No – no, thanks,' said Detective Dooley. 'I've been stopped by the shades a couple of times and the last thing I want is to lose my licence.'

'Sit down, anyway. What's this job about, then?'

Detective Dooley nodded towards Patia. 'Is it all right to talk about it in front of her, like?'

'You're all right. Patia don't know shite from chocolate.'

'Will you ever stop *talking* about me like that?' whined Patia.

'Oh, shut your gob,' said Beval.

Patia pouted sulkily but she didn't argue. Detective Dooley couldn't even guess what her relationship was to Beval – whether she was his wife or his girlfriend or his daughter, or just some stray spicer who had wandered in off the halting site. He sat down next to her anyway and she shuffled up nearer to Beval to give him more room.

119

'I have a friend in Kilmichael who has some horses to be taken care of,' said Detective Dooley. 'Nine altogether.'

'Nine? I can handle nine no bother at all,' said Paddy.

'The problem is that none of them is fit for human consumption, so my friend can't sell them to the slaughterhouse. All but two of them's thoroughbreds and if they're not full of xylazine they're full of bute or steroids. But you told me when we was talking together in Waxy's that you could get rid of horses cheap-like, without having to pay the full charge to the knackery.'

Paddy took out a cigarette and tucked it between his lips, so that it waggled when he talked. 'That's right, like. All the knackeries have whacked up their prices lately, more than thirty-three per cent some of them, so by comparison I can offer you a very economical service. For a full-grown horse, Fitzgerald's will sting you anything up to a hundred and fifty yoyos, depending on its weight, like, and how far they have to go to pick it up. But for nine horses, I could dispose of them for you – let's say – five hundred the lot.'

Detective Dooley raised his eyebrows. 'That don't sound too bad at all. You couldn't make it four fifty?'

Paddy lit his cigarette with a Zippo and shook his head without saying anything.

'That's rock bottom, five hundred,' put in Beval. 'You won't get nobody to do it for you cheaper than that.'

'Okay,' said Detective Dooley. 'I'll give my friend a ring, see what he says.'

'He has all of their passports, like?' asked Paddy.

'So far as I know, yes, and I believe they've all been chipped. That's not a problem, is it?'

'No, not at all. They can have their names embroidered on the arses for all I care.'

'So, ah, what you would be doing with them exactly?'

Paddy tapped the side of his nose with his finger. 'Trade secret, boy. If I told you, then you'd be fecking doing it instead of me and putting me out of work.'

Detective Dooley took out his iPhone and held it up. He prodded it and then he said, 'No, I'm not getting any decent reception in here, I'll have to go outside.'

'Don't forget to ask your friend when he wants the job done,' said Paddy. 'There's a few race meetings coming up at Mallow and Greenmount Park that I'll be off to and there's a rake of other jobs I've got in me diary. No fecking peace for the wicked.'

Detective Dooley went outside and called Detective Inspector O'Rourke. As soon as he answered, he said, 'Dooley, sir. I'm up at Spring Lane. I just spoke to Paddy Fearon and a butty of his. He says he can dispose of nine horses for me for five hundred euros.'

'Good work, Dooley. How long is it going to take us to get nine horses together?'

'I've talked to two trainers already – Michael O'Malley and Kevin Corgan. O'Malley can let us have five that are ready for the knackery and Corgan can let us have another four. We could set this up for Saturday or Monday, depending on Fearon.'

'All right, then. That's grand. Go ahead.'

As he was talking, Detective Dooley saw Tauna standing on the opposite side of the halting site, still chatting to her friends. When she caught sight of him she blew out cigarette smoke and then she blew him a kiss. Jesus, he thought. I wonder what my friends and my family would say if I turned up on the doorstep with a twenty-four-year-old Traveller, with her ponytail and her dangly earrings and her barrel arse, not to mention her four young kids?

He climbed back up the steps into Paddy's caravan.

'Well?' said Paddy. 'What did your friend have to say to ye?'

'He says five hundred is acceptable and he'd like you to do it as soon as you can.'

'Okay,' Paddy told him. 'I'll be away this weekend, but I can probably manage it Monday or Tuesday. It'll take a while, like, because I can only carry three horses at a time, but, yes, we can do that for him. If you come back tomorrow morning with his address and the grade.'

'You want all of the money even before you've done it?'

'Those are my usual terms of business, yes.'

'And what if you take the money and I never see you again?'

Paddy grinned at him, and so did Beval, but their grins were threatening rather than amused. 'That's the kind of suggestion I don't take kindly to,' said Paddy. 'If you don't think you can trust me, then why don't you take three steps back and fuck yourself.'

'Don't worry, I was only messing,' said Detective Dooley. 'I'll be here tomorrow with the necessary.'

Paddy spat copiously into the palm of his hand and held it out. Detective Dooley shook it, looking straight into his bloodshot eyes.

After he had climbed back into his car, he took a plastic bottle of lemon-scented antibacterial gel out of the glovebox and washed his hands with it, over and over.

Sixteen

Chief Superintendent MacCostagáin came into Katie's office and said, 'Good morning, Katie, and a grand sunny morning it is, too! We can start excavations at the Bon Sauveur whenever you're ready. We have most of the team assembled now and we won't need ground-penetrating radar or the mechanical digger until later, if at all. It depends what we find.'

Katie looked up from the vet's report that Tadhg Meaney had sent her. The preliminary toxicology test on each of the twenty-three dead horses had revealed that all of the one- and two-year-olds had traces of xylazine or detomidine, drugs that were administered either to sedate a horse so that it could be medically treated or else to slow it down on the racetrack.

'So what's the roster?' she asked. She pushed aside the vet's report and picked up the search warrant for the Bon Sauveur Convent, as well as a copy of the sketch map that Sister Rose had emailed to Detective Sergeant Ni Nuallán.

'Fifteen altogether. Three technicians, four officers and eight reservists. Sergeant O'Farell is just about to give them a briefing and then they'll be ready for the off. Kyna Ni Nuallán told me that you were keen to serve the search warrant yourself.'

'Yes, I am. From what she's told me about Mother O'Dwyer, I think I need to meet her face to face. If experience has taught me anything about mother superiors, it's that they're all as wily as foxes and about as straight as a drawerful of corkscrews.'

'That's a little *harsh*, isn't it?' said Chief Superintendent MacCostagáin. He almost managed to smile.

'Take my word for it, sir, they'll do anything to protect themselves from the outside world, these nuns. Not straight-out lying maybe, but lying by what they don't tell you. Look what happened at Tuam, and I pray to God we don't find anything like that here. Kenny Horgan used to say that the church taught the gospels of Saint Mark, Saint Luke, Saint John and Saint Matt-the-liar.'

Chief Superintendent MacCostagáin looked depressed again. 'Yes. Kenny Horgan. The commissioner's been in touch, by the way, about holding a state funeral for him.'

'He deserves it. They did it for Detective Donohue in Dundalk, didn't they?'

They were both silent for a moment, thinking about Detective Horgan, but then Chief Superintendent MacCostagáin said, 'So, Katie, what's your plan of action?'

Katie looked up at the clock. 'I have to be in court at two-thirty for Michael Gerrety's plea hearing, so I think I'll go up to the Bon Sauveur now, while the search team are finishing off their briefing. The sooner we get started, the better. There's something going on there, connected with those holy sisters, I'm convinced of it.'

'They didn't identify that flying nun as one of theirs, though, did they?'

'Didn't or wouldn't,' said Katie. 'Patrick took her picture her up there yesterday evening and they all denied knowing who she was, Mother O'Dwyer included. What really struck him, though, was that some of the sisters scarcely seemed to give the picture a glance. He definitely had the feeling that they'd been *told* to say that they didn't recognize her.'

'You can't read too much into that, Katie. It's fair off-putting to look at the picture of a dead person, especially if you might have known them.'

'Well, all right, I agree with you there, and none of the sisters at any of the other convents recognized her, either. We showed her picture to all of them – the Poor Clares, the Ursuline Sisters, the Good Shepherd Sisters, the Mercy Sisters, the Little Sisters of the Assumption, the Presentation. The convent schools, too. But I still have that feeling about the Bon Sauveurs.'

'Just don't be vexing this Mother O'Dwyer. I don't want Bishop Buckley coming down on me like a ton of bricks.'

'I think you know me better than that, sir. I'll be all sweetness and light.'

Chief Superintendent MacCostagáin looked at her for a moment, with his head tilted to one side, and then he said, 'You won't get vexed yourself if I pay you a compliment?'

Katie couldn't stop herself from feeling suddenly and uncomfortably hot. It was almost unheard of for 'Chief Superintendent Aingesoir' to say anything complimentary about any other officer, or indeed about anything. He couldn't eat a ham sandwich in the canteen without complaining loudly halfway through that it tasted of nothing very much at all.

'You're blooming,' he said. 'I don't know what it is, but you have a shine about you.'

'Thank you, sir,' said Katie, trying to make her reply sound as official as possible. 'Kind of you to say so.'

* * *

Mother O'Dwyer put on her spectacles and read through the search warrant with a frown, her lips moving as she did so.

'I don't understand,' she said when she had finished. Her hand was trembling. 'Why in the name of God would you wish to carry out a search *here*?'

Katie said, 'It's only routine, Mother O'Dwyer. As you can see from the warrant, a young child's jawbone was discovered in the gardens and we have to make sure that there are no further remains.'

'Further remains? What do you mean by *further* remains?'

'Any more bones of the child whose jawbone was discovered. Or any other children, for that matter.'

'That's absurd!' protested Mother O'Dwyer. 'Our sisters tend our gardens daily. We grow all our own vegetables. Cabbages, potatoes, turnips. And our own flowers, too. If there were further remains to be discovered, surely we would have discovered them by now.'

'I understand completely,' said Katie. 'It's just that the law requires us to be sure. I'm very sorry for any disturbance that we may be causing you.'

'So who was it who found this child's jawbone?' Mother O'Dwyer demanded. 'No outsiders have access to our gardens. You're not telling me that one of our sisters came across it.'

'I'm not at liberty to tell you that, I'm afraid.'

Mother O'Dwyer opened and closed her mouth as if she were struggling for air. 'We are a community here, Detective Superintendent. More than a community, we are a family, all related in the sight of God. If one of us has transgressed in any way, it is essential that the rest of us are aware of it.'

'Reporting to the Garda that you have discovered a young child's jawbone is hardly a religious transgression, Mother O'Dwyer.'

'Well! That's what *you* say! But our congregation depends on complete openness and mutual loyalty! You realize that I will have to ask each sister in turn if it was she who contacted you?'

'I'm afraid I have to require you not to do that,' said Katie. 'It could obstruct our enquiries.'

'I am the mother superior of this convent, Detective Superintendent. It's my duty.'

Katie tried to sound light-hearted but at the same time she wanted Mother O'Dwyer to understand that she was deadly serious. 'If you attempt to question your congregation regarding the discovery of this bone fragment, Mother O'Dwyer, I shall have to consider arresting you under the Public Order Act, 1994, section 19. That could mean a fine or six months' imprisonment, or both. I've never had occasion to arrest a mother superior before, not in my whole career, but you know what they say. There's always a first time.'

Mother O'Dwyer slowly removed her spectacles and stared at Katie as if she had uttered the greatest blasphemy that she had ever heard in her life. She inhaled deeply, so that her nostrils flared, but she didn't reply. *You have great Christian self-restraint*, thought Katie, *I admire you for that, at least.*

At that moment, Detective Sergeant Ni Nuallán appeared in the doorway of Mother O'Dwyer's office. Close behind her there was a young novice nun, dressed in white. Detective Sergeant Ni Nuallán gave a little knuckle tap on the open door and said, 'Ma'am? Sorry to interrupt you, ma'am, but the search team's arrived.'

'With your permission, then, we'll make a start,' said Katie to Mother O'Dwyer, although both of them knew that it would make no difference at all if she refused it.

'Very well, then,' said Mother O'Dwyer. But as Katie turned to go she said, sharply, 'I assume you've had no luck at all in finding Sister Barbara?'

'No, regretfully not,' said Katie. 'We had tracker dogs out looking for her yesterday afternoon and they picked up a scent outside her rest home, but they lost it after only twenty metres or so. That would indicate that she was probably taken away in a waiting vehicle – willingly or unwillingly, we have no way of telling. We've issued a description, of course, but no response so far. You've probably seen it yourself on the news.'

'I haven't, no,' said Mother O'Dwyer. 'I've been praying and meditating. Sister Barbara is in the hands of God, as are all of us. We should never forget that our achievements are His, our failings are our own.'

Katie knew that this was a subtle dig at the Garda's inability to solve the murder of Sister Bridget and to find out what had happened to Sister Barbara, but all she did was to give Mother O'Dwyer the weakest of smiles and say, 'Thank you for your cooperation. We'll try to keep damage to your garden to a minimum and create as little disturbance inside the convent as we can.'

'Suspicion of any kind is always a disturbance, and it always leaves a trail of irreparable damage behind it,' retorted Mother

O'Dwyer.

'Yes, well,' said Katie. 'In the meantime, perhaps you'd be kind enough to show Detective Sergeant Ni Nuallán where your records are kept, especially the records relating to the Bon Sauveur's years as a home for single mothers. We'll need to see them at least as far back as 1950.'

'Sister Rose, go and find Sister Caoilainn, would you?' said Mother O'Dwyer. 'Sister Caoilainn keeps all the books. There's a room here where you can look through them, if you wish. I assume you won't be needing to take them off the premises.'

'It depends what we find, if anything,' said Katie.

Mother O'Dwyer looked up at her with her lips tightly pursed. Katie was only five foot four, but Mother O'Dwyer could barely have been more than four foot eleven inches. As tiny as she was, she looked as if she could explode with such a devastating blast of anger that she would demolish the entire convent.

'If you need me,' she quivered, 'you can find me in the chapel. I shall be praying that God grants you discretion and sound judgement, and that He forgives you any sins of commission or omission.'

She turned and walked out of her office before Katie could think of a reply that wouldn't bring Bishop Buckley down on Chief Superintendent MacCostagáin like a ton of bricks.

* * *

Katie went out into the convent garden. The technicians had already started work, kneeling in the flower bed around the spot where Sister Rose had marked the X on her sketch map. The rest of the team that had been assembled so far were standing around talking and clapping their hands together to keep warm.

Bill Phinner had turned up and was drinking coffee from a cardboard cup. Although the morning was so sunny and the sky was bright blue, the high convent wall kept the south side of the garden in shadow so that it was damp and bone-chillingly cold.

'Jesus,' said Bill as Katie came up to him. 'It's baltic out here. I should have stayed in the lab and finished those drug tests.'

'I don't know if we're going to find anything here,' said Katie, looking around. 'That jawbone could have come from almost anywhere. A dog or a fox might have dug it up somewhere totally different and just dropped it here.'

'Well, there's always that possibility,' said Bill. 'We'll find out soon enough. By the way, I went up to your office earlier but you'd already gone out. I left a report on your desk about the balloons that were used for that flying nun.'

'Oh yes? Anything interesting?'

'They were weather balloons, you can buy them online from any number of sources, such as Weather Balloons 'R' Us, and they don't cost much. They were all inflated with helium, but so far we don't know where that might have come from. We've contacted all the industrial suppliers in the area, even the party suppliers, but none of them have sold the quantity that would have been required to lift a forty-four kilo woman off the ground.'

'Where else would anybody get that that amount of helium? From a factory, maybe? They might have some over at Collins Barracks for army balloons. How about the UCC Physics Department? Or the weather station up at the airport? Do they send up balloons from there, or would they get in the way of the planes?'

Bill shook his head. 'I had a word with Sergeant O'Farrell. Nobody's reported any missing helium up until now.'

Katie said, 'I still can't work out why anybody would go to all that trouble. If you want to murder a nun, why not just murder her and bury her where nobody's ever going to find her. Putting on a show like that, with those balloons, it hugely increases your risk of being caught.'

'Well, you know as well as I do, ma'am, a lot of murderers are out to make a point. Whoever strung up that nun to those balloons obviously believed that they had something important to say. Only God or the Devil knows what it was.'

'I agree with you,' said Katie, watching as one of the technicians carefully sieved soil through a garden riddle. 'Look at Sister Bridget, assaulted with that statuette. I'll bet you money that there was some significance to that, if only we could work it out.'

'One of my guys had an explanation, but I won't repeat it.'

'I'll leave you to it, then,' said Katie. 'Give me a ring if you come up with anything.'

She was already walking away when the technician with the riddle raised his hand and called out, 'Here! Over here, sir! I have something here!'

Bill crossed the lawn and Katie came back to join him. The technician was on his knees in the flower bed, about halfway between the place where Sister Rose said she had found the jawbone and the grey limestone wall of the convent. He held up the riddle for Katie and Bill to see what he had found. It was a stick-like bone, about eight centimetres long, mottled brown by the soil in which it had been buried. Bill pulled on his black forensic gloves and picked it up. He examined it closely and then he said, 'Human, no doubt about it. It's a tibia, a shin bone. I'd say it came from a child about a year old, depending on how well nourished it was.'

'How long do you think it's been buried?' Katie asked him.

Bill stuck out his lower lip. 'Hard to say offhand. But if it belongs to the same child as that piece of jawbone, then we're talking about forty years at least, give or take a couple of years. It certainly looks it.'

'And what if it belongs to a different child?' said Katie.

Bill raised his eyebrows, but said nothing.

* * *

Although it was getting late and Katie would soon have to go back to Anglesea Street to pick up the paperwork for Michael Gerrety's committal proceedings in the criminal court, she stayed for a while longer. She almost felt that she owed it to the lost children whose sad little remains had been found in this garden.

Detective Sergeant Ni Nuallán came out to join her. Katie nodded her head towards the technicians sifting soil. 'You see there? They've found another bone, a small child's tibia this time.'

'Oh God. I'm getting a bad, bad feeling about this place,' said Detective Sergeant Ni Nuallán. 'You should see some of the stuff we've dug up in the convent records and we haven't even scratched the surface yet.'

'What have you come up with so far?'

'A lot of what you'd expect, of course. The names of all of the unmarried mothers the Bon Sauveur sisters ever took in, and their children and the dates of their baptism. But there are files of correspondence, too, with adoption agencies in the USA.'

'What's wrong about that? Most of those girls wouldn't have been able to take care of their own children, would they, especially if they didn't have the support of their parents?'

'No, but when every baby was born the sisters used to make its mother sign away all of her parental rights. Then they routinely separated babies and young toddlers from their mothers, whether the mother liked it or not, and sent them off to be adopted by families in America. We can't be sure how many yet, but it could be more than a hundred. Maybe even twice that.'

Katie couldn't help thinking of the child that was growing inside her, and of the grief she had felt when she discovered little Seamus dead in his cot – which she felt still.

'Please don't tell me we've got another Philomena situation,' she said. 'I'm still getting ruptions from the diocese over those poor castrated choirboys.'

'I think it could be worse than that,' said Detective Sergeant Ni Nuallán. 'Judging by what we've found in the account books it looks as if the sisters were demanding payment from the adoptive parents, and not just nominal sums, either. We'll have to bring in that forensic accountant to check through the figures because they're not at all straightforward.'

'How much were they asking?'

'In some cases, eight or nine or even ten thousand dollars, and when you think what the dollar must have been worth back in the 1960s – seven times as much as it is now, easy. Some of the payments have been entered into the books as "expenses", but most of them are classified as "charitable donations to the Sacred Mission of the Congregation of the Bon Sauveur".'

'I see,' said Katie. 'Is there any record of what they actually did with all of that money?'

'It's not clear. Almost all the payments we've managed to identify so far just seem to vanish off the books. That's why we need to have them looked at by somebody who knows all about false accountancy.'

'But it looks as if the sisters might have been selling off the children of unmarried mothers for profit?'

'I wouldn't put it quite as blunt as that. Not to Mother O'Dwyer, anyway. But essentially, yes. It does look like that.'

'All right,' said Katie. 'I think the best course of action is to take all the books and records back to the station. You can do that, can't you, under the terms of the search warrant? If you're not sure that a book is relevant to this investigation, take it regardless. We can always give it back.'

She paused and then she said, 'Say nothing to Mother O'Dwyer or any of the other sisters. In fact, keep it to yourself as much as you can. It's remotely possible that this may have some relevance to Sister Bridget and that flying nun being murdered, and maybe that other nun who's gone missing. If it does, I don't want the offender to know that we know.'

'All right, I have you,' said Detective Sergeant Ni Nuallán, although she sounded a little guarded about it. She was always very procedural, rather than inspirational, which was one of the reasons Katie had detailed her to check the Bon Sauveur's records.

Katie heard the reservation in her voice and said, 'Listen, Kyna, it may turn out that there's no connection at all with those other nuns, but there are still plenty of people alive today who were involved in this adoption racket, if that's what it was, and I don't want *them* alerted, either. Not if it turns out that we can still build a case against them.'

'No, I understand,' said Detective Sergeant Ni Nuallán. She paused and then she said, 'Do you know something? You have only to look at those photographs in Mother O'Dwyer's waiting room, all those teenage mothers and their little children. You never in your whole life saw so many young people looking so sad and so hopeless, and now I know why.'

Katie took hold of Detective Sergeant Ni Nuallán's hand and said, 'You know me, I'm usually dead set against jumping to conclusions before I have all the evidence, but we're dealing with the church here and the church are past masters in deviosity and they count on us being reverential towards them just because they wear the cloth. In this case, I would rather be proved disrespectful than gullible.'

She wound her scarf around her neck and turned to leave. Before she could, though, Bill called out to her, 'Detective superintendent!' and beckoned her back across the grass. He was holding something in the palm of his black-gloved hand that looked like a broken teacup. As she came closer she realized that it was a tiny pelvis. It was completely undamaged but as mottled as the tibia.

'I don't think there's any question about it now,' he said. 'This wasn't dropped by a dog or a fox. There's a whole child here somewhere in this flower bed and it was buried here deliberate by a human being. Or some creature that passed for a human being.'

Seventeen

Sister Barbara opened her eyes. She was lying on a single bed in a bare bedroom bright with winter sunlight. The walls were of unpainted plaster, as if they had once been wallpapered but now it had all been scraped off. The single window had no curtains and the floor was uncarpeted. Apart from the bed, the only furniture was a wheelback chair.

Gradually, she managed to pull herself up into a sitting position. Her head was banging and she found it difficult to focus. She couldn't think where she was. The last thing she could remember was sitting in her chair in the rest home talking to that sister who had come to visit her from the Bon Sauveur Convent – what was her name?

She heard voices outside and a car door slamming. Then she heard the car drive away and somebody shouting. There was a moment's silence, but that was soon broken by the clopping sound of a horse's hooves. Then more voices and the horse impatiently snorting.

Where in the name of the Holy Father am I? she thought, *and how did I get here?*

She stood up. She felt swimmy at first and the floor rose and fell underneath her feet like a sluggish incoming tide. However, she managed to grip the brass rail at the end of the bed to steady herself and after a while she regained her sense of balance.

She took one step towards the window, and then another. The last three steps she took in a hurry and clutched at the window frame to stop herself from falling over. She had only been drunk once in her life, when she was seventeen years old, at her Uncle Bernard's birthday party, but that was what she felt like now, as if she were drunk.

She looked out of the window and saw that there was an asphalt yard below, with a row of stables on the right-hand side with white-painted doors. Directly below, a black-haired woman in a brown tweed jacket was talking to a grizzled-looking man who was holding the reins of a large bay horse. Sister Barbara couldn't make out what the woman was saying but it sounded as if she were giving the man down the banks for something. Her voice was harsh and barking, and she kept prodding at him with her finger.

On the far side of the yard there was an asphalt road, with a row of lime trees on one side of it, with their leaves turned yellow, and a fenced-in field on the other, where five or six horses were grazing. Beyond the field there were rusty-coloured woods and beyond the woods rose hazy green hills. If there was one thing of which Sister Barbara was absolutely certain, it was that she had never been here before in her life.

She stood staring out of the window for a while, unsure if she could manage to walk safely back to the bed. Her head still thumped and her mouth felt dry. After a while the black-haired woman in the brown tweed jacket gave the grizzled-looking man a dismissive wave and he led the horse away. The woman turned around and as she did so she looked up and saw Sister Barbara. She didn't acknowledge her, but walked quickly to the left and disappeared out of sight.

Sister Barbara took three deep breaths and then released her grip on the side of the window frame. Very slowly, she started to stagger back towards the bed, her arms outstretched as if she were a zombie. She was only two steps away from the bed when the room seemed to slope and she pitched over sideways, hitting her left cheek and her shoulder hard against the floor.

She lay there, half stunned, unable to climb back on to her feet, twitching with pain and helplessness.

'*Saint Anastasia, please protect me,*' she whispered. '*You who suffered so terribly because you refused to deny your belief, please relieve my suffering.*'

She wasn't lying there long, however, before she heard footsteps climbing the stairs. It sounded like more than one person, and she heard a woman's voice, although it was very deep for a woman.

The bedroom door opened and the black-haired woman she had seen down in the yard walked in. Sister Barbara saw her tan-coloured high-heeled boots first of all. Then, when she managed to raise her head a little and look up, she saw that she had taken off her brown tweed jacket and was wearing a beige turtleneck sweater, with a silver oval medallion around her neck, and a dark-chocolate skirt.

She was closely followed into the room by a short bald man in a tight black T-shirt and jeans. He had a squashed-looking face, like a Hallowe'en turnip lantern, and protruding ears with silver earrings in both of them. He was broad-chested but his legs were bandy, as if he had been riding horses all his life. He was carrying a soiled canvas bag which looked as if it contained a number of heavy objects and clanked when he set it down on the floor.

'Why, Sister Barbara,' said the black-haired woman. 'What are you doing down there, girl, when you have a perfectly good bed to have a nap on?'

She crouched down beside her and tilted her head to one side so that she was looking directly into Sister Barbara's face. Close up, Sister Barbara could see that she was the same woman who had come to visit her at the Greendale Rest Home dressed as a nun and claiming to be Sister Margaret from the Bon Sauveur Convent.

Now, though, Sister Barbara could smell a strong jasmine perfume on her, so strong that she could taste it, and from where was she was lying she couldn't avoid seeing up her skirt and her white satin knickers.

'Dermot,' said the woman, standing up, 'help me to lift this old wan on to her feet, would you?'

'Who are you?' asked Sister Barbara tremulously. 'You're not genuinely a sister from the Bon Sauveur, are you?'

'Oh, there's no pulling the wool over your eyes, is there, Sister Barbara?' said the woman. 'You were always the cute one.'

She grasped Sister Barbara's right arm and although Sister Barbara tried to flap her away she kept a tight grip on it, so tight that it hurt. The man called Dermot took hold of her left arm, tugging it out from under her, and between them they hauled her upright. She swayed and staggered, but they heaved her over to the bed and dropped her flat on her back. She tried to sit up but the woman pushed her back down.

'You just stay lying there. You could do with the rest.'

'Who are you?' said Sister Barbara. 'Where is this place? What do you want with me?'

'Don't you recognize me?' the woman asked her. 'Well, no, I don't suppose you would after forty-one years. That's how long it's been, Sister Barbara. Forty-one years.'

'I still don't know who you are.'

'Then let me refresh your memory, sister. Riona Nolan. Skinny little Riona Nolan, fifteen and a half years old, dragged around to the convent by her own mother because she was pregnant and had consequently brought everlasting shame on the Nolan family. I'm Riona Mulliken these days, but skinny little Riona Nolan is still here inside me, just as scared as she was that day, and skinny little Riona Nolan will never forget what you gave her all that time ago when all she needed was Christian kindness.'

Sister Barbara tried again to sit up, but again Riona pushed her back down.

'The way you treated me, you heartless sanctimonious witches, all of you. The way you treated my Sorley.'

'So you were one of the fallen girls we took in?' said Sister Barbara.

'Fallen! Fallen! You made us sound like horses dropped dead in the field! The only thing I'd ever fallen was pregnant and that wouldn't have happened if my mother had better educated me, and if the church hadn't forbidden the use of condoms, or abortion.'

'I confess that I don't remember you,' said Sister Barbara. 'However . . . if you believe that I failed to give you the comfort that you needed, or if I inadvertently mistreated you in any way, then I am truly sorry and beg your forgiveness.'

'Forgiveness!' said Riona. She turned around to Dermot, who was standing by the window with his arms folded, as if he were waiting. 'Did you hear that, Dermot, she begs my forgiveness!'

Dermot shrugged and sniffed and wiped his nose with the back of his hand, as if he couldn't give a continental. Riona turned back to Sister Barbara.

'There's all kinds of things that you can beg forgiveness for and a person will forgive you. But if you ruin a person's whole life, then I don't think you can expect forgiveness for that, do you? If you take everything away from them – their self-respect, and their confidence, and their family, and their friends, and on top of that you take away the child they gave birth to, which is the only one thing they have left to love, the only one thing that makes them feel that they have any worth in this world – if you take that away, too, do you really think for a single moment that you can expect forgiveness, or deserve it?'

'I'm sorry, that's all I can say to you,' said Sister Barbara. 'Was your child sent off for adoption?'

Riona puckered her lips and nodded, and there were tears sparkling in her eyes.

'Then I *am* sorry,' Sister Barbara told her. 'But you have to remember that times were very different then. People were nowhere near as liberal-minded as they are today. We would have considered very carefully before putting your child up for adoption. You say you were only fifteen. I'm sure you can understand that we thought it would be best for your child, and for you, too. My goodness, you were only a child yourself.'

'Oh, that's what you thought, is it? You never asked me. You never said, "Riona, do you think it might be better for you and Sorley if we separate you and you never see each other again?"

You never said that, did you? I just went to his cot that morning with his bottle all warm and he was gone. I never even had the chance to kiss him goodbye.'

Sister Barbara closed her eyes for a moment. Then she opened them and licked her lips. 'Do you think that I might have a drink of water?' she asked.

'No,' said Riona.

'My mouth is fierce dry. Did you drug me? I can't seem to remember us leaving Greendale.'

'You don't seem to remember anything very much, do you? You don't even remember giving my little boy away to total strangers. How can you not remember that? Well, no, I suppose I can understand it. Sorley wasn't the only child you gave away, was he? Not by a long chalk. My friend Clodagh – twin girls she had and you gave those away, too. Do you know what happened to Clodagh? Do you?'

'I'm sorry, I don't remember her, either.'

'She hanged herself, Clodagh, on her seventeenth birthday. Her twins were taken away but her parents still wouldn't have her back home and it was her birthday and nobody gave her so much as a birthday card and so she hanged herself. I went to her funeral and I was the only one there.'

'Life can be very cruel sometimes,' said Sister Barbara.

'No, Sister,' Riona retorted. 'Life isn't cruel. *People* are cruel. You used to tell me over and over all about your precious Saint Anastasia, how cruelly she was treated by the Romans. What you never understood was that you and your sisters at the Bon Sauveur were just as cruel to us as the Romans were to Saint Anastasia. You didn't torture us, like the Romans tortured Anastasia. You didn't cut off our hands and our feet and our breasts and burn us at the stake, but you might just as well have done. Clodagh ended up dead, and she wasn't the only girl to take her own life, and most of the rest of us suffered mental torture that will last until *we're* dead and buried, too.'

'I don't know what I can say to you,' said Sister Barbara. 'I never realized. I always thought that the discipline we imposed on you girls would correct your morals and bring you back to Jesus, and that by sending your children for adoption we were relieving you of a burden that you were far too young to bear, as well as being a lifelong reminder of your shame.'

'Shame? What shame? I had sex with Tony O'Riordan in the back of my brother's van! *Once*! I wasn't ashamed! I would have done it again if he hadn't copped off with that Bernadette Gibney!'

She leaned over Sister Barbara, breathing deeply, as if she had just run upstairs. Sister Barbara looked up at her and said, 'Why did you bring me here? Just to tell me how badly we all treated you? I'm an old woman now, Riona. That was all a long time ago, as you so rightly say, and to be perfectly honest with you, I've forgotten most of it.'

'Just because you've forgotten it doesn't mean you didn't do it. Just because you've forgotten it doesn't mean you no longer deserve to be punished for it.'

'How can you punish me more than time has punished me already? I pray all day every day for Saint Anastasia to take me away.'

Riona stood up straight. 'How would you like your prayers to be granted?'

There was a moment of utter silence in the bedroom and none of the three of them moved. Then Dermot opened his mouth and started to worry a fragment of food from between his two front teeth with his thumbnail, and the window rattled softly, and from outside came the echoing clatter of a horse's hooves.

Sister Barbara crossed herself. 'What are you going to do?' she asked, so quietly that her voice was barely audible. 'Are you going to kill me?'

Eighteen

As Katie parked outside the courthouse in Washington Street, already five minutes late, her iPhone rang. It was Dr O'Brien calling from the hospital and she was tempted not to answer, but he kept on ringing. She climbed out of her car and hurried up the courthouse steps in between the tall Corinthian pilasters. A small crowd of reporters had gathered outside the front doors, as well as lawyers and relatives and members of the public, including a red-bearded young man with a handwritten placard reading FREE THE WATER METER THREE!

'Yes?' said Katie, pausing before she entered the building. 'Listen, Ailbe – I'm just about to go into court. Can I call you back later?'

'Phew!' said Dr O'Brien. 'I was worried I wouldn't catch you in time.'

'Why? What is it?'

'You're going in for the Michael Gerrety hearing, right?'

'That's right. But I'm really pushed for time.'

'Please, listen. You know when you visited the mortuary to see the flying nun, there were two floaters under wraps, waiting for me to issue death certificates?'

'Go on. But do hurry. The court usher's waving for me to go in.'

'You won't need to go in.'

'What? What are you talking about?'

'The young female floater. One of your gardaí came in about twenty minutes ago with another body that was found in a ditch beside the N71. He saw the girl lying there on the table and he recognized her immediately. We checked on PULSE and there's no doubt about it. It's Roisin Begley.'

Katie felt as if she had been punched hard in the midriff. She leaned back against the nearest pilaster and said, 'I can't believe this. Roisin Begley? Is it really her?'

'Sorry. Absolutely no question at all. She even has the same small mole on her left upper lip.'

Katie took a deep breath, and then another. Her abdominal muscles were rock-hard and she rubbed her stomach slowly to try and relax.

'All right, Ailbe,' she said. 'I suppose I'm glad you caught me when you did. God Almighty, though, I'm not looking forward to seeing the smug look on Michael Gerrety's face when he finds out that the only witness against him is deceased. There are no signs of foul play, I suppose?'

'She could have been pushed into the river, but there's no suspicious bruising on her body and she definitely died of drowning. There's no alcohol or drugs in her system and only some partially digested pizza in her stomach.'

'What a tragedy. That silly young girl. And so pretty, too. I'll have Detective Dooley call round to see her parents, so they'll probably be coming over to the hospital later to make a formal ID. I'll sort things out here at the courthouse and then I'll get back to you.'

She paused and then she said, 'Sometimes I could curse out loud, Ailbe, do you know what I mean? It's all so pointless. It's all so sad.'

'Yes,' said Dr O'Brien. 'But that's life for you, in the end, isn't it? Myself, I see the proof of it every day, stretched out on the table. Young and old, pretty and not so pretty. You're absolutely right, Katie. It's pointless and it's sad.'

* * *

Katie hurried into the courtroom. Finola McFerren was talking to the beetroot-faced clerk of the court and when Katie appeared she raised her eyebrows in relief.

'Oh, you made it! Thank God! I thought I was going to have to ask for an adjournment.'

'Are you all set, DS Maguire?' asked the clerk. He beckoned to the tipstaff sitting at the side of the courtroom to go and tell the judge that the hearing was ready to begin.

Katie could see Michael Gerrety sitting in the dock with a garda next to him. Handsome as ever, with his broad face and his wavy chestnut hair, wearing a white shirt and purple silk necktie and a navy designer suit. A pink ribbon was pinned to his lapel, to show his support for the Irish Breast Cancer campaign. *Jesus*, thought Katie, *you don't miss a trick, do you?*

He didn't look at her, although he was obviously aware that she was looking at him because he yawned, as if the hearing was completely futile and nothing but a waste of his time.

'You don't – you don't have to call the judge,' said Katie. 'We're dropping this case, as of right now.'

'*What*?' said Finola. She was a tall, hawk-like woman and even sitting down she was formidable, especially in her wig. She picked up some of the papers that were spread out in front of her and crumpled them in frustration. 'Detective Superintendent Maguire! This has taken us weeks to prepare. *Weeks*! I thought you had your teeth into Gerrety. What's changed?'

'Roisin Begley has been found drowned. The pathologist called me not five minutes ago.'

Finola dropped the papers back on the bench. 'Holy Mary, Mother of God. That's terrible. Have her parents been told?'

'I've sent a detective round to tell them now. I'll go and see them myself after.'

'So, that's it, then?' the clerk chipped in. 'You won't be pursuing this prosecution any further?'

'Given that our only complainant has passed away – no,' said Katie.

'Well, I'm very sorry to hear that,' said the clerk. 'I'll go and inform the defendant.'

143

Finola McFerren stood up, took off her wig, and started to gather her documents together. 'Was it suicide, do we know? Did she leave a note or anything?'

'I haven't heard yet,' Katie told her. 'If she did, we'll probably find it at her home or on her phone.'

All the time she was watching Michael Gerrety intently. She wanted to see his expression when the clerk told him that the prosecution was entering no evidence against him and that the case was being abandoned. If she saw the merest glimmer that he already knew that Roisin Begley was dead, that would be incentive enough for her to set up a full-scale investigation into how she had drowned, even if she had left a suicide note.

But if he did already know, Michael Gerrety was clever enough to do nothing but frown slightly when the clerk spoke to him, and then nod. No hint of a smile. No over-reaction. Just grave acknowledgement. As the garda ushered him out of the dock, he turned to Katie and caught her looking at him and his face was unreadable.

'So, what do we do now?' asked Finola.

'There's only one thing we can do. Keep up our surveillance on Gerrety and wait for him to make another mistake. There's plenty of crimes we can entrap people into committing, but pimping an underage girl isn't one of them.'

They walked out of the courtroom. On the steps outside, Michael Gerrety was talking to Fionnuala Sweeney from RTÉ, as well as reporters from the *Examiner* and the *Echo*.

'It's a tragedy, yes,' he was saying, 'and for me part of that tragedy is that I will never have the opportunity to prove to the world that I never took advantage of that unfortunate girl. Roisin was a free spirit – beautiful and vivacious. She did what she wanted to do and there was nobody could stop her. We don't know yet how or why she died, but I am totally certain in my own mind that it had nothing whatsoever to do with her career with Cork Fantasy Girls.'

Martin Docherty from the *Examiner* lifted up his voice recorder. 'That's all very well for you to say that, Mr Gerrety, but the critical question is that, did you have sex with her?'

'Roisin was underage,' said Michael Gerrety.

'With respect,' said Martin Docherty, 'that wasn't the question.'

'I know, but that's the only answer you're going to get out of me. If you want to suggest in your newspaper that I had intimate relations with a girl who was under the legal age of consent, then go ahead and I shall have the considerable pleasure of seeing you back here in court, faced with an action for libel.'

Michael Gerrety's solicitor, James Moody, stepped forward then and called a halt to the questioning. In any case, Fionnuala Sweeney had caught sight of Katie and came hurrying down the courthouse steps with her microphone, followed by her cameraman.

'Detective Superintendent Maguire! As a woman police officer, you must be very upset that this case has had to be abandoned.'

'All I'm upset about today is the loss of a lovely young life,' said Katie. 'As far as the case against Michael Gerrety is concerned, that can wait.'

'You've said more than once, though, that you're determined to clean up Cork's sex trade.'

'I have said that, and I'm determined to. But that's the only comment I'm going to make at the moment, except to send Roisin Begley's family and friends my personal condolences and to pass on the deepest sympathy of the whole of the Cork City Garda.'

A shiny black Mercedes drew into the kerb and Michael Gerrety and James Moody climbed into it, accompanied by a shaven-headed man in a black nylon bomber jacket who looked as if he could break slates with his teeth.

Before he ducked his head down into the car, Michael Gerrety glanced up the steps at Katie and again his expression was utterly lacking in emotion.

She could guess what he was thinking, though. *Did I have Roisin Begley drowned? Wouldn't you like to know?*

Nineteen

Riona sat on the wheelback chair while Dermot rummaged in his canvas bag, sniffing repeatedly as he did so.

'We really thought that we were doing the best for you,' Sister Barbara repeated. 'You'd gone astray, you girls. Your families had rejected you. The whole of decent society had turned its back on you. We were the only ones who were prepared to take you in and care for you. What would you have done without us?'

'Oh, we would have struggled, no question about it,' said Riona. 'Some of us might even have died, if you hadn't given us shelter. But did it ever occur to you that we weren't fallen women, we were only silly young girls who had done nothing worse than give in to the feelings that God Himself gave us?'

'We never judged you! We opened our hearts to you!'

'No, you didn't, you sanctimonious hypocrites! You made our lives unbearable! Instead of taking us in, why didn't you tell our parents to show us some Christian forgiveness, instead of dragging us around to Saint Margaret's, like they did, and disowning us? My own mother threw my suitcase at me and it broke open and all of my clothes fell out on the ground, and it was raining.'

'You have to understand that you'd brought shame on them,' said Sister Barbara. 'You can't deny that. Their friends and neighbours would never have spoken to them again.'

'Then maybe you should have gone around to their friends and neighbours and told *them* to show us some mercy, too,' said Riona. 'Oh, sure, you probably fooled yourselves that you were being saintly, but all you were doing was agreeing with the whole lot of them that we were sluts. What about the lads who knocked us up? None of *them* got shut up in monasteries and had to work like slaves for nothing. Where were the laundries for the boys who couldn't keep their kecks zipped up?'

Out of his bag Dermot had now produced a pair of Powerkut ratchet secateurs, the sort gardeners used to cut through thick and obstinate branches. He walked around to the end of the bed with them, snipping at the air, then he held up his left hand so that Sister Barbara could see that half of his little finger was missing.

'Wish I'd had these when I cut my own fecking finger off. They don't cut all the way through, not the first go.'

Sister Barbara looked at him anxiously but all he did was give her a snaggle-toothed grin.

'What are you going to do?' she asked in a hoarse, whispery voice.

But Riona said, 'You took our children away from us, Sister Barbara. Our own children. Our babies. I don't know how many you neglected so badly that they died, but I know that it was more than a few. Even when they managed to survive you stole them from us, you stole them right from out of their cradles, and you sent them away to be adopted. You changed their names on their birth certificates. You even changed the date they were born and *where* they were born so that even when they grew up they wouldn't ever be able to find us again. Do you have any idea at all of the pain you caused? Not just to us, but our children, too? Do you know how many tears have been shed, and are still being shed, because of you? We could have filled the Atlantic Ocean twice over with our tears!'

'You weren't fit and decent mothers,' Sister Barbara retorted, and now she began to sound angry. 'They didn't ever belong to you, those children. They belonged to God. That was why we had them adopted.'

'And all the ones who died of pneumonia, or the flu, or choked to death on biscuits they shouldn't have been given? What about them?'

'They were all God's children, too. Not yours. It was God who decided to take them back into His arms. Who are we to tell what dismal lives He was saving them from?'

'Who was God to know whether their lives were going to be dismal or not? And even if they were going to be dismal, didn't you always teach us how holy it is to bear the worst of our sufferings without complaint?'

'Well, yes, that much is true,' Sister Barbara agreed. 'So why are you complaining now?'

'Because I never pretended to be holy, unlike you and your sisters at Saint Margaret's,' said Riona. 'But now I'm going to give you the chance to show me how holy *you* are.' She stood up, crossed over to Sister Barbara, and sat down on the bed close beside her.

'What are you going to do?' asked Sister Barbara.

'Do you remember, when my Sorley was very little, you used to come into the dormitory at bedtime and sing him that little song?'

'No, I'm sorry. I don't remember you or your son. There were so many girls. So many babies.'

'I was allergic to you doing it. The way you used to talk to us girls, it used to set my teeth on edge. But what could I do? I was fifteen and you were a holy sister. I could hardly tell you to go and feck yourself, could I?'

'What song?' said Sister Barbara.

Riona leaned over her and grasped both of her skinny, blue-veined wrists, pinning them down hard against the horsehair mattress. Her face was now so close to Sister Barbara's that their noses were almost touching and it was clear from the way Sister Barbara was blinking that she was finding it difficult to focus.

Riona's large breasts were pressing down against Sister Barbara's chest and she could feel the wires of the firm support bra underneath her sweater.

'Do you know something, Sister Barbara?' said Riona. 'Your breath smells. It smells like chicken that's gone off and the insides of old women's handbags. You know what it smells of, most of all, though? It smells like you're dead already.'

'I don't care what you do to me,' said Sister Barbara, her eyes swivelling in all directions to avoid looking at Riona directly. 'Saint Anastasia told her torturers to do their worst because that would only mean that she went to meet Jesus even sooner.'

Riona said, *'Dear little bare feet, dimpled and white.'*

'Oh, *that* song!' said Sister Barbara. 'Of course I remember it! But I used to sing it to all the babies, not just yours!'

'In your long nightgown, wrapped for the night,' Riona continued, still staring into Sister Barbara's face from only an inch away. *'Come, let me count all your queer little toes . . . pink as the heart of a shell, or a rose.'*

She paused. She didn't turn around to Dermot, or give him any sign, but he reached down and took hold of Sister Barbara's left foot. She tried to kick herself free, but Dermot was far too strong for her and she couldn't move her foot even a millimetre, as if she were paralysed. He opened the curved blades of the secateurs and inserted her big toe between them.

'No!' said Sister Barbara. 'Please, don't do this! I admit that I didn't forgive you all those years ago for your sinful behaviour, but I do now! I do! I will pray for you and your son every day for the rest of my life!'

'What? I thought Saint Anastasia told her torturers to hurry up and get on with it.'

'That was in another time, Riona, in another place. That was in the third century, in what is now Serbia.'

'And what difference does that make? Pain is pain, Sister Barbara, no matter when you feel it, or where. Do you think I suffered any less than Saint Anastasia when I lost my Sorley? *More* probably, because I've been suffering my pain for more than forty years.'

'I am pleading with you not to do this,' said Sister Barbara. 'What purpose will it serve?'

'It's your punishment, that's the purpose!' said Riona. 'Don't you think you *deserve* to be punished for what you did?'

'If I have done wrong, then God will punish me!'

'That's always assuming that there is a God.'

'Of course there's a God! What are you talking about?'

'Yes, but supposing there isn't? If there isn't a God, you'll go to your grave unpunished, and I couldn't bear the thought of that. Don't you think it's painful enough, knowing how many Bon Sauveur sisters have already died without my having the chance to hurt them as much as they hurt me?'

There was a long silence. Sister Barbara clearly couldn't think of anything else to say and she began to breathe in short, shallow gasps, partly because Riona's breasts were pressing so hard against her ribcage, and partly because she was terrified.

'*One is a lady that sits in the sun*,' sang Riona, very softly.

'Please,' said Sister Barbara, but it was then that Dermot squeezed the handles of the secateurs and they cut through the skin and flesh of her big toe.

Sister Barbara quivered and let out a sound that was more like a laugh than a cry of pain. Dermot squeezed the handles again and this time the secateurs had ratcheted up so that they cut halfway through the bone. They made a crunch that could easily have been mistaken for a thick tree branch being chopped off.

This time Sister Barbara screamed. It was such a high-pitched scream that it was almost beyond the range of human hearing, although it was probably less out of pain than the realization that she was going to lose her toe.

Dermot squeezed the secateurs a third time. There was another crunch, and Sister Barbara's toe dropped on to the mattress with a spurt of blood.

'Dear Lord, dear Holy Mother of God, dear Saint Anastasia, please save me from this purgatory,' Sister Barbara babbled, and Riona could feel her spit against her face. She wanted to rub it off but she was determined to keep Sister Barbara pinned down. When she was a young girl, Sister Barbara had done far worse than spit on her and she could bear it until she and Dermot were done with her.

'*Two is a baby*,' she sang.

'Oh God, please, oh God, please! Please, don't do this, oh God, please!' begged Sister Barbara. But Dermot took hold of her second toe and positioned the secateurs on either side of it and clipped it off with only two squeezes. His hands were bloody, so he wiped them on the mattress.

Sister Barbara cried out '*dah*!' and then '*dah*!' and then '*dah*!' She was in such pain that she couldn't even think straight, let alone appeal for Riona and Dermot to stop torturing her. It was taking all of Riona's strength and weight to keep her flat on her back.

'. . . *and three is a nun*!' sang Riona, with spiteful emphasis on the word *nun*!, and Dermot clipped off her third toe. Sister Barbara's face had turned so pale that she looked like a wrinkled ghost of herself and her eyes had rolled upwards so that only the whites showed. She was still conscious, though, because she kept on letting out intermittent cries of '*dah*!' and '*oh*!' and little flinching screams.

'*Four is a lily with innocent breast*,' sang Riona. *Scrunch*. And *scrunch*.

'These clippers are me daza,' said Dermot admiringly. 'I'll have to buy some meself.'

'*Five is a birdie asleep in its nest*.' *Scrunch*, and Sister Barbara's little toe dropped off.

There was another silence and then, 'Now what?' asked Dermot.

'What do you think?' said Riona. 'She has ten toes altogether, doesn't she? Now I'll sing it again.'

Twenty

Katie had meant to leave Anglesea Street early, but by the time she had finished all her paperwork it was past six and the sun was setting. The clocks would go back this weekend and so at this time on Sunday it would already have been dark for nearly an hour. She hated the early winter nights. They always reminded her that little Seamus hadn't lived to see his second Christmas.

She closed the file on her desk and stood up. As she did so, Detective Dooley came in, still wearing his brown oilskin jacket.

'Oh, good. Glad I caught you, ma'am. I just came back from the Begleys.'

'How are they taking it, as if I have to ask?'

'Very bad altogether. Mrs Begley is in a terrible state. I left the counsellor with her, to calm her down if she could.'

'I'll see if I can't visit them myself tomorrow, but I don't really want to intrude.'

Detective Dooley held up a transparent plastic folder with a sheet of paper inside it. 'Roisin left a note. It was tucked under her pillow in her bedroom, so they didn't find it till it was too late.'

He handed it to Katie. The paper was A4 size, lined, and looked as if it had been torn out of a school exercise book. The writing on it was large and scrawly, in blue liquid-ink pen.

Dear Ma and Pa and Shauna and Keeva and Tom, you will hate me I know but I cannot face going to court and having to tell everyone what I did. I love you all so much but I wish I had never been born. Everything was so wrong inside my head and the only way I can think of putting it right is to switch off the light for ever. Try to think good things about me. Love and love and love again Roisin XXXXX.

Katie read it a second time and then handed it back. 'Holy Mary,' she said. 'It's enough to bring the tears to your eyes. Poor girl.'

'I took one of her schoolbooks as well, so the technicians can make a comparison and verify her handwriting. They'll be checking the paper for dabs, too, of course, and DNA, although I doubt if they'll find much of that.'

'Thanks, Robert. I'm sorry you had to do the news-breaking duty.'

'No, you're grand. It had to be me. Her mum and dad knew it was me that got her out of that so-called massage parlour. She was a beautiful girl, you know. Just too frisky for her own good.'

Katie put on her duffel coat. The last of the evening sun was gleaming on the green glass windows of the Elysian Tower and she could see the lights shining in Michael Gerrety's top-floor apartment. She wondered what he was thinking right now – whether he had Roisin Begley on his mind at all, or had completely wiped her from his conscience already. Whether Roisin had genuinely drowned herself or not, he was still responsible for it.

'Everything all right, like?' asked Detective Dooley.

'Yes, sure, fine, thanks, Robert. Just a little tired, that's all.'

'You remember what you said to me my first day here?'

Katie switched off her desk lamp. 'I can't say that I do.'

'You said, "You can't take care of everybody, just give the best care possible to the people you can."'

'Did I say that? That was very philosophical of me.'

'You also said, "There is often the look of an angel on the Devil himself."'

Katie closed her office door behind her and walked along the corridor with him. 'My granny used to say that. I think she was talking about her local priest, but it's equally true of criminals. And politicians. And one or two assistant commissioners, too.'

And David Kane, who used to live next door to me and made me pregnant.

* * *

John was out when she arrived home, although he had left the porch light on for her, and a table lamp in the living room, as well drawing the curtains.

There was a note on the kitchen table: *Gone to Bishopstown. Won't be late. Barney's been walked. Made my spicy shepherd's pie. Love you, Det. Supt!*

Katie changed out of her grey tweed work suit into jeans and a sloppy white sweater. The waistband of her jeans was becoming a little tight, so she left the top button undone, but the sweater covered it and she hoped John wouldn't notice She sat down in the living room with a glass of Tanora and switched on the television. *Fair City* had just started, but she had missed so many episodes that she couldn't follow what Callum was trying to do to help Dermot and Jo.

She was still channel-hopping, looking for something else to watch, when she heard John's car arriving outside. She went to open the front door for him, with Barney jostling excitedly around her knees.

John came in carrying a large black artist's portfolio, over a metre wide. He took it into the living room and propped it up against the sofa, then he removed his tan corduroy coat and hung it up in the hallway. Katie put her arms around him and kissed him, and he kissed her back.

'So, what did you go to Bishopstown for?' she asked him.

He walked back into the living room, ruffling his hair. 'For this. It's a lunchbox for giant sandwiches.'

'Oh, stop codding.'

'It's my drawings and my paintings. When I sold the farm I put them into storage at William O'Brien's. I always imagined that when I went to San Francisco I'd be far too busy to be doing any art. But now I'm back here, well, I have a reasonable amount

154

of free time, so I can take it up again. And I was vain enough to think that you'd be interested to take a look.'

'You never told me you were good at art,' said Katie.

'There were three or four of my landscapes up on the walls at the farm, and a portrait of my ma, God bless her.'

'Well, yes, I remember them. But I didn't realize *you*'d painted them.'

'I've always liked drawing. I was top in art at school. Look.'

John unzipped the portfolio and laid it open on the floor. Inside were twenty or thirty sheets of cartridge paper with sketches of fields and trees and drinkers sitting in pubs. He lifted these out and underneath lay at least a dozen oil-painting boards with landscapes and riverside scenes and portraits of local people, mostly women. All of the paintings were rendered in sombre colours, varying shades of grey and green, but John had caught the greyness of Cork on wet and cloudy days, and his portraits were so highly finished that their sitters almost looked as if they were alive and would open their mouths to speak at any moment .

'John,' said Katie, 'these are *fantastic*. I had no idea.'

She looked through them all, one by one, until she came to the last one, which was a picture of a thin naked girl looking out of a window at a rainy garden. She had long brunette hair tied up in a grey velvet ribbon and she had her face turned coyly towards the artist.

'Who's this?' asked Katie.

'Erm, well, that's my ex, Belinda.'

'She's a very pretty girl.'

'Pretty, yes, but argumentative. Whatever I said to her, she'd say different. If I said chalk was cheese, she'd say it was champ.'

Katie laughed, 'Sounds like my sister Moirin. She disagrees with me on principle. She'd eat a bowlful of spiders for her breakfast if I told her that I couldn't stand the taste of them.'

John carefully stacked the paintings and drawings back into the portfolio and zipped it up again.

'The thing is, Katie, it's you who's inspired me to take up painting again.'

'Oh yes? And how did I manage to do that?'

'Serious, I want so much to show you how much I love you. If I can paint you, it will give me a way of proving how committed I am to us being together. And apart from that, goddamnit, you're beautiful. I really want to celebrate that beauty in a portrait.'

'You don't mean nude, like Belinda?' asked Katie.

John shrugged. 'If you'll let me. You have the most fantastic body.'

'I've put on weight lately. Too many boxty lunches in the canteen.'

'Oh, come on. You look great. You're not overweight at all.'

'John – I'm a senior Garda officer. I'm not sure that posing for a portrait in the nude is exactly prudent. Supposing somebody else gets hold of it.'

'Like who? We'll hang it on the bedroom wall and keep it to ourselves. Katie – I love you, darling, I'm crazy about you, and it would give me so much pleasure. Musicians write songs for the women they love, don't they? "Lady in Red", "Wonderful Tonight", "Layla", songs like that. Painting this picture would be the same kind of thing for me.'

'I don't know, John. I love you, too. I really, really do. But maybe wearing one of those lovely Sarah Pacini dresses I bought last week. Or just head and shoulders.'

John held her close and kissed her, again and again. 'Katie Maguire, I want you naked, just as you are. I want to paint every inch of you.'

She smiled, and kissed him back. 'Let me think about it.'

'Of course. Think about it, and then say yes. I'll be waiting, darling – with my palette all filled up and my brush poised ready.'

Katie laughed and gave him a playful push. 'You're a sex maniac, do you know that?'

'And why do you think that is?' asked John. 'Because of you.'

* * *

At about two in the morning, John reached across the bed and started to lift up Katie's nightgown. He stroked her thigh and then he began to reach around her hip.

'No, John, please,' she told him and pushed her nightgown down again.

'What's the matter?' he asked her. 'When was the last time we made love?'

'I'm sorry.'

'You don't have to be sorry. Just tell me what's wrong. Is it something I've done? You're upset because I want to paint you? Is that it?'

She twisted herself around in bed and stroked his prickly cheek. 'It's not that at all. It's just that work has been fierce traumatic lately, what with Kenny Horgan getting shot like that, and then today there was Roisin Begley.'

'What about her?'

'She was found in the river. It looks like she committed suicide because she couldn't face giving evidence against Michael Gerrety.'

'Jesus, Katie. Why didn't you tell me? No wonder you're upset.'

'I don't like to bring my work home, that's all. What am I supposed to do, sit at the supper table and talk about people being glassed in the face and smashed up in car crashes and choking on their own vomit?'

John held her close and kissed her forehead and ran his fingers through her hair. She thought that it felt dry and that, last time, her hairdresser had cut it too short. 'Hey,' he told her, in that American way he had picked up while he was working in San Francisco. 'I've known right from the very beginning what you have to cope with. Look what happened at Knocknadeenly, that was enough to give anybody the screaming ab-jabs for the rest of their life, those women getting all cut up like that. I still have nightmares about it.'

'I'm sorry,' Katie repeated.

'Don't be sorry. You don't have a single thing to be sorry about, believe me. But I love you, darling, and you turn me on and I would like to think that we can have a good sex life together.'

Tell him you're pregnant.

No, I can't. Not now. I'm too tired and stressed and he's all stressed, too, even though he's trying to sound so calm and reassuring.

They held each other for a while in silence. Somewhere in the distance, in Cobh, a clock struck three, a clock she never heard in the daytime. A clock for the lonely and those who couldn't sleep.

She touched his cheek again. 'I'll do it,' she said.

'Do what?'

'The portrait. I'll pose for you.'

'I don't want you to feel like you're obliged to do it.'

'I don't. I'll do it. I won't be able to sit very still for you, you know that. My mother always used to call me Fairy Fidget. But I'll do my best, I promise. It's something you want, and if you want it, then I want it, too. I love you, John. Don't ever forget that, no matter what happens.'

John kissed her. 'Do you know what my ma used to say to my da? "Sometimes I hate the face off ye, but I couldn't live without ye."'

'Very romantic woman, your mother, wasn't she?' said Katie. 'Now I need to get some sleep.'

Twenty-one

The two investigating officers from the Garda Ombudsman arrived from Dublin at 11:30 the next morning, while Katie was talking on the phone to Dr O'Brien. They knocked at her open office door and she waved them inside.

They sat down in the two chairs facing her desk, giving her brief, uncomfortable smiles. Both of them wore grey suits. One was a barrel-chested man with rough red cheeks and a greasy comb-over. The other was a very thin woman with a large complicated nose and sad eyes, who looked as if she might start silently weeping at any moment. One of them smelled of liniment, although Katie couldn't be sure which one.

'I've completed the post-mortem on Roisin Begley now,' said Dr O'Brien. 'I'm still waiting on the hair follicle tests for drug metabolites, but I should get those by late tomorrow or the day after. There are no drugs or alcohol in her blood or urine. You can tell the Begleys that they can send the undertakers round to collect her now.'

'Thanks a million, Ailbe. Let me know the minute you get the results from the hair tests.'

She put down the phone and walked around her desk to shake the two GSOC officers by the hand.

'I'm Enda Blaney and this is my deputy, Partlan McKey,' said the woman, in a sharp D4 accent. 'We're here to investigate a complaint that's been lodged against you by former Acting Chief Superintendent Bryan Molloy.'

'Yes,' said Katie, sitting down. 'I was notified by Chief Superintendent MacCostagáin and I received your email. What I don't understand is why he made his complaint to the GSOC and what your justification is for following it up. I thought you only handled complaints against Garda officers from the public.'

'Well, that's right,' said Enda. 'But with Bryan Molloy we're dealing with what you might call a grey area, in that he's resigned from the Garda and is now legally a civilian.'

'That might well be the case,' Katie told her. 'But surely his complaint relates to the time when he was still a serving officer.'

'That's part of what makes this a grey area,' said Enda. 'But there's an added complication. We have a related complaint from a woman called Jilleen Quaid. She says you coerced her into providing you with false evidence – specifically that her brother Donie had been hired by Bryan Molloy to execute a Limerick gangster called Niall Duggan.'

'*Coerced* her? Coerced her how? She gave me her evidence of her own free will. She handed me the very gun that Bryan Molloy had supplied to her late brother so that he could shoot Niall Duggan, and a letter signed by Donie confessing to what he'd done. I still have them.'

Partlan opened a pale-green folder on his lap and said, 'Ms Quaid told us that before she met you in the Cauldron Bar in Limerick she had never seen either the gun or the so-called letter of confession. You told her that you were dead set on ousting Bryan Molloy from his position as acting chief superintendent, and if she helped you to prove that he had paid Donie Quaid to murder Niall Duggan, that would be the finish of him. Your actual words were, "he'd be hockeyed".'

'She was talking *raiméis*, if you'll excuse my saying so,' Katie replied. 'I don't think I've ever said "hockeyed" in my life. Besides, I have a very reliable witness. I was introduced to Jilleen Quaid by Gary Cannon, who used to be a sergeant at Henry Street, and he was sitting right next to us in the Cauldron when Jilleen gave me the gun and the letter.'

Enda tugged at the tip of her nose as if she were moderately surprised to find that it was still there. 'We're aware of that, Detective Superintendent. Ms Quaid told us that it was former Garda sergeant Cannon who arranged for her to meet you. I'm sorry to have to inform you, though, that he was found deceased at his house on Thursday last week.'

'He's *dead*?' said Katie. 'How? What happened?'

'Apparent suicide,' put in Partlan. 'Shot himself in the mouth with a shotgun. Almost took his head off.'

'Did he leave a note?'

'You know as well as we do that only one in six suicides leaves a note,' said Enda. 'In this particular case, no, he didn't.'

'Was he married?'

'Yes, he was. His wife said that he had been depressed about not finding work, and it seemed he had some serious gambling debts, too.'

'Had he talked to his wife about Bryan Molloy? Or to any of his friends?'

'His attitude towards Bryan Molloy was generally resentful and he blamed him for his losing his job at Henry Street. That may have been why he was willing to assist you in fitting up Bryan Molloy with false evidence.'

Katie said, 'Now, you listen. You're talking as if I actually did falsify the evidence against him, but I didn't. I had the pistol checked by the Technical Bureau and they confirmed that it was a Garda-issued weapon with the serial number filed off it, although it didn't come from Limerick. It was signed out of Tipperary Town Garda station by Inspector Colm McManus, who happened to be a fellow Freemason and golfing partner of Bryan Molloy's. Inspector McManus claimed that he had lost the weapon while pursuing a suspect who was trying to escape along the River Ara. But, quite clearly, he wasn't telling the truth.'

'Have you interviewed Inspector McManus?' asked Enda.

'No. He's another deceased witness, I'm frustrated to say. Of all the ways for a Garda inspector to go, he was poisoned by carbon monoxide while he was on a caravan holiday in Killorglin.'

'So you have nobody to rebut Jilleen Quaid's allegation against you?'

Katie was growing increasingly impatient with Enda and Partlan's questioning, but she was trying very hard to keep her temper in check. 'Apparently not,' she said. 'But the material evidence is conclusive enough, whether I have any living witnesses or not. I have Donie Quaid's confession and I can have the handwriting checked to confirm that he wrote it. Most important, though, the bullet that was retrieved from Niall Duggan's body was definitely fired from the gun that I have in evidence, and where would I have got that gun from if Jilleen Quaid hadn't given it to me?'

'It's possible that Gary Cannon gave it to you,' said Partlan. 'He was just as determined to see Bryan Molloy lose his job as you were.'

'You can suggest that Gary Cannon gave it to me until you're black in the face,' Katie retorted. 'The plain truth is that he didn't, and where would *he* have got it from? If anybody wanted anybody else to lose their job, it was Bryan Molloy who was taking every conceivable opportunity to undermine *me*. You have only to see what he said about me at media conferences, and read his reports.'

'Well, we have,' said Enda. 'He *is* critical of you, but with some justification. It seems clear that you mishandled your investigation into a series of kidnappings, to say the very least, and the consequence was that two young gardaí lost their lives.'

Partlan held up a sheet of paper from his folder. 'We also have a report on that case from Assistant Commissioner O'Reilly, and what he says supports and corroborates Bryan Molloy's complaint. His specific comments are that you behaved "rashly and unprofessionally, and that you took unnecessary risks before you had sufficient intelligence to deal with all foreseeable outcomes".'

'That doesn't surprise me,' Katie told him. 'Assistant Commissioner O'Reilly has an overwhelming motive for wanting to be rid of me, just like Bryan Molloy. And I also happen to have a letter from Detective Inspector Fennessy that confirms what they were up to. Extorting money from public funds.'

'We've seen that letter,' said Partlan. 'By his own admission, Detective Inspector Fennessy was mentally unstable at the time that he wrote it. And, of course, we have no idea where he is – whether he's alive or dead. There's a strong suggestion in the letter that he might have been considering suicide.'

Katie was about to answer him when her phone rang. She picked it up and said, snappily, 'DS Maguire.'

'It's Kyna, ma'am. You need to come up to the convent, as soon as you can.'

'What is it? That Mother O'Dwyer's not giving you ire, is she?'

'Mother O'Dwyer? No. She's shut herself up in her study and isn't talking to anybody. No, it's what's been found in the garden. We've uncovered a disused septic tank and it's filled up with children's bones. It looks like it could be hundreds of them. It's Tuam all over again. It may even be worse.'

'I'll be right there,' said Katie. 'You have Patrick with you there, don't you?'

'Yes, and Sergeant O'Farrell, too. He's sealed off the convent, but discreet, like, so that we don't attract any attention from the media.'

'Good. I shouldn't be more than ten minutes so.'

She put down the phone. Enda and Partlan were both staring at her expectantly.

'I'll have to wind this up,' she said. 'Something critical has come up, and I'll have to love you and leave you.'

'We've come down specially from Dublin,' said Enda. 'This interview has been prearranged for days.'

'I know. But you can't prearrange fate, I'm afraid. This is much more important. Besides, I don't really have anything more to say to you, not at this stage. I'll need to see the complaint in writing, in full, with any substantiating evidence, not just supposition and unfounded accusations. I'll be talking to my lawyers and they'll be getting back to you.'

'We have a lot more questions for you, Detective Superintendent,' said Enda.

'That's as may be, but right at this moment I'm not prepared to give you any more answers. Have you arranged to meet anybody else here in Cork?'

'No. We came only to see you this morning. We spoke yesterday to Assistant Commissioner O'Reilly at Phoenix Park. I must say this is all very unsatisfactory. At the very least we were expecting some kind of response from you about Bryan Molloy's complaints of bullying and harassment.'

'This is totally off the record,' said Katie. 'But let me put it this way: for Bryan Molloy to complain that I bullied him is like an Irish Staffie saying that a woman provoked it into biting her leg because she made a point of looking too defenceless.'

'I don't think Irish Staffies can talk,' said Enda.

'And neither any more will I,' Katie told her. 'Now, I have to go. Good luck to you so.'

* * *

It had started to drizzle again and the two gardaí who were standing at the gates of the Bon Sauveur Convent were looking wet and miserable, but they gave Katie a salute as she drove into the car park.

Detective Sergeant Ni Nuallán was waiting for her in the garden at the back of the building, wearing a dark-blue raincoat with a tall peaky hood that made her look like a character out of *The Lord of the Rings*.

The garden was crowded with at least thirty reservists and technicians and even more gardaí. Katie could see the pale faces of some of the sisters watching them from the windows. A small yellow Hanix digger had been brought in now and it was jolting backwards and forwards on its caterpillar tracks, scraping up the turf from the lawn to expose the wet grey concrete of the septic tank underneath it. Part of the flower bed had already been dug up and a large heap of soil had been piled up against the convent wall.

Bill Phinner came over, looking as miserable as everybody else.

'Hard to believe this,' he said. 'First those kiddies' skeletons in County Galway and now here. It seems to have been the nuns' default method of disposing of dead babies.'

He led Katie across the garden to an area next to the flower bed where the grass on top of the septic tank had already been scraped away. A metal lid about forty-five centimetres square had been lifted up, giving access to the chamber beneath it. Bill shone his Scorpion forensic flashlight down into the hole and beckoned Katie to take a look.

'Holy Mother of God,' she said. The chamber was filled almost to the top with a tangled clutter of diminutive bones. She could see baby-sized skulls and tiny ribcages and pelvises even smaller than the first one that they had discovered in the flower bed. Kyna had been right: the bodies of hundreds of little children must have been dropped in here.

The smell was like nothing she had ever smelled before. Usually she thought that death smelled green, but this was dark brown.

'I only pray they were dead when they were disposed of,' she said.

'Well, me too,' said Bill. 'But I don't think that even the sisters of the Bon Sauveur would have been so callous as to sling a living baby into a septic tank.'

'It's going to be a fierce brutal job getting them all out of there,' said Katie. 'You're not thinking of trying to fit them all together, are you?'

'That was what I was going to ask you about,' said Bill. 'This is your fairly average septic tank, which means it has three chambers, each with a thousand-gallon capacity. If all three chambers are filled up with bones like this one, God alone knows how many skeletons we have here. Fitting them all back together will mean that we have to test almost every single bone for a DNA match. The cost would be astronomic. Like, the overtime alone.'

'No, I wouldn't expect you to try,' said Katie. 'Even if you did manage to fit them all back together, we wouldn't necessarily know who they were, not unless their mothers came forward – and those mothers who aren't deceased would probably be very reluctant to admit that they once gave birth to an illegitimate child.'

She peered down into the septic tank again. One tiny skull seemed to be frowning at her, as if it were saying, *Where am I? What am I doing down here? I should be in my own little coffin, in a cemetery, with a gravestone to mark who I was.* It even had some stray blonde hairs still attached to it.

Bill said, 'We'll be able to calculate how long they've been down here, and how old they were when they died, and what sex they were, too. Girls have more advanced skeletal maturation than boys after birth, but boys' bones have higher mineral density and their long bones tend to be larger. There are plenty of other tests, too, although some of them are less reliable than others.'

Katie turned to Detective Sergeant Ni Nuallán. 'Those books that Mother O'Dwyer handed over, do they include a record of all the children who were born here but died?'

'No,' said Detective Sergeant Ni Nuallán. 'All we've seen so far is live births. If they did keep a register of stillborns, or deaths, she didn't produce it.'

The digger chugged into silence and two of the technicians began to prise up the next access cover with crowbars. It took them a minute or two to lift it, but when they had done so they shone flashlights down into the second chamber of the septic tank. Detective O'Donovan took a look inside and then came across to Katie with a serious expression on his face.

'There's more,' he said. 'At least as many again, I'd say.'

Katie went over and looked into the second chamber for herself.

'All right,' she said. 'Keep at it. I think now's the time that I need to have a word with Mother O'Dwyer.'

She heard a harsh croaking sound. She looked up and saw that six or seven hooded crows were perched on the convent roof, ruffling their feathers to shake off the rain.

Twenty-two

By now, Sister Barbara's voice was nothing more than a hoarse, delirious mumble, punctuated by occasional high-pitched squeals which sounded more like a puppy yelping than an eighty-three-year-old woman in pain. Riona was still holding her pinned down to the mattress, but she was semi-conscious and offering hardly any resistance, apart from shivering as if she were suffering from flu.

Dermot cut off the last of her toes. He had left the big toe until last, because it was easier to get a good grip on it with the secateurs when the toe next to it had already been removed. He still had to squeeze the handles together three times to ratchet up enough power to cut right through the bone. Sister Barbara was silent when he did it, so that the crunch sounded even louder.

'That's it then, Riona,' he told her. 'Now she'll take notice of ye. No-toe *bene*, like. You know, like *nota bene*.'

'I can't believe you sometimes, Dermot,' said Riona. 'You thought that Ebola was a rock band and yet you just made a joke in Latin.'

Dermot was picking up the bloody severed toes from the bed and dropping them into a plastic food bag. 'The Christian Brothers taught me. There was three things you came out of that school with any kind of a qualification for, and one of them was Latin. Very handy, Latin, if you wanted to be a motor mechanic, like, or a plasterer.'

'So what were the other two things they taught you?'

Dermot sniffed and wiped his nose with the back of the hand in which the bag of toes was dangling. 'Sodomy, and how to duck your head so that you didn't get hit by a cheeser.'

'Those Christian Brothers,' said Riona, in the same tone of voice she might have used to say 'cockroaches'.

Sister Barbara groaned and coughed and licked her lips and then she opened her eyes.

'My feet hurt,' she said. 'My feet hurt so much. What have you done to me?'

'No-toe *bene*,' Dermot grinned, holding up the bloody bag and waving it from side to side so that Sister Barbara could see it.

'Could I please have a little water?' said Sister Barbara.

'No,' said Riona.

'I'm so thirsty. I'm begging you.'

'I don't care if your mouth is as dry as Gandhi's flip-flop. This is all part of the Saint Anastasia experience. You always wanted to be a martyr like her, didn't you? Well, this is your chance.'

'I'm in fierce terrible pain,' said Sister Barbara. Tears were sliding from the sides of her eyes. 'Please don't hurt me any more. I can understand now how much we wronged you at Saint Margaret's, taking your babies away from you. But please. That was a long time ago and the world – the world – it was all very different then.'

'Do you remember that picture of Saint Anastasia you had hanging above your bed, Sister Barbara?' said Riona. 'One day about a week before my little Sorley was born, you took me into your room and you showed me that picture and explained what all of the symbols meant, Saint Anastasia's attributes. A palm branch there was, to represent her peace-making, and a medicine pot, because she was a healer and an exorcist. But a bowl of fire, too, because she was martyred.

'Oh, I remember you telling me all about her attributes like it was yesterday, and how you told me how shameful I was, and how I didn't have a scrap of decency, not compared with your blessed Saint Anastasia.'

168

Sister Barbara groaned again and winced, although she managed to keep her eyes open.

'I don't have a bowl of fire to martyr you with, I'm sorry to say,' Riona told her. 'What I do have, though, is what you might call the up-to-date equivalent. Dermot? Can you do the honours?'

Dermot went back to his canvas bag. He rummaged around some more and then he lifted out a kitchen food processor with a heavy black base and a glass blender jar. He unwound the cable as he came back across the bedroom and plugged it in at the end of the bed. Sister Barbara tried to lift her head up to see what he was doing, but Riona was still pressing down on her too heavily and obscuring her view.

Sister Barbara let her head drop back down on the mattress. 'I hope that the Lord forgives you for what you are doing this day, Riona. I know that you have suffered, child, but the suffering you will have to endure in hell for all eternity – that suffering will far exceed anything you have had to endure in your life so far.'

'I don't believe in hell, Sister Barbara,' said Riona. 'I don't believe in hell any more than I believe in heaven. What you did to me and my Sorley, you shook my belief right down to the very core of me. Maybe there is a God. Somebody had to make the world and everything in it. But so far as I'm concerned, there are kind people and there are cruel people, that's all, and sure enough the cruel people can make you suffer, but the people who can make you suffer worst of all are the kind people who think they know what's best for you.'

'You – you may have lost your faith in God, Riona,' said Sister Barbara. She was shivering so violently now that she could barely get the words out. 'But God still has faith in you.'

'Dermot,' said Riona over her shoulder. 'The bowl of fire, will you?'

Dermot had fitted the blender jar on to the food processor. He tilted it up at an angle so that he could fit Sister Barbara's bloodied left foot into it, as far as it would go, with the stumps of her toes pressed right up against the metal cutting blades.

Sister Barbara closed her eyes again. '*Veni, Santa Anastasia, et salva me,*' she whispered. Then Dermot switched the food processor on to pulse and there was a crashing sound of blades against bone and flesh, and blood sprayed out of the blender jar all over the mattress, and Riona even felt it pattering against her sweater at the back. She kept Sister Barbara pressed against the bed and she didn't mind the blood. Sweaters could be washed, but there was no detergent that could ever wash away forty years of grief.

Dermot kept the blender running for nearly a quarter of a minute, but then Sister Barbara's foot bones jammed between the blades and he had to switch it off.

'Stall the ball for a minute,' he said. 'I need to dig out some of this shite.'

As he said that, though, Sister Barbara convulsed. Her bony chest heaved against Riona's breasts and then she shuddered and let out a thin, airy squeak.

'Sister Barbara?' said Riona. '*Sister Barbara!*'

But Sister Barbara stayed utterly still. Her eyes were open and she looked as if she were staring at the lampshade on the ceiling, but her face had turned a chalky beige, almost the same colour as the plastered walls.

'Sister Barbara?' Riona repeated, and shook her, but there was no response.

'What's up?' said Dermot, who was poking a spatula into the blender jar to clear out the fragments of bone and ribbons of skin and bloody lumps of flesh. He peered over Riona's shoulder and said, 'Jesus, she's horrid shook-looking. She hasn't passed away on us, has she? We've only just got fecking started.'

Riona let go of Sister Barbara's wrists and shook her, but all Sister Barbara did was jiggle lifelessly on the bed.

'Sister Barbara! Can you hear me? Sister Barbara!'

She slapped Sister Barbara's face, first the left cheek and then the right, but Sister Barbara didn't even blink.

'Maybe you should try that seepy thing on her,' Dermot

170

suggested. He gave the food processor two quick whizzes to make sure the blades were clear.

'What seepy thing? Oh, you mean CPR. Firstly, because I don't have any idea at all how to do it, and secondly, because I think it's too late.'

Dermot came around the side of the bed and frowned at Sister Barbara. 'You're right. She's brown bread. Not surprising, I suppose, at her age, do you know what I mean? The old ticker probably couldn't take it.'

Riona stood up, dry-washing her hands. 'That was a pity. It looks like her precious Saint Anastasia took her after all.'

'Well, it wouldn't be worth praying to them if the saints never showed us any mercy, would it?'

'I still want her to look like she's been tortured in the same way as Saint Anastasia,' said Riona.

'She's gone to meet her maker, Riona. What's the fecking point of that?'

'The point is that I'm making a point, and I want everybody to know that I'm making a point. What those sisters did was pure murder.'

'They never murdered your Sorley.'

'They might just as well. They might just as well have murdered me, too, while they were at it.'

They both stood beside the bed, looking at Sister Barbara. Very gradually, Sister Barbara's clenched fingers opened up, as if she were letting go of the last faint ghost of life, and then her chin sagged. With a sharp click her false teeth came detached from her palate, and Dermot jumped.

'Jesus, I thought she was going to say something to me then. I fecking did.'

'She'll be saying something to whoever finds her, don't you worry. She'll be saying, "Look at me, this is what happens when you treat an unfortunate young girl like a whore and her child like a whore's melt."'

'So what do you want me to do?' Dermot asked her.

'I want you to do what I was after telling you before.'

'What, the diddies and everything?'

Riona turned to him. There was a faraway look in her eyes, as if her thoughts were somewhere else altogether, and at that moment the low winter sun shone in through the window and illuminated her face and the thick black hair that crowned her. She had that Spanish appearance that some people call Black Irish, although these days her hair was dyed rather than natural.

Suddenly she focused. 'Yes, Dermot. Everything. That's what I'm paying you for, isn't it?'

Dermot shrugged and said, 'No bother whatsoever. It's your yoyo.'

'I'm going to get myself changed now,' said Riona, twisting her head around and tugging at her sweater so that she could see the blood spatters on it. 'Call me when you've finished and I'll tell you where we're going to take her.'

'Not more balloons, is it?'

'No. Saint Anastasia was supposed to have worked all manner of miracles, but Saint Anastasia never flew.'

Twenty-three

Mother O'Dwyer's study door was closed, so Detective Sergeant Ni Nuallán gently knocked on it. While they waited for an answer, she gave Katie a quick, hesitant smile. Katie read something in that smile that disturbed her. It wasn't conspiratorial, or humorous, or wry. It was more like the smile of somebody who needs to come out and make a confession but hasn't yet summoned up the courage to do so.

She was about to ask Detective Sergeant Ni Nuallán if there was anything wrong when the door opened and Mother O'Dwyer appeared in her jet-black habit, breathing hard, like a diminutive Darth Vader.

'Yes?' she demanded.

'I don't mean to disturb you, Mother O'Dwyer,' said Katie.

'Well, I'm afraid that you are. I have one of the vicars general on the phone.'

'You must know by now what we've uncovered underneath your garden.'

A moment's silence. Two harsh breaths. Then, 'Sister Brenda Murphy has made me aware of it, yes.'

'We'll be needing to ask you some questions about it,' said Katie. 'Is it all right if we come in?'

'I can't respond to any of your enquiries at the moment, Detective Superintendent,' said Mother O'Dwyer. She raised her hand towards the door as if she were about to close it again.

Katie raised her hand, too, as if she would stop her if she tried. 'Mother O'Dwyer, we've discovered the skeletal remains of what must be hundreds of infants. Not just a few. *Hundreds*. You're the mother superior in charge of this convent, so I don't think it's unreasonable for me to assume that you knew of their existence.'

'I told you, I'm not saying anything to you,' said Mother O'Dwyer. 'I've already contacted the Right Reverend Monsignor O'Leary at the diocesan offices once this morning. In fact, that's him who's waiting on the phone for me now.'

'And what did *he* say when you told him what we'd found?'

'He's instructed me to wait until the bishop has been informed, and until he's had the opportunity to talk the principal church legal adviser, Diarmuid O'Catháin.'

Katie said, 'I've told you before that if you refuse to assist us, I could arrest you for obstruction.'

'You'll have to do whatever you think fit,' Mother O'Dwyer retorted.

'All these children – do you have records of their deaths?' Katie asked her. 'You didn't give any to Detective Sergeant Ni Nuallán here. Were they registered with the coroner, as they should have been?'

'Stillborn children don't have to be registered.'

'I know that, but you can clearly see from the size of some of the bones in your septic tank that most of them were considerably older than newborns.'

'I have no comment about that.'

'Let me ask you this, though, Mother O'Dwyer. Straight out: did you know that they were there?'

'I've nothing at all to say about that, either. I'm sure that Mr O'Catháin or one of his associates will be in touch with you shortly. My only comment is that illegitimate children could not be baptized and anybody who had not been baptised could not be buried in consecrated ground.'

It took all of Katie's self-control not to ask Mother O'Dwyer how she would like her own body to be disposed of when she died? Dumped naked into the wastewater plant at Carrigrenan? She thought of the funeral they had held for Seamus, and the flowers, and the reverence with which his little casket had been buried. Apart from the hymns, they had sung "Morning Has Broken". She thought of the tiny life that was growing inside her even now.

'We'll let you get back to Monsignor O'Leary,' she said. 'We don't want him cribbing that you might be spilling the beans, do we?'

Mother O'Dwyer bowed her head and said, 'Good day to you so, detective superintendent. May the Lord be with you.'

* * *

Katie held her daily briefing later that afternoon than usual. After coming back from the Bon Sauveur Convent she had spent over two hours with her solicitor, Casie Driscoll, discussing how she should respond to the investigation by the Garda Ombudsman. Casie wore a loud suit of yellow and black checked tweed and huge horn-rimmed glasses, and her maroon-coloured hair was always a mess, but in spite of her appearance and her assertive attitude she advised Katie to be reactive rather than aggressive.

'Whatever Bryan Molloy did and said about you, Katie, *you* did nothing wrong at all. Everything you did as far as I can understand it was totally by the book. So don't be slinging any mud back at them. It will only dignify the mud that they're slinging at you.'

Katie wasn't sure how you dignified mud, but she understood what Casie was saying to her.

The daily briefing afterwards was short and frustrating. They had made hardly any progress at all in trying to find out who had murdered Detective Horgan. A silver Mercedes S-class of the type from which the shot had been fired had been found burned out behind Tesco's at the Manor West Retail Park in Tralee, in Kerry. It had originally been supplied by Frank Hogan Motors in Limerick, who had sold it to William Innes, an insurance broker who lived in Castletownroche. William Innes's son had borrowed the Mercedes and badly damaged it, so he had sold it to a man called Devine for cash rather than lose his no-claims bonus.

'Do we know this Devine fellow?' asked Katie.

Detective Inspector O'Rourke said, 'No. Your man gave Mr Innes a business card with a Limerick address on it, but the address turned out to be Donkey Ford's chipper in Cathedral Square and the phone number was the Samaritans.'

'Where is the car now? Have the Technical Bureau had the chance to examine it?'

'It's here now. We had it brought in about an hour ago. We took a quick sconce at it, but there's nothing obvious in it in the way of forensics. No cartridge cases or anything like that. It may not even be the same car as the one that was used to shoot at you, so we're still looking.'

'Any luck with the flying nun?' asked Katie.

Detective O'Donovan shook his head. 'No luck at all. We must have shown her picture to everybody in Cork who's taken holy orders, and of course it's been shown on the TV, too, and in the papers. She may not have been a genuine nun at all, of course, but whoever killed her dressed her up like that.'

'And what do you think the motive might be for that?'

'God knows. What was the motive for cutting her tripes out and floating her up the Glashaboy?'

Katie said, 'If we can work that out, Patrick, we'll have a much clearer profile of our offender.' She paused. 'Either that, or we'll be even more confused than we are now.'

'Nothing more to report on Roisin Begley,' said Detective Dooley. 'She was picked up on CCTV crossing over Pana at 10:34 p.m. on Sunday evening. Her parents thought she was in bed at that time. She was wearing the same pink coat that she was wearing when they fished her out of the river. She's on her own, though, on Pana and there's no obvious indication that she's being followed.'

'Was that the last sighting of her?'

'It was, yeah. She must have gone into the river soon after, whether she jumped or was pushed.'

'How about the horses?' asked Katie.

'That's all going according to plan. I went up to Spring Lane this morning and took Paddy Fearon his five hundred and he was very appreciative to say the least. He's going to pick up the first three horses at Kilmichael early Monday morning and then come back for the other six during the course of the day.'

'He won't be able to tell where the horses really came from?'

'No. All of their passports will be fakes and they'll all be fly-grazing in a field about three kilometres from Josh O'Malley's stud farm. We'll follow Fearon wherever he takes them and hopefully catch him before he does them any harm. I doubt if it will be Nohaval Cove, though – that's been too much on the news lately.'

'But you're quite sure he doesn't suspect you?' asked Katie. 'He's not just going to keep the five hundred and fail to show up and deny all knowledge of what you asked him to do?'

'I don't think so, ma'am,' said Detective Dooley. 'I think I've convinced him that he's met me before. One of my Pavee girls told me that he was in Waxy's one night and a friend's dog pooped on his shoe. I made out that I'd been there, too, that night and it was then that he'd he tipped me the wink that he could dispose of horses on the cheap. He must have been so stocious he couldn't remember if I was there or not.'

'A dog pooped on Paddy Fearon's shoe?' said Detective Sheedy. 'Jesus! I'm surprised the poor creature lived to tell the tale.'

'How about the dead horses?' asked Katie. 'Have we heard any more from Tadhg Meaney?'

'Nothing much at all,' said Detective Dooley. 'The vets are sure now that the horses must have been alive when they were driven off the cliff. Most of them have traces of performance-inhibiting drugs in them, but not enough to kill them. That backs up Tadhg Meaney's first impression that they died from the fall, rather than being dead horses that were thrown off the cliff just to get rid of them.'

'We haven't been able to discover where any of these horses came from?'

'Weatherbys have been very cooperative, but since they don't have any record of their chip numbers there isn't a whole lot more they can do. These were like the ghost horses that never were, do you know what I mean?'

'All right,' said Katie. 'DS Ni Nuallán called me just before we started this briefing and so I can bring you up to date on the progress we're making up at the Bon Sauveur Convent. They've lifted up the access cover to the third chamber of the septic tank and *that* chamber, too, is almost completely filled up with children's bones. It's impossible at the moment to tell how many.

'The technical experts are taking photographs and measurements, but they're going to be leaving the bones undisturbed for tonight. They'll start removing them tomorrow, but that's going to be a very slow and painstaking business altogether.'

Detective Byrne put up her hand and said, 'Will they be able to reassemble each child's skeleton? You know, like individually, so they can give each child its own coffin?'

'It's doubtful, Maureen,' Katie told her. 'If we can find a record of their names, that would be a start, but so far the convent hasn't produced one. Apart from that, we'd have to test the DNA of nearly every single bone and that would be hugely expensive and time-consuming. To be honest with you, I think the best we can hope for is a decent mass burial and a memorial stone put up. They all had short lives, those children, and unhappy ones, too, most likely, but at least we'll be giving them some acknowledgement that they existed – which is more than the sisters at the Bon Sauveur ever did.'

'Well, amen to that,' said Detective Brennan, crossing himself.

'We might have found the skeletons in the septic tank, but I don't think we can stop searching,' said Katie. 'As you know, we were originally alerted to the existence of these remains by one of the sisters who had found part of a child's jawbone in the flower bed, and when we started digging we found a pelvis and a leg bone in the flower bed, too. It may very well be that more children were buried in other locations in the convent garden.

'Because of this, I'm going to request that we bring in RMR Engineering. Detective Inspector O'Rourke is going up to Dublin this weekend in any case for a security conference and he'll discuss it with RMR while he's there. They have a radar scanner that can detect any signs of human activity under the ground, no matter how long ago it took place – like grave-digging or other soil disturbances.'

'Can they locate actual bones?' asked Detective Brennan.

'No, they can't,' said Katie. 'But if they pick up any anomaly beneath the lawns, we can then call in another contractor to dig a series of slit trenches at regular intervals. If there are any bones there, that should find them for sure.

'I've checked out the cost of doing this. It's about two thousand euros a day and RMR say they can complete the survey in three days or less. I think that's a small price to pay to find out how so many children died, and who was responsible for them dying, and who disposed of their bodies as if they were nothing but waste matter, to put it politely.

'It's far too early to say for sure, but I believe we could be looking at the possibility of some criminal prosecutions.'

She suddenly felt faint and swimmy. She sat down, rather abruptly, and then said, 'Sorry. It's been a long day.'

'You're all right, ma'am?' asked Detective Inspector O'Rourke, close to her ear.

'Of course, yes, thank you, Francis,' said Katie.

She looked around at all the detectives in the room and said, 'Everybody – I just want to say this. Some of the major cases that we're working on at the moment, they're unusually difficult, and highly sensitive, too – especially the remains we've found at the Bon Sauveur. I want to thank you all of you for the work you've been putting into them, which has been exemplary. If you have no more questions, that's it for today.'

She remained seated while everybody left the room, all except for Detective Inspector O'Rourke, who was sitting beside her. He poured a glass of Ishka spring water from one of the small bottles on the table and passed it over to her. He didn't say anything, but she could see a look in his eye and she knew that he was far from stupid.

'May the roof above us never fall in,' she said, lifting the glass.

Detective Inspector O'Rourke smiled, but he didn't complete the toast she was giving him. *And may we, as friends, never fall out.*

Twenty-four

Before she drove home, Katie went shopping at Dunne's Store on Patrick's Street. She needed to do a full shop because her fridge was almost empty, but that would have to wait until Sunday. She picked up some pork chops and green beans for tonight, as well as muesli and grapefruit juice and coffee for breakfast.

While she was standing in the queue at the checkout, a short, heavily built man came past her, wearing a long brown raincoat that almost reached the floor. He had greased-back hair and a single gold earring, and a squashed-looking face that looked as if he was being pressed very hard up against a shop window.

When he saw Katie, he stopped and grinned at her. Although he was so ugly, he had immaculate white teeth. She pretended that she hadn't seen him, because she knew who he was: Dovydas Karosas, one of the pimps who worked for Michael Gerrety. She had tried several times to have him deported back to Lithuania, but he had family here and she had never been able to prove beyond reasonable doubt that he was involved in the sex trade.

She knew that he was grinning at her because she had been forced to abandon her prosecution of Michael Gerrety, and that made her feel even more depressed than she was already. She couldn't help thinking about Roisin Begley, and all the hundreds of children's bones at the Bon Sauveur Convent. When it was her turn to pay she found that she had left her purse in her car and she had to swallow hard to stop tears coming to her eyes.

What's the matter with you, Katie Maguire? she asked herself as she walked back along Patrick's Street. *You're a grown woman, not a girl. More than that, you're a detective superintendent. It's your responsibility always to be strong and to take care of other people, not to be pussing just because you're feeling emotional and you've forgotten your purse.*

As she unlocked her car, though, and reached across to the passenger seat,to pick up her purse she suddenly felt very lonely and vulnerable, as if she had nobody to take care of *her*. She knew she had John waiting for her at home, but how long would that last once he discovered that she was pregnant?

On her way back to Dunne's, she passed Dovydas Karosas, who was standing outside Gentleman's Quarters, the menswear store, talking to a dark-haired young woman in a short leopard-print coat. He grinned at her again and called out, '*Labas vakaras, mano numylétinis. Gera matyti tave!*'

She had no idea what he had said, but she ignored him. She took a deep breath and went back into Dunne's to pick up the basket that she had left by the checkout. She felt stronger now, but she also felt conscious of all the gloomy clouds that were looming in her life. After she had graduated from Templemore her father had said, 'I'm fierce proud of you, Katie, but you're a garda now, and I have to tell you this: no matter what the weather, for you it'll always be lashing.'

* * *

After she had stepped out of the shower that evening and towelled herself dry, she looked at herself in the steamy full-length mirror on the back of the door. There was no doubt that she had developed a slight tummy, but she didn't look as pregnant as she felt.

She put on her thick pink bathrobe and went through to the living room. John was sitting on the couch with a large sketchpad on his knee, drawing pictures of Barney in terracotta crayon. Barney seemed to understand what he was doing because he was sitting patiently by the fire with his tongue hanging out, not moving. He didn't even get to his feet when Katie came into the room.

Katie knelt on the couch next to John and said, 'John, those are *wonderful*! You've really caught him.'

'I was thinking of painting a proper full-size portrait of him in acrylic,' said John. 'That's after I've painted you.'

'Why don't you paint him first?'

'You're not backing out on me, are you?' he asked her. 'I was hoping I could do some preliminary sketches tonight. I'll be free for most of the day tomorrow so I can make a start.'

'No, no. I'm not backing out on you. A promise is a promise. It's just that I don't think I'm looking my best at the moment. My hair's a bird's nest and my eyes are all puffy. I don't know how you can even find me attractive.'

John leaned sideways and kissed her. 'You're beautiful, that's why I find you attractive. You're always beautiful. And if you're worried about your eyes being puffy, I can always paint them un-puffy. Artistic licence, that's what we call it. Next best thing to cosmetic surgery.'

Katie picked up a cushion and hit him on the head with it. 'If that wasn't the most backhanded compliment anybody ever paid me!'

John laughed, then closed his sketchpad and stood up. 'Do you want to pose now? It'll only take twenty minutes or so.'

'I'm pure racked, John. Maybe tomorrow.'

'You don't have to do anything. Just lie on the couch looking delectable.'

'Well . . . only for a short while, though. And I'm going to shut Barney in the kitchen.'

'He's a dog, Katie. He's not going to get excited if you take off your clothes.'

'You don't know that. He's a boy dog, after all.'

John laughed and shook his head. 'Okay, then, but you can fetch me another beer while you're in there.'

When she came back, Katie took off her bathrobe and sat naked on the couch. She wasn't embarrassed, but it felt strange, the way John was looking at her now, with his eyes narrowed, as if she were a stranger rather than his lover.

'Okay . . .' he said, 'put up your legs . . . that's it. And lift your right arm and lean on the cushions. That's perfect. And turn your head slightly to the left – a little more, that's it, but turn your eyes towards me. And try to look seductive, as if you don't already.'

'What about my hair?'

'Don't worry about your hair, I can sort that out later. It's your general pose I'm trying to catch now.'

He sat down in the armchair opposite, with his legs crossed, and started to draw, the tip of his tongue held between his teeth, his eyes darting up and down over the top of his pad as he sketched her outline.

'You're sure my boobs don't look droopy in this position?' Katie asked him.

'You have amazing boobs. Don't worry about it.'

'They're much too big. Can't you paint them smaller?'

'You want me to misrepresent you? Detective Superintendent, I'm surprised at you!'

He carried on drawing for a few minutes. When it was obvious that he was drawing her face, Katie deliberately squinted.

'Oh, *that's* attractive,' said John. 'The cross-eyed Venus, that's what I'll call it.'

'One of our cleaners is cross-eyed,' said Katie. 'I'd hate to have to interrogate him because you never know if he's looking at you or not. He's so cross-eyed that when he cries the tears run down his back.'

John drew for a little longer and then he frowned. 'Can you raise your left knee a little higher?' he asked her. 'No, not like that, that's too far. Look – let me show you.'

He put down his pad and came over to her. He took hold of her left knee and gently bent it.

'That's it,' he said. 'Perfect.'

He ran his hand all the way down her calf to her ankle and took hold of her foot and tickled it. She said, 'Don't do that! You don't know how ticklish I am! You'll make me wet myself!'

John smiled and said, 'Yes, but that's how I like you, when you're wet.'

He knelt down beside the couch and kissed her forehead, and then the tip of her nose, her cheek, and then her lips. While they were kissing he caressed her arm and then her side, sliding his fingertips down until they reached the sensitive nerve in her hip, which made her jump.

He held her left breast in his hand, gently squeezing it and rotating the ball of his thumb around her nipple until it started to stiffen.

'John . . .' she said, when they both came up for air.

He kissed her again and then he stood up, crossing his arms to take off his navy-blue sweater. As he did so, static electricity made the crucifix of dark hair on his chest rise up, like some minor miracle.

'John – ' Katie repeated, but she knew that she wanted him just as much as he wanted her. He unbuckled his braided leather belt and pulled down his jeans, kicking them aside. His pale-blue boxer shirts only emphasized how stiff his erection was and when he pulled those off, too, it gave a little bounce as it caught on his elasticated waistband. Katie reached out and grasped the shaft of his penis in her left hand, holding it very tight and looking up into John's eyes with defiance, as if she were saying, *Whatever you believe, this is mine, this belongs to me, and always will*. She rubbed it slowly up and down, and John let out a low murmur and half-closed his eyes.

'You know what you look like?' said Katie. 'You look like a god.'

She reached behind her back and caught hold of the corner of one of the cushions so that she could fling it across the room. That allowed her to lie back flat on the couch and open up her thighs. John climbed in between her knees and leaned over to kiss her. He was breathing hard and his breath smelled of beer. Without releasing her grip on his penis, she guided it in between the lips of her smooth waxed vulva. She could feel how wet she was, much wetter than usual, and her lips opened with a soft, sticky click.

John started to weigh down on her and push the head of his penis into her, but she still kept her grip on it even though she was aching to feel it right up inside her as far as it would go.

'John,' she said, very quietly.

'What?' he asked her.

'Gently, won't you? Very, very gently.'

He said nothing at first, but she could see from his eyes that he was looking for an explanation of why she had said that. When they had first started their relationship, their lovemaking had occasionally been slow and gentle and long drawn-out, almost soporific, especially when they were both tired or had drunk too much. But most of the time Katie had wanted him to force himself into her as hard as he could. She liked it deep and a little rough. She would wrestle with him, laughing, so that she could get on top and press herself so far down on his erection that it touched the neck of her womb and made her flinch.

'Okay,' said John. 'If you want gentle, I'll be gentle. Hey – I'll be like a cat, creeping through the grass.'

'You know how much I love you, don't you?'

'Yes. And I love you.'

She released her grip on his penis and he slid himself into her until she could feel his pubic hair tickling her bare skin.

'Now that's heaven,' she murmured.

'That's weird,' said John. 'That's exactly what I was thinking.'

He was strong and muscular but she could feel how much he was restraining himself. He pushed himself into her very slowly and rhythmically, and at the same time he massaged her breast and rolled her nipple between finger and thumb. She could feel her pelvic floor tightening, much sooner and tighter than it usually did, and her stomach muscles were rock-hard, too. But John continued to be gentle and restrained, even though his penis was now so stiff and curved that it felt like a slippery tusk.

He was beginning to breathe harder and push a little more forcefully when Katie's iPhone rang. He stopped and opened his eyes.

'Ignore it,' she panted.

'What if it's work?'

'It won't be. It can't be. Ignore it.'

But it kept ringing and ringing and she knew it had to be somebody at the station calling her, and that it had to be urgent. They never disturbed her at home without a serious reason.

John lifted himself off her and she sat up and reached across to the coffee table to pick up her phone.

'Detective Superintendent Maguire.'

'It's Patrick O'Donovan, ma'am. I hope I haven't interrupted you in the middle of anything important. I would have called Inspector O'Rourke but he's left for Dublin already.'

'No, Patrick, no bother at all. What is it?'

'Another dead nun. We think it could be the one that went missing from that care home in Douglas. It looks like her, any road, from the photograph they gave us.'

'Where was she found?'

'In the fountain on Grand Parade of all places. We don't have any idea at all how she got there because the whole area was crowded with drunken kids at the time. They're always jumping in and out of it when they're langered, but this time they noticed there was somebody lying in it who didn't get out.'

'Has the body been removed yet?'

'Not yet. The technical boys have only just arrived and I thought you might want to take a sconce at it, too. The media are all here, of course. I don't know who tipped them off.'

'All right, Patrick. Thanks. Give me half an hour tops and I'll be with you.'

John stood up, his erection already subsiding.

'I'm sorry,' said Katie. 'They've found another dead nun. Grand Parade this time, in the Berwick Fountain.'

'Do you want me to drive you?'

'No, I'll be grand, thanks. I may have to stay in the city tonight.'

'You don't have to apologize, Katie.'

'Oh, but John.'

'It's not just your job, sweetheart, it's who you are. I get that now, even though I didn't understand it before. I know you have to go, so go. At least you've had something to eat and a shower.'

'Not to mention half a flah.'

'Hey . . . if I ever used dirty language like that my ma used to shove a bar of coal-tar soap into my mouth. I can still taste it now.'

Katie went up to him and put her arms around him, pressing her breasts against him and feeling his still-sticky penis against her bare stomach. She kissed the hair on his chest and said, 'Nothing is dirty when you're in love.'

He stroked her dark-red hair and said, '*Katie Maguire*,' and the way he said it made it sound like a declaration of love in itself, or the words a man speaks in his sleep when the bed next to him lies empty.

Twenty-five

The ornamental fountain in the middle of Grand Parade had been cordoned off for fifty metres in all directions and the street was crowded with Garda patrol cars and vans from the Technical Bureau, and an ambulance. Although it was chilly and the pavements were still shiny and wet it had stopped raining about an hour ago and beyond the Garda crime-scene tapes there was a rabble of drunken young people, still chattering and whistling and hooting.

A garda lifted aside the tape so that Katie could drive through. She turned right into Oliver Plunkett Street directly opposite the fountain and parked. Detective O'Donovan came over and opened her car door for her.

'This is beginning to look like a pattern,' he said.

'What makes you think that?' asked Katie as she climbed out.

'Well, three elderly nuns murdered in the same week, for starters. And all of them killed like it was some kind of ritual or something, do you know what I mean?'

Katie gave him a pat on the back of his nylon windcheater. 'Sorry, that was only me codding. It does look like somebody has an agenda, doesn't it? I mean, they've all been killed in very different ways, haven't they, these nuns? But I'm sure you're right, and there's a connection here.'

They walked across to the fountain. It had a lower basin about seven metres across, shaped like a clover leaf, out of which rose a pedestal with a second basin on it, about two and a half metres

189

across, and then a third basin, about one and a half metres across, which was topped by a fourth small basin supported by a dolphin. The water had been turned off, but normally it would spout from the top of the fountain and cascade down from one overflowing basin to the one below it.

Three technical experts were gathered around the side of the lower basin, one kneeling and taking photographs. The body of the nun was lying close by, covered with a dark-green sheet, with two glum-looking gardaí standing next to it.

Bill Phinner, the chief technical officer, was there, in a thick bronze padded jacket with a fisherman's sweater underneath it, although Katie could see from his collar that under his sweater he was wearing blue-striped pyjamas.

'Three lads fished her out because they thought she was drowning,' he said, taking out a handkerchief and wiping his nose. 'But she was stiff as a board, so they realized she was well past saving.'

'I've talked to the lads,' said Detective O'Donovan. 'It was the birthday party of one of them and they were all daring each other to jump into the fountain, like they do. They say that loads of them were doing it and all of them were totally langers. The deceased must have been carried across the street somehow and dropped into the basin there, but none of the lads saw that happen. All they know is one of them jumped in and found her body floating around in there.'

Katie turned around and checked the location of the CCTV camera that overlooked Grand Parade. 'We should have some footage of her being carried over to the fountain,' she said. 'And how about the lads? Were any of them taking pictures or videos?'

Detective O'Donovan unfastened the pocket of his jacket and took out two iPhones, both in separate evidence bags, with the names and addresses of their owners written on them. 'One of them was taking a video, although he says that he can't guarantee how steady it is because he wasn't too steady himself, and it may contain strong language, like. The other was taking photos of a couple of girls who were paddling in the fountain and flashing their knickers. That was just before the body was first discovered, so there could well be something useful in the background. I've taken a quick lamp at the video myself but there are so many kids looning around in it that it's hard to make out anything for certain, like.'

'Thanks, Patrick,' said Katie. 'If we can get those back to the station as soon as we can and see if we can't enhance them. And run through the CCTV footage , too.'

She looked around again. 'It's pure amazing that an offender should dump a victim's body in the middle of one of the most crowded streets in the city on a Friday night. They must have known they'd be caught on camera.'

Patrick nodded. 'It's like they're sticking up two fingers, like, do you know what I mean?'

Bill said, 'We've completed taking pictures of the victim and the fountain. We've taken some water samples from the fountain basin, too. There's a chance that they might tell us if the victim was still bleeding when she was dumped into the water – in other words, if she was alive or dead.'

'Is she ready to be removed?'

'Once you've taken a sconce at her, yes, she'll be on her way to the Wilton Hilton.'

'Jesus, Dr O'Brien's going to be happy out. He was hoping to get back to Dublin tomorrow. It's his birthday.'

'Are you ready?' asked Bill. He held out his hand towards her in what was almost a fatherly way and Katie felt that he had sensed her reluctance to view the dead nun's body. *Is it that obvious that I'm feeling hormonal?* she thought. *First Francis O'Rourke and now Bill Phinner. I might just as well walk around with a large placard announcing Pregnant Woman, Handle With Care Or I'll Cry. Or Be Sick. Or Lose My Temper.*

They walked over to the nun and a young female technical expert lifted the sheet that covered her. Both gardaí who were standing there made a point of turning away.

The nun was dressed in a black tunic, with a black scapular over it. Her head and neck were covered with a white coif, but her black veil was missing. Her face was pale grey, the colour and texture of a papier-mâché mask. Her eyes were open but clouded over and her mouth was gaping downwards, as if in terrible dismay.

Bill crouched down beside her and lifted up her tunic so that Katie could see her feet. All of her toes were missing. Not only that, the skin on both feet had been shredded and tangled, and the flesh underneath had somehow been ripped away so that the jagged toe bones protruded like a set of broken teeth.

'I hope to God she wasn't alive and conscious when that was done to her,' said Katie.

'No way of telling at the moment,' said Bill. 'But that's not all.'

He folded back the nun's outer sleeves and showed Katie that both of her hands had been mutilated in the same way. Her fingers had gone and her hands were badly mangled so that they resembled paws.

'We don't know yet if she's suffered any other injuries. She's already in rigor and her body temperature indicates that she's probably been dead for six to eight hours, depending on where she's been. The ambient temperature is seven degrees right now and the water temperature in the fountain is just under five, so that may have cooled her down a little, but she couldn't have been in the water for very long. We'll be able to tell a whole lot more when we get her into the mortuary.'

'And we think this is the same nun who went missing from the Greendale Rest Home?' Katie asked Detective O'Donovan.

He prodded at his iPhone and then showed her the picture of Sister Barbara that had been given to them by Eileen O'Shea. Katie took it and looked at it closely and then held it over the body to compare it.

'I'd say that it's her, all right. What was her name again?'

'Sister Barbara Flynn. She spent nearly fifty years at the Bon Sauveur Convent.'

'Well, now we know for sure that two out of the three murdered nuns were members of the Bon Sauveur. But nobody at the convent recognized the flying nun?'

'They all swore that they didn't, any road.'

'Well, maybe they didn't, Patrick, and maybe they did. I'll tell you this, though. In the waiting room outside the mother superior's office there's a whole collection of group photographs hanging on the walls. I don't know how far they go back, but there's all of the sisters in them, as well as the young mothers and the babies that the sisters were supposed to be caring for.'

'I'll go up there tomorrow first thing and see if I can't pick her out in one of them, then,' said Detective O'Donovan.

'Good. And don't take any nonsense from Mother O'Dwyer. If you can't identify the flying nun immediately, the search warrant gives you the authority to requisition the photographs as possible evidence and bring them into the station so that you can take a look at them closer.'

The ambulance was backed up closer to the fountain and Sister Barbara's body was lifted on to a stretcher. Bill came up and said, 'They're ready to take her off to the mortuary now. I'll go along there myself with Tyrone and Eithne and we'll start the preliminaries straight away. It'll be Christmas before we know it and we could all do with the overtime.'

'Oh stop,' said Detective O'Donovan. 'I hate fecking Christmas.'

'How about you, ma'am?' Bill asked Katie. 'I'll give you an update in the morning. What time do you think you'll be getting in, like?'

Katie said, 'No, Bill. I think I'll come with you. I want to see what's been done to this poor woman.'

Bill raised one black eyebrow like a crow taking off from a rooftop. 'You're sure about that? It's going to be taking us three or four hours at least. Maybe longer.'

But Katie thought of going home to John, who would still be awake and waiting for her, and would probably want to carry on where they had left off. She knew that she would be lying next to him trying to be responsive while all she would be able to picture in her mind would be Sister Barbara's mutilated feet.

'No, I'll come along,' she said. 'I'm wide awake now, and besides, it's about time I came and breathed down your neck while you're at work.'

'Please yourself,' said Bill. 'Just don't be overdoing it, like, okay?'

'Bill, are you trying to tell me something?' she asked him.

'Nothing that you don't know yourself already, ma'am. But I have three daughters and I've been working for the Technical Bureau for twenty-three years next February, so I've encountered women in all kinds of conditions. So let's just leave it at that, shall we?'

He gave her a small, conspiratorial smile and walked off. Katie stood there for a moment watching him go, feeling partly upset that he had noticed the change in her, but partly relieved, too, that somebody else knew she was pregnant, or had guessed, at least, and that the knowledge wasn't a secret any more.

Detective O'Donovan was standing over by the fountain now, so she waved to him and called out, 'Patrick! I'm off to the hospital! I'll see you after so!'

* * *

Outside Cork University Hospital the car park was in chaos. A coach carrying thirty-two Cork supporters back from a hurling match against Kerry had overturned on the N22 at the roundabout with Model Farm Road. Seventeen people had been injured, three of them seriously. The rest were wandering around outside the hospital, dazed and still drunk. Some of them were bruised and bloodied and sitting on the wall with their heads in their hands. Others were teetering about, shouting and swearing.

Katie went through reception and made straight for the mortuary. After all the commotion outside, it seemed even more deathly silent in there than usual. Bill Phinner was already there, with his two technical experts, as well as a mortuary assistant whose white coat was buttoned up wrongly and whose hair was sticking up as though he had just got out of bed. They were down at the far end of the mortuary and only the fluorescent lights immediately above them were switched on, so that they looked as if they were on a stage set. They were standing around the body of Sister Barbara who was lying on a steel autopsy table. They had taken off her coif and scapular, but she was still wearing her tunic, with a belt of woven black wool.

'Ah, here you are, ma'am,' said Bill.

'That's one hell of a rumpus outside,' said Katie.

'The perils of drinking and driving,' said Bill. 'I was talking to the garda outside and he said the coach driver had fifty-three micrograms of alcohol in his breath and couldn't even pronounce his own name. Fair play, though, his name was O'Siodhachain.'

Katie approached the autopsy table. She felt calmer than she had before, and more detached. Sister Barbara was still in rigor, so that she looked more like a fibreglass dummy from Brown Thomas's window than a real nun.

Bill said, 'We've taken another body temperature reading and we've examined her eyes. I'd say the time of death was fifteen hundred hours yesterday afternoon.'

'That's very precise of you.'

'Well, to be honest with you, it could have been an hour either side of that. But I'm a great believer in what the eyes can tell you. They're a much more accurate indicator of t.o.d. than rigor mortis or livor mortis. Here, take a closer look. See . . . they're cloudy, because the potassium in the red blood cells has broken down, and the eyeballs themselves have flattened because of the loss of blood pressure.'

Katie looked down at Sister Barbara and Sister Barbara stared blindly back at her, with her mouth still dismally drawn down as if she were saying, *Dear God in heaven, what did I ever do to deserve this?*

'We'll be taking off her clothing to see what other injuries she might have sustained and take all the necessary pictures and measurements, but then we can leave the rest to Dr O'Brien. Who could wish for a better birthday present? Go ahead, Tyrone.'

Tyrone was a serious-looking young man with rimless spectacles and spiky black hair. He picked up a pair of surgical scissors and began to cut into the black fabric of Sister Barbara's tunic. Normally, a nun would have been wearing two underskirts, a top skirt of black serge and a skirt of black cotton, but as Tyrone snipped all the way up to her woollen belt, her blotchy, stick-like legs appeared and they could see that she was naked underneath.

'She didn't have on a holy habit when she went missing from the rest home,' said Katie. 'Whoever killed her dressed her up like this on purpose.'

'Believe me, ma'am, I'm glad that you're the one who has to work out the motive,' said Bill. 'All I have to do is work out what was done to her. You remember that fellow who was stabbed to death in Sallybrook and the fellow who killed him dressed his body up in his mother's clothing, underwear and all? You never did find out why he did that, did you?'

'Ah, he was nothing but a header,' said Katie. 'I don't think he knew himself why he did it.'

Katie watched as Tyrone finished cutting Sister Barbara's tunic all the way up to the coif, including the sleeves. Bill and Tyrone then lifted her up so that Eithne could tug the tunic out from under her and then fold it and drop it into a large evidence bag. Eithne was a very pretty girl, with blonde hair cut like a dandelion, and although she had only been attached to Bill's team for five months, she was already proving herself to be highly professional as a forensic artist as well as a technical expert.

'Holy Mary, Mother of God,' said Katie, as Sister Barbara's body was fully exposed. 'The state of her la.'

It looked as if Sister Barbara had been viciously whipped. Her body was striped with scores of purple diagonal furrows, all the way down from her neck to her knees, and across her upper arms. Most of the furrows were less than five centimetres apart, although they were lumpier and more concentrated around the lower part of her stomach and her genitals, where some of them had broken the skin.

It was what had been done to her breasts, though, that Katie found the most disturbing. Her pale-brown nipples hadn't been touched, but all around them the flesh of each breast had been scorched and blistered in a pattern like the rays of the sun, about fifteen centimetres in diameter. At the top of each pattern there was a small cross, although this was more pronounced on the right breast than the left.

Bill reached out and stroked one of the furrows on Sister Barbara's right thigh with his black-gloved finger.

'I'd say she was whipped with something like a cat-o'-nine-tails. Multiple thongs of thin cotton cord, knotted at the end. You can tell by the way the contusions are bunched up and how they've criss-crossed over each other. Very painful if you're alive.'

'But you don't think she was?'

Bill shook his head. 'Dr O'Brien will have to do some tests to make absolutely certain, but I'd guess she was dead already. It's often difficult to tell for sure, especially if a body's been handled roughly, but you'll find a chemical present in bruises that were inflicted when a person was still alive, leukotriene, which is what causes inflammation. It's noticeably absent in post-mortem bruises, which I'd say these are.'

'How much hatred would you have to be feeling to whip somebody like this when they couldn't even feel it?' said Katie.

'Like I say, ma'am, I only collect the evidence. I leave the motivation up to you.'

'What about her breasts? That pattern around them, it looks almost like a monstrance.'

Bill peered at Sister Barbara's breasts more closely. 'Eithne? What do you think?'

'I think Detective Superintendent Maguire is absolutely right,' Eithne said, so quietly that Katie could hardly hear her. 'It looks as if somebody's taken the luna out of the middle of a monstrance

197

and then heated it up red-hot and pressed it over each of her breasts. My grandma has a monstrance almost exactly like that, with the cross on top of it and everything.'

'And that was done post-mortem?' asked Katie.

'Again, I'd guess so,' said Bill. 'I can't be one hundred per cent sure, but the reddening looks less severe than it would been if she had been still alive.'

'What about her hands and her feet?'

'I'm fairly certain that she was alive when her toes were severed, and maybe her fingers, too, but it wouldn't surprise me if it was the shock of that that killed her. She was an elderly lady, after all. We won't know what kind of a condition her heart was in until Dr O'Brien examines her, or we can lay our hands on her medical records.'

Katie took a long look at Sister Barbara's mutilated body, with the sun-ray burns around her breasts. Maimed and whipped and branded like this, she could almost have been the victim of some ancient Gaelic punishment from the days of Tuatha Dé Danaan, the mythical gods who ruled Ireland before the arrival of Christianity.

'So,' she said, 'we have three murdered nuns, and all three of them interfered with in some ritualistic way after they were dead.'

'Well, they were either dead or so close to death that it would have made no difference,' Bill put in. 'In any case, I doubt if they would have been conscious of what was happening to them.'

'That's precisely my point,' said Katie. 'If they weren't conscious of what was happening to them, why do it?'

Bill shrugged. 'I wouldn't have a clue, to tell you the truth. Like you say, maybe the offender was just being vengeful.'

'I think there's more to it than that,' said Katie. 'I don't think their bodies were mutilated to teach *them* a lesson. I think it was done to show *us* – and when I say *us* I mean the whole of society, you and me and the church. All of us. But the church more than anybody else.'

'Well, that narrows it down a bit,' said Bill. 'Introduce me to one middle-aged person in Cork who isn't still bearing a grudge against some nun or priest from when they were younger and I'll show you a kipper that can sing "Jesus Wants Me for a Sunbeam".'

Twenty-six

It was growing light by the time Katie returned to Anglesea Street, although it looked as if it was going to be another grey, drizzly day. She had a shower and changed her underwear and then she went to the canteen for breakfast. She felt tired but she didn't feel like going to bed, not yet. There was too much milling around in her head and she knew that even if she lay in the dark with her eyes closed, she wouldn't be able to fall asleep.

She was sitting by the rain-spotted canteen window with two boiled eggs and a plate of toast when Detective O'Donovan came in. He looked even more dishevelled and exhausted than he usually did.

'Good morning to you, ma'am. Chief Superintendent MacCostagáin told me you were back. Okay if I sit down for a minute? I don't want to interrupt your breakfast, like.'

'No, go ahead,' Katie told him, and he pulled out the chair opposite her.

'That nun, that Sister Barbara?' he asked her. 'What sort of a state was she in, like?'

'Worse than you can imagine, believe me. Her fingers and toes were cut off, you saw that for yourself, but she'd also been lashed all over with some kind of a whip and both of her breasts had been burned. It looked like her killer had heated up a monstrance until it was red-hot and pressed it against her chest like a branding iron. It's unthinkable.'

'Mother of God,' said Detective O'Donovan. He looked down at Katie's boiled eggs and said, 'I'm not surprised you didn't order the bacon.' Then, 'Sorry. Bad joke. Sort of thing that Kenny Horgan would have said.'

Katie shook her head to show him that she was too tired to care. 'Did you get the chance yet to run through the CCTV footage and the video?'

'I did, yeah. That's why I came to find you. There's a CCTV camera on Property House on the corner of Oliver Plunkett Street and it picked up two fellers with the nun in between them coming out of Tuckey Street opposite. They carry her straight across the pavement to the fountain and heave her into the basin. Then they stroll off again the same way they came.'

'And nobody noticed them doing it?'

'There were so many kids there messing around and they were all totally langered. There was even some girls jumping into the fountain while the two fellers were dropping her in.'

'What did they look like, these two fellows?'

'Both of them are wearing black hoodies, so you can't see their faces, and for most of the time they stay on the blind side of the fountain from the camera, like they're hidden behind the basins and you can't see them clearly at all. They're both of them chunky, though, do you know what I mean? They're carrying that nun between them, but you'd swear to God that she's walking on her own. It's only when you look at the footage closer that you can see her feet trailing along the pavement.'

'Does the iPhone video show them any clearer?'

'Not really. The young feen who was taking it was just as langered as all of his mates, so it's jerking and jumping around, and you can only see the two fellows for a split second, like, turning their backs after they've dropped the nun into the water.'

'You have some photographs, too, though, don't you?' asked Katie.

'Well, I was coming to that,' said Detective O'Donovan. 'There's seven pictures altogether, all of them showing these three young girls dancing in the fountain and pulling up their skirts and flashing their knickers. But in one of them you can see half of the face of one of the two hoodie fellows. He's turned his head to look at the girls and the camera's caught him. Like I say, it's only half of his face but he's a right mog and it should be enough for somebody to reck him. He's got an earring, too, so that should help.'

'Good work, Patrick,' said Katie. 'As soon as I've finished this I'll come and take a look. Meanwhile, why don't you call Eithne O'Neill, if she hasn't gone home to bed yet? She was working last night on Sister Barbara's body. See if she can use some of her computer wizardry to turn half a face into a whole face.'

'Not a bother at all,' said Patrick, clicking his tongue. 'Any excuse to chat up Eithne.'

Katie glanced up at him sharply and he said, 'Sorry. Sorry. I'm sorry. I'm on the wrong side of knackered, that's all. I'll see you after.'

Katie's second egg had gone cold now and the yolk had mostly solidified, but she made herself eat it. She sat there for a while looking down at the car park while the rain dribbled down the window. For the first time in a long time she wondered if she had sacrificed too much to her sense of duty.

* * *

When she had finished her breakfast she went down to the CCTV room to see for herself the footage of the two men in hoodies carrying Sister Barbara from Tuckey Street to the fountain and dumping her into the water. Detective O'Donovan had been right: as they crossed the pavement, the two men were jiggling her along between them and any casual observer would have assumed that she was walking unaided. They certainly wouldn't have realized that she was dead.

A young man was climbing out of the water as the two men approached the fountain, and three girls jumped in immediately after him, which was when Sister Barbara's body was dropped in, face-down. The two men then walked unhurriedly back towards Tuckey Street and out of camera range.

She also asked for the iPhone photographs to be displayed on a screen for her. The second to last shot showed the man who had turned to look at the girls, and Detective O'Donovan had been right about him, too. He was flat-faced and ugly: 'bone ugly', Katie's grandmother would have called him – meaning a child so hideous that his mother would have to tie a bone around his neck before the family dog would play with him.

There was nothing much more Katie could do today. Excavation work at the Bon Sauveur Convent had halted for the weekend and the ground-radar equipment wouldn't be brought in from Dublin until Tuesday next week at the earliest. The investigation into the shooting of Detective Horgan was making no progress at all. Forensic examination of the burned-out Mercedes had given up no clues whatsoever. As for the twenty-three dead horses, Detective Dooley had still been unable to trace who had forged their passports or where they had come from. It might well have been Paddy Fearon who had thrown them over the cliff, but they were in no position to prove that, either.

She drove herself home. When she got there, she found John sitting at the coffee table in the living room with a small table-top easel and a palette and a box of acrylic paints .

'Hey, sweetheart,' he said. He put down his brush and came over to give her a hug. 'Did you get any sleep last night?'

'No,' she said. 'None at all. I spent most of the night in the mortuary.'

'Oh, wonderful. The mortuary! Come on, you must be exhausted. Why don't you get some sleep now? You don't have to go back to the station today, do you?'

'No,' she said. Barney came up and she patted his head and tugged at his ears. 'I don't feel like going to bed, though. Not yet.'

'Have you eaten?'

'Yes. I had some breakfast. I wouldn't mind a cup of coffee, though.'

'Sure. Come and sit down. I'll move all these paint things out of the way.'

'Is that the picture of me?' she asked, nodding towards the art board on the easel.

John angled it sideways so that she couldn't see it. 'Yes, it is. But it's not finished yet. So – no peeking until it is.'

'If it looks anything like I feel, I don't want to see it anyway.'

But John smiled at her and gently stroked her cheek, and she could see from the look in his eyes how much he loved her and it made her feel more comforted already. She sat down on the couch and Barney came to sit next to her, very upright, as if to guard her.

By the time John came back out of the kitchen with her coffee, she was asleep.

Twenty-seven

Riona was walking out of the parade ring with Saint Sparkle and his owner, Gerry Brickley, when Paddy Fearon caught up with her. He glanced furtively around like a pantomime villain to make sure that no TV cameras were pointing in their direction, and that there weren't any gardaí close by, and then said, 'Riona? I need a word with ye, girl. Urgent, like.'

Gerry had been talking to Riona about the stud fees they could charge for Saint Sparkle and he frowned at Paddy in annoyance. He wasn't the kind of man who was used to being interrupted.

'It'll have to wait, Paddy,' Riona told him, without looking at him, and smiling instead at the crowd behind the railings. 'We've less than ten minutes to go before the flag.'

Saint Sparkle's colours were scarlet and white and she was wearing a scarlet woollen suit to match, as well as a conical scarlet hat with feathers in it and scarlet shoes. Gerry sported a red silk rose in the lapel of his velvet-collared Crombie, which clashed with the terracotta colour of his face. It was Sunday afternoon, the first race day of the year at Mallow, and the course was thronged with thousands of racegoers.

'I think you'll be wanting to hear this, like,' said Paddy, holding the collars of his sheepskin coat together with one hand, as if he were worried that somebody in the crowd might be reading his lips.

Although their jockey, Josh Teagan, had already mounted Saint Sparkle in the parade ring, the four-year-old bay was still being led by Riona's grizzled-looking stable lad – the same stable lad that

Sister Barbara had seen her shouting at, from her upstairs window.

'Take him on for me, Ryan, would you?' said Riona. Then, to Gerry, 'Sorry, Gerry. This won't take a moment. I'll catch up with you.'

Gerry frowned again at Paddy and said, 'There's not a problem, is there?'

'No, no, everything's grand altogether. I won't be two ticks.' She kept on following Saint Sparkle around the side of the grandstand, but she slowed down until Gerry was ten metres ahead of her and out of earshot. Then she turned back to Paddy and said, 'Well, come on, then. Make it snappy. I don't have all day.'

'I'll be quick, then,' he said. 'But a feller came to see me at Spring Lane a couple of days ago and said he'd met me one evening in Waxy's, though I don't remember seeing him there myself, like.'

The noise of the crowd and the echoing announcements from the public address speakers made it difficult for Riona to hear what Paddy was saying, so she had to lean closer to him than she would have liked. He smelled strongly of cigarettes and whiskey.

'Go on, then,' she said, keeping her eyes on Saint Sparkle's glossy brown haunches and his swishing black tail.

'Any road, the feller asked me to dispose of some horses for him, nine altogether. He said I'd told him at Waxy's that I could do it for cheap. He gave me five hundred yoyos and I'm supposed to be picking the horses up tomorrow morning.'

Riona stopped dead. 'And what were you planning to do with them? Throw them over a cliff, like you did with mine?'

'Hey, come on now! Fair play! They were never yours, those horses. I took yours to the knackery. Besides, that wasn't me who did that.'

'Of course it was you. It's been all over the news, in case you hadn't noticed. Twenty-three thoroughbreds found on the beach at Nohaval Cove.'

Riona's stable lad had halted now and was waiting for her, so she started walking again, even more quickly. Paddy caught up with her and said, 'That *proves* it, though, doesn't it? You never gave me twenty-three to get rid of. Only eleven. Well, fifteen with the foals.'

'That proves nothing except that some other unsuspecting eejit paid you to get rid of their horses, too. Hop off, Paddy, I want nothing more to do with you.'

'Wait, you haven't heard this. The feller who wanted me to dispose of the horses for him, one of the girls up at Spring Lane took a shine to him, like. Tauna.'

'Paddy, in case you hadn't noticed, my horse is just going in for the biggest race of the day.'

'Yeah, I know, but the thing of it is, Tauna saw this feller yesterday morning in the city centre. He was standing on the steps outside the Garda station on Anglesea Street, talking and laughing with two gardaí in uniform. He's not some chancer at all. He's the filth.'

Riona stopped again. She stared up at Paddy with her eyes narrowed and her scarlet lips puckered. 'You know what that means, don't you? It means the guards have a strong suspicion that it was you who dumped those horses on to the beach, and that they're setting you up.'

'*Riona*!' called out her stable lad.

'Of course they're setting me up,' said Paddy. 'That's fecking obvious. But I thought I'd warn you. If they're on to me, then they could be on to you, too. So if they come sniffing around, like, I hope you won't be telling them that it was me who disposed of them horses for you.'

'And why not? Didn't you just say that you took them to a knackery, legitimate like?'

'Riona!' her stable lad repeated. 'The stewards are telling us to make a bust or else we won't be running at all!'

'You didn't take them to any knackery, did you, Paddy?' said Riona. 'You threw them off the cliffs. It was you, you lying pox! You kept the money I gave you and you threw them off the cliffs!'

'I'm not saying nothing,' Paddy told her. 'I'm warning you, that's all.'

'Holy Mary, Mother of God, I can't believe you. What did you do with their passports?'

'I probably burned them. Well, if it had been me I would have done.'

'Ri-*ona*!' shouted her stable lad, and now he sounded desperate. Even Gerry shouted out, 'Riona! What's the hold-up?'

Riona said, 'I have to go, but I'll talk to you after the weigh-in. I'll text you so and tell you where to meet me.'

'No, don't text me. It wouldn't surprise me if the shades were hacking my phone. I'll meet you up in the Owners, Trainers and Members' Bar.'

'Don't tell me that you're a member?'

Paddy tapped the side of his nose, turned around, and elbowed his way into the jostling crowd. Riona stood there for a moment, the red feathers on her hat ruffled by the breeze, and then hurried after Saint Sparkle.

* * *

'What was all that about?' asked Gerry as they made their way to the rails to watch the start. There were eleven runners in the O'Grady Insurance Group Steeplechase and they were all prancing around now, waiting for the flag.

'Oh, he's a vet,' said Riona. 'One of my foals has epiphysitis and he was asking if he could put him on steroids.'

'I don't see what's so urgent about that,' said Gerry, looking over his shoulder to see if Paddy was still in sight. ' Besides, he doesn't look much like a vet.'

'Doesn't he? I don't know. What are vets supposed to look like?'

'Not so much like bookies' runners, I suppose,' said Gerry. He turned back and shaded his eyes with both hands so that he could focus on the start. 'I'll tell you something, though, Riona. Saint Sparkle is looking the best I've ever seen him. I'm really delighted the way he's been coming on. Top of the range.'

'Well, he really scored over the timber at Ballinrobe, didn't he?' said Riona. 'Let's hope he does even better today. Thirty-two and a half thousand euros if he wins it.'

Suddenly the flag waved and the horses were off. A roar went up from the crowd in the grandstand and the new pavilion, and a smartly dressed girl next to Riona began to jump and down and squeal, 'Lucky William! Go on, Lucky William!'

As they reached the first fence the field was still tightly bunched, with Saint Sparkle in fourth place. They all jumped over smoothly and by the time they reached the second fence they were still close together. Over the first ditch, though, one horse fell and two of them collided as they landed, and the rest of the field began to thin out more. Saint Sparkle still seemed to be running strongly and he moved up to third place.

'He's going to do it, isn't he?' said Gerry, gripping Riona's arm. 'He's only going to fecking do it!'

Riona patted his hand and said, 'Don't start counting your prize money yet, Gerry! But he's going brilliant, isn't he? Just look at him! Come on, Josh! Now's your moment! Come on, boy, *now*!'

As the horses came around the last bend Saint Sparkle was still in third place. On the final straight towards the winning post there were two regulation fences with a ditch in between them, which were designed to test the horses' stamina to the very last furlong. The sound of the crowd began to swell even louder now, so that it sounded like a gale-force wind blowing through a concrete tunnel.

Saint Sparkle jumped the first of the two fences, but he stumbled badly and was overtaken by Lucky William, and then by White Russian.

'*Come on!*' Gerry bellowed. 'Come on, Josh, for the love of God! You can still do it, boy! Come on!'

Josh tried to whip Saint Sparkle back up to speed, but the horse had completely lost his momentum and as he approached the ditch he dipped his head two or three times to show that he didn't have the strength, or the willpower, to clear it. Josh circled him around, but there was no point in attempting to jump the ditch a second time. He steered Saint Sparkle off the track and guided him back towards the grandstand.

There was an even greater roar from the crowd as Gentleman Jim passed the post first. Gentleman Jim's starting price had been 10-1, while Saint Sparkle's had been 7-2.

Gerry's face was purple with anger and disappointment. 'What the *feck* went wrong there?' he demanded. 'He should have *walked* it and he didn't even finish!'

Riona shook her head and said, 'I'm sorry, Gerry. I'm really sorry. He should have walked it, like you said, but you could see that he landed badly after that fence. I just pray he hasn't broken his ankle.'

'You and me both, Riona. If he's broken his ankle, that's the end of him. I can't fecking believe it.'

They pushed their way through the crowds to the grassy ring at the back of the pavilion, where Josh had already dismounted. Two girls from Riona's stables were holding Saint Sparkle and patting him to calm him down. He was sweating and breathing harshly, and snuffling repeatedly. Ryan, the stable lad, was bending over to feel each of Saint Sparkle's fetlocks and pastern joints in turn.

'Well?' demanded Gerry. 'Has he broken anything?'

Ryan felt the last of the horse's ankles and stood up straight. 'Not that I can tell, sir. He could have sustained a fracture, but he seems to be comfortable standing, like, and he's walking okay.'

'So what went wrong?' asked Gerry. 'He was right up there, ready to go to the wire, and he just ran out of steam. He didn't do that at Ballinrobe. He went like a fecking express train at Ballinrobe and he would have kept running all the way to Castlebar if you hadn't reined him in.'

'I have to say I felt him fading at the fourth fence,' said Josh, the jockey, taking off his red and yellow cap. He had a pointy nose and glittery, near-together eyes. 'He was bowling along great to start with. He was jumping high, like, giving all of the fences plenty of air, but that didn't seem to be slowing him down at all.

But then, click! like, do you know what I mean? It was just like somebody switched him off.'

'He's a horse, not a fecking TV,' snapped Gerry. 'I just pray to God he doesn't have the virus.'

'There's no Lyme disease in my stables, Gerry,' Riona retorted. 'Sparkle's always been nervy, you know that. For some reason, he lost his confidence today, that's all.'

'Oh yes? And what reason would that be? You're his trainer, Riona. You're supposed to know all this horse psychology.'

'I don't know yet, Gerry, but I'll find out, and I'll do everything I can to make sure that it doesn't happen again.'

'You do that. Put him on the couch and get him to talk to you about his unhappy childhood or whatever it is that caused him to lose his confidence. He's only lost his confidence, but I've lost the chance to win thirty two thousand five hundred euros. Even if he'd only come second I would have won nine thousand, for Christ's sake!'

'Gerry, I've told you I'm sorry,' said Riona. 'But it's the luck of the track, isn't it, as always? I'll have Sparkle thoroughly checked over by the vet and I'll call you if it's anything serious, or even if it isn't.'

Gerry turned around in a circle, trying to think of something else to say to vent his anger, but all he could manage was, 'Jesus, I need a drink!'

* * *

Riona found Paddy sitting on a stool at the end of the bar, furthest away from the windows, with a large glass of whiskey in front of him. He looked like a shabby old brown bird perched on a gatepost.

'What are you having, girl?' he asked her, without looking at her.

'From you, Paddy, nothing at all, thanks very much. What's on your mind?'

'You'll be wanting to dispose of that horse, too, won't you,

211

and sharpish? Lost his sparkle today, didn't he? Not that he was Sparkle to begin with.'

'I thought I made it crystal-clear that I want nothing more to do with you,' said Riona. 'How in the name of God did you think that you were going to get away with throwing all those horses off the cliffs? You must be cracked.'

'They did it in Clare and got away with it. Not that I'm saying that it was me.'

'So what are you going to do about the horses that this garda has paid you to get rid of?'

'Well, nothing at all, of course. For what he's paid me I can't afford to take them to Fitzgerald's.'

'And you think the guards are just going to forget about it? If you don't show up to collect those horses they're going to be knocking on the door of your not-so-mobile home before you know it. What will you say to them then?'

'I'll deny everything,' said Paddy. 'I'll deny I ever saw your man before in the whole of my life.'

Riona shook her head in exasperation so that her scarlet feathers nodded. 'You're even dimmer than I thought, Paddy Fearon. If your man was an undercover cop, don't you think he would have been recording everything you were saying? He might even have a video of it. They have cameras in their coat buttons these days.'

'Well, I don't know, feck it. I'll think of something,' said Paddy.

'That's entirely up to you,' Riona told him. 'But what you will *not* do is give the guards even the slightest hint of my name, do you hear? Because if you do, it won't just be horses that's going over the cliffs at Nohaval Cove.'

Paddy was about to put his whiskey glass to his lips, but now he lowered it and stared at her.

'I mean it,' she said. 'You don't know who you're dealing with when you're dealing with me, and you'd be better off not finding out.'

At that moment Gerry came in from the balcony that overlooked the racecourse and weaved his way across the bar.

'Ah, Riona!' he called out as he approached. 'Come up here to drown your sorrows? And your vet! He's still here! I thought he went off to treat your foal for its effy – its eppy – do you know something, I can't even fecking pronounce it.'

'He was just on his way, weren't you?' said Riona, staring at Paddy without blinking.

Paddy knocked back the last of his whiskey and climbed off his bar stool.

'G'luck to you so,' he told Riona and left.

'And good luck to you, too, boy,' said Riona under her breath. 'You're going to need it.'

Twenty-eight

Katie arrived at Anglesea Street early on Monday morning. It was a bright, dry day and even though it was chilly she knew that the search team up the Bon Sauveur Convent would have made a start already. Not only that, Detectives Dooley and Brennan would be following Paddy Fearon after he had picked up the first three horses from the field at Kilmichael – and she had been called late the night before and told that customs officers had arrested a number of handicapped people at the ferry port at Ringaskiddy, all of whom had been carrying substantial quantities of heroin concealed in their clothing.

It was common practice for smugglers to use mentally challenged people or children to carry drugs for them. Under the law, a person could only be searched if they understood the reason for the search.

A stack of notes and reports was waiting for her when she arrived in her office, but when she glanced through them she saw to her relief that there was nothing further about the Ombudsman inquiry. She was doing her best to keep that out of her mind, because she knew that she was right and that she could prove that she was right. It wasn't going to be easy, though, since it sounded as though Bryan Molloy was doing his very best to subvert her witnesses.

She was prising open the lid of her cappuccino when Detective O'Donovan came in, carrying a framed black and white photograph. He looked very much fresher this morning, as if he had managed to get a good night's sleep, and he was smartly dressed in a yellow shirt and tan corduroy jacket. Katie said nothing, but she was pleased that he looked less stressed. She made a point of watching for the slightest signs of fatigue and nervous tension in her detectives, especially since Detective Inspector Liam Fennessy had so comprehensively fallen apart when his marriage had broken up. Liam had left her a letter that appeared to be a suicide note, but there had been no sign of him for nearly three months, alive or dead.

'It's your wan all right,' Detective O'Donovan told her and laid the photograph on top of the files in front of her.

It was a picture of the sisters of the Bon Sauveur Convent, with the mothers and babies and small children in their charge, dated 7 March 1972. The nuns looked grim, the mothers looked miserable, and the babies and children looked bewildered. Detective O'Donovan pointed to a nun on the right-hand side of the photograph, at the back.

'That's her,' he said, and next to the photograph he held the post-mortem picture of the flying nun that they had been circulating around all of the convents and schools and day centres. 'There's over forty years between these two pictures, but we checked it with the facial recognition system and there's no doubt about it. In both of them she looks as if her head is wrecked, but that was a help. Bill said that the biometric software can get confused if the subject's smiling.'

Katie examined both photographs closely. 'Well . . . maybe she looks so angry because she wasn't enjoying her life at the convent. And I certainly don't think I'd be smiling if I'd been gutted like she was and sent off up in the air. How about a name for her? Do we know who she was?'

Detective O'Donovan turned the framed photograph over. On the back there was a yellowing label with the names of all of the sisters handwritten on it. None of the young mothers, the 'fallen women', were identified, and neither were their babies or little children.

'Pure amazing, isn't it?' said Katie. 'These girls and their wains might just as well have not existed at all as far as these holy sisters were concerned. All they cared about was themselves.'

'Sister Mona Murphy, that's her name,' said Detective O'Donovan. 'And look, standing right next to her, there's Sister Hannah O'Dwyer – now *Mother* O'Dwyer, the mother superior. Yet didn't Mother O'Dwyer tell us barefaced without the slightest hint of a hint of a blush that she didn't recognize her?'

'Unfortunately you can't arrest somebody for claiming to have a poor memory,' said Katie. 'Otherwise half of Cork would be behind bars, especially on a Sunday morning.'

'But this does show us, doesn't it, that all three of the nuns came from the Bon Sauveur Convent? And that must mean something.'

'Yes, of course. I don't know if three is enough to establish a pattern but it's looking increasingly likely. What interests me, though, is what was done to each of them. Sister Bridget assaulted with a figurine of Mary; Sister Barbara with her fingers and toes chopped off, and branded; and now this Sister Mona, disembowelled and floated through the air. All three of them sisters from the same convent, but all three of them tortured or mutilated in completely different ways.'

'Well, those are the differences, like,' said Detective O'Donovan. 'But I think there's a really important similarity between them, and that's their age. All three of them were in their eighties, so all three of them must have been resident at the convent at around the same time, do you know what I mean?'

Katie studied the framed photograph again. 'What you're suggesting is that whoever killed them was also at the convent at the same time they were, and for some reason still bears a grudge against them? Yes, that's a fairly obvious supposition. Maybe it was one of the unmarried mothers they were supposed to be taking such good care of?'

She looked at all the sad, pale faces of the 'fallen women', but there was no guarantee that whoever had murdered the nuns was one of them. The killer could have been a girl from any of the twenty-odd years that the three sisters had been contemporaries at the convent. Every year Saint Margaret's Mother and Baby Home had taken in an average of twenty-three girls from Cork City and the surrounding area, and that meant that Katie's detectives would have to track down more than four hundred and fifty potential suspects.

'You can see the problem, can't you?' she said. 'Detective Sergeant Ni Nuallán says that the books the sisters kept are very scant when it comes to detail. They recorded the girls' names and home addresses when they first arrived, and they recorded the births of their children. But they kept no record at all of the children's deaths, and you only have to take a quick sconce at all the skeletons we've discovered to see that there were hundreds. The main trouble for us, though, is that they kept no record of when the girls eventually left the home, or where they went.

'Even if their families still live at their original home addresses, I doubt if many of them kept up contact with the parents who threw them out. I expect almost all of them went off somewhere and got married and changed their names. It's not going to be feasible for us to go looking for them all. We don't have the manpower and we don't have the money. Besides, it's only a supposition that one of the girls is responsible. We could be barking up the wrong tree altogether. It might be some rapacious old priest who took advantage of them when they were younger and doesn't want anybody to find out about it.'

'I can't see an eighty-year-old priest hanging a dead nun off of a bunch of helium balloons. I mean, serious.'

'Well, maybe not, but stranger things have happened. Think about that old fellow in Doughcloyne who cut his wife's stomach open and stuffed her with apples and fed her to the pigs.'

'I've just had an apple for my breakfast, so I'd rather not, if it's all the same to you,' said Detective O'Donovan. He picked up the photograph and held it up in front of him, his eyes focused on it intently, as if one of those despondent faces might magically come to life and give him a clue. A nod of the head, a movement of the lips, anything.

'So, any road, what's the plan?' he asked Katie, still staring at the photograph.

'The plan is we don't really have a plan. But we carry on searching the convent garden for more remains and we try to identify the ugly fellow who dropped Sister Barbara's body in the Berwick Fountain.'

'That shouldn't be too hard, the head on him. Rough as a bagful of mangled badgers.'

'Well, maybe *he*'s the one who's been murdering the nuns. He could have been a home boy and you know what those home children suffered. My father said he had some home children in his class at school. The nuns always made them wear big noisy wooden clogs because they never wore out, and they got treated like they weren't even human, even by the other kids. If my father misbehaved in class the teacher made him sit next to one of the home boys and that was supposed to be a punishment. Well, it was, because they smelled.'

'Don't ever talk to my ma about home children,' said Detective O'Donovan. 'She told me that she and some of the older girls played a trick on a home girl once. They wrapped up a stone in an empty sweetie wrapper and gave it to her, saying that it was a treat. When the girl opened it she burst into tears because they were never given sweeties in the children's home. My ma still feels guilty about it after all these years.'

'What do you think, Patrick?' asked Katie. 'Suffering a childhood like that, is that motive enough to murder three nuns and abuse their bodies?'

'I couldn't say for sure, like,' said Detective O'Donovan. 'But I would reckon it's possible, do you know what I mean? My ma said the nuns were always cold as ice to the children in their charge because they were illegitimate, and the teachers treated them as if they were dirt, so the other kids did, too. If you're brought up like that, who knows what that can do to your mind psychologically?

218

It wouldn't be something you'd forget, would it? If my ma can't get that stone wrapped up as a sweetie out of her mind – and she was seven years old when she did that – what about the girl she gave it to?'

Katie stood up and walked over to the window. Unconsciously, she laid her hand on her stomach. Down in the street below she could see a little girl of about three skipping along beside her mother. She wondered if her own baby was going to be a girl. Somehow she felt that it was. She was due at the hospital for a scan soon, but even so it would be too early to tell.

'Are you all right, ma'am?' asked Detective O'Donovan. *God* – sometimes she wished she wasn't surrounded by detectives. If anybody was feeling even slightly out of kilter, they picked up on it immediately. She could only be grateful that John didn't seem to have the same hypersensitive antennae.

'I'm grand, thanks, Patrick. That was good work, identifying Sister Mona. Have you found out where she was living?'

'As far as I know, in a downstairs flat in Upper Lotabeg Road. According to the register of electors, she was sharing it with another woman. Stall the ball, I have it written down here somewhere – another woman called Enda McMahon, *Mrs* Enda McMahon. I'll be calling round there directly myself in person to see if she can help at all.'

'Grand. The sooner the better. Meanwhile I think I'll get myself up to the Bon Sauveur and have another word with Mother O'Dwyer.'

'You can tell Mother O'Dwyer from me that she's some spoofer. And that's me being polite.'

Twenty-nine

Detectives Dooley and Brennan had been sitting in their car outside the Kilmichael Bar for over two hours before they began to suspect that Paddy Fearon wasn't going to make an appearance.

'This is so fecking typical,' said Detective Brennan. He was big and broad-shouldered, with a bulbous nose and acne-scarred cheeks that looked as if they had been peppered with airgun pellets. 'You can't even trust these fecking knackers to incriminate themselves.'

Detective Dooley looked at his watch and said, 'What do you think? Give him another half-hour? Maybe the horsebox broke down.'

'No, feck it. Let's go look for him. I know that Paddy Fearon from way back. A right scobe. I wouldn't trust him to hold my dog's lead even if there was no dog on it.'

In the field diagonally opposite the pub, nine ill-assorted thoroughbred horses were grazing. Most of them were retired racehorses with their glory days behind them, although three were young horses that had suffered injuries or sickness and would never be able to race. Detective Dooley had arranged with the owner of the field to let the horses loose in it for twenty-four hours and yesterday afternoon Michael O'Malley and Kevin Corgan had sent their stable lads with three horseboxes to deliver them. If any harm came to any of them, the agreement was that their trainers would be compensated by An Garda Síochána to their full meat-processing value, whether they were actually fit for human consumption or not.

Detective Dooley climbed out of the car and stood there for a while, listening. All he could hear was the wind. Kilmichael was out in the middle of nowhere, up back of leap, and the only signs of human habitation were the yellow and red painted Kilmichael Bar and the single petrol pump on the opposite side of the road that served as the filling station.

It was famous for the IRA ambush in November 1920, when Tom Barry and thirty-six local volunteers had stopped two lorries full of Auxiliaries and killed seventeen of them. After that, though, Kilmichael had been famous for nothing at all.

No cars drove past. No planes flew overhead. Occasionally one of the horses snorted, but that was all. Detective Dooley got back into the driver's seat and fastened his seat belt.

'I reckon he sussed you for the law,' said Detective Brennan.

'I don't see how he could have done. If I was the law, how could I have known about that night at Waxy's? And one of the girls at the halting site kept giving me the eye. She wouldn't have done that if she'd any idea at all that I was a cop. Jesus, I'd have been lucky if she spat at me.'

'He's not turning up, though, is he? And there's only one way to find out why.'

Detective Dooley started the engine. As he did so, the owner of the Kilmichael Bar came out of the pub's front door in a brown zig-zag patterned sweater and stared at them.

'Sorry, my friend,' said Detective Brennan. 'We'd love a drink but we're a little pressed at the moment.'

* * *

They arrived at the Spring Lane Halting Site just after noon. Detective Dooley parked close to the entrance but out of sight of the mobile homes.

'Watch out for that beour who has the hots for you,' said Detective Brennan. 'If she tries to drag you into her caravan for a bulling, give me a ring on my moby and I'll come and save you.'

'Oh, g'way, will you,' said Detective Dooley. He left Detective Brennan in the car and walked into the halting site. Six or seven children were playing there, but he was relieved that there was no sign of the cluster of women who had been smoking and gossiping there the last time he visited. Most of the pool of brown sewage water had drained away, too. He went past the toilets to Paddy Fearon's caravan. The brindled pony was still tethered outside, and more importantly, Paddy's horsebox was still parked on the hard standing opposite.

Detective Dooley knocked on the caravan door and stepped back down to wait for it to open. Nobody answered, so he stepped back up again and knocked a second time.

After a long pause, the door opened and Paddy Fearon appeared in a cloud of cigarette smoke. He was wearing only a grubby vest and a pair of navy-blue trackies with food stains on them.

'Yes?' he said, taking his cigarette out of his mouth. 'What d'ye want, boy?'

'I thought you were going to come and collect my horses. That was the arrangement, wasn't it?'

Paddy blinked, as if he were mystified. 'What horses? What arrangement?'

'You know what horses and you know what arrangement. The arrangement I paid you five hundred euros in cash for. The arrangement to pick up my horses and get shot of them for me.'

Paddy took a long drag at his cigarette. 'I don't have the first idea what you're talking about. Sorry. I don't know who the feck you are or what the feck you've been drinking, but if I was you I'd switch to something that doesn't give you the galloping delusions.'

'Don't give me that,' said Detective Dooley, 'You know perfectly well who I am. Now, are you going to go to Kilmichael and collect those horses for me and dispose of them like you agreed to?'

'Kilmichael? Why in the name of feck should I go to Kilmichael?'

'Because I paid you to, that's why, and you agreed you'd do it.'

Paddy slowly shook his head. 'No, kid. Not me. Why don't you try that caravan over there? That yellow one. Maybe you're colour-blind, like. Whatever the reason, I'd say that you've made a mistake, wouldn't you? And you know what happens to people who make mistakes. They have to live with the consequences.'

As they were talking, four young men appeared from the direction of the toilets. They walked up to Detective Dooley and stood close behind him, with their arms folded. He recognized them as the same young men who had been trying to get the motorbike started. They had shaven heads or close-cropped hair and tattoos on their necks and earrings. At least one of them smelled strongly of Lynx aftershave, which for some reason Detective Dooley found more menacing than if they had smelled of beer or ganja.

He glanced at them over his shoulders, first left and then right. They stared back at him, expressionless, ceaselessly chewing gum. One of them had a squint. Detective Dooley guessed that Paddy must have called them the first time that he had knocked at his caravan door. He was carrying his SIG Sauer automatic in a shoulder holster, but he could imagine what would happen if he pulled it out. Somebody would end up seriously injured, or dead, and it could easily be him.

He turned back to Paddy and said, 'Yes, Paddy. I think you're right. I must have made that arrangement with somebody else altogether. What am I like, eh? I'll forget my own name next.'

'No bother at all, boy,' said Paddy, with smoke leaking out of his nostrils. 'You're forgiven.'

Detective Dooley turned to go. For a nerve-wracking moment the four young Travellers barred his way and he stayed where he was, trying to avoid eye contact. *Don't look at them. Even a look they might take as a challenge. Just try to appear as if you've been humbled and all you want to do is get away from here without being hurt.*

'*Stafa tapa hu, feen!*' called out Paddy hoarsely. Detective Dooley knew that in cant that meant 'Long life to you, feller!'

223

When he said that, the young men stood aside, still chewing gum, still with their arms folded. He made his way back across the halting site, dodging the potholes in the asphalt. Halfway across, he caught sight of Tauna at one of the caravan windows, watching him. As soon as she realized he had seen her, she lifted her middle finger at him and then turned her back. It was only a gesture but it was enough to tell him that the Travellers had found out that he was a garda. If he had simply been some gomie that Paddy had duped out of five hundred euros, she wouldn't have felt any animosity towards him. But she had discovered that he was a shade, and what was worse, she had fancied him.

He climbed back into the car. It was cold in there because Detective Brennan had been smoking with the passenger window wide open.

'Well, did you bog the ginnet?' Detective Brennan asked him. 'Full marks for speed if you did.'

'No. And you were right. Somehow they've twigged who I am. Maybe one of them recognized me, I don't know. Fearon made out like he'd never seen me before in his life. I never asked him to dispose of any horses for him and I never gave him five hundred euros to do it.'

'You're messing! What an eejit!'

'I know. All he had to do was give me the money back and say he wasn't going to get rid of the horses for me because he couldn't afford it. Or he could have said that he'd only been boasting and he didn't really do that kind of thing. If he'd done that, I wouldn't have been able to stick anything on him at all. Now I've got him for extorting money with menaces.'

Detective Brennan put up his window. 'I don't know what the feck the super's going to say. She was dead set on catching him red-handed throwing horses off a cliff. Still, if you can charge him under section 17, that might give us some leverage.'

'You'd best call Michael O'Malley and Kevin Corgan,' said Detective Dooley as they drove out of Spring Lane towards

Ballyvolane. 'Tell them they can go back to Kilmichael and collect their horses, and thanks for the loan of them, like.'

'Oh, they'll be well pissed off about that,' said Detective Brennan. 'They were hoping to see the last of those old nags and make a bit of a profit out of it, too.'

'The more you want something, the less chance you have of getting it, that's what my nan used to say.'

'Mine, too, or something like that,' said Detective Brennan. 'She always dreamed of marrying Christy Ring, and what did she get? My dipso of a grandpa. Mind you, he may not have been Cork's greatest hurler, my grandpa, not like Christy Ring, but give him ten pints of Murphy's, point him at an open window, and he could hurl with the best of them.'

Thirty

Katie was buttoning up her red duffel coat when Detective Dooley called her to tell her what had happened.

'So Fearon found out somehow that you were the law?' she said. 'Oh well, there was always a risk of that. But good, yes, it may be second-best but we can charge him with extortion. I'm on my way now to the Bon Sauveur Convent to talk to the mother superior, but as soon as I get back we'll go up to Spring Lane and pull him in. Jesus, you almost have to feel sorry for them sometimes, these poor eejits like Paddy Fearon, don't you?'

She was already on her way along the corridor when Eithne from the Technical Bureau stepped out of the lift and came towards her, waving a black plastic folder.

'Eithne, what's the story?' asked Katie. 'How did you get on with that ugly fellow's face?'

'I've done that, ma'am. I've just given a copy to Detective O'Donovan, and I have one here for you.'

She unzipped the folder and took out a full-face computer image of the man in the hoodie who had dumped Sister Barbara's body into the fountain.

'Holy Mary,' said Katie.

'No, he's not pretty, is he?' said Eithne. 'He may not look exactly like that in real life, but the software is very good at extrapolating facial structure – like it takes into account that one side of your face is not a mirror image of the other.'

'All right,' said Katie. 'I'm on my way out now, so if you could leave that on my desk.'

'This is not really what I came to see you about,' said Eithne. She brought out a sheet of paper in a transparent plastic cover. 'We've been examining the note that Roisin Begley was supposed to have left under her pillow.'

'*Supposed* to have left?'

'Superficially, you'd think that she wrote it. But – look, this is the note and this is a page from her biology notes from school.'

'They look the same to me,' said Katie.

'Well, at first sight they do, I agree. There's distinct similarities, like the way the *g*s and the *y*s have that sharp-angled tail, and the *i*s have the long mark, the *fada*, rather than dots. But the *a*s and the *e*s are formed in totally different ways – you see how Roisin almost goes around them twice – and all of her writing in her schoolbook has a measurable left-leaning slope to it, which the note doesn't.'

Katie looked more closely at the two samples of handwriting. Eithne was right. At a glance, they seemed to be almost identical. But apart from the differences in some of the letters, it was apparent that whoever had written the note had been pressing much harder, as if they had been writing slowly and carefully. Copying, in fact.

'I'd stand up in court and testify that Roisin herself didn't write this note,' said Eithne. 'There's no DNA on it, and no fingerprints, but it was written with a blue liquid ink pen that we couldn't find in Roisin's bedroom and that's another indication that it was written by somebody else.'

'But somebody who had access to Roisin's bedroom, and to her schoolbooks,' said Katie.

Eithne said nothing. Katie handed back the note and the handwriting sample. 'Thank you, Eithne,' she said. 'I've been putting off paying a visit to the Begleys, but it looks like I'll have to now.'

* * *

As she parked outside the Bon Sauveur Convent, Detective Inspector O'Rourke called her. He was on his way back from Dublin and wanted to tell her that he made all the arrangements for RMR to bring their ground-radar equipment down to Cork tomorrow.

'I'm catching the three o'clock from Heuston so I'll be back at five-thirty. There's a couple of things I need to talk to you about that I can't do over the phone.'

'Now you have me worried,' said Katie.

'Well, it's best that you know what's going on,' Detective Inspector O'Rourke told her. 'How's it going generally? Did Dooley catch Fearon chucking his horses off the cliff?'

'That all went pear-shaped. The Travellers found out that Dooley was a cop. I don't know how, but it's not a total disaster because we have a plan B. I'll give you the SP when you get back. I'm just off to talk to Mother O'Dwyer. We've identified the flying nun and she used to be a member of the Bon Sauveurs.'

'Mother O'Dwyer definitely said that she wasn't, didn't she? How about that? We have the flying nun and the lying nun.'

'That's true. Take care, Francis. I'll see you later so.'

Before she went into the convent building, Katie walked around to the garden to see what progress the search team was making. Seven or eight reservists were still carefully raking through the flower bed and sifting the black peaty soil through riddles, while another three had started on the vegetable garden. They had dug up scores of potatoes and winter cabbages and piled them beside the wall.

The technical experts had erected a large blue nylon tent which completely sheltered the septic tank. The triangular entrance flap was tied back and as she walked across the grass Katie could see the technicians in their white Tyvek suits with masks over their faces, kneeling beside one of the open access ports. They were lifting the bones out of the septic tank with an Unger pick-up tool,

228

which had rubber-covered claws to prevent the bones from being marked or damaged. As they were retrieved, the bones were laid out on a groundsheet and the technical experts were making every effort to reassemble them as individual skeletons.

Bill Phinner was there and he was wearing a Tyvek suit, too, and had obviously been helping. He never looked particularly happy. He always reminded Katie of Peter Cushing when Dracula's ashes start to come back to life, pinch-faced and anxious. Today, though, he seemed to more serious than ever.

'How many so far?' she asked him.

He snapped off one of his latex gloves and ran his hand through his thinning grey hair. 'Eighteen so far. Of course, that has to be an estimate. The way they're all jumbled together, we can't be sure whose skull belongs to whose vertebrae, or which ribcage is which. But when we're finished we'll be able to work out how many exactly were disposed of here, and at least we'll be able to give their remains something that the nuns never did, and that's a respectful burial.'

'How many more have you found in the garden?'

'Three in the flower bed, but that's only a guess because we haven't located all of their skeletons yet. None in the vegetable garden so far. The mother superior was giving us a hard time because we're digging up all their vegetables and what are they going to do for food over the next few months? I politely suggested she went up to Dunne's Stores like everybody else, like it's only up the road, like.'

'Well, they're bringing the radar scanners down tomorrow, so if there are any more to be found, we'll find them.'

Bill looked down at the tiny skeletons laid out in three rows, not all of them complete. Some were still missing legs or arms and two of them had no skulls. 'What a way to end up, eh? Just because their mothers weren't married. I hope there's a playground for them up in heaven – although I very much doubt it.'

'Bill!' said Katie, laying her hand on his shoulder. 'I didn't realize you were so sentimental!'

'Oh, I'm not sentimental at all, ma'am. I'm bitter, if you must know. I've probably been in this job too long, but I can never come to terms with what human beings are capable of doing to each other, the weak and defenceless most of all. Look at them. They were so little, they never even found out what they were supposed to have done wrong.'

'Bill, you're going to make me cry in a minute.'

Bill looked at her and gave her a weary smile. 'No, I'm not. You're harder than that, Detective Superintendent Maguire. And you're in this job for the same reason I am. So that the scumbags who hurt innocent kiddies like this don't get away with it.'

Katie nodded but didn't say any more. She didn't need to, the children's skeletons laid out on the groundsheet spoke for her.

'Sir!' called out one of Bill's technicians. They had brought up another small skull and Bill said to Katie, 'I'll see you after, ma'am,' and went over to take a look at it.

* * *

Mother O'Dwyer was sitting at her desk with a Bible in front of her. Sister Rose showed Katie into her study and as she did so, Mother O'Dwyer stood up. The deep lines around her mouth made it appear as if her lips had been sewn together by headhunters.

'Good afternoon, Detective Superintendent,' she said, and her voice was precise and cold. 'Is it too much to hope that you have come to tell me that you have almost finished ravaging our gardens?'

'I'm afraid we still have a lot more to do, Mother. We did advise you that we were thinking of bringing in ground-radar scanners to see if there were any more bones buried under the lawns. They should be here and starting work tomorrow.'

'I see. You do understand that you have shattered our lives? Our peace, our tranquillity, our ability to meditate? We have done nothing but devote ourselves wholly and completely to God and the service of others, but you have even dug up our cabbages.'

Katie said, 'May I sit down? I have something serious to ask you.'

'I told you the last time you were here, I have been instructed by our legal adviser to say nothing to you at all. Mr O'Catháin or one of his representatives should be in touch with you shortly.'

Katie pulled the bucket-like chair around and sat down anyway. 'My detective showed you a post-mortem picture of the nun who was found dead in Glanmire. You said that you didn't know her, but it was recognizably Sister Mona Murphy, who used to belong to this congregation. In one of the photographs we borrowed from you she is standing right next to you. There's no question at all that you knew who she was, so why did you lie to us?'

Mother O'Dwyer didn't answer, but went back to her desk and sat down. She laid her hand on the open Bible and stared at Katie as if she didn't understand what she was doing there, or as if Katie had asked her a question in a foreign language.

'Mother O'Dwyer?' said Katie. 'I really need to know why you didn't tell us the truth.'

'I was afraid,' said Mother O'Dwyer. She sounded as if she had barbed wire in her throat, to try and catch her words before they came out.

'You were *afraid*? Afraid of what? The sooner we find out who's been killing these sisters, the better it will be for everybody.'

'Will it? Is that what you think?'

'Of course it will,' said Katie. 'You don't want any more sisters to be murdered, do you? And whoever did this, you want to see them punished, don't you?'

'Sometimes it is better to die than tell the truth,' said Mother O'Dwyer.

'Oh, really? And under what circumstances is that?'

Mother O'Dwyer was silent for almost half a minute, her lips tightly pursed, but Katie didn't ask her any more questions because she could sense that she was carefully thinking of what she was going to say.

'I knew it was Sister Mona as soon as I heard about it on the news,' she said. 'And then when Sister Barbara was found, mutilated as she was, I was absolutely certain.'

'Go on,' Katie coaxed her. 'Certain of what?'

'I was certain that somebody was taking their revenge on the sisters of the Bon Sauveur, and that more might be killed.'

'And why did you think that?'

'Because of the abuse that was inflicted on Sister Bridget, and the way that Sister Mona and Sister Barbara were tortured. It could only have been done by somebody who knew each of them intimately.'

'Why?'

Mother O'Dwyer was highly agitated now. She stood up and went to the window. Outside, she could see the blue nylon tent and the reservists digging up the gardens. She lifted her hand as if to bless them, or as if she were commanding them to stop. Katie stayed where she was and waited for her to answer.

'As you probably know, Detective Superintendent, many sisters are devoted to one particular saint and see in that saint's experience their own path to divine ecstasy. Some see their way to Jesus in the miracles that their chosen saint might have worked. Some see it in their martyrdom. Some see it in both, for many martyred saints worked miracles before they went to meet their maker.'

Again, she was silent for a long while, and then she said, 'Sister Bridget was passionate about the Immaculate Heart of Mary. She believed that if she lived as the Blessed Virgin had lived, with a pure and forgiving heart, she would eventually reach God.'

'All right . . .' said Katie. 'So, what you're suggesting is that whoever suffocated her and then used the figurine of the Immaculate Heart of Mary to violate her, there was a strong possibility that they knew that.'

'Exactly. As for Sister Mona, her spiritual ideal was Saint Gemma Galgani, known as the Lover of the Cross.'

Katie shook her head. 'I'm afraid you'll have to enlighten me there. Who was Saint Gemma Galgani?'

'Just a simple girl who worked in the kitchen of a wealthy Italian family about the beginning of the twentieth century. But because of her great love of Jesus she would often pause in her work to contemplate the large crucifix that hung on the kitchen wall. It aroused such a passion in her that it made her heart beat faster, and one day she cried out, 'Let me come to you, I am thirsting for you!'

'I see,' said Katie. 'And then what?'

Mother O'Dwyer turned away from the window. 'The Corpus on the cross came to life, and His right hand detached from the cross, and with a loving look in His eyes He beckoned Gemma to come to Him. Gemma rushed over to the crucifix and flew up in the air so that Jesus could embrace her. He pressed her lips against the wound in His side, so that she could drink His blood, and all the time she remained floating in the air – "as if resting on a cloud", according to her biographer.'

'So she *flew*, this Saint Gemma? And her killer made sure that Sister Mona flew, too.'

'That was what convinced me more than anything,' said Mother O'Dwyer. 'If Sister Bridget had been the only one, I would have certainly had my suspicions. But then there was Sister Mona, and now what was done to Sister Barbara really confirms it.'

'We've given out hardly any details about Sister Barbara except that her hands and feet were mutilated.'

'That was enough. Sister Barbara was devoted to Saint Anastasia, who was a healer and an exorcist. She was martyred in the third century under the persecution of the Roman Emperor Diocletian. She was tortured by having her fingers and toes cut off and her breasts burned with red-hot irons, but she refused to deny her faith. Some legends say that she was beheaded, others that she was drowned.'

Katie didn't say anything immediately. Although the Garda press office had released some details of Sister Barbara's condition when her body was found in the fountain, they had held back the information that her breasts had been branded. So Mother

O'Dwyer's suspicions about the murderer could very well be correct, and he or she was somebody who had known all three nuns intimately.

'What I want to know is, why didn't you tell us any of this before?' Katie asked her. 'I'm not saying that it could have prevented Sister Barbara from being abducted, but it could have helped us a great deal in narrowing down our list of possible suspects.'

'I've *told* you!' snapped Mother O'Dwyer, as if Katie had forced her into giving so much away. 'I was afraid. I shall confess my cowardice, and I shall beg the Lord for absolution, but I was afraid, sorely afraid – and I wanted to protect the good name of the Bon Sauveurs, and the diocese.'

'What were you so afraid of, Mother?' Katie asked as gently as she could.

Mother O'Dwyer's eyes were crowded with tears. 'It was the way we treated the young mothers that we took into Saint Margaret's, and their babies, too. At the time, we sincerely believed that we were doing right by those girls, showing them how sinful they had been and guiding them back to the path of righteousness. We believed that we were doing our best for the children, too, even though they had been conceived in acts of immorality and were born invested with their mothers' shame. If we hadn't been so strict with those children, Satan would have claimed them for his own – which, of course, they were.'

'What about the children you sent for adoption?' asked Katie. 'I thought you believed that they belonged to God and that was why you could take them away from their natural mothers and give them to somebody else.'

'Some of the children behaved well and grew up healthy; it was clear that God had smiled upon them and accepted them. It was those children we sent for adoption, so that they could be raised in a God-fearing family and not be tainted by the sinfulness of their conception.'

'I don't understand why you were so afraid to speak out,' said Katie. 'All this happened nearly thirty years ago. Times were different then, as you say, and you thought that you were doing the right thing by those girls and their babies. Who knows what might have happened to them if Satan had kept them in his clutches.'

'I'm not a fool, Detective Superintendent,' Mother O'Dwyer retorted. 'I don't appreciate sarcasm, either. I am quite aware of how the world has changed and how our treatment of those girls is regarded these days. What was considered to be a righteous Christian upbringing in the 1970s is now considered to be cruelty. What our priests believed was the selfless giving of affection to children who had known no love at home is now considered to be paedophilia.

'I am telling you this in the strictest confidence. There were seven sisters who were known among us to be the most devout, but they were also the strongest disciplinarians. If a young mother was wilful, or blasphemous, she would be chastised, or made to stay up all night praying for forgiveness. If a child misbehaved or was disobedient, it went without food. I admit that there were casualties from that, from sickness mostly, or malnutrition.

'Sister Bridget and Sister Mona and Sister Barbara were three of those seven. You can only imagine what the media would do to the Bon Sauveurs if this were to come out. That is why I said nothing. That is why I told your detective an untruth about recognizing Sister Mona. If this became public knowledge, it would mean the end of the congregation as we know it.'

Katie waited while she tugged a tissue out of a box, took off her glasses, and wiped her eyes. Instead of looking like a diminutive Darth Vader, she now looked like a small, miserable child who had inexplicably grown old before her time.

'We've found the bones, mother,' said Katie. 'There's no point in trying to protect the Bon Sauveurs now. The evidence is there for everybody to see.'

'I mustn't say any more,' said Mother O'Dwyer. 'I'll have to talk to my legal advisers first. I don't even know why I told you all of that.'

'You told me all of that because in spite of everything you have a heart,' said Katie.

Mother O'Dwyer gave her a quick, twisted smile and then she opened a drawer in her desk and took out a notepad and a black address book. 'I suppose you'll be wanting the names of the other four sisters from the Sacred Seven.'

'Is that what you used to call them? The Sacred Seven?'

'That is what they called themselves, although they thought that none of the other sisters knew. Here, I'll write them down for you, along with their last known addresses. I don't know for certain if all, or any, of them are still alive, to tell you the truth.'

Katie waited while she wrote down the names and addresses. Outside in the garden she saw one of the reservists holding up a bone that she had found in her riddle, and Bill walking towards her.

'What I've told you today, you won't be disclosing it to the media, will you?' said Mother O'Dwyer, as she tore out the sheet of paper from her notebook and handed it over.

'Do you really think it will make any difference if I do?' Katie asked her. 'It might help to save the lives of these other four, if they're still with us.'

Mother O'Dwyer remained at her desk, looking defeated. 'It's a disaster, isn't it? How can an act of charity that you did in the past turn out to be a crime in the future?'

Katie stood up. 'There's only one person who knows the answer to that, Mother, and you know Him very much better than I do.'

236

Thirty-one

Katie went to find Detective Sergeant Ni Nuallán, who was still in a side room in the convent with Sister Caoilainn, systematically checking the records of all the mothers and babies who had been taken in by Saint Margaret's Mother and Baby Home before it had been closed.

The room was gloomy and smelled of oak panelling and old books. At the far end there was a stained-glass window with an image of Jesus on it, holding up a lamp. Sister Caoilainn was sitting underneath it, a large pasty-faced woman with a dark moustache. She was biting her thumbnail and looking bored.

'Could you excuse us for a moment, please, Sister?' asked Katie. 'I need to have a word with Sergeant Ni Nuallán here.'

Sister Caoilainn stood up and bustled out of the room, making it plain from her upturned nose what she thought about being ordered around by the Garda. When she had gone, Katie closed the door and passed Detective Sergeant Nuallán the list of sisters that Mother O'Dwyer had given her. Very briefly, she explained who they were and what Mother O'Dwyer had told her about them.

'You can leave these records for a while. It's urgent that we locate these four women, if they're still alive, and put them under immediate protection. If you can go back to the station and organize that with Superintendent Pearse.'

'Right, I'll do that,' said Detective Sergeant Ni Nuallán. 'I'll come back to these records after, though. If what Mother O'Dwyer has told you is true, our offender could well be one of these young women. There's not just lists of names here, there's a whole rake of correspondence with adoption agencies in America, and daily reports on the young girls' behaviour. Some of them protested when their children were taken away from them for adoption. Some of them self-harmed and attempted suicide, and others actually attacked the sisters. One of them set fire to a rubbish bin and nearly burned the whole convent down.'

'What a can of worms,' said Katie. 'Listen, I'll leave it with you for now. I have to pay a visit to the Begleys.'

'The Begleys? I don't envy you that. Dooley said they were in bits.'

'Well, there's more to it than meets the eye. It turns out that Roisin's suicide note was probably a forgery.'

'You're codding!' said Detective Sergeant Ni Nuallán. 'Do we know who might have done it?'

'I'm dreading finding out, if you must know.'

'You don't think . . . Jesus.'

'I'm thinking nothing at all at the moment, not until I talk to the Begleys. I promised anyway that I'd call by to give them my sympathies and let them know how our investigation was coming along. This is going to make it all rather awkward, to say the least, but I think I'm probably the best person to be doing it. I'll be back at the station no later than five, I should have thought. Inspector O'Rourke's on his way back from Dublin and apparently he has something of great moment to tell me.'

'I, ah . . .' Detective Sergeant Ni Nuallán began.

'What is it, Kyna?'

'No, it's nothing at all. No bother.'

'Go on, tell me.'

'No, like I say, it's nothing. I'll get back to Anglesea Street directly and start looking for these four old sisters.'

'There's nothing wrong, is there?' Katie asked her.

Detective Sergeant Ni Nuallán shook her head. 'Nothing wrong at all. If anything, it's all too right.'

She lifted her blue wool jacket from the back of her chair and shrugged it on, then she scruffed up her short blonde hair. Katie waited for a moment, but it was obvious that whatever she might have had on her mind, Kyna wasn't going to tell her what it was. Not yet, anyway.

* * *

The Begleys lived in a modern new-build house on Montenotte Road, on the steep northern slope that overlooked the River Lee. It was white and angular, with a swimming pool in front of it and a balcony that gave them a panoramic view of the city.

Montenotte Road was walled and narrow, with cars parked in it, and it took a seven-point turn for Katie to manoeuvre into the Begleys' driveway. She pulled up behind Jim Begley's red Range Rover Sport and climbed out. The house was lit up inside and she could see a huge plasma TV flickering in one of the downstairs rooms. The swimming pool was empty, with a few dry leaves scurrying around in it. A chilly breeze was blowing from the south-west and Katie shivered.

She walked up the steps to the white-painted front door and pressed the doorbell. It played the opening bars of Beethoven's 'Moonlight Sonata'. She waited, rubbing her hands together to keep warm, and just as she was about to press the bell again she heard footsteps and the light in the hallway was switched on. The door was opened by Aileen Begley, who blinked at her and said, 'Yes?'

Katie produced her badge. 'Detective Superintendent Maguire, from Garda headquarters at Anglesea Street. I think Detective Dooley told you that I'd be calling around to see you. This is not a bad time, is it?'

'At the moment, Superintendent, any time is a bad time, as I'm sure you can understand,' said Aileen. 'But come in anyway.'

'I can come back tomorrow if it's better for you,' said Katie.

'No, no, since you're here. You can't make things any worse.'

She opened the door wider so that Katie could step inside. She was a dark-haired, bosomy woman of about forty-five and she had been eye-wateringly over-generous with the Estée Lauder Beautiful. She was wearing a black wool dress that was a size too small for her, so that Katie could see where her midriff bulged over the top of her tights. Her face was puffy, probably from too many years of vodka cocktails, but Katie guessed that she must have once been just as pretty as Roisin.

Inside, the Begley house was plain and minimalist, with white leather couches and revolving armchairs, and sparkling chandeliers made of triangles of glass. On one living-room wall hung a large landscape by the Cork artist Maurice Desmond, the top half a lurid blue and the bottom half sludgy brown. On the facing wall hung a large crucifix, and Katie couldn't help thinking of Saint Gemma levitating into the air to drink the blood of Christ from the wound in His side.

'I wanted to offer my condolences to you and your husband on behalf of the Garda,' said Katie. 'Is your husband here?'

'He'll be down directly,' said Aileen. 'Can I get you a drink at all?'

'No, thank you, I'm grand altogether,' Katie told her, but noticed Aileen glancing towards a cut-glass tumbler on one of the side tables with ice cubes and a slice of lemon in it. 'But, please, don't let me stop you. This must have been a terrible time for you. Roisin was the only child you had living at home, wasn't she?'

'That's right. We have two sons, Darragh and Coileán. Darragh's in Dubai just now, working for a construction company, and Coileán's at UCC, studying architecture. They both take after their father, thank God.'

'And Roisin? Who did she take after?'

'God knows. That girl, may she rest in peace. It's not right to speak ill of the dead, I know that, but she was trouble from the very moment she was born. Jim used to wonder if we'd offended the Lord in some way that we weren't aware of, to be burdened with a child like her.'

At that moment they heard Jim Begley coming down the stairs.

He walked into the living room in a cloud of cigar smoke, like a demon making his entrance in a pantomime.

'I thought I heard the front door,' he said, in a harsh, phlegmy voice.

'This is Detective Superintendent Maguire, Jim,' said Aileen. 'She's very kindly come to offer her condolences.'

Jim was a tall, heavily built man with a wave of white hair. Everything about him seemed larger than a normal human being. He had a huge, long face with deep-set eyes and a lantern jaw, and there was a cleft in the end of his nose. He was wearing a light-grey Adidas tracksuit top and white trackie bottoms, almost a parody of the millionaire property developer relaxing at home. When he held out his hand to Katie, she could see that he was wearing a massive gold ring with a crest on it.

'It's good of you to take the trouble,' he said. 'We're holding the funeral mass at St Joseph's on Thursday. It'll be a quiet affair, under the circumstances. Close family only.'

'None of her school friends? She was very popular at school, I understand.'

'Yes, but suicide. Self-murder is a mortal sin and there was a time when we couldn't have held a mass at all. As for inviting her school friends, I didn't consider that at all appropriate. They'd be weeping and wailing and saying what an angel she was. A funeral isn't a time to eulogize the dead. It's a time to worship Christ's victory over death and to console those left behind.'

'We don't yet have definitive proof that Roisin took her own life, Mr Begley. That's another reason I've come to see you today.'

'What are you talking about?' asked Jim. He sucked at his cigar until the end glowed red and then blew a long stream of smoke out of the side of his mouth. 'She was ashamed of giving evidence in court about prostituting herself and so she drowned herself in the river. What more proof do you need than that?'

'Do you mind if we sit down?' said Katie.

'Help yourself,' said Jim and pointed to one of the armchairs. When Katie had perched herself on the edge of the seat, he lowered himself on to the couch next to her, with his belly in his lap, tapping his cigar ash into a large glass ashtray. Aileen retrieved her drink and took a sip of it, and then another, and then sat down on the other end of the couch, keeping her distance from him.

'So, what's the problem?' asked Jim.

'The note that was found under Roisin's pillow, that's the problem.'

'I don't see why that should be. She made it perfectly clear that she was mortified by what she'd done and that she wanted to end it all. She wanted to turn out the light, that's what she wrote.'

'I agree with you, Mr Begley, that's what the note said, but the high probability is that Roisin didn't write it. Our technical experts have examined it and they're ninety-nine point nine per cent certain that it's a forgery.'

'*What?*' said Aileen. 'What do you mean, it's forgery? I found it myself, under her pillow. There was nobody else in the house that night but us. Who else could have written it but Roisin?'

Katie said nothing but looked at Jim and raised her eyebrows. Jim had been about to take another puff of his cigar, but now he lowered it. He turned to look at Aileen and then turned back to face Katie.

'Jim?' said Aileen.

Jim ignored her and heaved himself to his feet. He loomed over Katie and said, in that brick-harsh voice, 'I think you'd best leave, Detective Superintendent.'

'We're talking about the death of your daughter, Mr Begley. The unexplained death of your daughter. If you refuse to discuss it now, I shall have to ask you to come down to Anglesea Street Garda Station and answer questions about it there, under caution.'

'And if I refuse to do that?'

'Well, I'm very much hoping that you won't, but if you do, I shall detain you.'

Jim continued to loom over her, breathing hard. The smell of his cigar smoke was so acrid that it made Katie feel as if she had been smoking a cigar herself and she began to feel nauseous.

She thought about standing up herself and leaving and sending Detective Dooley around tomorrow to bring Jim in for questioning. But just as she was about to get to her feet, Aileen said, 'Jim? It wasn't *you* wrote the note, was it?'

Jim opened and closed his mouth like a huge landed salmon. Then he sat down again and Katie could see that he was trembling.

'Jim?' said Aileen. 'Tell me it wasn't you. Please, Jim, tell me it wasn't you.'

'She was prostituting herself,' said Jim. 'Our own daughter. I had to make it look as if she was feeling at least some remorse for bringing so such shame on us.'

'So you wrote the note?' asked Katie.

He closed his eyes and nodded. 'Have you any idea at all what it's been like, sitting in church every Sunday morning at Mass, and everybody's eyes on us, and whispering. "That's the Begleys. You know what their daughter Roisin does for a living? She's only a hoor!"'

'One of our oldest friends came up to us and told us that she didn't know how we had the nerve to come and take communion alongside decent folk.'

He opened his eyes and looked at Katie as if he were asking for understanding, but she could tell that he was still more angry than sorrowful. *I thought I had a beautiful clever daughter and she turned out to be a brasser. What she would have said in court, that would have ruined our reputation for good and all.*

'Oh, Jim,' said Aileen and reached across and laid her hand on top of his.

'Are you satisfied?' Jim asked Katie. 'Maybe you can leave now.'

'You know there's one more question I have to ask you,' said Katie. 'Was it you who drowned her?'

The silence was so total that Katie could almost have believed that she had gone deaf. It was broken only by Aileen making a suppressed mewing sound, like a kitten that had been shut in a cupboard. At last Jim stood up again. His cigar had gone out but he sucked at it all the same.

'I asked you to leave, Detective Superintendent.'

'I will at once, if you answer my question.'

'I don't have to answer a question like that. Coming from a senior Garda officer like you, that's an outrage. Don't you have any idea who I am? I'm a county councillor for Cork City South-East, for one thing. For another thing, I could buy and sell you in the same street.'

Katie stood up. 'I'm sorry you feel unable to give me a straight answer, Mr Begley. But I think you're capable of understanding why I had to ask you. I'm not going to take this any further at the moment, but when I get back to the station I'm going to be meeting Detective Dooley, who's been handling Roisin's case. We'll be wanting to talk to you again.'

'Not without my lawyer,' said Jim.

'Not a bother,' said Katie. 'I'll have Detective Dooley ring you to make an appointment.'

Jim was about to say something else, but Aileen stood up and took hold of his arm and shook her head, warning him not to. She showed Katie to the front door. The draught that blew in when she opened it was damp and cold, and they could hear an oil tanker mournfully hooting as it made its way down the river and the dry leaves crackling in the swimming pool.

'I'm sorry,' said Katie.

Aileen shrugged, as if to show Katie that she didn't believe her.

'I'm sorry you lost Roisin, and there's something else that I'm sorry about. I may never again get an opportunity to prosecute the man who pimped her and because of that he's going to go on exploiting scores of other young girls just like Roisin, only they won't be able to escape from him like she did.'

'Well, that's your problem, Detective Superintendent,' said Aileen. 'You can't expect us to sacrifice our family's good name just because you can't do your job properly.'

'Goodnight to you, Mrs Begley,' Katie told her and left. Aileen closed the front door very quietly behind her.

Katie didn't leave immediately, though. She stood by the empty swimming pool, listening, and almost at once she heard Aileen shouting and Jim shouting back at her. Their voices grew louder and louder, and it sounded as if Aileen was following Jim from one room to another. Katie heard a crash, and then another crash, and another, and a bump like an armchair tipping over.

Then Aileen screaming, quite distinctly, 'How could you? How could you? She was our daughter! She was our daughter, no matter what!'

After that she heard Aileen sobbing, then silence. She walked down the sloping driveway back to her car. She felt far more sad than satisfied, although she was almost certain now that she would eventually get a confession. She knew from experience that it was those who had committed criminal acts in the name of righteousness who always ended up feeling the most guilty. Mother O'Dwyer was a prime example. The real criminals like Michael Gerrety never felt a moment's remorse.

Driving back down Summerhill into the city she saw a young blonde girl waiting to cross the road who looked so much like Roisin that it gave her a prickly feeling of shock. As she crossed over the Brian Boru Bridge, it occurred her that Jim and Aileen Begley would be liable to the same kind of shock whenever they saw a Roisin lookalike, and that would be a life sentence in itself.

Thirty-two

She stayed at Anglesea Street until 7.45 p.m., drawing up a plan of action with Superintendent Pearse to arrest Paddy Fearon. If he had been an ordinary suspect, they simply would have sent two uniformed gardaí around to knock on his door and take him into custody.

Paddy Fearon, though, was a prominent figure among the Travellers, which made his arrest much more contentious and political. Not only that, they were going to arrest him at the Spring Lane Halting Site, which because of its condition had been the subject of fierce protests from the Pavee community for years. As Superintendent Pearse said, it would be as sensitive as the American police arresting a black activist in a rundown ghetto.

He looked around at the twenty gardaí assembled in the briefing room and said, 'No matter what verbal provocation you get from the Travellers – and you know as well as I do that they'll be giving you an earful – you are not to respond.'

'What if they start tossing rockers?' asked one young officer.

'Then, of course, that's different. It's possible that you may have to resort to physical force in order to effect the arrest, or to keep the peace, or to protect yourselves from injury. If you do, though, you must apply only the very minimum force necessary. It doesn't matter what you think of Travellers, or what kind of a slabbering they give you, they're human beings, and I don't want to see you clubbing them like seals.'

'What time are you planning on going in?' Katie asked him.

Superintendent Pearse pointed at the map of Ballyvolane spread out on the table. 'I want everybody assembled at the entrance to the halting site *here* by 07.00 hours sharp. Sunrise is at 07.22 tomorrow and that's when six officers will enter the site to surround the Fearon caravan and knock on his door. I don't want us being accused of making the arrest under cover of darkness, even though it should be well light by then, and I don't want us being accused of going in mob-handed.'

'And if you get trouble?'

'If Fearon resists arrest, or if we're attacked by any of the other residents, we'll have a further fourteen officers in riot gear waiting out here in the roadway, ready to take immediate action. Now, as far as bringing Fearon back here to Anglesea Street for questioning is concerned – '

Detective Dooley's iPhone buzzed. He checked the screen and then he raised one hand and said, 'Sorry to interrupt you, sir, but I've just had a text from the press office. Somehow the media have got wind of this.'

'How in the name of all that's holy did that happen?' said Superintendent Pearse. He glared at the gardaí crowded all around him, but all they could do was turn their heads around and look at each other and shrug. 'That's absolutely what we *don't* need, the media! If the Travellers think they're going to be shown on the telly, they'll only play up all the more.'

'Don't worry about it,' said Katie. 'I'll come along myself and deal with the press. You just worry about bringing in Paddy Fearon. As you know, this arrest is just one part of our investigation into the racehorses that were found at Nohaval Cove, but I don't want the media to make that connection just yet. I'll tell them that he's suspected of extorting money with menaces, and that's all.'

'And if they ask you for details? Like who he's extorted money from, and for what?'

'I'll give them my sweetest smile and say, "No comment at the present time", like I usually do.'

* * *

Just before she left the station, John texted her to say that he would be out when she arrived home because he was meeting a new pharmaceutical supplier at the Silver Spring Hotel. However, he had fed and walked Barney and he had made a lasagne for supper.

I love u, he had added. *But strictly no peeking at the painting! XXX J.*

When she let herself in, the curtains were drawn, the lamps in the living room were lit and the house was comfortably warm. Barney circled excitedly around her and she patted his head, but it was growing foggy outside and she was seriously grateful that she didn't have to take him out.

She went into the bedroom and changed into her sloppy white sweater and a pair of green tracksuit bottoms and slippers. She frowned at herself in the mirror and she was sure that her face was rounder, but maybe it only looked that way because she was tired and her eyes were swollen.

She filled the kettle to make herself a cup of tea and then went back into the living room to switch on the television. John's painting was standing on the bookcase next to the fireplace, facing the wall. He had obviously been working on it today because he normally covered it with one of Seamus's old cot sheets when it was dry, and there was a smell of acrylic paint in the room.

Once she had made herself a mug of tea, she sat down on the couch to watch the nine o'clock news. The headline story was about a homeless man and woman whose bodies had been pulled out of the River Lee by naval divers early that afternoon, close to the Port of Cork sign. Katie knew about that already, and there were no suspicious circumstances. A sad double suicide. The rest of the news concerned the struggling Irish economy and she was relieved when Eileen Dunne, the presenter, went on to the weather forecast without making any mention of the continuing search for children's skeletons at the Bon Sauveur Convent.

Her iPhone pinged while she was in the kitchen and it was John telling her that he would be back home in less than half an hour. She glanced back into the living room, at the painting facing the wall. *No peeking,* John had cautioned her. But if she did take a quick sconce at it, how would he know?

She walked into the living room and Barney must have sensed her indecision because he stood up and looked at her seriously, wagging his tail. *Mother of God,* she thought, *it seems like everybody I know can read me like yesterday evening's* Echo, *even my dog.*

'Listen,' she told Barney, 'what I'm about to do now, you didn't see me do it, and even if you did, you won't go telling himself when he walks through the door, will you?'

Barney made an extraordinary creaking sound in the back of his throat, but stayed where he was, watching her, with his tail beating rhythmically against the couch.

Katie went across to the bookshelf. She turned around the small wooden easel on which the painting was supported, taking care not to touch the painting itself. It was possible that the paint hadn't fully dried and she didn't want to risk leaving a fingerprint in it. *Detective Superintendent Leaves Tell-Tale Dab At Scene Of Prohibited Peeking.*

When she saw John's painting she slowly raised her hand and pressed it over her mouth. She stood there for nearly a minute, staring at it in disbelief. So far, he had only sketched out the lines of her naked body in umber acrylic and roughly shaded in some of the background in the same dark-brown colour. Her face, however, was nearly finished. It was unmistakably her, with her bottle-green eyes and her distinctive cheekbones and her slightly pouty lips, but he had given her such a warm, seductive expression. He had caught her likeness exactly, but he had also made her look beautiful.

He had taken scores of photographs of her recently, especially when they went out for walks, but this painting was how he saw her through his own eyes and she understood now how deeply he must love her.

She carefully turned the painting back to face the wall.

'Remember, Barns, you never saw me do that,' she said. 'You say one single word and I swear to God you're a dead setter.'

Barney made that creaky noise again, almost like an old door opening, and vigorously shook his head.

* * *

John was dog-tired when he came home, and he smelled of whiskey, but he was in a good mood. The meeting with his new suppliers had gone well and he expected to increase his online turnover of antibiotics by at least seven per cent.

Katie had heated up the lasagne in the oven and they ate it in the kitchen. She lit a red candle in the middle of the table and switched off the main light.

'Hey,' smiled John, putting on his American accent. 'This is very roh-mannick.'

'Maybe I love you,' she said.

'You're only saying that because I can make a mean lasagne.'

Katie smiled back at him. God, he was handsome, especially now that his dark curly hair had grown a little more. She was so tempted to say to him, *No, it's nothing to do with your lasagne, it's because I've found out now how you see me, and you love me, too.*

'I have to get up early tomorrow,' she said.

'Who's thinking about tomorrow? Tomorrow can take care of itself.'

'We're arresting a Traveller up at the Spring Lane Halting Site. He's a well-known figure in the Travelling community, so we may have some trouble. Not only that, the media have found out about it, which is why I have to be there.'

'What time do you have to get up?'

'Five-thirty at the latest. There won't be much traffic at that time of the morning, but the forecast is fog.'

'Hmm,' said John, looking at his watch. 'That gives us seven hours and eleven minutes. That's unless you want a second helping of lasagne.'

'I couldn't,' said Katie, pressing her hand against her stomach. 'I'm stuffed as a goose.'

She stayed where she was at the table, watching him scrape the plates and stack them in the dishwasher. *Stuffed as a goose*, she thought. *I wish I hadn't said that.*

* * *

When she came out of the bathroom after brushing her teeth she found that John was already asleep. She climbed carefully into bed and switched off her bedside lamp. Then she turned over and put her arm around him, pressing herself against his back so that she could breathe in the smell of him and stroke the hairs on his chest.

From Cobh she heard the clock chiming, the clock she only ever heard at night. She closed her eyes and hoped that she would fall asleep before the morning.

Thirty-three

Katie was driven up to the Spring Lane Halting Site by Detective Dooley. Detective Brennan came, too, sitting in the back seat eating a sausage sandwich and swigging tangerine-flavoured Tanora from the bottle. It was still foggy, but it was nearly sunrise and the fog was beginning to glow bright.

Five patrol cars were lined up along the access road to the halting site, as well as two marked Nissan Terranos and a Mercedes van that was used as a mobile command centre. Three media cars were there, too, as well as an outside broadcast van, but Sergeant O'Farrell had made them park in the commercial estate just off the Ballyvolane Road, out of sight.

'I don't want them tinkers getting the idea that they're film stars,' he told Katie, as she walked up to join him. The six uniformed gardaí who were going to make the arrest were standing around clapping their hands to keep warm, while the officers in riot gear were waiting in their vehicles.

Dan Keane from the *Examiner* was there, in a pork-pie hat, looking as if he was suffering from a severe hangover. So was Fionnuala Sweeney from RTÉ, bundled up in a sheepskin jacket and a turquoise knitted hood.

'Good morning, Detective Superintendent,' said Fionnauala. 'We hear that you've come to the Spring Lane Halting Site this morning to arrest Paddy Fearon, one of the leading figures in the Cork Pavee community. Can you tell us what he's being charged with?'

'No comment at the moment, Fionnuala,' said Katie.

'Would this be anything to do with horses now?' asked Dan Keane. 'Paddy Fearon has been in trouble with the law before for supplying unfit horses for slaughter.'

'I'll be holding a media conference later, when we've had the opportunity to ask Mr Fearon a few pertinent questions,' Katie told him. 'Meanwhile I have nothing to say at all.'

'It looks like you're expecting ructions,' said Dan Keane, nodding his head towards the gardaí in riot gear sitting in their Terranos.

'Simply a precaution,' said Katie. 'This is a sensitive place to be making an arrest and we want to make sure that nobody gets hurt.'

Sergeant O'Farrell came up to her, wearing a yellow and white high-visibility jacket that made him look even bulkier than he usually did. 'All right, ma'am. We're ready to go in now.'

'Very good. But, everybody, please remember what Superintendent Pearse said yesterday evening. We want this arrest to be as low-key as possible.'

Sergeant O'Farrell led the six gardaí into the entrance to the halting site. As they did so, two scruffy young boys of about seven and five came out of the toilet block and saw them. They immediately ran across to the nearest caravan, shouting out 'Mam! Mam! There's shades here! Mam! There's shades here!'

'Oh, fantastic,' said Sergeant O'Farrell. 'Just what we needed. I was hoping to lift Fearon nice and quiet before the rest of these tinkers woke up.'

'Travellers, Kevin,' Katie corrected him.

'Oh yeah, sorry. At least it's not as bad as what my oul' fella used to call them.'

They made their way between the water-filled potholes until they reached Paddy Fearon's caravan. His brindled pony was standing outside in the fog, with a heavy brown blanket over it, looking mournful. The six gardaí surrounded the caravan, four in front of the steps and two around the back, in case Paddy Fearon attempted some ridiculous escape, like trying to climb out of one of the windows. Katie knew from experience that there was no limit to the stupidity of criminals trying to get away from the law. They had once had to rescue a seventeen-stone shoplifter who had got herself wedged in a manhole in Paul Street.

One of the gardaí knocked sharply on the caravan door with his baton and called out, 'Paddy Fearon! This is the Garda, Mr Fearon! Would you open up, please?'

While they were waiting for Paddy Fearon to answer, several caravan doors around the halting site were thrown open and at least a dozen Travellers appeared, including the four men had who threatened Detective Dooley the last time he was there. There were several women, too, some of them with nylon curlers in their hair and two of them wrapped up in frayed satin dressing gowns. One of them was still wearing her dead-white face pack.

'Jesus,' said Detective Brennan. 'Zombies.'

Sergeant O'Farrell looked around at the approaching Travellers and then turned back and said, 'Give Fearon another knock, Connor. If he's not going to open up, we'll have to make a forced entry.'

A fat woman in a shiny purple shell suit came waddling up to Katie and Sergeant O'Farrell, breathing hard. She reeked of cigarettes. 'What in the name of feck do you think you're playing at?' she demanded. 'As if we don't suffer enough persamacution from the shades already.'

'There's nothing for you to get upset about, ma'am,' said Katie. 'We just want to have a few quiet words with Paddy Fearon, that's all.'

'A few quiet words? Is that why you've fetched a whole fecking army with you?'

'All we want to do is keep the situation calm,' Katie told her. 'I apologize if we've disturbed you at all. As soon as Mr Fearon comes to the door, we'll be off and leave you in peace.'

'Well, that's all well and good you saying that,' the fat woman retorted. 'But what's he supposed to have done? You people seem to think you have some divine right to treat us like shite because we don't live in houses.'

'I can't discuss it with you, I'm afraid,' said Katie. 'Mr Fearon hasn't been charged with any offence yet and he's entitled to his privacy, like anybody else.'

The garda standing on the steps of Paddy Fearon's caravan beat a postman's knock with his baton, even harder than before.

'Paddy Fearon! Garda! If you don't open up immediately we'll have to break the door open!'

'He *is* in there, I hope?' said Katie.

'His horsebox is there and his car's there right next to it,' said Detective Dooley.

'Oh, he's home all right,' said the fat woman in the purple shell suit. 'I sees him early on looking out the windy.' She was about to say something else but she started coughing and couldn't stop herself and in the end she was thumping herself on the chest with her fist and spitting out long strings of mucus.

'God, I'm so glad I had that sausage sandwich,' said Detective Brennan, pulling a face and turning to look the other way.

The garda at Paddy Fearon's door took out a bunch of skeleton keys and tried them out one by one. Eventually he managed to find one that turned in the lock, but when he tried to open the door it wouldn't budge. 'Bolted!' he called out.

Another garda pushed his way out of the halting site through the gathering crowd of Travellers and after a short while returned with a crowbar. One of the young Travellers shouted, 'You're racists, that's what you are! You're fecking racists! Why don't you the feck off the lot of you and leave us in peace?' Others were pacing edgily backwards and forwards as if they were waiting for any excuse to start a fight.

There were now twenty or thirty of them and Katie was growing increasingly worried that the situation was going to turn violent. She glanced across at Sergeant O'Farrell and he gave her a thumbs up to indicate that he shared her concern. He switched on his R/T and spoke to the riot officers waiting outside. 'Grady? Everything's still on the simmer at the moment, like, but there's a few skangers here throwing shapes. So be ready to come in here quick if we need you.'

The garda with the crowbar climbed the steps of Paddy Fearon's caravan and inserted the flat end of it into the side of the door. He tugged at it, but as he did so Katie was deafened by a massive bang. Paddy Fearon's caravan burst apart in front of her eyes. Its windows were shattered in a blizzard of broken glass and its aluminium carcass was ripped into weird distorted shapes, like rags, and flags, and leaping horses.

Katie was thrown backwards by the force of the explosion, hitting her head and her right shoulder on the asphalt. Detectives Dooley and Brennan and all of the gardaí were knocked over, too. The two gardaí who had been trying to open the door were both killed instantly. Their mangled, legless torsos were blown almost fifteen metres into the crowd of Travellers, landing with a double thump and spraying blood in all directions. They were immediately followed by a clattering shower of saucepans, china ornaments, cutlery and bottles.

A ball of orange fire rolled up out the wreckage of the caravan, but it turned almost at once into a mushroom cloud of thick grey smoke. The sound of the explosion echoed and re-echoed and scores of hooded crows took off from the telegraph wires along the Ballyvolane Road, scrawking in panic.

Katie sat up, her ears ringing. Her hair was thick with dust and her duffel coat was sparkling with thousands of specks of broken glass. She had a cut on the heel of her hand where she had instinctively lifted it to protect her face. Her stomach muscles were rock-hard and she prayed to God that the foetus inside her hadn't been harmed.

Pieces of debris were still dropping from the sky, fragments of wooden shelving and sheets of paper, and three tattered bed sheets were floating high up in the shining fog like ghosts. The first thing she saw was Paddy Fearon's brindled pony, first collapsing on to its knees, then falling over on to its side. A large triangular shard of aluminium had sliced into the lower side of its neck severing its cranial vena cava and dark red blood was pouring out of it in a thick glossy stream.

Detective Brennan helped Katie to her feet. He said something to her, but she could hardly hear him and the voices of everybody around her sounded like children in a playground far away. She looked around. There was chaos, with people running everywhere. Apart from the two gardaí who had been killed, however, it didn't look as if anybody else had been seriously injured, although she could see one woman with a deep diagonal cut on her cheek from flying glass and several of the young men were still sprawled out on the ground, shaking their heads as if they were half concussed.

Katie walked over to the two bloodied bodies lying on the ground. The water in the potholes around them was streaked with crimson. Both dead gardaí were wearing their shoulder numbers, but she couldn't recognize either of them because their faces were so swollen and battered. Their thighs looked like dark-red joints of meat. She was so shocked she couldn't believe that any of this was really happening, and when she turned around again she almost lost her balance.

Detective Brennan caught her arm to steady her and then immediately said, 'Sorry, ma'am—'

'No, no. God. Thank you. I nearly fell. Oh God, this is appalling.' She crossed herself. 'Those poor men.'

'Here, come away, ma'am,' said Detective Brennan. 'There's nothing at all we can do for them now. Well, we can pray for their immortal souls, but that's about all, like.'

Sergeant O'Farrell was on his R/T, calling loudly for the army bomb squad from Collins Barracks, which was only a little more than five minutes away, and for ambulances, and for the Technical Bureau.

'We need to evacuate the whole halting site immediately,' said Katie.

'What?' said Detective Brennan, cupping his hand to his ear.

'I said we need to clear everybody out of here! There could be more bombs in some of the other caravans for all we know! This could be some kind of racist attack!'

'I'll get it done, ma'am,' said Detective Brennan

'Tell Sergeant O'Farrell to call Bus Éireann. Ask them to send up half a dozen buses from the bus station as fast as they can, but only as far as the Ballyvolane Road. And have him call the Reverend McSweeney at Saint Joseph's in Mayfield. Ask him if we could use the parish hall for a few hours to house all these people.'

'Yes, ma'am.'

Katie saw the injured pony trying to lift its head. 'That pony!' she said. 'Can't we do anything to save it?'

Detective Brennan turned his mouth down and shook his head. 'Not a hope, ma'am. He's a goner, that one.'

Katie looked around again. Some of the Travellers were still milling around, dazed, but all of the women had retreated back to their caravans and hustled their children inside. Already, though, seven or eight gardaí from the riot team were fanning out around the halting site, knocking on mobile home doors and trying to direct the Travellers towards the entrance. Through her temporary deafness, she could hear shouting and arguing and swearing.

Fionnuala Sweeney was circling the wreckage of Paddy Fearon's caravan with her cameraman, giving a gabbled commentary. Katie guessed that she was probably reporting live now. She reached over and patted Detective Dooley on the shoulder and shouted, 'Get her out of here, would you, Robert?'

Detective Dooley was clearly as deaf as she was, but he nodded. Katie waited while he went over to Fionnuala and spoke to her and her cameraman, then ushered both of them well away, past the toilet block. Then she walked over to the side of the caravan where the pony was lying. There was a stench of scorched metal and burned rubber in the air, although the last of the debris had settled now.

The pony rolled its eyes and looked up at her. *Jesus,* she thought, *what a miserable life you've led, and what a miserable way to end it. Let's hope there's a pony heaven, with fresh grass and blue skies and other ponies romping around.*

She unbuttoned her duffel coat and tugged her revolver out her hip holster. Then she went down on one knee and aimed at the pony's forehead. She knew from her firearms training how to put down horses. She imagined an X drawn from each of the pony's ears to its opposing eye and she positioned the muzzle where the X met in the middle, at a slight downward angle, so that the bullet would go through its brain and into its spine.

The pony let out a soft, regretful sigh, as if it understood what she was going to do but accepted it, and then she fired. She was still so deaf that the shot sounded muffled and flat. The pony's legs puppet-jerked and then it lay still.

When she stood up, Sergeant O'Farrell touched her shoulder and said, 'Come on, ma'am, we need to get you away from here. I don't personally think that any anti-knacker fanatic is set on blowing this whole place up, but you never know. And if it's the Provos, they have a nasty habit of setting a booby trap for the first responders.'

'Of course,' she said. She slid her revolver back into its holster and followed him around to the other side of the caravan, glancing back at the pony as she did so. It was still staring at her and she hoped that it forgave her.

* * *

It was more than three hours before the bomb squad had completed their examination of the wreckage of Paddy Fearon's caravan. They had also thoroughly searched every other mobile home on the Spring Lane Halting Site for any further explosive devices. All of the residents meanwhile had been taken in buses to Saint Joseph's parish hall where they had been given tea and sandwiches and seen by a doctor and a nurse.

Katie waited in the Mercedes command van, keeping in touch with Chief Superintendent MacCostagáin and Mathew McElvey in the press office. Gradually her hearing returned to normal, but the back of her head was still sore from her knocking it so hard on the ground.

She had just finished talking to Mathew when Detective Dooley climbed up into the van.

'I think you'd better come and take a lamp at this, ma'am,' he said. He caught sight of the sugared doughnut that one of the gardaí had brought her with a mug of tea, and said, 'I wouldn't eat that just yet, like, if I was you.'

They walked back through the halting site. Sergeant O'Farrell and three gardaí were standing amongst some of the junk with which Paddy Fearon had surrounded his caravan – a bedside table, a gas boiler, and the skeleton of a baby's Tansad pushchair They were all staring down at the tussocky grass that had been flattened by the blast, but as Katie appeared they all looked up at her uneasily.

'We'll have to have him formally identified, of course,' said Sergeant O'Farrell. 'I'm fair confident, though, that it's your man.'

Katie looked down. Behind the gas boiler, half hidden in the grass, his squinchy eyes narrowed as if he were playing hide-and-seek, was a man's severed head. He had tousled grey hair, roughly pitted cheeks and a broken nose. His prominent Adam's apple was still intact, but below that the unshaven skin of his neck was ripped into lacy red tatters and his trachea coiled out of it like the pink body sac of a squid.

Katie said, 'It certainly *looks* like Paddy Fearon, doesn't it? But who in the name of Jesus would want to blow *him* up? He hasn't annoyed the Provos, has he?'

'Oh, he had a fierce number of enemies, as far as I know,' said Detective Brennan. 'You'll have to ask Inspector O'Rourke, he's the expert when it comes to cultured individuals and all the feuds between them. I know that Fearon got himself on the wrong side of Tómas Ó Conaill a couple of years ago, and there's a sham-feen you wouldn't want to upset if you valued your mebs.'

Katie looked at the twisted remains of the caravan. Its entire upper half had been blown off, leaving the cooker and kitchen worktops exposed, as well as a jagged diagonal section of the plywood shelves on which Paddy had kept his ornaments.

'So where's the rest of him?' she asked.

Detective Dooley beckoned her nearer so that she could see what was left of the caravan's interior. The brown Dralon couch was still mostly intact, although one corner of it had been torn open and a fold of burned white sponge was bulging out of it, with a stray spring in the middle. The rest of Paddy Fearon was still sitting there, in his trackie bottoms, up to his midriff. His intestines were piled on to the gold satin cushion next to him, with three or four bloodstained strings of them trailing over to the torn metal edge of the caravan in the direction of his detached head.

'No sign of his ribcage or his arms yet,' said Detective Dooley. 'They'll be scattered about, though. We'll find them. The bomb squad have found the detonator. It's an ordinary commercial detonator, same as the Provos use. That doesn't necessarily mean that the Provos did this, though. Not unless Fearon was up to something that upset their Republican sensibilities, like selling ketamine without giving them a share of the proceeds.'

'Is this is a coincidence, though?' Katie asked him. 'Or was he deliberately killed this morning so that we couldn't arrest him?'

'Well, now, that's the sixty-four million euro question. The media knew that we were coming here to lift him, so whoever planted this bomb in Fearon's caravan, maybe *they* knew, too. But who knows how?'

'I've already asked Fionnuala Sweeney and Dan Keane, but they're not telling me. Thank you, supreme court. It makes you wonder what's more important, doesn't it, protecting the freedom of the press or catching the scumbags who break the law?'

She paused and looked again at the slippery beige heap of Paddy Fearon's innards on the couch. 'I really don't mean that,' she said, more to herself than anybody else. 'I just get so frustrated at times.'

She walked back to the entrance of the halting site. The fog had all cleared now and the morning was sunny and sharp. Fionnula

Sweeney and Dan Keane came up to her, as well as Jean Mulligan from the *Echo*, and she gave them a brief statement.

'Two gardaí were killed instantly this morning when a bomb was detonated in a static caravan at the Spring Lane Halting Site in Ballyvolane. The owner of the caravan, Mr Paddy Fearon, was also fatally injured.'

'Fatally injured?' she heard Detective Brennan mutter, close behind her, to Detective Dooley. 'Blown to fecking smithereens, more like.'

'Mr Fearon was a prominent member of the Travelling community,' Katie went on. 'The police had come to Spring Lane to question him on a routine matter, but that is all I'm able to tell you at the moment. We will be contacting as many of Mr Fearon's relatives as we can find, but it will take some time as we've been told that he had eighteen children.

'The families of the two gardaí who lost their lives have yet to be informed and until then we won't be releasing their names or any further details. Everybody at Anglesea Garda station is extremely shocked and distressed, and I know that feeling will be shared by members of the Garda throughout the country, as well as ordinary men and women.

'After the explosion all the residents of the Spring Lane Halting Site were evacuated for their own safety. However, the site has been thoroughly searched by the army bomb disposal team and should soon be all clear for its residents to return.'

'Just one question, Detective Superintendent Maguire!' Jean Mulligan called out. 'Do you know if Paddy Pearon had been threatened at all? Was there any prior warning about the bomb?'

'That's two questions, Jean, and the answer to both of them is no.'

'You weren't just going to *question* Paddy Fearon, though, were you?' asked Fionnuala. 'You came here to arrest him.'

'I'm not prepared to discuss that yet, Fionnuala. This tragic incident has only just occurred and I'll be holding a full media conference as soon as we have it in perspective. At the moment, to be honest with you, we're all still in shock.'

Fionnuala didn't answer, but frowned and suddenly came towards her, with her left hand uplifted. Katie took a step back, wondering what she was doing, but Fionnuala said, 'It's okay, ma'am, just hold still for a moment.'

She came right up to Katie, lifted the hair at the right side of her head and then tugged gently at her earlobe. Then she held up in front of her a hard, dark-red droplet that looked like an earring. 'Dried blood,' she said. 'You've grazed your ear, that's all.'

Thirty-four

As soon as she passed the open door of his office, Chief Superintendent MacCostagáin called out, 'Katie!'

She stopped and went back.

'How are you?' he asked her, standing up and coming around his desk. 'You weren't hurt at all, were you?'

'Couple of minor cuts, that's all,' said Katie, holding up her right hand to show him her sticking plaster, as if she were swearing an oath of allegiance. 'But honestly, sir, I'm in bits. We're all in bits. Those two young guards. We were ready for a bit of trouble, like, but nothing like that. Do you have their names yet?'

Chief Superintendent MacCostagáin went back to his desk and picked up a sheet of paper. 'Garda Darragh Mullan, he was twenty-three years old, and Garda John Burns, twenty-two. Garda Mullan only passed out of Templemore eighteen months ago, and Garda Burns had only just got married. Michael Pearse has already gone off to notify the families.'

They stood there in silence for a few moments, with Chief Superintendent MacCostagáin looking more mournful than ever. Then he said, 'You'll take yourself for a check-up, Katie, just to make sure?'

'I'm grand, don't worry. I just need to brush myself down and give my hair a quick wash.'

'You should go home and have a good rest. I don't want you coming down with that what-d'ye-call-it, that post-traumatic stress disorder. Francis O'Rourke can keep things ticking over for you.'

'Really, sir, I'm shaken, I admit, but I'm grand altogether and I want to get straight back to this investigation. It'll help me get over the shock. Besides that, I want to catch up with anything new that they might have found up at the Bon Sauveur Convent.'

'Oh yes. The Bon Sauveur Convent. We had the diocesan legal advisers on the blower this morning. I've left a note on your desk. They were asking for a meeting with the assistant commissioner, but he's away in Kinsale today and won't be back till tomorrow. There was somebody else called for you, too. Those two wastes of space from the Ombudsman. I told them you'd been involved in a major incident and that you probably wouldn't be back into the station for a couple of days at the earliest.'

'I – oh – thank you, sir,' Katie told him. She didn't know what else to say. Up until now she had never heard Chief Superintendent MacCostagáin use any kind of derogatory language about anybody. Not only that, he had never treated her so protectively. She couldn't say that he had been actively hostile towards her appointment as detective superintendent, unlike some of the other male officers at Anglesea Street. On the other hand, he had always appeared to be indifferent – more wrapped up in his own perpetual gloom than concerned about her welfare.

'So, what's the current situation up at Spring Lane?' he asked her.

'It's stable now. We've sealed off the area all around Paddy Fearon's caravan and the technical team are down on their hands and knees picking up the bits. Before it gets dark, we should be able to allow most of the Travellers to go back to their homes. I have to say, though, that this incident has done no good at all to our relationship with the Pavee community. Some of them have even got it into their heads that it was *us* who blew up Paddy Fearon – a controlled explosion to force open his caravan door that got out of control – even though two of our officers got killed.'

'What about witnesses? Did any of the Travellers see anybody acting suspicious around Fearon's caravan?'

Katie shook her head. 'No. But even if they had, they wouldn't tell us, would they? Travellers never rat to the law. I know it sounds racist, but I think Detective Dooley has a point. When he went there to set up that knackering deal with Fearon, he said that everybody on the whole site seemed to be acting suspicious. It's just the way that Travellers are. They don't trust anybody and nobody trusts them.'

'So what are you going to do now?'

'Have a cup of coffee and a cheese sandwich if the canteen have any left. Then I'm going up to the Bon Sauveur to see how the search is getting on – they should have the ground radar working by now. First of all, though, I want to see if Detective Sergeant Ni Nuallán has made any progress in locating the remaining four nuns from the Sacred Seven that Mother O'Dwyer told me about. That's if any of them are still alive. It'll save us all a fierce amount of work and worry if they've all passed away already.'

'Very good,' said Chief Superintendent MacCostagáin. He looked down at his desk with two fingertips pressed against his lips, as if he were having trouble remembering something. As Katie turned to leave, he said, 'You will be very careful, won't you? I mean, after what happened to Detective Horgan, and now this.'

'Of course,' she said, with half a smile. 'I'm always careful.'

He raised his eyes. She could tell that he didn't really want to say this, but if he didn't he would never forgive himself later. 'It's just that you're a very attractive woman, Katie, and we don't want a similar tragedy befalling you, do you know what I mean?'

'Thank you, sir,' said Katie, and left his office. Walking along the corridor towards her own office, though, her eyes were wide open and she could hardly believe what he had just said to her. *You're a very attractive woman?* Denis MacCostagáin had called her a very attractive woman? And what a moment to choose, when she and everybody else in the station was still deeply in shock.

Perhaps that was why he had chosen this moment, thought Katie. Perhaps he had believed that he couldn't shock her any more than she was shocked already.

She went into her office, hung up her coat, and immediately went across to her bathroom. She switched on the light, locked the door and leaned back against the wall, facing the mirror over the washbasin. Her stomach felt as hard as a medicine ball.

Please God, let everything be all right. Whatever trouble this child is going to cause me, please don't let any harm come to it.

She unfastened her holster and laid her revolver on top of the waste bin. Then she unzipped her skirt and tugged down her thick black tights and her thong. To her relief she could see that she had wet herself a little, probably when the bomb went off, but that was all. She stood there massaging her stomach, her eyes closed, and gradually her muscles began to relax.

When she came out of the bathroom, carrying her holstered gun in her hand, she found Detective Inspector O'Rourke waiting for her.

'Mother of God,' he said, shaking his head. 'The only lucky thing about it was that more of us weren't killed.'

Katie sat down at her desk. She held out her hands in front of her and they were trembling uncontrollably. 'Look at me!' she said. 'Still got the shakes! The worst thing about it, there was no warning at all. And it was obvious that Paddy Fearon wasn't expecting it. But whoever planted that device, I'm seriously wondering if they knew that we were coming for him.'

'Well, the media were tipped off, weren't they, so what are the chances that half of Cork knew about it, too? Next time we're planning on making an arrest perhaps we ought to cut out the middleman and announce it ourselves on Red FM.'

'There's no future in being bitter about it, Francis,' said Katie. 'We had the same problem when Bryan Molloy was in charge. The whole station was leaking highly classified information like a colander – mainly for Molloy's financial benefit. I'm not going to let that happen again and I'm not going to tolerate any more lives lost.'

Detective Inspector O'Rourke sat down opposite her. He watched her for a moment as she tried to steady her hands and then he said, 'When you're suggesting that the bombers might have known that we were coming to lift Fearon, and that was why they bombed him, I think you're thinking in the right general direction.'

'I'm convinced that they were specifically out to get him,' said Katie. 'I certainly don't believe that it was a racist attack against the Pavees in general.'

'I agree with you, ma'am. Sure, there's been bad blood for donkey's years between the Travellers and the residents of the Park Court estate overlooking the halting site, but I can't see any of those council tenants taking things that far. No – instead of asking ourselves who may have gained the most from Paddy Fearon being killed, I think we should be asking ourselves who would have lost the most if he *hadn't* been. I've known him by reputation for years and I can tell you that he was known for ratting on people if ever he found himself in an awkward situation, like. He was lucky he didn't get himself killed a few times before. Tómas Ó Conaill always swore that he'd a stick a chisel in him if he ever got the chance.'

'Like he did with his pregnant girlfriend?'

'Yes, not a pleasant feller at all, Ó Conaill. A total scumbag, in fact. He'd sell you the eye out of your own head and stab you if you couldn't pay for it.'

Katie said, 'I'm going to get myself a coffee. Do you want to come with me? I think that you and I share a very similar feeling about Paddy Fearon. Dooley feels the same, too. Once he found out that Dooley was the law, Fearon was a fool to himself to keep the money that he'd paid him. That meant we could arrest him and put some pressure on him and I'll bet you anything at all that whoever killed him didn't want him to talk to us.'

'About those racehorses thrown off the cliff, you mean?'

'What else? As far as we know, the only other shady dealings that Fearon was involved in were stripping copper wire from the railway and fencing stolen bicycles – hardly worth taking the risk of blowing him up for.'

They walked along the corridor towards the lifts. As they waited for one to come up from the ground floor, Katie said, 'Think about it, Francis. There's mega money in horse racing. In my opinion, it's become even more urgent for us to find out who those horses originally belonged to, and why they wanted to dispose of them, and why they chose Paddy Fearon to do it. I think he got seriously out of his depth.'

'You do realize this is all guesswork,' said Detective Inspector O'Rourke as they joined the queue at the canteen counter. 'It might not have been Paddy Fearon who threw them off that cliff at all, in which case we'll have to start looking for somebody who simply wanted to blow him up.'

'Like I say, that wouldn't really make sense,' said Katie. 'And if all they had wanted to do was kill him, they would simply have knocked on his door and shot him when he answered it. This was done by somebody who really wanted to make a point. Like, if you mess with me, this is what you get. Not just *pop*! you're dead – you get blown to kingdom come in a massive explosion, and two gardai get killed, too, even if that wasn't the intention.'

She carried their coffees over to a table by the window and then she said, 'Whoever we're looking for, Francis, they're not scared of anything. They're not scared of the Travellers and they're not scared of us. Blowing up Paddy Fearon's caravan and killing two of our officers was like putting two fingers up to the world.'

'That means that they must have one hell of a motive,' said Detective Inspector O'Rourke.

'Oh, yes,' said Katie. She was feeling much steadier now and she appreciated Detective Inspector O'Rourke's reassuring presence, but all the same she still wasn't far away from tears.

* * *

Katie had finished her coffee and was pushing back her chair when Detective Inspector O'Rourke said, 'Before you go, ma'am.'

'Yes, what is it?'

His expression was serious, so Katie slowly sat down again.

'That security meeting at Phoenix Park I went to, ma'am.'

'What about it?' she asked him. 'You're going to write me a report on it, aren't you? And you told them all about the new screening procedures we've set up at Ringaskiddy and the airport?'

'I did, of course. But I thought you ought to know that in the bar after the meeting I earwigged on a couple of conversations between some of the officers who were present. Naming no names, but if I say Limerick and Kilkenny I think you'll get the gist of who I'm talking about.'

'What were they saying?'

Detective Inspector O'Rourke pulled a face. 'I couldn't hear all of it, and because I'm stationed here in Cork now they were obviously being cautious about what they said. But Bryan Molloy has a fair amount of support from some of those fellows and I believe that you and I know why. They all had a good thing going back in the days when they called themselves the High Kings of Erin – all that dropping of charges and wiping clean the driving licences of the rich and famous. They were making some very comfortable extra income out of that, but you helped to put a stop to it. I don't think you have any notion how much they resent you, those stonecutters. Well, apart from the fact that you're a woman. They'd be happy to see you dead, and I'm not codding.'

Katie suddenly thought of the bullet coming through the windscreen of their car when she and Detective Horgan were driving away from Dromsligo. But then she thought, *No, it couldn't be, they wouldn't take a chance like that.* Surely it was enough for Molloy's old cronies that she was being investigated by the Garda Ombudsman.

'Thank you, Francis,' she told him, laying her hand on top of his. 'I appreciate your loyalty.'

He shrugged. 'I've always said it, ma'am. If we don't look after each other, nobody else is going to.'

* * *

Down in the squad room she met up with Detective Sergeant Ni Nuallán, who was still sitting at her desk trying to trace the four remaining sisters of the Sacred Seven.

The squad room was hushed, although phones were still ringing and detectives were still tapping away at their laptops. The shock of the Spring Lane bombing had affected everybody in the whole building and there was none of the usual laughing and banter.

Detective Sergeant Ni Nuallán looked up from her keyboard. 'This is fierce difficult,' she said. 'I've checked with the General Register Office in Roscommon and Sister Grainne McNevin died eight years ago, but unless somebody failed to register their deaths the other three are still with us.'

'Oh, okay,' said Katie. 'I don't mean to be callous, but I was rather hoping they would have peacefully passed away by now.'

'I thought I'd tracked one of them down, Sister Virginia O'Cleary. She was living with her younger sister in Rochestown but her younger sister died of the cancer and so she was moved to a rest home in Carrigaline. I've just tried to contact the rest home but it was closed two years ago and now it's somebody's private house and they don't have any idea what happened to any of the old folks who used to live there.'

'What about the others?'

'Sister Nessa Bolan left the convent fifteen years ago to work with the Bon Sauveurs in Malawi. They had set up a school for children blinded by Vitamin A deficiency or measles. However, the school closed after two years because of lack of funding and I can't find out what happened to Sister Nessa, whether she came back to Ireland or stayed in Africa. She didn't return to the convent here in Cork.

'Sister Aibrean Callery, she had to leave the congregation seven years ago when she developed kidney disease. She spent three months being treated at CUH but then she was discharged and

271

so far I can't find any record of where she went or who might have taken her.'

'All right. Well, keep trying,' said Katie. 'Let's hope that if we can't find them, our killers can't find them either.'

As she turned to go, Detective Sergeant Ni Nuallán said, 'Ma'am – I need to talk to you.'

'Yes, what is it? There's no problem, is there?'

'Well, yes and no. Maybe this isn't the right time.'

'Kyna, if something's bothering you, you should tell me about it,' said Katie. 'That's what I'm here for.'

Detective Sergeant Ni Nuallán raised her eyes to her and her lower lip protruded like a sad child. She looked so miserable that Katie went back across to her and laid a hand on her shoulder.

'*Kyna*, what is it? Tell me.'

'I'm thinking of applying for a transfer,' she said. 'Dublin, if there's any vacancies.'

'But why? Aren't you happy here? Don't tell me you're bored with living amongst us culchies?'

Detective Sergeant Ni Nuallán said, 'No, I love it here. But that's the trouble. I love it because of you.'

Katie took her hand away. 'Kyna,' she said.

'I know. It's insane. It's insane and it's impossible and there's no way that anything is ever going to happen between us. But I can't help it. I've tried to meet other women and stop thinking about you, but every day I come into the station and there you are and I'm in love with you and it *hurts*, and the only way I'm going to be able to stop it from hurting is if I apply for a transfer and move away and never see you again, ever.'

Detective Brennan was sitting on the opposite side of the squad room, laboriously typing with two fingers. He glanced up at Katie and Detective Sergeant Ni Nuallán, but he was too far away to hear what they were saying. Katie wished she could take Kyna in her arms and hold her close and kiss her and tell her how fond she was of her, and how much she would miss her if she left, but of course she couldn't.

'Let's talk about this later,' she said. 'Don't go rushing off before we've had a chance to discuss what your options are.'

'There are no options. Being in love is not an option. You've put a *geis* on me and there's nothing I can do about it.'

'I'll meet you after, anyway, Kyna. I don't want you being upset.'

She said nothing, but went back to her keyboard. Katie stayed beside her for a few moments and then said, 'Smile, would you, just for me?'

Detective Sergeant Ni Nuallán looked up and smiled, although her eyes were filled with tears.

* * *

By the time Katie drove up to the Bon Sauveur Convent, the sun had gone down behind the three spires of Saint Finbarr's Cathedral in the centre of the city and it was growing grainy and dark.

When she parked, however, a dazzling array of halogen lamps were shining behind the convent chapel and lighting up the garden as if it were a sports stadium, and she could hear the hum of generators and the clanking of shovels. The car park was crowded with cars and vans from the Technical Bureau and RMR Engineering.

She walked around into the garden and found Eithne O'Neill talking to two men in yellow high-visibility jackets and hard hats. They were standing around a wide machine on wheels that resembled a lawnmower without any blades. Eithne herself was wearing a pale-blue Tyvek suit that looked as if belonged to somebody much bigger than her, and her hair was sticking up like a fledgling that had fallen out of its nest.

'Oh, good, Detective Superintendent Maguire,' she said. 'This is Stephen Murtry, the technical director of RMR, and this is his ground-radar expert, Dermot Brooke. They're showing me what they've discovered under the ground so far.'

Both men shook hands with Katie. Stephen Murtry had a trim salt-and-pepper beard and horn-rimmed spectacles, and could almost have been a menswear model for the older man, while

Dermot Brooke was young and overweight with florid cheeks.

'It seems to me that you have something of a delicate situation here, Detective Superintendent,' said Stephen, looking around. 'Excavating a convent garden, with the nuns still in residence. At least in Galway the nuns had already sold their building and gone.'

'Before they left, though, didn't they, the nuns in Galway made sure that they exhumed their dear sisters who had been buried there?' put in Eithne. 'They gave them a fine reburial in County Mayo, with a blessing from the parish priest and all, and a memorial stone with all their names on it. Not like the bodies of all the infants they left behind, thrown into a hole like so much rubbish.'

'Sorry – hold on for a moment, could you?' said Stephen. 'We need to do some adjustments if we're going to start scanning deeper.'

He and Dermot bent over their ground-radar machine to fine-tune its frequency settings. As they did so, Katie frowned at Eithne and lifted her fingertip to her lips. She agreed with her absolutely, but however strongly they felt about the cases they were investigating, it was not the place of technical experts or rank and file gardaí to express their opinions publicly.

Stephen turned back to Katie and said, 'So far we've covered only the north-west side of the lawn here, but we've already found two anomalies under the ground where it looks as if the soil has been disturbed by human activity. Inside both of these anomalies we've identified a number of objects of higher density than the surrounding soil, so I'm recommending that you bring in another contractor to dig some exploratory slit trenches.'

'How deep are these objects buried?' asked Katie.

'One of the anomalies is very deep indeed and so far we've only managed to scan the top of it. I mean, what we have here is one of the latest ground-radar machines, the RIS-K2. It costs the thick end of a hundred thousand euros and it can detect underground anomalies up to three metres deep. But this anomaly goes a whole lot deeper than that and it's been partially covered, too, maybe with sheets of plywood. In my opinion, whoever dug it was trying to conceal the objects they were burying for good and all.'

'But you have no way of telling for sure if they're bones?'

'Not until we dig them up and see them with our own eyes. That's the only way to tell for certain.'

'I'll see that we bring in somebody to start trench digging first thing tomorrow morning,' said Katie. 'What area will you be scanning next?'

'Underneath that vegetable bed next. You've already discovered several bones there, close to the surface, so I should imagine that the bodies there weren't buried nearly so deep.'

Dermot switched the ground-radar machine on again and began slowly to roll it across the grass. Katie watched him at work for a few moments and then she said to Eithne, 'How's it going with the septic tank? How many have you managed to fish out so far?'

'Come and see,' said Eithne. Then, as they walked across the lawn, she said, 'That bombing today at Spring Lane, that was terrible. You were there, weren't you? Holy Mary. Are you all right? You weren't hurt at all, were you?'

'I'm okay, but I'm still slightly deaf,' said Katie. 'Bill Phinner hasn't left the halting site yet, has he?'

'No. As a matter of fact, he called me only about five minutes ago. It's probably going to take them most of tomorrow before they've finished combing the ground around the caravan. Then they're going to tow it in to Anglesea Street examine it. He says he has a strong suspicion about who built the device, but he's not one hundred per cent sure yet.'

'Oh, Bill's very good at that,' said Katie. 'He only has to smell the residue from an IED and he can tell who put it together. He's better than a sniffer dog when it comes to Semtex. Anyway – these bones.'

Since her last visit to the convent garden the brightly lit blue tent had been extended towards the eastern wall and more groundsheets laid out. She stopped at the entrance to the tent and she could hardly believe what was laid out in front of her.

There were now eight rows of tiny skeletons arranged on the groundsheets, close together, and in each row there must have been more than thirty.

'We've counted two hundred and seventy so far,' said Eithne, snapping off her black forensic glove so that she could push her hair out of her eyes. 'Of course, we can't be sure that all the individual bones belong to the correct skeletons, but we're being very careful to photograph them in situ before we move them. We've measured every bone, too, and that's given us quite an accurate idea of how old they were, taking their poor diet into account.'

'So what ages were most of them, when they died?' asked Katie. She couldn't help thinking of the small white casket that her late husband Paul had carried by himself into the church, with little Seamus inside it, in his best blue romper suit.

Eithne said, 'This is only the roughest of estimates, but so far we think that about twenty-five were stillborn, while the majority of them were eighteen months to two and a half years old. Some are obviously much older, though. You see that skeleton on the end of the second row there? That child was at least seven when she died, although her growth was well below average for a girl of her age, almost certainly because her diet was badly lacking.'

'You know it was a girl?'

Eithne nodded. 'It's her teeth that give her away. Up until the age of five or six, there's no difference between the dental development of boys and girls. After the age of six, girls start to outstrip boys, particularly in the growth of their mandibular teeth.'

Katie walked over and crouched down beside the girl's skeleton.

'You sad, hard-done-by little girl,' she said. 'I wonder what your name was.'

Two middle-aged reservists in blue anoraks came waddling up to Eithne and said, 'We've finished sifting through that end of the flower bed now. We've found no more bones, like, but Sergeant O'Farrell says he wants us back tomorrow morning.'

'Okay, grand, thanks. I'll see you tomorrow so,' Eithne told them.

Katie stood up and together she and Eithne left the tent. Stephen and Dermot were still plodding slowly up and down the lawn with their ground-radar machine, occasionally stopping to frown at the screen.

'By the way,' said Katie. 'I paid a visit to the Begleys regarding Roisin's suicide note.'

'And?'

'After a whole lot of huffing and puffing, Jim Begley finally admitted to me that he had written it himself.'

'*Serious*? He actually admitted it?'

'He didn't have much choice, did he? When Roisin went missing there was nobody else in the house, only the Begleys. He said that he had written it so that it would look as if Roisin was penitent for working for Cork Fantasy Girls and hadn't wanted to shame her family any further.'

'That's fantastic,' said Eithne. 'I mean, it's tragic, but it's fantastic. But it doesn't help to explain how she died, does it? It makes it more of a mystery than ever.'

'I asked Jim Begley outright if he'd drowned her. He gave out with a whole lot more bluster, but he wouldn't give me a straight answer. I told him that I'd be consulting Detective Dooley and that we'd almost certainly be wanting to question him further.'

'My God. Do you think he *did* drown her?'

Katie looked back at the children's skeletons lying on the groundsheets. As she did so, one of the reservists untied the tent flap and hid them from view, and she was glad of that. They had been given little enough respect when they were alive.

'Oh, I think he's quite capable of it,' she said. 'He's like thorny wire and he's very protective of his family's good name. In other words, he can't tolerate people looking down their noses at the Begleys during Mass because their daughter's a slapper.'

'But to actually drown her? What kind of a father would do that to his daughter, even if she was a bit of a slut?'

'I don't know, Eithne, to tell you the truth. I stopped speculating about people's motivations a long time ago, especially when it comes to religion.'

As if to emphasize her point, Mother O'Dwyer appeared around the side of the chapel and stopped and stared at her. Her eyes were bright and hard, as if two steel nails had been hammered into her face. Katie considered walking over to tell her the latest count of infants' skeletons they had lifted out of the septic tank, but she decided that she would rather keep her in suspense until they had all been recovered. Unless, of course, she knew already how many there were.

Thirty-five

Riona was riding Saint Sparkle around and around the back field when Andy Flanagan came driving into the stud farm in his dusty green Range Rover. Dermot was leaning on the fence watching Riona and smoking a cigarette and Andy stopped beside him and climbed out.

Riona rode over to them and dismounted. She handed the reins to Dermot and said, 'Take him back to his stall for me, would you, Dermot? The vet will be here soon, anyway.'

'He's looking in real fine fettle,' said Dermot. Then, turning to Andy, 'What's the craic, boy? Keeping you busy are they, all those adulterish husbands?'

'Oh, it's the wives, they're the worst,' grinned Andy. 'They're all doing the messages online these days and having the delivery fellows from Tesco and SuperValu around when their husbands are at work. It's like the milkmen used to be in the old days. Tesco Direct? Tesco Erect, more like!'

It was a grey, overcast morning and the clouds were moving only slowly, although there was enough of a chilly breeze for the lime trees to be whispering to each other. Dermot smacked Saint Sparkle affectionately on his shiny brown flank and then led him away. Andy took out a packet of cigarettes himself and offered them to Riona, but she shook her head.

'Handsome-looking horse,' he said, flicking his lighter three or four times before he got a flame. 'He didn't do too well on Sunday, though, did he?'

'You didn't bet on him, did you?'

Andy blew out smoke and shook his head. 'I only bet when it's a fix and I'm in on it. Since you declined to tell me where he was going to finish, like, or if he was going to finish at all, which as it turned out he didn't, I wisely decided to keep my money in my wallet.'

'He wasn't mentally hyped up for it, that's all,' said Riona. 'He's physically strong, Sparkle, but he's a pessimist. He's like a lot of people . . . if he realizes that he's not going to make it past the post first, he gives up. But he's entered into the BoyleSports Tied Cottage Race Day at Punchestown the Sunday after next and I can tell you for sure that he'll run away with that one.'

'He'll be up against Jezki, though, won't he, and Tiger Roll? What's his price?'

'Paddy Power are giving an early bird of tens.'

'But you think he's going to win it easy?'

'God willing, yes.'

Andy looked at her with his eyes narrowed so suspiciously that he appeared to have no eyes at all. He was a huge man, at least six foot four inches, with a head that looked too big for his brown trilby hat. His cheeks were blotchy and embroidered with fine crimson veins, his teeth were all brown and crowded, and his nose was broken. He wore a flappy white trench coat and raspberry-coloured corduroy trousers that didn't quite reach his ankles. If he were a building on Adelaide Street he would be well past derelict and ready for demolition.

'You said that you'd located Sister Aibrean Callery,' said Riona.

'I have, yes. It wasn't easy, I can tell you, but I've found her all right. She's living with her eldest granddaughter in Waterfall Road, Curraheen. Up until last February she was being looked after in the Marymount Hospice, but her granddaughter's husband died of a haemorrhage about a year ago and so she offered to take her in, for the company, like.'

'Well, that was good work, Andy,' said Riona. 'Can I ask how you found her, or is that one of your trade secrets?'

'No, it's no secret. It's knowing the right people, that's all. I talked to Canon O'Flynn, who used to hold Mass at the Holy Family Church on Military Hill, and he knew all of the penguins up at the Bon Sauveur. He visited Sister Aibrean when she was in hospital with her kidneys and he kept in touch with her afterwards, too. The one critical thing he told me about Sister Aibrean was that she always insisted on wearing the full penguin outfit, even after she left the convent.

'One of the porters I know at the Wilton Hilton tipped me off that after she was discharged from there she was sent to the Marymount. The trouble was, the Marymount refused to tell me where she had gone to after that. But I reckoned that if she was still wearing the full penguin outfit, like, she must either be sewing it herself, like a lot of the nuns do, or else she was buying it from one of the very few places that still supply religious clothing. Since she's so old, and she has the arthritis, I doubted that she was doing her own sewing, so I checked with some of the suppliers of holy vestments.

'You wouldn't believe it. Most church stuff is sold online these days – copes, albs, candles – even the fecking sacramental wafers. All on the Internet. I'm surprised they don't supply choirboys, too, with their bums ready-buttered. But after I'd tried ars.sacra. com and churchsupplies.ie, I got third time lucky with Mary Fitzpatrick who runs her own vestment business in Carrigaline, called GloryBe.com. She'd been making habits for Sister Aibrean for years, and when I explained to her with tears in my eyes that I was Sister Aibrean's long-lost cousin Conor from Australia, she told me at once where she lived.'

'And you've checked that she's actually there?'

Andy produced his iPhone from out of his raincoat pocket, jabbed at it with a dirty fingernail, and then passed it over. Riona could see a white-painted detached house with a hedge outside and a tall elderly woman in a nun's habit standing in the open doorway, her face as pale as a plateful of porridge. She had one hand lifted as if she were waving somebody goodbye.

'I took that myself this morning,' said Andy. 'Right near the corner of Waterfall Road and Bandon Road.'

'And you're certain that's her?'

'I talked to the girl behind the counter at Mac's Cafe in Bishopstown Road. She knows her. She's in there as soon as they open every morning. Tea, no milk, no sugar, and two plain oat biscuits.'

'That's good work, Andy. How are the other two coming along? Sister Virginia and Sister Nessa?'

'I think I have a break on Sister Virginia. The other one's a little more knotty, like. But don't worry. I'll track them down, the both of them. They don't call me Find 'Em Flanagan for nothing.'

'Who doesn't?'

'Well, nobody. I just made that up. But it sounds good, what do you think?'

Riona looked totally unamused. For some reason Andy found himself staring at the pink face powder that clung to the very fine hairs on her upper lip. Perhaps he didn't have the nerve to look her straight in the eyes. Although he would have found it hard to explain why, she was one of the most frightening people that he had ever met, and that was including a Slovakian drug-dealer called Vicki who had once threatened to cut his mebs off with serrated kitchen scissors.

'Come into the house and I'll pay you for finding Sister Aibrean,' said Riona. 'You do understand, don't you, that the second that money passes from my hands into yours, you have never heard of anybody called Sister Aibrean and nobody has ever asked you to find anybody of that name and you have never been looking for her?'

'Mother of God, Riona. For what you're paying me, I'd be happy to forget my own name, let alone hers.'

'I wanted to make that crystal-clear, that's all,' said Riona. 'I wouldn't like you to end up as the victim of a misunderstanding.'

Andy left his Range Rover where it was and followed Riona across the stable yard and into the house. As they approached the back door he didn't know what to do with his cigarette, so he nipped it out between finger and thumb and tucked it behind his left ear.

Thirty-six

Almost as soon as she had returned to the station and hung up her coat, Katie's phone rang. It was Garret MacTeague, from Scully & MacTeague, who were Jim Begley's solicitors. He spoke with a thick lisp, almost as if he were half langered, but Katie had faced him many times in the district court and she knew that he always sounded like that, and that he was a very formidable lawyer.

'My client informs me that you may want to interview him regarding the tragic death of his daughter.'

'That's correct, yes. Has he told you about Roisin's suicide note?'

'He's admitted that he wrote it himself, if that's what you're referring to. I know you have the necessary evidence so there's no point in us beating about the bush and trying to make out that he didn't. However, he totally denies any responsibility for her drowning.'

Katie sat down and slowly rubbed her stomach. She had been suffering from indigestion ever since she had left the Bon Sauveur Convent. Not only that, she had the beginnings of a headache. Her normal painkillers contained caffeine as well as paracetamol and she knew that she shouldn't be taking those now that she was pregnant.

'Why don't you bring your client into the station about eleven tomorrow morning?' she suggested. 'I'm very tied up at the moment, what with the Spring Lane bombing and all.'

'Of course, yes,' said Garret MacTeague. 'You have my firm's sincerest condolences for that. I'll contact my client, but I don't think there'll be any problem with him coming in tomorrow. He's very anxious to get this matter resolved as soon as possible. So is *Mrs* Begley, as I'm sure you can imagine.'

Katie hung up and then rang for Detective Dooley, who had also returned to the station only a few minutes before. When he came up to her office he looked almost as if he had been in a brawl. His brushed-up Jedward hairstyle was windswept and his jacket collar half turned up at the back.

'State of you la,' she said, and she couldn't help smiling. 'How's it going up at Spring Lane?'

'Oh, slow – painful slow. The technical experts are still picking up all of the doonchie little bits of human flesh and aluminium with tweezers. They have the patience of Job, those people, I tell you. But me and Brennan have finished interviewing all of the residents, which is why I've come back. We talked to every one of them, even the kids.'

'So what did they have to say for themselves, the residents?'

'They're Travellers, what do you think? The politest response I got out of them was, "Go wash the back of your bollocks," if you'll excuse my language, and that was from a little girl of six.'

Katie raised her eyebrows. 'Oh well. Maybe Inspector O'Rourke will have more luck. He has very good connections with the Pavees. Meanwhile, I've just had Jim Begley's solicitor on the phone. Jim Begley's coming in to the station tomorrow morning to answer questions about Roisin's drowning.'

'He's coming in voluntarily, like?'

'Yes. Voluntarily. At eleven. I want you there, too, please.'

'If he's coming in voluntarily he must be feeling confident that we can't stick it on him. He totally denied that it was him who drowned Roisin, didn't he, when you went round to see him? If he goes on denying it, it's going to be fierce problematical for us to prove it.'

'He's very religious, so maybe his conscience will get the better of him,' said Katie. 'That's always supposing that he really *did* do it.'

'We don't have any forensics, that's the trouble,' said Detective Dooley. 'There was no bruising on her to speak of, and none of her fingernails were broken or had skin under them, like if she'd been fighting somebody off. All right, Jim Begley might have confessed that he forged her suicide note, but what's that proof of? Only proof that he was ashamed of her, nothing else.'

'It goes to motive, if nothing else,' said Katie. 'But I've been thinking what evidence we might be able to find. What about her phone?'

'Well, yes, her phone might have been helpful, but we couldn't find it. It wasn't in her bedroom or anywhere else in the rest of the house. We tried tracking it, but we couldn't get a GPS signal. In the end we had to assume that she'd had it with her when she went into the river and that it wasn't waterproof – and if that was the case, the chances of locating it are not much better than zero. We'd have had to call in the navy divers to look for it – and even then . . .'

'Didn't you find out from her parents what network she was connected to? They could provide you with all of her recent texts and tweets and emails and whatever.'

Detective Dooley looked flustered. 'I was intending to, of course, but at the time we thought the suicide note was genuine so there didn't seem to be too much urgency. I'm sorry. What with this Spring Lane bombing and all, it kind of slipped down the list of priorities.'

'It's all right, Robert,' said Katie. 'I've piled a heap of work on you lately, I know that, but with all the cutbacks we've been suffering lately I haven't had much choice. But let's think about it. Roisin Begley was a teenage girl, and how do teenage girls share all their worries these days? If she was stressed or thinking about taking her own life, it's highly probable that she would have used her phone to tell her friends how bad she was feeling.'

'You're right, of course,' said Detective Dooley. ' I'll get on to it immediately.'

Katie looked up at him. His hair was sticking up even more than it had before, and he looked so young and anxious that it was hard for her to think of him as an experienced detective. 'Have you had a break today?'

'Not yet.'

'Then go and have a break now and something to eat and then get on to Roisin's phone messages after. So long as I can see them before her father comes in to the station tomorrow morning.'

'Yes, ma'am. Thanks a million.'

* * *

When she arrived home that evening the living-room curtains were still open and when she climbed out of her car she could see John bent over the coffee table, tapping away at his laptop.

He didn't look up when she came into the room, but raised one hand to greet her. 'Be with you in a second, sweetheart.'

The house smelled of bolognese sauce, but it also still smelled faintly of acrylic paint. Katie leaned over him and kissed the back of John's neck. 'You're working late.'

'In Montreal, it's only three-twenty in the afternoon,' he told her. 'I'm just closing a deal on resveratrol tablets. Sorry, but it's the only way I'm ever going to become a billionaire.'

He tapped the keyboard with a flourish and then he said, 'There, that's it, order complete. I got a fantastic discount, too.'

Katie peered at the screen. 'Resveratrol, never heard of it. What's it for? Shyness?'

'No, no. It gives you all of the life-enhancing benefits of red wine without the deathly after-effects of a hangover. Maybe you should try some now you've given up drinking. I'm really impressed, the way you've stuck to it. The last time I went on the wagon I think I lasted five hours before I tumbled off again.'

'I'm up the walls at the station these days, darling,' said Katie. 'I couldn't possibly cope if I went into work every day feeling like thirteen tinkers after a wedding. I know, I know – politically incorrect, but I'm too tired to be PC.'

She nodded towards the painting on the sideboard, facing the wall. 'You managed to do some more painting today, then?'

'Just an hour or so, but it's coming on. Maybe you can pose for me again after supper.'

'I don't know. I'm pretty much beat out.'

'You don't have to do anything. Just sit there looking gorgeous.'

'We'll see. I don't *feel* gorgeous, believe me. I'll probably feel better once I've had something to eat. When are you going to show it to me?'

'Not yet,' said John, closing his laptop. 'Not until it looks so much like you that I can't tell for certain which is which.'

'As long as you don't try to take it to bed, instead of me.'

Barney had been standing by the kitchen door, sniffing and slowly wagging his tail. Suddenly he let out a sharp bark, and then another, and scuffled his paws on the carpet.

'What's the matter, Barns?' Katie asked him. She turned towards the living-room window, where she could see herself reflected in the darkness outside. 'Is there somebody there? It'll only be old Pauly from the shop, taking his dogs for a dander.'

She walked over to the window and took hold of the curtain cord. 'I can't see anybody out there, Barns. Maybe it's next door's cat.'

She tugged the cord and the curtains started to jerk across the window, but as they did so there was a splintering crack. The right-hand curtain billowed inwards as if it had been violently poked from behind with a walking stick, and then fell back again. A Celtic Weave plate on the sideboard was smashed apart and Katie could see a black hole in the wall right behind it.

'*Get down!*' she shouted at John, breathless, almost screaming.

John hesitated and she threw herself across the room, grabbed his red plaid shirt and pulled him down behind the couch. He rolled over and stared at her, wide-eyed.

'What the hell is that? Is somebody shooting at us?'

'Stay there,' Katie told him. She lifted herself up on to her hands and knees and crawled over to the door. Once she was out in the hallway she stood up and reached around for the living room light switch, clicking it off. Then, when the living room was in darkness, she hurried along to the nursery and retrieved her revolver from the chest of drawers.

'Katie? What do you want me to do?' John called out.

'Call 112. Tell them where we are and who I am, and tell them that we're being shot at from somewhere outside the front of the house. Tell them to send the Regional Support Unit.'

'The what? The Regional Support Unit? Okay, I'm doing it.'

Katie went back into the hallway, holding her revolver raised in both hands, with the hammer cocked. Keeping her back close to the wall, she went up to the front door, reached across and slid off the safety chain. Then, dodging quickly across to the other side of the hallway, she opened the door two or three inches and peered out into the night. The temperature was three or four degrees above freezing, but there was a cold wind blowing inshore from the harbour, which made her shiver.

She could hear John talking to the emergency services, and then he said, 'Katie! *Katie*! You're not going outside, are you?'

Katie said, '*Ssh*! I'm just trying to see if there's anybody here!'

But there was nobody standing in the driveway in the front of the house and as far as she could tell there was nobody crouching behind their cars. The hedge on the right-hand side cast an inky triangular shadow, but she couldn't see anybody hiding there, either.

She opened the door wider, although she still kept herself close to the frame with her revolver held up high in front of her. She was about to take a step outside when she heard the roar of a car engine starting up and the screech of a fan belt, and a silver Mercedes appeared from behind the next-door hedge and sped away northwards. It happened so fast that Katie couldn't see its registration plate or what model of Mercedes it was. She couldn't even be sure if it was a Mercedes at all and not an Audi. After a few moments she smelled scorched rubber in the wind and half-burned diesel.

John came to the door and laid his hand on her shoulder.

'Was that them?' he asked.

Katie waited for a moment and then she said, 'I should think so. Nobody else round here drives like that. Holy Mary, I'm shaking like a leaf.'

'Do you want to speak to the call-handler? She said they're sending armed back-up right away. "Armed back-up" – Listen to me! I sound like a character in a crime film.'

'Well, darling, you are,' said Katie. Her heart was thumping so hard that she was sure that John could actually hear it. She waited a few moments longer and then she closed the door and slid on the safety chain. 'It's a miracle that neither of us got killed.'

She went through to the kitchen, which was dimly illuminated by the street light on the corner. Even though she was fairly sure that the shooter had driven off in that Mercedes and wouldn't be coming back, she was going to keep the house in darkness until the RSU arrived. It was quite possible that whoever had taken a shot at her had arranged for a car to make a show of driving away but had left a second gunman behind so that he could pick her off as soon as she switched on the lights and appeared in one of the windows.

John took her in his arms and held her close and kissed her hair. 'I hate to say this,' he said. 'I'm not a cop, but it does seem to me that somebody is seriously out to get you.'

'I don't think you have to be a cop to work that out,' said Katie. 'That car looked very much like the same one that Horgan was shot from over in Dromsligo.'

'I thought you'd found that one, all burned out.'

'We found a car that answered its description, all burned out, but there was nothing in it to prove that it was actually the same one.'

'You need to move away from here for a while, sweetheart, at least until you find out who's taking pot-shots at you. Can you do that? You have some safe houses, don't you, for witness protection, that kind of thing?'

'No, I'm not moving,' said Katie. 'If I allowed myself to be frightened out of my house every time some scumbag wanted to see me dead, I wouldn't be living here at all. I'll arrange to have a couple of officers parked outside for a few days. It'll be more cost-effective than moving, and besides I'm thinking of *your* security, too.'

John kissed her again and stroked her back. 'I love you, Detective Superintendent Maguire. If I lost you, I don't know what the hell I'd do.'

* * *

It was over twenty-five minutes before two blue and yellow Volvo station wagons arrived outside, their blue lights flashing and GARDA ARMED SUPPORT UNIT scrolling across their roof racks.

John looked cautiously out of the living-room window and said, 'The cavalry's here. Didn't exactly hurry, did they?'

'That's budget cuts for you,' said Katie. Cobh Garda station was less than two kilometres away from Carrig View, but financial restrictions had recently forced its closure and now Cobh and Carrigtwohill were served from Midleton, eighteen kilometres away to the north-east.

Six armed gardaí in dark-blue uniforms and body armour scrambled out of the Volvos and immediately fanned out around Katie's front garden. Katie opened the front door for them and two officers came inside – a sergeant with a battered face like a former boxer and a woman garda with choppy brown hair and heavy eyebrows. They were both weighted down with Glock pistols and ammunition pouches and tasers and handcuffs and two encrypted radios each, and they jingled and clanked as they walked.

'What's the story?' said the sergeant. 'Somebody's taken a shot at you, is that it?'

'About half an hour ago,' Katie told them. She took them into the living room and showed them where the bullet had pierced the window and buried itself in the wall.

The sergeant crouched down, so that his eye-line matched the bullet's trajectory and he could make a rough calculation of where the shooter had been standing when he fired. 'Right next to your front gatepost, I'd say. Okay. We'll make a thorough search of the area, of course, but what? You think he's well away, do you?'

'A car went speeding off like a bat out of hell as soon as I opened the front door,' said Katie. 'It was silvery-coloured, a Mercedes maybe, but it could have been an Audi or a BMW. It went that way, north, probably heading for the N25. I've alerted Traffic to look out for it, but I can't say that I'm very optimistic.'

'At least you weren't hit, ma'am, and that's a blessing,' said the woman garda.

'Yes, thank God,' said the sergeant. 'And there's no further call for you to worry about your security, not tonight. We won't be leaving until we're totally satisfied that there's no other potential offenders in the locality who might be a threat to you. Even so, I'll be posting two armed officers outside until we can relieve them in the morning.'

Another RSU garda appeared in the porch, holding a Heckler & Koch sub-machine gun at a slant. 'Technical Bureau's here, ma'am. And three patrol cars. And a vanload of reservists.'

'Jesus, when one of your own gets threatened you people really take it serious, don't you?' said John. Outside, on the pavement, floodlights were being erected and the front of Katie's house was being cordoned off with crime-scene tapes.

The RSU sergeant looked at John and it was obvious from the twitch under his left eye that he found that remark deeply unamusing. 'We take it serious when *anybody* gets threatened, sir. That's our job.'

Five reservists spent over two hours on their hands and knees on the pavement searching for a spent cartridge case, although they couldn't find one. Meanwhile, the technicians took photographs of the tyre tracks that had been left by the silver saloon and photographs of the bullet holes in Katie's living-room window and curtain, and the hole in the wall opposite.

When Katie went back into the living room she found that Eithne was there, her blonde hair covered by a black woolly bobble-hat, measuring the room with a laser.

'Don't mind if I move this out of the way, ma'am?' she said, pointing to the painting on the easel, which was still facing the wall.

Katie shrugged. 'Yes, go ahead, if you have to.'

Eithne picked it up and turned it around. John had finished painting Katie's face and hair, and now he had painted her breasts as well and part of her left arm. Eithne stared at it in embarrassment.

'Oh, I'm sorry, ma'am,' she said. 'I didn't realize—'

'That's all right,' Katie told her. 'My partner's a very good artist, so how could I refuse?'

Denis McBride, the ballistics expert, had just walked into the living room and he caught sight of the painting, too. He blinked and took off his owlish glasses and furiously started to polish them with the end of his tie.

Katie took the easel from Eithne and set it down on the small occasional table in the corner, facing the wall again. Eithne said, 'Fair play to you, ma'am, it's beautiful. He's really done you justice.'

'Well, justice, that's what we're all here for, isn't it?' said Katie. To her surprise, she didn't feel at all disconcerted about Eithne or Denis seeing the painting. In fact, in a strange way, she felt proud of herself. She remembered from carrying Seamus how different her attitude had been about her body – how womanly she had felt, but not at all shy about showing herself. Any man could find her arousing, but he couldn't make her pregnant.

Denis opened up his metal box of tools and started to examine the bullet hole in the wall with a magnifying-glass. Katie went through to the kitchen. Fortunately, John had been in here when Eithne had turned the painting around, talking about hurling to two of the gardaí.

'Anyone for coffee?' she asked. 'I think we can all forget about sleeping tonight.'

She made four mugs of instant coffee and a glass of warm milk for herself, and then she sat down at the kitchen table, although she didn't join in the men's conversation about Pa Cronin and the Bishopstown hurling team and how well they expected to score this season. Being shot at in her own home had badly disturbed her. She had been threatened so many times, ever since she was a young garda on traffic duty and crowd control at GAA matches. One drug-dealer had even screamed in open court that he would give her a blood eagle, which meant breaking her ribs at her spine and pulling her lungs out of her back. But this sniping felt very different and very much more personal, as if somebody was trying to kill her because of who she was, not simply because she represented the law.

After about twenty minutes, Denis came in, holding up a bullet in a pair of forensic tweezers.

'Well?' asked Katie.

'Same type of bullet that was used to shoot Detective Horgan,' he said. '7.62 × 54 millimetre R. Of course, I'll have to take it back to the lab and compare the striations, and as you're aware there's anything up to a ten per cent error factor, but considering both bullets were fired in your direction, it wouldn't surprise me at all if they came from the same weapon.'

'What did I say?' put in John. 'It really looks like somebody's out to get you.'

'Yes, it does,' said Katie. Barney was standing close to her, looking as desperately worried as only Irish setters can do. She patted him on the head and said, 'I'll just have to make sure that I get them first.'

Thirty-seven

Sister Aibrean always woke early, before it was light. This morning she was woken even earlier than usual by the rumbling of a thunderstorm over Ballyburden to the south-west and the flashing of lightning behind her thin, rose-patterned curtains.

She switched on her bedside lamp and climbed out of bed. It was 6.16 a.m. As she did so, it started to hammer down with rain, almost ridiculously hard, drumming on the roof and bouncing off the window sill. She went over to the window and looked out and she could see that the gutters along Waterfall Road were already overflowing. She stood there for a while and lightning flickered again. For some reason she felt it was an omen that something terrible was going to happen to her today, although she couldn't imagine what. All she was planning to do was help with the jumble sale at the Church of the Real Presence on Curraheen Road.

She let the curtain fall back and picked up the triangular cream-coloured scarf that was folded on the seat of her armchair and covered her head with it. She eased herself carefully down on to her knees on the thin maroon mat beside her bed, clasping her hands together and raising her eyes.

On the wall beside her bed there was a small shelf with a gilded icon of Saint Eustace on it. He was mounted on a grey horse with his red cloak flowing behind him, and surrounded by stags. On either side of the icon stood two plaster figurines, one of Jesus with his arms outstretched and one of Mary with the Infant Jesus in her arms.

Sister Aibrean whispered her usual morning prayer and then a novena to Saint Eustace.

'Almighty and eternal God! With lively faith and reverently worshipping Thy divine Majesty, I prostrate myself before Thee and invoke Thy supreme bounty and mercy. Illumine the darkness of my soul with a ray of Thy heavenly light and inflame my heart with the fire of Thy divine love, that I may contemplate the great virtues and merits of Saint Eustace in whose honour I make this novena, and following his example imitate, like him, the life of Thy divine Son.'

After five minutes of meditation she climbed stiffly to her feet again, opened her bedroom door and tiptoed to the bathroom, so that she wouldn't disturb her granddaughter Fianna and her husband Paul. She wouldn't flush the toilet until Fianna and Paul woke up, because the cistern made so much noise.

Once she had dressed in her nun's vestments, she crept downstairs. She could see through the kitchen window that the rain was still lashing outside and so she put on her hooded black raincoat and sat on the stairs to pull on her black rubber rushers. Then she let herself out of the front door, closing it very quietly behind her, and started to walk up Waterfall Road. She didn't take an umbrella. She liked to look up to the clouds so that God's raindrops trickled down her cheeks, like the tears of those who had cried when Christ was crucified and when Saint Eustace and his family were so cruelly martyred.

The worst of the storm gradually passed over and the thunder made a crumbly sound as the dark grey clouds rolled away over Glanmire. Even though it was growing lighter the rain persisted, steady and soaking, and Sister Aibrean guessed that it was in for the day. She walked as far as Bishopstown Road and went into Mac's Cafe, with its green-painted frontage and steamy windows. As usual at this time of the morning, there were only three or four customers sitting in there, a postman and two men in high-visibility jackets with Ervia printed on the back, which was the new name for Bord Gáis.

As she crossed over to her usual table, though, she saw that a squat, bald man in a shiny grey puffer jacket was sitting half hidden in the alcove next to the counter, underneath a photo-mural of Blackrock Castle on a day just as grey and wet as today. To Sister Aibrean, he looked like the hideous hungry troll who had been waiting under the bridge for the Billy Goats Gruff to come trip-trapping over. He grinned at her and winked as she took off her raincoat and she gave him a weak, distracted smile in return, feeling ashamed of herself for having had such an uncharitable thought about him. She would apologize later to Saint Eustace.

She sat down by the window and wiped the steam off it with her sleeve so that she could see out. Anna, the plump, ginger-haired waitress, came over and said, 'Usual cup of tea is it, Sister? I have some of them Boland's jam mallows in this morning if you'd care for a change. They're fan*tas*tic! I'm desperate to sell them before I eat them all myself.'

'We can only get to heaven by way of self-denial,' said Sister Aibrean. 'I'll just have my two plain oat biscuits, thank you.'

'Well, please yourself, but I don't think the Lord would exactly throw a sevener if you ate a couple of jam mallows, do you know what I mean? There's nothing about eating jam mallows in the Bible.'

'There's nothing about running people over in motor cars, either,' Sister Aibrean replied. 'That doesn't mean to say that we have God's permission to do it.'

Anna shrugged and went off to fetch Sister Aibrean's tea. As soon as she did so, the troll-like man stood up from his table and came walking, bandy-legged, across the cafe. Sister Aibrean glanced up at him and tried not to appear alarmed. He looked even more troll-like now that he was closer, with two silver earrings in his ears. He had a smell about him, too, of horses and balsamic horse liniment and stale cigarettes and body odour.

'Buy you a cup of tea, Sister?' he asked.

'That's very charitable of you,' said Sister Aibrean. 'However, there's really no need.'

'Don't mind if I join you, though?'

'Forgive me, won't you, but I usually use my time here to meditate.'

'You don't mind if I join you while you meditate, though?'

'I won't be very good company.'

The troll-like man grinned again and scraped out one of the chairs on the opposite side of the table. 'I don't mind that, like. I promise I won't interrupt you. I'll be silent as the gravy. Listen, all I want is to sit close to somebody holy. You know, so that some of your holiness might rub off on me, like. I've been a sinner all my life, Sister, I have to confess that to you. Ever since I first saw the light of day.'

'Perhaps you should go to church and confess your sins to a priest,' said Sister Aibrean.

'Whoa, I'm not sure about that. Go to church! I'd be afeard to.'

'There's nothing to be scared of. God welcomes everybody in to His house, even sinners. In fact, sinners more than anybody else.'

The troll-like man sniffed and wiped his nose with the heel of his hand. 'I don't think that He'd welcome *me*, Sister – not after all the fierce terrible things that I've done. The second I stepped over the threshold I reckon he'd strike me down with a fecking great thunderbolt. I'd be nothing more than ashes to ashes, with a puff of smoke coming out of the top of my head, and I can't say that I wouldn't have deserved it. No – I'll just sit here with you, if that's not too much of a bother, and hope that I absorb some of the goodness that's radiating out of you. You know, like sitting next to a sunlamp.'

Anna brought over Sister Aibrean's tea with two plain oat biscuits in the saucer. 'You still sure I can't tempt you?' she said, widening her eyes and licking her lips.

Sister Aibrean narrowed her eyes but said nothing. The troll-like man kept on grinning and flapping his hands towards his chest as if he were trying to wave more of her divinity into himself.

'What's your name?' she asked him.

'Dermot,' he said. 'After my father, and my father's father, and my father's father's father, and so on. It's been an interminable fecking line of Dermots in my family – as far back as the fecking dinosaurs as far as anybody knows. Dermot the Dinosaur. I'm sorry. Sorry about the language. I can't help myself. Even my granny used to swear worse than Mrs Brown.'

'I won't ask you what your trespasses have been, Dermot,' said Sister Aibrean. 'Only a priest as a chosen representative of God has the power to grant you absolution. But I will say that today could be the day when you put all of your misdeeds behind you and begin a fresh and conscientious life. Today could be the day when you embrace Jesus and Jesus embraces you.'

Dermot sat back and pulled a face. 'Is that right? Serious? A fresh and conscious life?'

'Conscie*nti*ous,' Sister Aibrean corrected him, but nodded. 'All you have to do is make confession and show how contrite you are.'

'But that means going to church and I've told you what I think about that. I'd be shitting myself. God will strike me dead as I soon as I put one foot inside the door, I swear it.'

'No, He won't, Dermot. He's not a vengeful God.'

Dermot thought for a few moments and then he said, 'How about you coming with me? I'd feel a whole lot safer if I was with you. He's not going to zap me if I'm with a nun, is He?'

Sister Aibrean thought to herself that there was nothing in the world she would less like to do than accompany Dermot to church, or anywhere else for that matter. On the other hand, perhaps that explained the ominous feeling that she had experienced this morning that something terrible was going to happen to her. If she refused Dermot's request, perhaps in some unexpected way God would make her suffer for it.

'Very well,' she said. 'I was going to the Curraheen Road Church later this morning in any case. Just let me finish my tea and after that there's something I need to do back home. Then I could meet you here in, say, twenty-five minutes?'

Dermot gave the cafe window another wipe. 'Look, it's rotten out there. I have my car right outside. I could you drive you back to your house and wait for you, and then I could drive you to the church and you wouldn't get wet at all.'

'I'm not sure, Dermot.'

Dermot spread his hands wide. 'This is the day that I embrace Jesus, Sister. This is the day that Jesus embraces me.'

'All right, then. Thank you. Are you having another cup?'

'No, Sister. If I have any more I'll be pissing like a Belgian racehorse. I'll just watch you. I'll just sit here basking in your holy goodness. There – look at me – here I am, sitting back, basking. You take your own sweet time.'

* * *

Dermot gripped Sister Aibrean's elbow as they crossed the road to the car park outside the Bishopstown Pharmacy. She tried to twist her arm free when they reached the opposite pavement, but he kept a tight hold of it and guided her towards a grimy blue Toyota Avensis estate.

'Perhaps we could do this later,' said Sister Aibrean, as he opened the passenger door for her. 'There's a jumble sale at the church starting at eleven o'clock and I have to be there anyway.'

'No, come on, Sister, you've inspired me now,' said Dermot. 'Strike while the iron is hot is what I always say. Later on, who knows, the pubs will be open and I'll be hearing Murphy's calling me much louder than Jesus.'

The wind had risen so that the rain was sweeping across the shiny asphalt car park and Sister Aibrean had to admit to herself that she was feeling very cold. 'All right, then,' she agreed. 'So long as you drop me off home first. It's not far, only at the corner of Waterfall Road and Bandon Road.'

She climbed into the passenger seat and fastened her seat belt. The rear seats of the estate car were folded down and the back was crammed to the ceiling with cardboard boxes filled with dirty old sheepskin numnahs and saddlecloths and bridles, two racing exercise saddles, at least half a dozen large tins of Ronseal varnish, a bicycle with no wheels, three paper sacks of cement and a terracotta pot with a spidery dead umbrella plant in it.

Dermot sat in the driver's seat, slammed his door and started the engine. 'There now, off we go,' he told her, grinning at her again, his face so close to hers that she could smell his bad breath and a speckle of his spit landed on the shoulder of her raincoat. 'A journey in search of Jesus.'

He reversed out of the car park and turned left.

'I have to say that I felt when I woke up this morning that something momentous was going to happen to me,' said Sister Aibrean. She had decided now that God was testing her and that this was how she was going to prove her devotion. If she managed to bring Dermot into the bosom of the church, so that he confessed all of his sins and became a better man because of it, surely a golden star would be placed beside her name in heaven. Saint Eustace had suffered a thousand times worse than having to sit next to a malodorous man in a Toyota estate with worn-out suspension.

'Well, I felt much the same, Sister,' said Dermot. 'And I have to say that you're real stout for doing this. There's many a woman who would have passed by on the other side.'

They had almost reached Bandon Road now. Sister Aibrean said, 'Here – here – just here on the left is grand!' She was relieved to see that Fianna and Paul's bedroom curtains were still closed.

Instead of slowing down and drawing into the kerb, though, Dermot kept going and indicated that he was turning left down Bandon Road.

'You've passed it!' said Sister Aibrean, twisting around in her seat. 'You've passed it! That's my house, back there! The white one!'

'I know where your house is, Sister,' said Dermot.

'Then, please! You have to turn around and go back!'

Dermot didn't look at her, but reached into his inside pocket for a packet of cigarettes. He opened it one-handed and stuck a cigarette between his lips. 'We have somewhere else to go first, Sister.'

'Stop! Stop the car! If you're not going to take me home, then I want to get out!'

'Are you fecking deaf or something? I said we have somewhere else to go first.'

'If you don't stop, I shall throw myself out!'

'The doors are all locked,' said Dermot. 'Now, just shut your bake, will you? It's hooring out there and I'm trying to fecking concentrate.'

'What are you doing?' Sister Aibrean demanded. 'Where are you taking me? How do you know where my house is? I have to go back! I have to go back!'

'For the love of Jesus, Sister,' said Dermot. He lit his cigarette while he steered erratically around the roundabout that would take them down to the main Cork Ring. The rain was pelting down so hard now that the Toyota's half-perished windscreen wipers couldn't cope with it and he was driving almost blind.

'Please, if you sincerely repent of your sins, take me back,' Sister Aibrean begged him.

'Well, I've changed my mind,' said Dermot. 'I don't repent of them. Not a bit. If you want to know the truth, I'm looking forward to committing quite a few more.'

Sister Aibrean seized his left sleeve as he started to drive down the slip road to join the Cork Ring. The car slewed to the left, and then to the right, and a car close behind them blew its horn at them. Dermot lifted his elbow and jabbed Sister Aibrean hard on the cheekbone, just below her eye. She cried out and covered her face with both hands.

'You stupid fecking cow!' Dermot snapped at her, with his cigarette still in his mouth. 'You don't want to get to heaven that quick, do you?'

'Please take me back,' said Sister Aibrean, her voice muffled behind her hands. 'In the name of God the Father and Saint Eustace, please take me back.'

Dermot shook his head and kept on driving. He joined the ring road and headed west. Sister Aibrean kept her face covered but she started to sob – dry, husky sobs that sounded as if her lungs were made of wasps'-nest paper.

'Please, Dermot, take me back, it won't be too late.'

'I can't do that, Sister. I'm sorry. I sympathize, like, don't think that I don't, but if I don't fetch you back I'm going to be in shite right up to me fecking earrings, let me tell you that.'

'I have to flush the toilet,' said Sister Aibrean.

'What? What the feck are you talking about?'

'I left the house this morning but I didn't flush the toilet. If I don't go back and do it, I'm going to be mortified.'

Dermot shook his head. 'Unbelievable. You didn't flush the fecking toilet. Well, I'm sorry, Sister, but if it's a choice between your shite and mine, I'm afraid that mine takes priority.'

* * *

He left the main road at Farnanes and drove northwards up the winding country road towards Coachford. Sister Aibrean sat with her hands clasped in her lap, saying nothing, although she was thumbing through her purple rosary and silently praying inside her head for Saint Eustace to protect her. She had asked Dermot where he was taking her but his reply had been a long string of obscenities, so she had decided to remain silent and accept her fate.

Her life had been long and devout, and she believed that she had served God and Jesus to the utmost of her ability, as well as all the unfortunate young mothers and children that she had taken into her care. If God had decided that this was the day on which she was going to die, then He must have a reason, although she couldn't imagine what it was or why He should have decided that it should be so frightening.

They crossed the narrow bridge over the grey, rain-prickled water of the Taiscumar reservoir and as they did so she closed her eyes and tried not to think of the unflushed toilet. Perhaps that was God's way of demonstrating to Fianna and Paul that she was only human, after all. She had overheard Paul complaining to Fianna that Sister Aibrean seemed to think she was some kind of divinity.

They drove through Coachford, a strung-out collection of houses and shops, with two pubs facing each other across the main junction, O'Riordan's and O'Callaghan's. Sister Aibrean had hoped that there might be one or two early shoppers around so that she could knock on the window of Dermot's car and signal that she was being driven away against her will. But the only people she saw were two men smoking and talking to each other in a lumber yard and they were too far away to hear her.

Dermot drove on for another few kilometres. High straggly hedges grew on both sides of the road, which made it impossible for Sister Aibrean to see where they were or exactly which direction they were heading in. After about five minutes Dermot turned off left down a long single-track road and eventually they reached a gate with a white wooden sign with Clontead Stud lettered across it. He drove in through the gate and along an avenue of lime trees beside a field with several horses grazing in it. Then he turned into a courtyard surrounded by stables and parked next to a horsebox.

Sister Aibrean looked around. Next to the L-shaped stable block there was a large, green-painted house with a clock tower on top of its roof and a Father Time weathervane. Dermot climbed out from behind the wheel and walked around the car to open her door for her.

'Is this it?' she said. 'Are we here?'

'Yes, Sister. End of the road. Do you want to be hauling your rear end out of there so?'

'I suppose it's no good my throwing myself at your mercy and asking you to drive me back home?'

'You're bang on, Sister. No good at all.'

Just then, the side door of the house opened. A woman came out, with a long grey raincoat draped over shoulders, and walked briskly across to the open car door. She had a jet-black bob and a handsome, fiftyish face, with a short nose and a wide, strong jaw. Even though she didn't have her glasses on, Sister Aibrean could see that she had laid her foundation on too thickly and that she was wearing false eyelashes.

The woman gave Sister Aibrean a smile, although it was more of a smile of satisfaction than a smile of welcome.

'Sister Aibrean!' she said. 'Thanks a million for coming. It's been an age, hasn't it?'

'What's going on?' asked Sister Aibrean. 'Who are you? I'm not here for choicer, I can tell you that.'

'I didn't go to Saint Margaret's for choicer, Sister Aibrean. But that's life for you, isn't it? People who are stronger than us tell us what to do and we have to do what they say whether we like it or not, or they'll give us a beating. All for our own good, of course. All for the sake of our souls.'

'You went to Saint Margaret's?' said Sister Aibrean. 'Saint Margaret's was closed down years ago.'

'You can close down a mother and baby home,' the black-haired woman retorted. 'What you can never close down is the memories of what happened inside it.'

'I have no idea at all what you're talking about.'

'If you'd care to come inside, I'll explain it to you. Right at this moment my hair's getting wet and I've only just had it done.'

Sister Aibrean reluctantly unbuckled her seat belt and Dermot helped her out of the car. She followed the black-haired woman into the house, while Dermot stayed unnervingly close behind her, as if he was making sure that she couldn't turn around and make a run for it. As if she could, at her age, in the pouring rain, with the last house she had seen at least five kilometres away. In the whole of her life she had never felt so isolated and yet so trapped.

The black-haired woman led her into a large gloomy living room, with huge shabby sofas upholstered in chintz and a peat fire smouldering in the grate. On the walls hung oil paintings of thoroughbred horses, most of them with their heads too small for their bodies, and nineteenth-century prints of classic horse races, and framed rosettes.

'Sit down, and I'll explain why Dermot's fetched you here,' said the black-haired woman. 'There's no joy at all in getting your revenge on somebody if that somebody doesn't *know* that you're

305

getting your revenge on them. I could have told Dermot to tie you hand and foot and throw you in the reservoir. But what would have been the point of that? You would have thought that you were simply being murdered for no reason at all. Not punished for what you did, you and your six Sacred Sisters.'

Sister Aibrean remained standing. She clenched and unclenched her bony, liver-spotted hands, trying to summon up the strength to reply to this black-haired woman calmly and with confidence. *Remember*, she told herself, *the Lord is right behind you.*

'So,' she said, 'is it safe for me to presume that you were one of the fallen girls we took into Saint Margaret's?'

'That's right, sister. Riona, that's my name, Riona Nolan, although I doubt if you remember me.'

'Riona Nolan? I do remember you. I do clearly. You were very meek and obedient as far as I recall.'

'Browbeaten and intimidated, you mean. Every word you ever said to me was calculated to make me feel worthless and ugly and sluttish.'

'Holy Lamb of God! How can you say such a thing?'

'Because it's true. You were a witch and a bully, and so were all of your sisters. There was only one person in those days who made me believe that I had any value at all as a human being and that was my son Sorley. If it hadn't been for Sorley, I would have hanged myself, just like my friend Clodagh, and I mean that.'

Sister Aibrean slowly sat down, tucking a brown velveteen cushion behind the small of her back to support herself. 'But now, Riona. We looked after you. We gave you a roof over your head and a bed to sleep in. We fed you and clothed you. We kept you warm in the winter. We tended to you whenever you fell sick. We prayed for you constantly, that you should see the light, and we showed you how to lead an upright and moral life.'

Riona shook her head and kept on shaking it. 'You gave us the most miserable existence that anybody could imagine. You made all of us work like slaves. Our dormitory was freezing in the winter and suffocating in the summer. Our sheets were changed only once a month and we had to wear the same knickers for a week. Our food was gristle and cabbage and potatoes, and we were lucky if we got any gristle. And all the time you kept telling us that we were no better than common prostitutes.'

She stopped for breath. After what she had done to Sister Bridget and Sister Mona and Sister Barbara, she hadn't thought that she would still be boiling with so much anger. Yet she could easily have crossed the room and slapped Sister Aibrean across the face – twice, three times, left and right. Instead, though, she sat down next to her and leaned forward so close that Sister Aibrean couldn't focus on her and had to lean back.

'You made me feel like *nothing*,' said Riona. 'Not only that, you made me feel that even if I repented and begged God for His forgiveness that I would *still* be nothing. And, like I say, Sorley was all that stopped me from killing myself. He loved me because I was his mother, and he never judged me. And what did you do? You took him away from me. You *stole* him, you witch! You took away the only meaning that my life ever had.'

'Well – all I can say is that I'm sorry you feel that way,' said Sister Aibrean. 'As far as I'm concerned, we did the very best for you that we could, you and your son. You were in no position to bring him up yourself and, besides, he was God's child, not yours.'

Riona sat back as if this was an argument that she was no longer interested in pursuing. Instead, she said to Dermot, 'Can you go and get it ready?'

Dermot gave her the thumbs up and left the living room, and Sister Aibrean heard the side door slam.

'You always devoted yourself to Saint Eustace, didn't you?' said Riona.

'Yes, I did. And I am still devoted to him. He was one of the most inspirational of all the saints, although many claim that he was only mythical. I believe that he really existed and that the story of his martyrdom is true. I have felt his presence many times. I have heard his voice giving me encouragement.'

Riona said nothing for a moment and then she stood up. 'You know, of course, how Saint Eustace died?'

'Of course. Saint Eustace and his whole family, his wife and his sons. He had found Christ and so he refused to make a pagan sacrifice, and for that the Emperor Hadrian ordered him to be put to death.'

Riona went to the window. She could see that Dermot had opened one of the stable doors, directly opposite. 'Go on,' she said to Sister Aibrean. 'How exactly was he put to death?'

'Why are you asking me? You know already, don't you? I told you enough times when you were at Saint Margaret's. I even showed you pictures of it.'

'I'd like to hear you tell me again, that's all.'

'But why? If you hated Saint Margaret's and you despised me so much, why do you want to hear it now?'

'Just tell me,' said Riona. She could see her face faintly reflected in the rain-spotted window and she wondered if this is what she would look like after she had died and became a ghost, staring wistfully into the life she had left behind.

'The Emperor Hadrian had the statue of a huge bull cast out of bronze,' said Sister Aibrean. 'It was hollow, with a hinged lid in its side. Saint Eustace and his wife and sons were forced to climb inside it and the lid was locked. Then a fire was lit underneath the bull's belly, so that they would slowly be roasted to death.'

'Go on,' said Riona. 'Tell me about their screaming.'

'They screamed, of course they screamed, as anybody would,' said Sister Aibrean. 'But the statue had been made with special reeds in its nostrils so that their screams would sound instead like the bellowing of a bull.'

'How long did it take them to die?'

'Three days, according to the stories.'

'That's unlikely, wouldn't you think? Who could survive being roasted for three days?'

'God was protecting them, remember,' said Sister Aibrean.

'So God made him and his family suffer unbelievable agony

for three long days before He finally allowed them to die. Yes, I can believe that, considering my experience of God and all who believe they are acting on His behalf. Cardinals and canons and all the other gobshites who call themselves clergy.'

'I'm very sorry to hear you speak like that,' said Sister Aibrean. 'Without the church, and without those who serve it, there would be great desperation and hopelessness in the world. But why did you ask me to tell you about Saint Eustace again?'

Riona turned around. Sister Aibrean looked up at her, but she was silhouetted against the window and she couldn't see the expression on her face.

'Because I am going to give you the chance to prove that your faith is just as strong as his was. I think that's what you call killing two birds with one stone. You can be a martyr, like the saint you've adored for so many years, while I can get my revenge on you.'

Sister Aibrean stared at her in horror. 'What are you going to do to me?'

Riona turned back and looked out of the window. Dermot had appeared from the open stable door and waved to her.

'Come with me. You'll find out soon enough.'

Sister Aibrean crossed herself. 'Dear Jesus,' she said.

'Yes,' said Riona. 'My thoughts exactly.'

Thirty-eight

When Katie arrived at the station she was irritated to find that Enda Blaney and Partlan McKey from the Garda Ombudsman were waiting in reception for her. She ignored them and went over to the sergeant on the desk, shaking her umbrella. 'Jesus,' she said. 'The weather.'

'I know,' he said. 'Jesus.'

Enda stood up and came over to her with what she obviously imagined was a smile, although she still looked to Katie as if she were right on the verge of bursting into tears. 'Good morning, Detective Superintendent! It's teeming out, isn't it? We trust you can spare us a few moments more of your time.'

'As long as it's only a few moments, Enda. I have a heap of things to sort out this morning.'

'We think we might have some good news for you,' said Enda. '*Better* news, anyway.'

'All right, then. Let's go up to my office.'

Once they had taken off their coats and sat down in Katie's office, Katie said, 'All right, listen. I'm sorry I had to break off our last meeting so abruptly. I have two major investigations under way right now and the situation with each of them is developing almost hourly. You'll have heard about the bombing up at Spring Lane and two of our officers getting killed. That's apart from everything else I have on my plate.'

'We do appreciate that you're a very busy woman, Detective Superintendent,' said Partlan. The way he said 'woman' sounded to Katie as if he were comparing her to a harassed little housewife, but then again, she thought, perhaps she was being too sensitive.

'Yes, thank you,' she said, opening up the folder in front of her and starting to skim through it. 'So what's this "better news" you have for me?'

'Since we last talked to you, we've been looking further into the complaints made against you by Bryan Molloy and Jilleen Quaid,' said Partlan. 'Whatever anybody says about us Garda Ombudsman investigators, nobody has ever accused us of not being thorough.'

Partlan and Enda smiled at each other and then Enda said, 'We double-checked the ballistics tests that were carried out on the SIG Sauer pistol that was alleged to have been used to shoot Niall Duggan.'

'Oh yes?'

'There's not much doubt that the bullet that killed him was fired from the same weapon. And it's almost certain that it was Donie Quaid who fired the fatal shot. It was difficult to lift any latent fingerprints from the butt because of its criss-cross pattern, and, of course, you fired the weapon yourself, so the only clear fingerprint on the trigger was yours. But all the remaining bullets in the clip still had Donie Quaid's prints on them. And apart from that, we've verified where the weapon originally came from. It was definitely the Garda station at Tipperary Town and, as you said, it was signed out by the late Inspector Colin McManus.'

Partlan held up a sheet of paper, although Katie didn't look at it. 'Donie Quaid's letter confessing to the shooting was checked by our handwriting experts and that's almost certainly genuine, too. He had a unique way of forming his *f*s, like fish swimming.'

'Well, I'm glad you've confirmed what I knew already,' said Katie, still pretending that she was reading.

'There's more than that, though. Jilleen Quaid's complaint was that she had never seen the gun or the letter before she met you, but that you and Sergeant Gary Cannon intimidated her into saying that she had. That in itself would have been an act of gross misconduct on your behalf.'

'It would have been if I had done it, but I didn't.'

'That's the better news. We know you didn't. We went up to the prison yesterday on Rathmore Road and interviewed Lorcan Devitt.'

'Oh yes?' said Katie, looking up. Now she was interested. She had arrested Lorcan Devitt for his part in the murder and extortion racket that had been run by Niall Duggan's son and daughter, Aengus and Ruari. He had been one of the most feared members of the Duggan crime gang in Limerick, but ever since his conviction he had proved to be very obliging in providing information to the Garda – anything to reduce his seventeen-year sentence. Aengus and Ruari were dead now, so he had nothing to fear from them, and now that the Duggan gang had split up it was unlikely that any of the other one-time gang members would realize that he was grassing to the shades.

'Lorcan told us that his nephew Phelim and some of Phelim's classmates had been bullying Jilleen Quaid's son Sean at school,' said Enda. 'In the end the bullying got so bad that Jilleen told Sean that Donie had shot Niall Duggan, just so that Sean could prove to Phelim and the rest of them that he came from a hard family, and that they'd better lay off him.'

'Well, yes,' said Katie. 'Jilleen admitted to me herself that she'd done that. But now she's obviously going to deny it, isn't she? And her son will develop filial amnesia, more than likely.'

'Ah, but Phelim Devitt hasn't lost his memory, and neither have his pals at the Villiers Secondary School. We located them all, except one, and they all told us more or less the same story, that Sean came into school on the first day of summer term and boasted that his uncle had shot Niall Duggan and that his mother still had the gun in her possession. He told them that the gun had been given to Donie by Bryan Molloy and that was how Molloy had got rid of Niall Duggan and pretty much stamped out the worst of the crime feuds in Limerick, so they had better watch out.'

'They won't testify to this in court, will they, these lads?' asked Katie.

'They won't have to,' said Enda, and she looked pleased with herself now and much less weepy. 'We went back to Jilleen Quaid and told her what the boys had all said. We warned her that if she lied under oath in court she could be prosecuted herself, and even imprisoned. Would you believe that she withdrew her complaint then and there? "Oh," she said, "I think I must have been a bit confused." "Puggalized" was the actual word she used.'

'"Puggalized" isn't the word for it!' said Katie. 'But she's withdrawn her complaint? Fantastic! But where does that leave Bryan Molloy? Have you told *him* about this yet?'

'We'll be talking to his lawyers as soon as we've finished discussing this with you. Under the circumstances I'd say that it won't be easy for him to pursue his accusations of harassment against you. In fact, it's quite possible that he'll be facing criminal charges himself. It depends what the DPP thinks about it, although there may not be sufficient evidence and it might not be considered in the public interest.'

'That's up to her,' said Katie. 'But that *is* better news. I'm delighted.'

'We thought you'd be pleased,' Partlan put in. 'And *we're* pleased, too. We think this has gone a long way to clearing up some very dubious practices in the Garda, especially money and favours changing hands for the dropping of criminal charges.'

Katie said, 'I have to admit that I did feel a certain amount of hostility towards you two the last time we met. Fair play to you, though, you seem to be doing a grand job altogether. Very thorough, like you say.'

'We take the reputation of the Garda very seriously,' said Enda. 'Sometimes more seriously than many gardaí themselves ever do. It doesn't always make us very popular, but you won't find the word "popular" in our job description.'

'No,' said Katie. 'I don't think it's in mine, either.'

Hardly had Enda and Partlan left her office than Tadhg Meaney, the ISPCA inspector, knocked at her door. He was carrying two polystyrene cups of Costa coffee.

'Oh, you're a life-saver,' she told him.

'I saw you going up with those two and that you didn't have time to get yourself anything to drink. I guessed cappuccino. Is that right?'

'That's perfect,' she said. 'No wonder you're so good at taking care of animals.'

'Do you have five minutes?' he asked her. 'We've finished examining all of the horses now and we've come up with some fierce extraordinary findings.'

'Of course. Sit down. Do you want a biscuit? I have some chocolate gingers somewhere in my drawer here. I don't know why, but I've become addicted lately.'

As if I didn't know perfectly well why, she thought.

Tadhg laid a file on her desk and opened it up to show her at least forty shiny colour photographs of the twenty-three dead horses laid out at Dromsligo.

'Just as we thought, they're all thoroughbreds. I have a complete list here. We've estimated the approximate date of death of each of them, as well as what injuries were likely to have been caused by them being thrown off the cliff, and what injuries they might have sustained beforehand, and when.'

Katie looked carefully at the photographs, one by one. If their eyes hadn't turned milky and their lips weren't folded back in such a snarl, she could have believed that some of the horses were still alive.

Tadhg said, 'The list also shows what chemicals remained in their systems, if any. Most of them exhibited some traces of chemicals, not all of them illegal, although it was hard to detect any pharmacological activity in those animals that were the most decomposed. We call this "no effect".

'All the same, we did find some evidence of acepromazine, which is usually used to slow a racehorse's heart rate and can actually make it run more slowly, depending on how much you dose them up with. We also found Ritalin, which is a stimulant, and etorphine, which is another stimulant, highly controversial, and ractopamine, which is a muscle-builder usually used in pig farming to give you meatier bacon.

'I'll tell you, before I trained in veterinary medicine, I never realized just how many drugs we're eating and drinking and riding around on every day. It's amazing that humans and animals aren't all permanently stoned out of their minds. You buy a ham sandwich for your lunch and it's like you're eating two slices of bread and half of Phelan's Pharmacy.'

'Did you manage to determine if they were dead when they went over the cliff or still alive?'

'From our point of view, as veterinarians, we guessed that they were probably still alive. That was because of the high proportion of broken legs amongst them. They were probably driven to the edge, and jumped, and tried to land on their feet, but the impact, of course, would have shattered their bones.

'Your technical experts agreed with us, because of the distance from the foot of the cliff that their bodies were lying. If they had been dead already and simply tipped over the edge, they would have landed much closer. The tide had dragged some of the bodies out and then washed them back in again, so they weren't all positioned exactly where they first fell, but quite a few of them were impacted on the rocks and hadn't shifted at all.'

'Some people,' said Katie, shaking her head. 'They have no humanity at all, do they?'

'This isn't the worst case of cruelty to horses I've ever had to deal with, not by a long chalk,' said Tadhg. 'In terms of scale, though, it's the biggest, and until we completed our final tests we thought it was the most pointless. Throwing the poor creatures off the cliff instead of taking them to a knackery would have saved the offender a fair amount of money, but that didn't explain why they their owner wanted to be rid of them in the first place – owner, or owners plural, we're not sure which – but the indications are that they all came from the same stables.'

'But you have found out why they wanted to be rid of them?' Katie asked him.

'Let's just say that we believe we have a good idea. When we were testing for drugs we took hair samples from each of them, like you do when you test humans for drug use, especially if you suspect that they've stopped taking them for a while to avoid detection.'

'And?'

'And all of the horses except for the foals showed indications of hair dye.'

'Hair dye? You mean that their owners had been trying to disguise them or pass them off as other horses? Like, ringers? We thought they might have been, didn't we, right from the beginning?'

'Well, there are several reasons why horses have their hair dyed,' said Tadhg. 'The most innocuous is to cover up grey or white patches that might have appeared through sickness or age, so you can still show them off at dressage events. But of course horse thieves dye stolen horses to disguise them, and unscrupulous racehorse trainers dye horses to pass them off as other horses and fix the betting. Ringers, yes, in other words.'

'And what makes you think they all came from the same stables?' asked Katie.

'There's all kinds of indications. The majority of their racing plates all came from the same forge – Chinese, believe it or not.' He frowned at his notebook and said, 'The Qingdao Guanglongfa Precision Mould Forging Company in Beijing. They're cheaper than most of the Irish plates but they're very high quality.

'On top of that, most of the animals still had undigested food in their stomachs, and apart from the foals all of them had been fed on Gain Racehorse Mix, which wasn't really a surprise because that particular feed is used by dozens of Irish trainers. It's the dye that convinced us, more than anything. Their hair had all been coloured with varying shades of the same brand of dye.'

'Is there a special make of dye for horses?'

'There's no need. Horses' hair is no different from human hair. The only difference between dyeing a horse's hair and dyeing your own hair is the quantity you need. For a horse, of course, you need a bucketful. All the horses whose hair had been coloured had been dyed with Clairol.'

'I think I need to get Detective Inspector O'Rourke in on this,' said Katie. 'Detective Dooley, too. If you can hold a minute.'

She rang Detective Inspector O'Rourke, but Detective Dooley wasn't at his desk and when she contacted him on his iPhone he told her he was out in Mayfield, interviewing a witness, and that he wouldn't be back at Anglesea Street for at least half an hour.

Detective Inspector O'Rourke came into her office wearing a pond-green sweater that was half a size too tight for him. Katie asked Tadhg to bring him up to date on his post-mortem examination of the horses from Nohaval Cove and then she said, 'What do you think, Francis?'

'It certainly sounds to me like there's been some race-fixing going on,' said Detective Inspector O'Rourke. 'What with this exchange betting these days, there's a fortune to be made in ringing if you can get away with it. You can bet on a horse to win, but equally you can bet on a horse to come last, and if you paint up some clapped-out no-hoper to look like the best runner in your stable, it's ker-*ching*! you've made yourself a tidy little heap of euros.

'From what you've told me, it looks like there's one particular trainer who's been doing it big-time but wanted to dispose of the evidence. Unfortunately he made the mistake of hiring Paddy Fearon to do it for him.'

'Is it conceivable this same trainer might have planted the bomb in Paddy Fearon's caravan?' asked Katie. 'If there really is so much money at stake and he'd found out we were going to bring Paddy Fearon in and question him . . .'

317

'I'd be cautious about that,' said Detective Inspector O'Rourke. 'I know at least five Travellers who were more than happy out when they heard that Paddy Fearon had gone to meet his maker. One of them asked me who had done it because he wanted to shake them by the hand for saving him the bother. There's plenty of other scummers that Fearon upset, too, not just Travellers. He got on the wrong side of Lochian ó Bron once over some drugs business, and you never want to upset the Provos if you prefer to stay physically intact, like.'

'It's urgent in any case that we find out who this trainer is,' said Katie. 'If he was using buckets of Clairol, he must have been making unusually large purchases of it, so if you can initiate checks on who supplies Clairol wholesale and also who supplies it online. I'll ask Superintendent Pearse to have his officers make enquiries in all of the shops in Cork where you can buy Clairol, as well as all the hairdressers.

'At the same time, we need to do some subtle mingling with the racing community. We can have a quiet chat with that reporter from the *Racing Post*, can't we? What's his name? Peter Driscoll. And Declan O'Donoghue from the *Sun*. Don't tell me that one of them hasn't caught a whiff of this and has at least some idea who's been doing it.'

'Charlie O'Reilly from the Ennisbrook Stud, he's an old pal of mine,' said Detective Inspector O'Rourke. 'Him and me play golf together now and again. He knows just about everybody who's anybody in the racing game. They're very tight, though. They look after each other. It won't be easy to get any of them to make a direct accusation.'

'Well, let's try all the same,' said Katie. 'Meanwhile, thank you, Tadhg. You've done a fantastic job. What are we doing with the horses' bodies? I don't want them cremated until this investigation is completed.'

'I can arrange to have them stored in refrigeration trucks for now,' said Tadhg. 'That's if the Garda can meet the expense.'

'No bother, I'll sign that off,' said Katie. 'Good luck to you so.'

Tadhg Meaney gathered up his photographs, shook Katie's hand, and left. However, Detective Inspector O'Rourke stayed behind.

'I heard all about you being shot at last night,' he told her.

'Yes,' she said. 'But as you can see, they missed.'

'I'm sorry, but I don't find that very amusing myself. It does sound like there's somebody out to get you. They're having a triple funeral on Friday, for Horgan and those two young gardaí who got blown up. We don't want a quadruple funeral, for God's sake.'

'Francis, I have two armed protection officers posted outside my house and they're going to stay there, twenty-four hours a day, until we're satisfied that the threat of my being shot at again is over.'

'You need to be doggy wide, though. They may not shoot at your house next time. They may try to pick you off while you're shopping, or sitting in a café, or anywhere at all.'

Katie went over and patted his shoulder. 'Thank you, Francis. I appreciate your concern, believe me. But I can take care of myself. Really. In fact, it's my job to take care of you.'

Thirty-nine

Riona ushered Sister Aibrean across the stable yard, with the rain drumming on the large black umbrella that she held high over their heads. Sister Aibrean hesitated two or three times, but each time Riona pressed her hand against the small of her back and pushed her forward.

'You shouldn't do anything you're going to regret when you have to account for yourself to Saint Peter,' said Sister Aibrean.

'That's something that you and your sisters should have thought about when you were running Saint Margaret's,' Riona retorted.

'We never knew that you felt so hard done by. Why didn't you say anything at the time?'

'Because if any of us ever tried to complain, we'd get a hard slap, that's why, or have to go without our supper.'

They had reached the stable door now. Top and bottom were bolted together, but it was slightly ajar and Riona went to push it open wider.

'Isn't there some way that I can make amends to you?' said Sister Aibrean. 'I'm an old woman now, Riona. I'm not the same woman I was forty years ago. I know that I have never been perfect. I have never pretended to be. But if I did you such a grievous wrong, I am deeply penitent, believe me, and I will go to church as soon as I get back home and confess to it and beg for the Lord's forgiveness.'

'The Lord may forgive you, Sister Aibrean, but I don't and that's the difference. Anyway, you won't be going back home ever again, and you'll never be setting foot in a church again, either.'

Dermot must have heard them talking because he came to the stable door and opened it up wider.

'All ready for firing up,' he grinned and gave Riona the thumbs up.

Sister Aibrean leaned over to one side so that she could see past him. The stable was brightly illuminated by two fluorescent tubes in the ceiling, which gave it a flat, unnatural appearance, as if it were a stage set for a school Nativity play. On the brick wall at the back hung a metal hay feeder, still half filled with straggly hay, and the floor was spread with straw. A training saddle and other tack hung from the walls at the sides.

But Sister Aibrean's attention was caught most of all by the shining stainless-steel machine that was standing in the centre of the stable. It looked like a metal coffin on four legs with wheels. Its raised cover was in two hinged halves, with an oval glass window in each of them, and these had been opened and folded down on each side. Standing on the floor next to it, and connected to it by an orange hose, was a large red cylinder of propane gas.

'Come and take a look,' said Riona, pushing Sister Aibrean further forward. 'It's not a brazen bull, I'm afraid. You can't find anybody these days who hires out brazen bulls.'

Sister Aibrean approached the metal coffin and stared at it with mounting dread. Inside there was a long rectangular tray, which had recently been polished into shining semicircles with a scouring pad.

'What is it?' she whispered. 'What is it for?'

She knew very well what it was. She had seen different versions of it several times before, at weddings and church picnics. She was asking only because she wanted to hear Riona say that Dermot had set it up today for a different purpose altogether.

'It's a hog tray-roaster,' said Riona. 'I rented it from O'Malley's Barbecues in Macroom. Some people say that the tray-roasters can cook a hog much better than a spit, much more even, with better crackling. The most important thing about it, though, is that you can roast a much bigger beast on it than you can with most spits. Ninety kilos. What do you weigh, Sister Aibrean? Not as much as ninety kilos. Only half that, I'd say.'

Sister Aibrean turned to face her. 'If your intention was to frighten me, Riona, then you've succeeded. You've frightened me very much indeed. Now, why don't you please ask your man Dermot here to drive me back home and we'll forget any of this ever happened? I could make a complaint about you to the guards, but I won't.'

'You still don't have me, do you?' said Riona. 'You're going nowhere at all. You're going to suffer as I suffered – only you can thank that God of yours that your suffering isn't going to last a fraction as long as mine has.'

Sister Aibrean stared at her, with her lip quivering. She was about to say something in return, but she was so terrified now that she couldn't manage to speak. She sank slowly to her knees and had to grip the side of the hog roaster to ease herself down. She knelt on the straw-strewn floor of the stable with her head bent and closed her eyes, and clasped her hands together in prayer.

'If I were you, I would ask for some guidance from your precious Saint Eustace,' said Riona. 'If anybody understands what you're about to go through, then he does. That's if he's in heaven, which he doesn't deserve to be. What kind of a man allows his wife and children to be roasted alive because of his beliefs?'

She looked across at Dermot and nodded, and Dermot depressed and twisted the two gas-control knobs so that the burner bars that ran along each side of the roaster popped into life, two rows of small blue flames. Sister Aibrean felt the heat rising out of the open roaster immediately.

'Will you undress yourself or shall I?' asked Riona.

Sister Aibrean opened her eyes. '*What*? You expect me to undress?'

'Oh, come on, girl,' said Dermot. 'Did you ever see a hog that was roasted in a nun's habit? "I'll have a bit of crackling, please, boy, and a slice of that scapular."'

Sister Aibrean tried to climb to her feet, but she was too weak to manage it unaided and when she reached out to the hog roaster to ease herself up it was already too hot for her to put her hand on it. She let out a peculiar moan of despair and looked wildly around the stable, as if she were expecting some miracle to occur to save her – like the hog roaster being magically transformed into a harmless wooden table, or an angel with a fiery sword walking through the wall to strike the heads off Riona and Dermot and carry her away in his arms.

Riona, however, was growing impatient. She stood behind Sister Aibrean and wrenched off her raincoat, first one sleeve and then the other. Sister Aibrean struggled and grunted as her narrow shoulder blades were folded back. Riona, however, was far too strong and angry for her, and as she was yanking off the second sleeve Dermot came over and gripped Sister Aibrean's upper arms so that she couldn't fight back or pitch herself forwards or sideways on to the floor.

'You can't! You *can't*! You must *not*!' panted Sister Airbrean, but Riona ignored her and pulled off her scarf and her cowl, revealing her short, tufty grey hair, with all its bald patches. Then she dragged her long black scapular over her head, threw it aside, and reached down to untie her woollen belt.

'Help me! Help me! Oh, God in Heaven, will nobody help me?'

'You're absolutely right there, Sister,' said Dermot. 'Nobody will help you. There's only us and the horses here at the moment and the horses don't give a monkey's.'

Riona pulled up Sister Aibrean's habit, almost suffocating her as she tried to wrestle it over her head. After that, with Dermot holding her ankles to stop her from kicking, she forced her on to her back and took down her underskirts.

'No! Oh God, no!' wept Sister Airbrean, as Riona tugged down her large white Primark drawers. She couldn't reach down to cover herself because Dermot was holding her wrists. 'No man has ever seen me undressed, ever! Please, Riona! Please! I beg you, as a woman!'

'Chill the beans, would you, darling?' said Dermot. He looked down at her bony body with its wrinkly, fawn-coloured skin, dotted with moles and patterned with spidery red veins. 'I wouldn't climb on you to hang wallpaper.'

Riona went over to the bridles and reins and stirrups hanging on the wall and came back with two lengths of blue nylon cord. Grim-faced, she tied Sister Aibrean's ankles together, and then her wrists. She tied them so tightly that she clenched her teeth while she was doing it.

'I beg you, I beg you, I beg you,' said Sister Aibrean. 'Please, I beg you, don't do this. Please, think again. I will pray for you, I promise. I will pray for your forgiveness for sixty minutes of every waking hour. Don't think what you are doing to me, think what you are doing to your own immortal soul. I may burn here, yes, for a few terrible minutes, but you will burn in hell fire for ever.'

Riona bent over her and looked her directly in the face, unblinking. 'I don't believe in hell, Sister, any more than I believe in heaven. How could I, after the way that you and all your sisters treated me? You were the living proof that there *is* no merciful God.'

She stood up straight and said, 'Come on, Dermot. Let's get this over with. Every second that this witch stays alive is a second too long.'

Dermot forced his hands into Sister Aibrean's armpits, and Riona took hold of her ankles, and between them they lifted her up until she was level with the top of the open roaster. Sister Aibrean had her head thrown back. She was staring up at the ceiling and shivering uncontrollably, as if she had been caught naked in an Arctic draught.

'Ready?' said Riona.

'Ready,' said Dermot, and the two of them gave Sister Aibrean a little swing before dropping her down with a tumbling clang on to the hot metal tray of the roaster. Her bare skin sizzled and crackled, and she convulsed violently, jerking her arms upwards, even though her wrists were tightly bound together. She stretched her mouth wide open, exposing her brown and gappy teeth, but she was in too much shock to scream. Instead, she glared at Riona with unblinking fury even as she twitched and shuddered, as if to say, *How could you do this to me? How could you do this to any human being?*

Riona stared back at her for a few seconds, saying nothing. Even she was wondering to herself how she could be so emotionless. But she felt nothing for Sister Aibrean. To her, it was like watching a cockroach waltzing on a kitchen hotplate. What Sister Aibrean and her Sacred Sisters had done to her had emptied her of any pity. She thought that she might have had at least a little compassion if she had been able to understand why the nuns at the Bon Sauveur Convent had treated her so heartlessly, and why they had taken her Sorley away from her – but she couldn't understand it at all. What religion treats a pregnant teenage girl as if she is an irredeemable whore and steals the child that she adores?

'*Aaaaahhhhhhhhh,*' breathed Sister Aibrean, a soft expression of pain beyond any comprehension. Wherever her shoulders and her buttocks and her thighs were touching the metal tray, her skin was being scorched a livid scarlet and blistering, and the blisters were popping sporadically in the heat.

Dermot sniffed and then pinched his nose between finger and thumb. 'Lord lantern of Jesus, the hong off of that.' He sniffed again and then he said, 'The worst thing is, it almost smells like you could eat it. It's enough to give you the gawks.'

Sister Aibrean lifted her head and made one last effort to kick and hump herself off the roasting tray, but of course it was hopeless. Her head fell back against the metal with a resounding clonk and her hair began to shrivel.

'*Aaaaaahhhhhh,*' she whispered. She didn't even have enough breath to make a last appeal to Saint Eustace.

'Close it,' said Riona, and Dermot raised the two sides of the hog roaster's cover and fastened the clips that held them together. Sister Aibrean was still visible through the oval glass windows, which were designed so that the barbecue chef and his guests could watch their pig becoming steadily crisper without having to open up the roaster and lose any of its heat.

Riona stepped nearer and shaded her eyes with her hand so that she could see Sister Aibrean more clearly. *'Burn, you cruel creature,'* she said to herself.

As soon as the cover was closed, the temperature inside the roaster began to intensify and now Sister Aibrean was not just being seared by the metal tray but cooked. She must have dragged in two lungfuls of superheated air because now she let out a long and hideous scream. She knocked her knuckles against the windows and kicked her heels against the end of the roaster and her scream went on and on for so long that Riona thought it was never going to finish.

Eventually, though, it faltered and died away, and as it did so Sister Aibrean managed to lift her head so that Riona could see her face. It was vermilion-red now, like a demon's mask. Her eyes had rolled up so that only the whites showed and by now she was probably blinded, but in spite of that she appeared to be glaring at Riona with both desperation and utter hatred.

'Will you look at the scowl on her,' she said to Dermot. 'So much for dying in a spirit of forgiveness, like Jesus. Mind you, Jesus knew that He was going to come back to life again by the weekend, just in time for his dinner, and this one certainly won't be.'

'Oh, you're a hard woman and no mistake,' said Dermot, with a grin to show her that he meant no disrespect.

After another two or three minutes the knocking and kicking noises from inside the hog roaster gradually petered out. The last few knocks were barely audible and Riona guessed that they were probably caused by Sister Aibrean's tendons tightening in the heat, rather than her begging to be freed. Five minutes after that she could see that Sister Aibrean was lying completely stiff and still, and that her skin was turning orange. She heard a dripping sound in the metal tray underneath the roaster, and then another drip, and another. Sister Aibrean's body fats were melting.

'We should have fetched some baps,' said Dermot.

By now the whole stable was filled with the pungency of roasting flesh and Riona was nauseated to find that she had started to salivate. She retched and said to Dermot, 'I have to get out of here.'

'What do you want to do? She must be brown bread by now. Do you want me to turn the gas off?'

'No, leave it on till she burns. Let's cremate her, like the witch she is.'

They left the stable, closing the door behind them, and stepped out into the rain. Riona raised her umbrella and they stood for a while breathing in the smell of fresh air, and rain, and peaty soil, and horse manure.

'Who's the next one?' asked Dermot.

'I'm not sure yet. Either Sister Virginia or Sister Nessa. It depends which one Andy finds first.'

Dermot thought for a while, watching the rain falling in curtains across the stable yard. Then he said, 'What she said, do you think that's true, like?'

'What do you mean?'

'Do you think we'll be going to hell for this, you and me?'

'Do you believe in hell?'

Dermot shrugged. 'I don't know. I've been in Billy McReady's bar of a Saturday night and that comes pretty close, except that it's probably a fair bit hotter – Billy McReady's, I mean. But Carraig Mor, that was hell. That was definitely hell. The food was shite and everybody in the whole fecking dump was cracked.'

'And you weren't?'

'Of course not! I was the only one in who wasn't! And that included them doctors. They was cracked worser than most of the patients. They let me out, didn't they, when they realized their mistake?'

'They had to let you out, Dermot, because you'd served your time.'

Dermot stared at her. His bald head was bobbled with raindrops like the blisters on Sister Aibrean's skin. 'You're not trying to say that I'm a header, like, are you?' he asked warily.

'I wouldn't dream of it, Dermot. I may have a lot of faults, but stupidity isn't one of them.'

Forty

Katie was coming out of Superintendent Pearse's office when Detective Dooley caught up with her.

'Result!' he said, his face flushed, holding up his iPhone.

'With Roisin Begley, you mean? That's fantastic. Her father's due here in twenty minutes. What have you got?'

She pressed the button for the lift and the doors opened immediately. As they went up, Detective Dooley said, 'Roisin had a timeline on Facebook and a Twitter account, and her mobile phone service provider was Meteor. I went through all of her recents but there was nothing to indicate that she was anything but sound about the way that her life had turned out since we got her away from Gerrety.'

They reached Katie's office. She had been downstairs talking to Superintendent Pearse about continuing protection for herself and John, and about the arrangements for the public funerals on Friday of Detective Horgan and the two gardaí killed when Paddy Fearon's caravan blew up. She had been away less than ten minutes but another stack of folders had been left in her in-tray.

'Mother of God,' she said, picking up the pale-green folder on top of the pile, which was Cork County Council's new review of community relations. 'I'm thinking of changing my title to Paper-Pusher-in-Chief. Anyway, Robert, go on.'

'Roisin texted several of her friends to say that she was very nervous about giving evidence to the court against Gerrety. On the other hand, she said that she was determined to do it, because he deserved to be punished for what he'd done to her and to all the other young girls that he was pimping. She knew that she would be allowed to make her statement on closed-circuit TV, so she wouldn't have to face Gerrety in person, and that made her feel less anxious about it.'

'She didn't say that she was depressed, or thinking of taking her own life?' asked Katie. 'She hadn't logged on to any of those suicide websites?'

Detective Dooley shook his head. 'If anything, I'd say she was really optimistic about the future. She said that she was thinking of taking up guitar lessons and becoming a singer. She was a huge fan of Sinéad O'Connor and wanted to be just as famous as her. That's not the kind of thing that a would-be suicide talks about doing, is it?'

'I don't know,' said Katie. 'Sinéad O'Connor can be fierce miserable at times. "Nothing Compares to You"?'

'Listen,' said Detective Dooley, 'the last text message that Roisin received was from one of the girls who worked for Cork Fantasy Girls. This was at nine forty-seven on the night she was drowned. The girl's name is Abisola. She's a Nigerian and you can find her most nights at the Bodega or Havana Brown's. I met her myself when I first went looking for Roisin and I thought she was a real stunner, and a nice girl, too. Abisola said to meet her at Havana Brown's at eleven o'clock because she had some really fantastic news for her.'

'She didn't tell Roisin what it was, though, this fantastic news?'

'Not in the text. But I went to Havana Brown's last night and even though Abisola wasn't there I found out where she lives. That's where I was this morning when you rang me. She doesn't look like so much of a stunner when she's just dragged herself out of the scratcher, I can tell you. More like a week of wet washing that somebody's left a black sock in.

'It was obvious that she hadn't yet heard that Roisin was dead, and I didn't tell her in case she clammed up on me. She said that Dovydas Karosas had approached her and told her to meet up with Roisin and pass on a message from Michael Gerrety. Like, Gerrety was sorry about everything that had happened and he still owed her six and a half thousand euros for her last week of "massages" in inverted commas. If Abisola could fix it so that Roisin came to the club at eleven, Dovydas would be there to give her the cash.'

'So Roisin came?'

'Well, come on, Abisola had promised her that she had something fantastic to tell her. And she'd been living back home, too, with a father who thought she was nothing but a dirt-bird. She probably felt like a little taste of that clubbing again. You know, a couple of hours of freedom and Jägerbombs. And when they met up and Abisola told her that Dovydas was going to give her all that grade, she was really excited.'

'Was there any suggestion from Karosas that she would only be paid if she agreed not to give evidence against Gerrety?'

'Not that Abisola heard. But of course Roisin wanted the money. She felt that she'd earned it, after all, and she's a seventeen-year-old girl. What girl of that age wouldn't be tempted by six and a half thousand euros?'

'Did Abisola see Dovydas hand the money over?'

'No. And here's the thing. She didn't see Dovydas at all. Roisin had sneaked out of the house about ten o'clock and managed to get a pal from Henchy's Bar to drive her down to the city, so she arrived early. Roisin and Abisola had the time to knock back a couple of drinks together and catch up with the gossip and Abisola took a few selfies.'

He quickly prodded at his iPhone and then handed it to Katie to take a look. The first picture showed Roisin and Abisola hugging each other and laughing. Roisin was wearing a white V-necked sweater and a very short grey skirt and black tights. Abisola had her hair braided in cornrows and was dressed in a shiny turquoise blouse and black high-waisted leggings.

'Those are the clothes that Roisin was found in when they dragged her out of the river,' said Katie.

'That's right,' said Detective Dooley. He scrolled through the selfies that Abisola had taken, one after the other. 'But look at this picture, and this, and this. You can't see it in all of them, but take a sconce at Roisin's right wrist.'

Katie held up the iPhone and saw that Roisin was wearing a sparkly bracelet that looked like a cluster of flower petals. Each petal was fashioned out of dozens of tiny opalescent beads, with crystals forming the stamens.

'She was wearing only earrings when her body was recovered,' said Katie. 'What happened to that bracelet, I wonder? It's only costume jewellery, like, twenty or twenty-five euros at the most, so you wouldn't have thought that anybody would have considered it worth stealing.'

'I'll have some pictures taken of it and circulated around the markets,' said Detective Dooley. 'But any road, at about five past eleven a girl came into the club and told Roisin that there was somebody waiting for her outside.'

'Only "somebody"? She didn't mention Dovydas by name?'

'No. And like I say, Abisola didn't see Dovydas, either. Roisin picked up her coat and her purse and followed the girl outside, and that was the last Abisola saw of her. She asked me this morning how Roisin was, but all I said was "grand". Abisola isn't the type who reads newspapers or watches the news on TV and most of the time she's halfway out of her head on meow-meow. She doesn't even realize that I'm the law or wonder why I'm always asking her so many questions. She thinks I'm a DJ who works for Club D'Ville, the teenage disco. I wish.'

'Have you found *anybody* who saw what happened to Roisin when she left the club?'

Detective Dooley said, 'No. But I'm already having the CCTV footage checked from that evening and the manager gave me the home address of the doorman who was on duty outside.'

'Well, good luck with that. It sounds to me as if Dovydas was being careful not to be seen with Roisin. I'll bet you he has some fantastic alibi set up already. The only witness to any of this so far is this Abisola, and from what you've said about her she doesn't sound exactly what you'd call reliable.'

'Maybe she's not, ma'am,' said Detective Dooley. 'But I have a strong feeling about this. She might be halfway out of her head for most of the time, but I don't think she's a liar. In fact, these selfies prove it, don't they, because they have the date and time on them?'

Katie sat back, tapping a pencil against her desk. 'That's true. And I think that's sufficient reason for me to postpone this meeting with Jim Begley until you've checked out the CCTV and talked to the doorman. A possible scenario is that Jim Begley saw Roisin leaving the house and followed her down to Havana Brown's.'

'Begley? But how would Begley have sent in that girl to tell Roisin that somebody was waiting for her outside?'

'I don't know, but he might have done. She only said "somebody", after all. And even if it *was* Dovydas Karosas who sent the girl in, Begley might have waited until Karosas gave Roisin the money and left and *then* grabbed her. Maybe he didn't even have to grab her. Maybe all he had to say was, "I was worried about you and I followed you here and now I'll give you a lift back home." Only he gave her a trip to Kennedy Quay instead.'

'Well, yes, I suppose,' said Detective Dooley.

'I know what you're thinking,' said Katie. 'You're thinking that Detective Superintendent Maguire is always telling me not to theorise and now she's come up with this fantastical notion that Jim Begley really *was* guilty of drowning his daughter, after all. *And* that he might have pocketed the six and a half thousand euros that she made out of prostitution, in spite of his moral objections.'

'I hadn't considered him keeping the money, I must admit.'

'But this isn't theorising, Robert,' said Katie. 'I'm simply making sure that we leave no stone unturned. This is Michael Gerrety we're dealing with here and he's the cutest hoor in Cork,

332

so this case needs to be investigated logically and sequentially, especially in the light of this new evidence from Abisola. We don't want to jeopardise it by going off half-cocked. Supposing we arrest Michael Gerrety but he says there never was any six and a half thousand euros and that Dovydas Karosas was lying? Supposing we arrest Dovydas Karosas and then we find out that Jim Begley really did do it? Or vice versa? Or that neither of them did it and it was somebody who mugged her while she was walking home late at night with all that cash on her? Or that she'd had too many drinks with Abisola and fell into the river by accident?'

'So you're going to cancel this meeting with Jim Begley?'

'I'm going to postpone it, yes. Meanwhile, if you go down and check how they're getting along with that CCTV, and go to talk to the doorman, we'll be making some progress.'

'On my way, ma'am. I'll see you after.'

* * *

Detective Dooley went towards the office door, but as he did so he had to do a little dance to avoid Detective Brennan, who was on his way in.

'Stall for a moment, you should hear this, too,' Detective Brennan told him. 'Somebody's identified that ugly sham who dropped Sister Barbara into the fountain.'

'Now that *is* a result,' said Katie. 'Who is he?'

'His name's Dermot Gully and he used to be a patient at the big house at Carraig Mor. The woman who recked him was a psychiatric nurse. She didn't see the picture in the *Echo* when it first came out because she never reads it, only her husband, but she saw it this morning when she was crumpling it up to start the fire in her kitchen.'

'What was this Dermot Gully being treated for?'

'Hold on, I have it written here. "Antisocial personality disorder", that's what she told me. Apparently that means that he had no conscience at all about any harm or injury he caused to other people, and on top of that he didn't give a hen's knickers about the consequences. The nurse can't remember exactly when he was first admitted to Carraig Mor, but she knows he was sent there under a court order, and for most of his time there he was kept banged up in isolation.'

'Did she know what he'd done, to be sent there?'

'Put out a brasser's eye with a corkscrew, so she said, because she'd laughed at the size of his micky. Or the lack of it, presumably.'

'Well, he sounds like a nice enough fellow,' said Katie. But we shouldn't have too much trouble tracing him, should we, if he was under a court order? This psychiatric nurse, she didn't have any idea where he came from, did she?'

'Not specifically, like, but he was a Cork man, no question about that, and a Norrie, she thought, by the sound of him.'

'Had he been in work before he was committed?'

'I didn't ask her that, to be fair.'

'Can you get back to her and ask her, in that case, because whatever he did before, he could well have gone back to it. Unless he was unemployed, of course. And also ask her if he ever had any visitors that she can remember, especially regular visitors.'

'Sure, like, I did ask her that,' said Detective Brennan. 'There was a fellow who dropped in to see him now and again, and she thinks that was one of his brothers because he was almost as ugly as he was. Not long before they let him out, though, a nun came to see him and they spent a long time together, she remembers that. It was like the whole afternoon. She asked him about it after and he told her that she had promised him to save his soul when he was released.'

'That's interesting, considering he threw a dead nun into the fountain. Where did this nun come from? Did she know that?'

'I asked her that, too,' said Detective Brennan. 'She didn't know, but she thought it was odd because usually it'll be a priest who comes to visit the male patients, rather than a nun. The other thing that she thought was odd – and this must have really stuck in her mind, like. The nun smelled of perfume.'

'*Perfume?*' said Katie. 'What did that person in charge at the Greendale Rest Home tell us about the nun who visited Sister Barbara before she disappeared? Her eyebrows were plucked and her nails were varnished.'

'That's right,' said Detective Dooley. 'It sounds like it could be one and the same nun. Or nun at all. Sorry. That's a terrible Horgan kind of a joke.'

Katie lifted her hand to show him that she didn't mind. 'If we can remember the friends we've lost with a smile, Robert, then that's the best way. And you could be right. The nun who visited Sister Barbara and the nun who visited this Dermot Gully might have been the same person, and not a real nun – unless there's a convent in Cork I've never heard of where they all wear make-up and Prima Donna suspender belts under their habits.'

'Don't get me excited, ma'am,' said Detective Brennan. 'My doctor's been concerned about my blood pressure lately.'

Forty-one

Before she went home that evening, Katie visited her father, who lived in Monkstown, on the opposite side of the ferry crossing from Cobh. The rain had persisted all day, steady and heavy, which made his green-painted Victorian house look even more dreary and neglected than usual. The guttering around the front gable had broken so that water was clattering down the walls and streaking them with even darker green damp.

Katie had tried so many times to persuade him to move because the house was far too big for him, and far too expensive to maintain, but he had insisted that he wanted to stay there until he died, with all the memories of Katie's mother in every room.

When he answered the front door, he seemed to have diminished since the last time she had seen him, which was only two weeks ago. With each visit she thought he looked smaller. It was almost like watching somebody through a telescope, gradually disappearing into the distance.

'Katie! Grand to see you!' he said. His voice sounded hoarse and phlegmy, as if he had a cold. 'Come along in, I've just brewed some tea!'

Katie went up the steps and followed him inside. She had found him a new cleaner, a widow from Orilia Terrace who used to do the cleaning at Saint Mary's School but also cooked meals for the Roaring Donkey pub further down the road. Her name was Bláithín and the only thing about her that irritated Katie's father was her constant warbling.

'Sometimes I don't know if you got me a cleaner or an effing canary,' he grumbled.

All the same, the fire was lit and the house was warm and smelled of furniture polish. Her father might have been showing the signs of increasing age – his drooping grey cardigan appeared to be two sizes too large for him now, but at least it was clean and she could be happy that he was being well looked after.

'What's the craic?' he asked her, bringing in a second teacup from the kitchen. His hands trembled so that it rattled in the saucer. 'Would you care for some shortbread? It's only shop, I'm afraid. Not a patch on what your mother used to bake.'

She wasn't going to tell him that she had been shot at. That would only have distressed him and given him sleepless nights. Neither did she intend to give him all the grisly details about the nuns who had been murdered: he would have seen as much as he needed to know about that on the television news. But she did tell him about Enda Blaney and Partlan McKey, the two investigators from the Garda Ombudsman, and how they had found out that she was innocent of coercing Jilleen Quaid into giving false evidence.

'That has all the smell of Bryan Molloy about it,' said her father. 'But as you say, if you can prove that it was him who paid Donie Quaid to shoot Niall Duggan, or even raise the strong suspicion of it, he won't have much chance of pursuing a case against you. That's very good news. Mind you, it'll be even better news if he gets prosecuted and locked up in Mountjoy for the next ten years.'

Katie's father had been a Garda inspector, but he had blown the whistle on a group of senior officers who had been soliciting bribes in exchange for dropping criminal charges and he had been forced by his colleagues to resign. Among that group had been Jimmy O'Reilly, who was now assistant commissioner for the South-East region, and Bryan Molloy.

Katie stirred her tea and then carefully replaced her spoon in the saucer. 'I have some more good news for you, Dad.'

Her father raised his shaggy white eyebrows. 'Don't tell me that you and John are getting hitched? That *is* good news!'

'No, Dad, it's not exactly that. I haven't told anybody else, but I have to tell somebody or I'll burst and I thought that somebody would have to be you.'

'They're going to promote you, is that it?'

'It's not that, either, even if I deserve it. No, the good news is that you're going to be a grandfather again.'

'That's fantastic!' said her father, slapping his bony knees. 'Which one of you is it? Clodagh? Deirdre? Fenella? Don't tell me Moirin's having another one! I thought she had more than enough on her hands, looking after Siobhan!

'But, sure,' he added, shifting himself forward in his chair so that he could speak to her more confidentially, 'whichever one of you it is, I swear that I'll keep my mouth shut until she tells me herself, official-like!'

'You don't have to do that, Dad,' said Katie. 'It's me.'

Her father slowly sat back again. '*You*? *You're* having a baby?'

'That's right. Me. Just in time for Easter. A little Easter egg for you.'

There was a long silence. Her father took a clean white handkerchief out of his cardigan pocket, unfolded it, and carefully wiped his nose. Then he looked across at Katie and said, 'You two didn't hold your halt then, did you, you and John? How long has he been back from America?'

'Dad—'

'You *will* be getting married, though, you and John? I mean, before it gets too obvious, like? I'm not trying to be censorious or anything. I'm not the Pope. I'm just trying to think what your mother would have said.'

'Dad, I'm ten weeks' pregnant. It isn't John's.'

Another long silence. Katie's father opened and closed his mouth two or three times, rotating his jaw as if his dentures were uncomfortable. At last he said, 'I see. Well. Not that it makes all that much difference, I suppose. A child is a child. But you're still going to get married, aren't you?'

'I don't know,' said Katie. 'It depends how John reacts.'

'What do you mean, *reacts*? Doesn't he know?'

Katie shook her head. 'Not yet. I haven't been able to pluck up the nerve to tell him – mostly because I don't know how he's going to take it. When he came back he was so sure that we could carry on exactly where we left off, as if nothing had happened. But – Dad – I had no reason to think when he left me that he was *ever* going to come back. What was I supposed to do?'

'Oh, come on, I'm not blaming you for finding yourself another man friend,' said her father. 'You're still young, for goodness' sake. But to get yourself pregnant . . . whewf, I don't know. I always thought you were much more sensible than that. Who was it?'

'What?'

'Who was it? Someone at the station? Are you still seeing him? Don't tell me you're stringing them both along, John and this other fellow? Mother of God, Katie, you've totally knocked me sideways, I have to tell you!'

Katie said, 'Dad, it was a one-off. It was the fellow who had just moved in next door to me. He said he had trouble with his wife and, I don't know, I was feeling lonely and down and he was very good-looking and one thing led to another. It never happened again, even though he wanted it to.'

'So, this very good-looking next-door fellow, is he going to take any responsibility for this baby?'

'He can't, Dad. He's dead. That night the Duggans came round to my house and tried to shoot me . . . he was the one who took the bullet for me. David was his name. David Kane.'

Her father leaned forward again and took hold of her hand. Before Bláithín had started taking care of him his hands had always been dry and cold and his fingernails had always been dirty, but now they were clean and soft and warm, and his wedding ring was shiny. It was almost like having her hand held by a saint.

'Then, Katie, what can I say to you?' he told her. His voice was still throaty, but now it was very gentle. 'Since the father was the one who died saving you . . . you must have very mixed feelings about this child.' He watched her with a tender look on his face as a large teardrop rolled out of her right eye, and then the left. Then he patted her hand and said, 'However this turns out, Kathleen, I'll always love you, and I'll always be here to look after you, just so long as I have the breath. I'm your Dad, after all.'

Katie let out a hoot of misery and bent forward in her chair, covering her face with her hands. She sobbed and sobbed until her ribs hurt, while her father laid his hand on her shoulder to comfort her and occasionally patted her and said, 'There, now. There.'

After a while, though, she began to think of what Dr Murphy had told her when she had visited him last week. '*Remember from the last time, Kathleen. By now your little baby's major organs are starting to form, its tooth buds are visible, and you can even make out its fingers and toes. If you haven't felt it moving already, you will soon. It's going to be making its presence felt, believe me.*'

She sat up and wiped her eyes with the sleeve of her shirt, and blinked.

'I'm all right now, Dad. Thanks. Just a monster attack of the hormones.'

'So . . . are you going to tell John tonight, when you go home? You should, you know, sweetheart.'

'I don't know. I'll try. I'll see. I can't choose a name for it on my own, can I? So I suppose I'll *have* to tell him.'

* * *

When she arrived home, though, John was sitting hunched over the coffee table with his laptop and papers strewn everywhere and he was involved a lengthy Skype conversation with his bald-headed partner in San Francisco.

He blew her a finger-kiss and said, 'Sorry, darling, this is going to take a while. Do you want to order a takeaway? Or I could heat up that bolognese.'

'Ah, no, you're all right for now, thanks,' Katie told him. 'I had a decent lunch for a change. Maybe I'll just have a sandwich later, if that's all right with you.'

She changed into a loose stripey top and leggings, and then went into the kitchen to make herself a mug of green tea. She felt as if she had been living off almost nothing else for the past few weeks but green tea and chocolate ginger biscuits. She was pouring boiling water on to the teabag when her iPhone rang.

'Are you at home, ma'am? Oh, sorry about that. It's Bill – Bill Phinner.'

'Bill? You're working late.'

'I know, but I wanted to finish up all the forensics on the Spring Lane device. Besides, the moth has gone churchifying this evening and there's nothing on the telly.'

'So how's it going?'

'I think we're making some progress. It was what I suspected right from the beginning, because so much explosive was used, at least ten per cent more than was necessary for the job in hand. You don't need three hundred grams of Semtex to blow up a mobile home. You can bring down a two-storey building with fifteen hundred grams. I'm absolutely sure that this device was put together by Fergal ó Floinn, the same fellow we suspected of that Merchants Quay bomb.'

'Just because he used too much Semtex?'

'Ó Floinn was always what you might call *over-precautionary*. When he was blowing safes in Limerick for the Duggans there were two occasions when he didn't just blow the doors open, he blew the safes clear out of the buildings they were in and halfway across the street. But, no, it's just not that. Everything about the Spring Lane device says ó Floinn. It's the fussy way the wiring's been done, with the ends twisted into a figure of eight, and the detonator was one of a batch that was stolen years ago from that slate quarry near Killoran, which ó Floinn always used.'

'All right, Bill,' said Katie. 'Of course, there's already a warrant out for ó Floinn's arrest for the Merchants Quay bombing, but I'll talk to Superintendent Pearse in the morning to have another alert circulated. I'll also ask Mathew McElvey put out a new appeal through the media. The only problem is that even the latest

341

pictures we have of ó Floinn were taken about fifteen years ago. He probably has white hair by now, if he has any hair at all, and a beer belly on him.'

'Somebody must know where he is,' said Bill. 'After all, somebody hired him to blow up Paddy Fearon. How did *they* find him?'

When she had finished talking to Bill Phinner, Katie looked at her tea and saw that it had infused for so long that it was almost black. She tipped it away and switched on the kettle to make a fresh mug. She suddenly felt very tired. She could hear John still talking on Skype, and from what he was saying about pharmaceutical sales projections it sounded as if his conversation was going to go on for at least another half-hour.

She took her mug of tea into the bathroom and ran herself a peach-scented foam bath. When it was ready she wearily undressed and climbed into it. Her breasts were beginning to feel swollen and tender, and even if she didn't have a baby-bump yet there was no doubt that her waist was thickening. She thought it strange that she couldn't clearly remember her pregnancy with Seamus and this was almost like having a baby for the first time. Maybe that was God's way of making sure that women had more than one child. After each pregnancy, He wiped their memories clean, especially their recollections of how much it had hurt.

John came into the bathroom and sat on the side of the bath. 'How's my beautiful merrow?'

'Beat out, to tell you the truth. I went to see the father on the way home.'

'Oh, your dad. Good. And what did he have to say to you?'

He said: Tell him. You should.

'Not much. But he's looking so much better now that Bláithín's looking after him.'

Tell him.

'That's great, Listen, if you want to get yourself dry, I'll knock up a couple of sandwiches for us. Ham okay? Or would you rather have cheese?'

342

'Cheese would be grand. But just the Coolea. Not that stinky French stuff you got from the market.'

Once he had left the bathroom, Katie sank down into the water so that her breasts floated and she was bearded with bubbles. She had to tell him. She knew that he would be hurt, and jealous, and that it wouldn't be easy for him to raise another man's child even if he agreed to do it. So far, he had probably attributed the changes in her mood and her tastes to her usual PMT, but she wouldn't be able to hide it very much longer.

She heard him singing to himself as he made the sandwiches, 'The Fields of Athenry'. It brought tears to her eyes again and she had to tell herself, 'Stop crying, you fool, would you? Will you ever stop? You got yourself into this, now you get yourself out of it!'

Forty-two

It was after 11.15 p.m. when Riona walked along the stable block and knocked at the door of the small lean-to annex at the end where Dermot lived. She had to knock again before he opened up, and when he did he squinted at her as if he didn't recognize her. The living room behind him was foggy with cigarette smoke and he smelled of drink. On the table in the middle of the room she could see an open tin of tuna with a fork beside it, and a half-empty bottle of Paddy's.

'She should have cooled down by now,' she said. 'It's been more than an hour since you switched off the hog roaster.'

'Oh. Yes. Sure,' said Dermot. 'I'll get my jacket. Is it still lashing out?'

Riona didn't answer but waited under her umbrella while Dermot struggled into his jacket and then pulled on his mud-encrusted rushers.

They made their way across the rainy stable yard and Dermot pushed open the stable door and switched on the lights. The smell of roasted flesh still lingered, but it had almost faded now and the stable smelled more strongly of straw and horses.

'I took a lamp inside after I switched it off,' said Dermot. 'If that had been a pig, like, instead of a nun, I'd have said that she was fierce overdone.'

Riona said, 'The Romans were supposed to have roasted people in the brazen bull for days, until they were nothing but bones, and when they took the bones out they said they shone like diamonds. They used to make necklaces out of them.'

'Cracked, them fecking Romans, if you ask me.'

Dermot unlatched the hog roaster and with two loud clangs the stainless-steel covers dropped down on either side. Sister Aibrean was curled up on the metal tray with her knees bent and her hands up under her chin. Her skin was shiny and dark brown, so that she looked more like a giant insect than an elderly woman. Riona approached the hog roaster and looked down at her. In places her bones had broken through her flesh, so that Riona could see her elbows and her ribs and her pelvis.

So this is all she ever amounted to, she thought, *God's devoted servant, who bullied me and demeaned me and took away my precious boy. Underneath that frigid white skin she was nothing but a jigsaw puzzle of old bones, with a nasty, pious, self-righteous brain nestling inside her skull. Well, now that skin has been roasted and that brain has had all of that nastiness and piety and self-righteousness cooked right out of it.* She leaned over Sister Aibrean's brown, blind face and spat in it.

'Jesus, you really hate them fecking nuns, don't you?' said Dermot, shaking his head. 'What do you want to do with her? We could grind her up, like, and mix her with the horse cubes and then nobody would ever know what had happened to her, would they? I can't see the shades analysing nobs of horse shit, can you, to see if they can find a nun in one of them?'

'I *want* people to know what happened to her, Dermot!' snapped Riona. 'I *want* them to know how she suffered before she died! How many times I have told you that is the whole reason we're doing this? Why do you think we sent up Sister Mona with those balloons? For the fun of it? Why do you think I told you to throw Sister Barbara in the fountain? If they simply vanished, what would be the point of it? They'd be gone and after a week or so nobody would care that they'd vanished, or wonder where they'd gone to, or why.'

'If you say so,' said Dermot. 'I think we're taking a fierce risk myself. But then, you're the one who's paying.'

'Yes, Dermot, I'm the one who's paying. So can you go and wake up Conor, since he'll probably be asleep by now, and we can take Sister Aibrean down to Cork. I'll tell you where I want you to put her on show.'

Dermot frowned at the body in the hog roaster. 'I hope she's not going to fall to bits when we try to take her out of there.'

'No, she'll stay in one piece all right. Besides, I'm going to dress her again. That'll help keep her together.'

'You're going to *dress* her again? Lamb of the Lord Jesus, rather you than me!'

'You're going to help, Dermot. I can't manage it on my own.'

Dermot said nothing more. They both knew that he could walk out any time he wanted to, but then he would have nowhere to stay and no money, and where would a man with a record of criminal detention in a psychiatric hospital find work and a bed to sleep in?

Between them, Riona and Dermot lifted the metal tray out of the hog roaster and laid it on the floor. Dermot took out a clasp knife and cut the cords that were binding Sister Aibrean's wrists and ankles. Then he straightened out her arms and legs, with a crackle that sounded like pistol shots, kneeling on her knees with all of his weight and bending her arms back until he dislocated her elbows.

When he had done that he held her body up clear of the tray while Riona pulled on her habit, knotting it loosely around her waist, and then her scapular. She didn't bother with her drawers or underskirts. Finally, she fitted Sister Aibrean's cowl over her brown, grinning face, and pinned on her scarf.

'Would you look at the state of that?' said Dermot when Riona had finished dressing her. 'That's like something out of the nightmares I used to have about nuns when I was a kid. My mate Pauly told me that all nuns looked like fecking great spiders underneath their habits and that's why they only showed you their faces and their hands. Scared the living shite out of me, that did.'

'Go and wake up Conor,' said Riona. 'I'll go and get my coat and fetch the Range Rover around. Oh, and bring that cord, too. We're going to be needing it to tie her into position.'

Forty-three

Katie dreamed that she was standing in front of the grotto in Ballinspittle where, in 1985, the small statue of the Blessed Virgin had been seen to move and breathe, and which ever after had become a place of pilgrimage.

In her dream it was night-time and very dark, but the Virgin had a halo of stars which were lit up and illuminated her stone-white face and the huge red roses that had been placed all around her.

Katie had visited the grotto the week after little Seamus had died. She didn't really believe in miracles, and even the bishop of Cork and Ross had been very cautious about acknowledging that the statue might really have moved. But since the doctors hadn't been able fully to explain why Seamus had died, and in spite of all of her prayers God had remained silent, she had gone to Ballinspittle to see if she could find some kind of an answer.

She hadn't seen the Virgin move and she hadn't heard Her speak, but all the same she had found some measure of comfort standing in that country road, in the drizzle, with nobody else around. And here she was again, in her dream, although she wasn't aware that it was a dream.

She looked up at the Virgin and said, 'You know where Seamus is, don't you?'

The Virgin opened her eyes and turned her head to give Katie a tender smile. 'Yes,' she said, softly. 'Seamus is coming back to you.'

'You mean – *this* is Seamus? This baby I'm carrying now? I'm going to give birth to Seamus all over again?'

The Virgin nodded and closed her eyes, but Katie was so shocked that she woke up with a jolt, feeling that the ground had suddenly given way from under her feet.

She opened her eyes. It took her a few seconds to realize that she was in bed in her house in Carrig View. The bedroom was totally dark except for the red numerals on the digital clock – 3.27 a.m. She turned over to face John and she must have woken him up, too, because he shifted himself closer and said, 'Katie? Are you okay?'

'Ah, sure, I'm grand, thanks. I was dreaming, that's all.'

'Nothing too sexy, I hope,' he said, and kissed her forehead, and then the tip of her nose, and then her lips. 'Not having an orgy, were you, with a crowd of other fellows?'

She kissed him back and said, 'You don't ever have to be jealous of me, darling.'

He lifted the hem of her short nightgown and ran his hand right up her back, stroking her between her shoulder blades.

'Mmm,' she murmured. 'That feels good. You should have been a professional masseur.'

'What? Rubbing the arses of wobbly old women all day? No thanks. You're the only woman I want to massage.'

He slid his hand around and started to fondle her breast, gently rolling her nipple between finger and thumb until it stiffened. Even though her breast was so tender, she began to feel aroused. She could feel his breath against her face, and he was breathing harder and she could see his eyes glistening in the darkness.

She kissed him and said, 'Hold on,' and sat up in bed so that she could pull her nightgown over her head. Then, naked, she turned back to him and held him close to her. Somehow it made it more exciting that she could hardly see him in the darkness, but she could feel his muscular shoulders and the crucifix of hairs on his chest.

He caressed her hip, which made her jump, and then his fingertips trailed across her stomach and between her legs. She was already very wet and slippery, and he slid one finger up inside her while he slowly rotated the ball of his thumb over her clitoris.

'You're like a god, you know that,' she whispered. She opened her thighs wider and John knelt up between them. She reached down and cupped his balls in the palm of her hand and then she took hold of his stiffened penis and guided it into herself. When he entered her, she couldn't stop herself from letting out a long *oohhhh!* of pleasure and release. With John holding her and kissing her, and his hardened penis so far up inside her that it gave her little shivers, all of her anxieties seemed to dwindle into nothing but a single spark, and then even that spark winked out. All she could think of was him and how wonderful he was making her feel. His smell, and the tautness of his muscles, and the brushing of his hair against her bare skin.

'Oh, Katie,' he gasped, and he began to push himself into her faster and harder. 'God almighty, what you do to me.'

After a while, though, he drew himself out of her. 'Turn over,' he panted and laid his hand on her hip to help her get up. She knew what he wanted because they often used to do it like that, with Katie on her hands and knees. In that position, he could enter her even deeper, and even harder, until she could almost believe that his penis was going to come out of her mouth.

'No, John, not like that,' she told him. 'Not tonight.' She reached down and took hold of his penis again, pulling him back towards her. 'Let's just carry on like this.'

'Oh, come on, baby, you know how much you love it.'

'No, John, please.'

He must have caught something in her tone of voice, because he stayed perfectly still for a moment and she could hear that he was suppressing his heavy breathing. Then he dropped sideways, back on to the bed.

'What's wrong, Katie?' he asked her.

'Nothing's wrong. Everything's grand.'

'But you didn't want me to make love to you like that. You didn't think I was going to try to put it up the wrong hole, did you?'

'No, and you know I like that sometimes. It's too – it's too violent, that's all.'

'*Violent?*' said John, propping himself up on one elbow. 'What do you mean by "violent"? When have I ever been violent?'

'Sorry, "violent" isn't the word I was looking for, not at all.' She lifted her hand in the darkness and touched his unshaven cheek. 'What I meant was, when we do it like that, you go too far into me.'

'You never complained about that before. I thought that was the whole point of doing it like that.'

'Yes, but—' and now she couldn't stop the words coming out because they tumbled out all on their own, like children rushing out of school, and once she had spoken them she couldn't unspeak them. 'When we did it like that before, I wasn't pregnant.'

The silence that followed seemed to Katie to last for hours. John's breathing gradually returned to normal, but he didn't say anything and he didn't move. She almost wondered if he had fallen asleep again. Perhaps he had fallen asleep before she had admitted that she was pregnant, in which case the Blessed Virgin had granted her a few more days' grace.

'John?' she said.

He sat up, reached over and switched on his bedside lamp. His curly black hair looked wild and his eyes were puffy.

'Pregnant?' he said. 'How far gone?'

'Eleven weeks the end of this week.'

'I came back only seven weeks ago.'

'Yes.'

'So it's not mine, then? I mean, it's not ours – yours and mine? That's insane. How could it be?'

'No. No, it isn't.'

Katie had thought that when it came to this moment she might burst into tears and beg for his understanding, but now that she had actually told him she felt very calm, and also deeply protective of the child inside her. No matter what the circumstances, it had been conceived and she was going to be its mother.

John had walked out on her to go to America and she had believed that he would never come back, so why should she have stayed celibate? He might have refrained from having any affairs himself because he had missed her so much, but it was totally unreasonable for him to expect her to have done the same.

He stood up and walked naked across to the wardrobe. He still had crimson scratches from Katie's fingernails across one shoulder.

'Don't you want to know who the father is?' Katie asked him.

'What difference would it make?' he said, keeping his back turned to her. He took out a thick maroon roll-neck sweater and a pair of dark grey corduroy trousers.

'I think that if you knew the circumstances, you might find it easier to come to terms with it.'

'What do you mean, "circumstances"? The circumstances were that you fucked some other fellow. I don't need to know if he bought you dinner beforehand.'

Katie watched him as he dressed. Physically, she thought he was so beautiful. She didn't want to lose him, but already she was beginning to feel that dull emotional pain that she had experienced when he had left for San Francisco. As he pulled on his trousers she could see that his penis was still reddened and half swollen from their lovemaking, but his erection was dying fast.

'What are you getting dressed for?' she said. 'Why don't you come back to bed and we can talk about this in the morning. You're as tired as I am.'

'I'm going to take a walk, that's all.'

'John, don't be mental. It's not even four o'clock in the morning and it's teeming outside by the sound of it. Not only that, there's a very good reason why there's two armed protection officers sitting outside keeping a watch out.'

He turned around. She couldn't read the expression on his face at all. His eyes were always dark ocean blue, but now they looked even darker. 'Okay, then, I'll go for a drive.'

'Please, John, stay,' Katie begged him. 'I'll go and sleep on the couch if you don't want to sleep with me.'

'What kind of a scummer do you think I am? You think I'd throw a woman out of her own bed when she's eleven weeks' pregnant?'

'John – we need to talk about this. We really do.'

'Talk?' He tugged his fingers through his curls but only succeeded in making them even more tangled. 'Sure we do. You're right. We *do* need to talk. But give me a little time to think it over, would you?'

He left the bedroom, closing the door very quietly behind him, like a parent who doesn't want to wake a sleeping child. Katie thought about going after him, but she knew that John was never easily persuaded. He wasn't inflexible, but if he ever changed his mind about anything he had to believe that he had changed it himself.

She heard him going into the living room, and then a clatter and a noise like fabric tearing. She stayed where she was. If he was angry and he had broken some of her ornaments, she didn't want a physical confrontation. Apart from anything else, she could probably beat him in a fight, because she was a second-dan black belt at kick-boxing and still attended the Miko academy as often as she could, and she didn't want to humiliate him any more than she had already.

She heard the beeping sound of him switching off the burglar alarm and then the front door slamming. Soon after that, she heard his car start up and reverse out of the driveway. Then there was nothing but the pattering of the rain against the bedroom window.

She continued to lie in bed, but she kept the light on because she knew perfectly well that she wouldn't be able to sleep.

She said a prayer, asking God to protect John while he was feeling so angry and jealous and resentful, but also to help him understand how much she loved him, and that she hadn't slept with David Kane as a deliberate act of betrayal.

* * *

After about an hour the rain stopped. Katie climbed out of bed and took her thick pink bathrobe down from its hook on the back of the door. She went into the kitchen first and filled the kettle. Barney looked up from his bed, confused that she was walking around the house at this time of the morning, and wuffled at her.

'It's okay, Barns. It's only human beings behaving like human beings. Stone mad, in other words.'

While the kettle boiled, she went through to the living room. As soon as she switched on the light she saw that John's half-squashed tubes of acrylic paint were scattered all across the carpet, as well as his brushes and his wooden palette. Lying on the coffee table was the nude painting of her. He had torn it in half, diagonally.

Katie went over and picked up the two halves. It looked as if he had folded the board backwards and forwards several times before tearing it, so that it was damaged beyond repair.

Again, she didn't cry, although it grieved her so much that she had to sit down on the couch, still holding the two pieces, one in each hand. She understood the message. *You've torn me in half, so now I've torn you in half, too.* Barney came and stood in the living-room doorway, with his head on one side, and made that mewling sound in the back of his throat as if he were asking her what was wrong.

She had been sitting there only a few minutes when her phone rang, which made her jump.

'Detective Superintendent Maguire? It's Garda Sergeant Mulliken. Sorry to be calling you at this ungodly hour, ma'am, but there's something you need to be coming into the city to see for yourself first-hand. Detective Inspector O'Rourke and Detective O'Donovan are here already.'

'What is it ? Where?' asked Katie.

'Patrick's Bridge, ma'am. It's one of your nuns.'

Forty-four

She tried ringing John before she left the house, but he didn't answer. She walked across to the two protection officers sitting in their dark unmarked car in the rain and tapped on their window.

'I've been called into city and I doubt I'll be back until much later today. My partner's gone out for a drive but he didn't tell me how long he was going to be.'

'He had a word with us himself, ma'am,' said the garda in the passenger seat. 'He told us he'd be coming back in a couple of hours but he wouldn't be staying for long, like.'

'Oh,' said Katie. Then, 'Oh, yes, that's right,' trying not to sound surprised. 'What time are you going to be relieved?'

'06.00.'

'All right. Tell the officers who relieve you that as soon as my partner's come and gone, they can stand down. I'll sort it all out with your sergeant as soon as he gets into the station.'

'Yes, ma'am.'

'And – thanks,' she said. 'Do either of you need the toilet before I go?'

'No, we're grand. You have to have bladders of steel for this duty.'

Katie walked back to her car, climbed in and started the engine. She sat in the driveway for a few moments with the windscreen wipers squeaking from side to side. So John would be back but he wouldn't be staying for long. Did that mean that he was going to pack his bags and leave her? She tried ringing him again but he still didn't answer, so she left him a message.

'John,' she said. 'Call me. I have to go into the city, but we really, really need to talk. Don't walk out on me again, darling. I love you, and what happened was nothing to do with not loving you. So, please.'

She didn't know what else to say. She didn't think that she had to make excuses. When she had gone to bed with David Kane he had assured her that he had had a vasectomy, but why should she have to explain that to John?

She drove into the city. It was still dark and it was still raining hard. As she drove along Penrose Quay, however, she could already see dazzling halogen lights up ahead of her on St Patrick's Bridge, as well as blue and red flashing lights. When she turned off St Patrick's Quay on to the bridge itself she saw that it been cordoned off with crime-scene tapes and that it was crowded with squad cars and vans and an ambulance. At least fifteen gardaí were milling around, as well as three technical experts and a fire crew.

She parked behind a squad car and walked across the bridge. Detective Inspector O'Rourke and Detective O'Donovan caught sight of her and came up to meet her. Detective Inspector O'Rourke was wearing a baggy fawn raincoat and a brown brimmer that looked as if he had inherited it from his grandfather. Detective O'Donovan looked surprisingly smart in a short black overcoat, as if he had been out last night and hadn't been to bed yet.

'You won't believe this, ma'am, when you see it,' said Detective Inspector O'Rourke. 'This *has* to be the same offenders who threw that nun's body in the fountain and did for the other ones, too. You couldn't make this up, like.'

Four cast-iron lamp standards stood on the bridge's parapets, two on either side, with large glass lanterns on top of them. Lashed to the lamp standard on the south-east side was a sodden black figure, and as Detective Inspector O'Rourke and Detective O'Donovan led Katie towards it she could see that it was dressed in a nun's cowl and vestments. Two technicians who had been taking photographs of the figure stood aside so that she could step up close to it.

'Holy Mary,' she said, and crossed herself. The figure could have come straight out of a horror film. Its face was dark brown and shiny, like a tribal mask of varnished mahogany. Its eye sockets were hollow and dark, and its lips were stretched back in a hideous grimace. The cowl and scapular had been soaked by the rain and water was dripping from the blackened fingertips that dangled out of the sleeves, as well as the toes that hung below the hem of the habit.

'It's a woman all right,' said Detective Inspector O'Rourke. 'Like, they hoicked up her habit and took a quick lamp to make sure. Whether she's a genuine nun or not we can't tell just yet because she's been burned so bad. These are fourth-degree burns, easy. But she has a totally different look about her than most of the burns victims that I've ever come across, what do you think?'

Katie shaded her eyes against the halogen lamps and stared up at the figure's face. Detective Inspector O'Rourke was right. She had seen several victims of arson attacks herself, and people who had burned to death in car crashes. Where their skin had been exposed to the flames it had always looked blackened on the outside and red-raw where it had been split open by the heat. Sometimes people's faces looked as if they had melted, like Salvador Dalí's floppy watches. The skin of this victim's face, however, was glossy and taut and smooth. The only exception was her blistered lips, which were crisp and bubbly and ragged, as if somebody had been tearing bits away from them with pliers.

'I don't know,' said Katie. 'We'll have to wait and see what the pathologist has to say about it.'

'What I'm saying is, she doesn't look like she's had petrol splashed all over her, or that somebody's had a go at her with a blowtorch or chucked her on to a bonfire.'

'I have you, Francis. I know exactly what you mean. She looks more like she's been roasted in an oven.'

'Roasted nun, Jesus,' said Detective O'Donovan. 'I won't be ordering any black pudding with *my* breakfast this morning. But however they killed her, like, they dressed her *after* she was dead. Her clothes aren't burned at all. Not even scorched.'

'Any witnesses?' asked Katie. She looked around, checking where the CCTV cameras were positioned. There were two that covered the bridge, one on the north side of the river on the English College building, which used to be the AIB bank, and another on the corner of St Patrick's Street.

'It was a taxi driver who reported it,' said Detective Inspector O'Rourke. 'He was coming back from an early call to the airport. He said he saw two fellows tying something up to the lamp post, one of them standing right up on the parapet. He thought they might be council workers or something at first, fixing the lamp, but then he thought that was fierce queer, that time of the morning, and both of them were wearing black hoodies and not your high-vis jackets like you'd expect from council workers. So he turned around and went back to take a look. The two fellows were gone by then, but the body here was here all tied up to the lamp post.'

'Was that all he saw? Two fellows in black hoodies? He didn't see anybody else, or any vehicles nearby that might have been theirs?'

'No. Two fellows in black hoodies, that's all. Just like the two fellows who dropped Sister Barbara's body into the fountain. But at least we know who one of *them* was, even if we haven't found him yet.'

Katie said, 'I can see the press hovering over there. I'll have a quick word with them and then I'll go to the station and wake a few people up. We're going to need a pathologist, on the double, and we're going to need the footage from those two CCTV cameras. I think we'll be needing to pay another visit to the Bon Sauveur Convent, too. If this victim was one of their congregation, they may be able to help us identify who she was. Or *not*, of course – depending on how public-spirited Mother O'Dwyer happens to be feeling.'

'I was going to go up to the convent myself after,' said Detective O'Donovan. 'The search team told me they should be winding up their excavating later today, or sometime tomorrow at the latest.

They've finished digging up the vegetable garden and they've already taken up more than two thirds of the lawn'

'What's the latest body count?' asked Katie. 'Yesterday morning, Sergeant O'Farrell told me that it was up to three hundred and eighty.'

'More than that now, ma'am. It was well over four hundred by the time they stopped work in the evening. I reckon by the time they've finished it'll hit the five hundred mark, easy. Maybe even six. There were certainly four hundred in the septic tank and another hundred under the lawns and the flower beds.'

'It's a massacre,' said Katie. 'God knows how long it's going to take the pathologists to examine every one of them. And all we have is bones. It's not going to be easy to establish the cause of death, even if we can establish it at all. The real problem is we haven't found any record of their deaths, although I find it really hard to believe that there isn't one.'

'That's what I was thinking myself,' said Detective O'Donovan. 'Sure, the sisters believed that most of those poor children were the spawn of the Devil, but you would have thought that they would have made *some* note of them leaving this world, wouldn't you? It's bad enough for kids to die when they're only two or three years old – do you know what I mean, like? – especially when they've been nothing but hungry and unhappy all of their lives. But for nobody to have written down that they even existed, I think that's a tragedy.'

'It's more than a tragedy,' said Katie. 'It's going to be crucial in deciding what action we take against the Bon Sauveurs – that's if we decide to take any action at all.'

'Exactly,' nodded Detective Inspector O'Rourke. He was watching the technicians as they carefully cut through the nylon cords that had been used to fasten the stiff black figure up against the lamp post. One of them was standing on the parapet holding the dead woman's head to make sure that it didn't suddenly drop forward and snap her spine.

Katie said, 'At the moment, I don't see how we're going to be able to determine if the sisters were guilty of causing death by wilful negligence, or if the children simply died of natural causes.'

'For all anybody knows, they could have strangled them, like, or poisoned them, or drowned them,' said Detective O'Donovan.

'Well, I very much doubt it, but you're right, and there's no way of telling for certain.'

Without taking his eyes off the figure tied to the lamp post, Detective Inspector O'Rourke said, 'We could prosecute them for failing to report all of those deaths, couldn't we, and for disposing of their remains illegally?'

'Theoretically, yes,' said Katie. 'But I very much doubt if the DPP would go along with it. And what would be the point of taking action against a handful of doddery old nuns? They would have the diocese defending them in court, no expense spared, and even if they were found guilty, what would you do with them? They've spent most of their lives locked up in a convent in any case. It would be a complete waste of public money – not to mention bad publicity for us. There are still plenty of people who think that young women who get themselves pregnant out of wedlock are not much better than harlots.'

Oh God, she thought, even as she said it. *That includes me.*

Now the woman's body was being lifted down from the lamp standard and lowered on to a stretcher. She would be taken to the mortuary at CUH and Katie would have to call the cantankerous Dr Reidy to send down a deputy state pathologist to examine her, because Dr O'Brien had already returned to Dublin.

'If you could stall there for just a second, please,' Katie called out as the two technicians lifted up the stretcher. They waited patiently while she went over and pulled on a pair of black latex gloves. She took hold of the hem of the woman's rain-sodden habit and folded it back as far as the middle of her thighs. Unlike her face, her bare legs were amber rather than brown, but they were just as glossy, as if they had been lacquered, or suntanned. Where the skin was thinner, her kneecaps and shin bones had broken through, and the skin of her left thigh had split apart. What interested Katie was that the flesh that had been exposed underneath wasn't bloody and raw, as she normally would have expected in a severe burns victim, but a pale beige colour, like cooked pork.

She knocked against the skin of the woman's right thigh with her knuckle and it felt and sounded brittle.

Detective Inspector O'Rourke was standing close beside her. 'I think you're dead right,' he said. 'She's been roasted. But where would you find an oven big enough? At a bakery, maybe? Or a restaurant?'

'I think we need to find out who she is first,' said Katie. 'Then I think we'll be able to discover how she died.'

'Whoever she is, I hope for her sake that she was dead before they roasted her,' put in Detective O'Donovan as the technicians carried the stretcher away.

Katie snapped off her gloves. 'If she really is a nun, Patrick, and she was killed by the same person who killed those other three nuns, then I wouldn't count on it. If there's anything they all have in common, these three murders, it's maximum premeditated pain.'

* * *

She approached the small group of TV and radio and newspaper reporters who had been hanging around smoking by the statue of Father Mathew. They greeted her with a fusillade of coughs and 'g'mornings'.

'What's the story, Detective Superintendent?' asked Michael Malone from the *Examiner*.

'All I can tell you at the moment is that a deceased female dressed in a nun's vestments was tied to one of the lamp standards,' said Katie. 'An eyewitness saw two men in black hoodies tying her up there at approximately four thirty-five this morning. We're appealing for anybody else who might have seen this being done to contact us, or anybody who might have seen two men behaving suspiciously in the city centre in the early hours.'

'Was the victim actually a nun?'

'I can't give you any more details about her for the time being, but as soon as I know more we'll be holding a full media conference at the station.'

'From what I could see of her, I don't know, she looked like she was African,' said Jean Mulligan from the *Echo*. 'Do you think this could be a race-hate crime?'

'We don't yet know who she is or what her nationality might be,' Katie told her. 'I can assure you, though, that she wasn't black.'

'So why did she look like that? Was that something to do with the cause of death?'

'I can't answer any more questions at the moment,' said Katie. 'Mathew McElvey from the press office will be in touch with you later.'

'This is the fourth nun found murdered in Cork in not much more than a matter of days,' said Michael Malone. 'Like, not just murdered, but murdered in a really unusual way. Don't tell us there's no connection.'

'All I can say is that we're continuing to make enquiries and we're continuing to make progress in our efforts to find out who's responsible.'

'Well, that's a relief, because it's beginning to seem like less of a series of unrelated killings and more like a cull.'

* * *

Katie went into her office and switched on the lights because it was still dark outside. Even before she had taken off her wet raincoat she rang John again. His phone rang and rang but he still didn't answer.

She thought about leaving him another message, but she had already told him that she loved him and that she wanted to talk to him. What more could she say? Besides, he had said that he needed some time and some space to think, and it would probably be better if she allowed him to do that.

She had threatened to wake people up to get this investigation into motion, but in all seriousness she knew it was far too early to ring Dr Reidy and that it would also be several hours before they would be able to run through all of the CCTV coverage from St Patrick's Bridge and the surrounding streets. There were more than thirty high-definition CCTV cameras around Cork city centre and even though the radio room was manned by gardaí twenty-four hours a day it was impossible to watch every monitor screen continuously.

Still, she now had two or three hours of comparative peace in which she could calm down from the events of the night, have a latte and a Miracle Munch bar, and catch up with all of her paperwork.

* * *

Shortly after seven the rain stopped and the grey clouds cleared away and a wan sunlight shone into her office window. She was wondering whether she felt like another latte when Detective Dooley knocked at her door.

'Good morning, ma'am!' he greeted her. 'I think we might have a bit of a lead on Roisin Begley.'

'Really? Have you seen who she met up with?'

'Not directly. But I went through all the CCTV footage around Hanover Street around the time she left Havana Brown's. You can see her coming out of the doors and she stops and looks around, because there's nobody there to meet her. But then it seems like somebody's called out to her and caught her attention, because she starts walking quickly west towards Arthur's Bar on the corner. Of course, it's double yellows on both sides of the road outside Havana Brown's, so if somebody was waiting for her with a car they would have had to park in Cross Street.

'She walks out of our field of vision, so we don't see her meeting anybody or getting into a car, but after about thirty seconds we see a black Lexus GS driving east along Hanover Street, back past the entrance to Havana Brown's. It has dark tinted windows, so we can't identify the occupants. It turns right when it reaches South Main Street and then right again into French's Quay and after that we lose it, but it doesn't really matter because we have its registration plate.'

'Well, that's a break,' said Katie. 'And from the smug look on your face I'd say that you've traced who it belongs to.'

'Oh yes. Who said that Christmas comes only once a year? It's registered to Savitas Clothing Traders of Ballycurreen Industrial Estate. "Savitas" is Lithuanian for "distinctive", and the distinctive thing about Savitas Clothing Traders is that its principal partner is Dovydas Karosas.'

'Well how about that?' said Katie. 'We prosecuted Karosas about three years ago for stealing charity clothing bags from people's doorsteps in Glasheen. He was sending them off to Lithuania for processing and he was making a fortune out of it. That was quite apart from the pimping of underage girls that he's always been involved in, along with my dear friend Michael Gerrety.'

'You actually prosecuted Karosas? How did that turn out?'

'What do you think? Case dismissed for lack of evidence. In other words, case dismissed because all of our witnesses were threatened with having their tongues cut out with Stanley knives. Literally.'

'Jesus,' said Detective Dooley. But then he said, 'That CCTV footage, that's no proof at all that Karosas took Roisin. But I'll see if I can get a search warrant for his car. It's possible that she left fingerprints in it, or maybe hairs if there was any kind of a struggle.'

'That's fantastic, you do that,' Katie told him. 'But when you do get your warrant, and there's no reason why you shouldn't, let me know. If you're searching Karosas's car, I want to be there personally, just to enjoy his discomfort.'

'Ma'am?'

'Karosas is one of those scumbags who likes to taunt me because he thinks that I can never successfully prosecute him. Even if we don't find anything in his car, I want to see him squirm, that's all.'

A little over forty minutes later, Detective O'Donovan called her. He asked her to come down to the radio room so that she could watch the footage of the nun-figure being lashed to the lamp post on St Patrick's Bridge.

'It's not what you'd call enlightening, though, do you know what I mean?'

Katie went downstairs and after she had watched the footage being played back on one of the larger screens she had to agree with him. The CCTV cameras appeared to have picked up nothing more than they already knew. At 4.11 a.m. two bulky men in black hoodies appeared from Bridge Street, on the north side of the river, supporting the woman's body between them. They held her arms wrapped around their shoulders and her bare feet were trailing on the pavement. From a distance they could easily have been mistaken for two men who were helping home a woman who had drunk too much.

They crossed over to the south side of the bridge, lifted her up and lashed her to the lamp post. A white private-hire taxi drove past while they were doing it, but that was the only moving vehicle in sight. After they had finished tying her up the men walked quickly back the way they had come, their hands in their pockets, their faces always hidden in the shadow of their hoodies.

'But just watch this,' said Detective O'Donovan. After a few minutes, a hooded crow flew up and landed on the nun-figure's shoulder. It hesitated for a while and then it pecked at her lips. It was joined soon after by another hooded crow, which perched on top of her cowl and bent forward to peck at her eyes.

It wasn't too long, though, before the first squad car arrived, and then another, and the crows reluctantly flapped away. There was no sound, but Katie could imagine them cawing in annoyance.

'So that's why she didn't have any eyes?' she said. 'And that's why her lips were so lacerated?'

'Looks like it, doesn't it?' said Detective O'Donovan. 'Apart from that, though, this footage doesn't really help us too much, does it?'

Katie said, 'No . . . but run it again anyway.' She had been standing up to watch it, but now she sat down in one of the swivel chairs in front of the screen so that she could study it more closely. The two men in hoodies walked across the bridge. One of them climbed on to the parapet and took hold of the woman's body under her arms while the other one grasped her hips and started to lift her up.

'Freeze it right there,' said Katie. She leaned forward and peered at the screen intently. 'How much more can you zoom in?'

'Oh, quite a fair bit,' said the young blonde woman garda who was operating the CCTV monitor and she enlarged the picture until the two men and their victim almost filled the entire screen. They were nearly fifty metres away from the lens, but it was one of the new high-definition digital cameras that had recently been installed and so their images were only slightly blurred.

'Look,' said Katie. 'That fellow lifting her up. Am I mistaken, or is he missing the little finger on his left hand there?'

Detective O'Donovan leaned over her shoulder and said, 'You're right. He does have only the four fingers. You can see the stump.'

'So . . .' said Katie. 'We may not know who he is, not yet, but when we find him he's going to have a hard time proving that it wasn't him.'

Forty-five

Katie went in to see Superintendent Pearse. He was in the middle of eating a cheese baguette but he hurriedly opened his desk drawer, dropped it in, and shut it away.

'I didn't mean to interrupt your breakfast,' she smiled.

Superintendent Pearse waved one hand and said, 'No, no bother at all,' through a muffled mouthful of half-chewed bread. 'What can I help you with?'

Katie said, 'The thing is, my partner's going away for a while, which means we won't be requiring protection officers on duty during the day, not while I'm here at the station.'

'Oh. Okay. I see. Sergeant Willis did call me from Midleton, earlier on, and say something about that. When is your partner off?'

'Sometime today. I'm not exactly sure when. But as soon as he's gone they can stand down. I'll let you know this evening when I'm just about to leave for home.'

'Okay, thanks a million,' said Superintendent Pearse, jotting a note on his memo pad. 'Do you know when he's coming back?'

Katie was thinking about the painting, torn in half, and didn't answer him.

He looked up at her and said, 'Kathleen? Your partner. Do you know when he's coming back?'

'Oh, no. Sorry. No, I don't. It's business. He does a lot of business in Europe. Pharmaceuticals.'

Katie gave him another quick smile and left his office. When she turned around to close the door, however, she could see that Superintendent Pearse was still watching her and that he hadn't yet retrieved his cheese baguette from out of his drawer.

* * *

She rang Detective O'Donovan and asked him if he was ready to go up to the Bon Sauveur Convent. While she was putting on her coat, Denis McBride, the ballistics technician, appeared at her door.

'Denis,' she said. 'Is it anything important? I have to shoot out.'

'I just wanted to tell you that I've completed my tests on the round that I extracted from your living-room wall. It was definitely fired by the same rifle that fired the round that killed Detective Horgan.'

'I see,' said Katie. 'So it sounds like somebody really is gunning for me, doesn't it?'

'Well, that's up to you to decide,' said Denis. 'I only do the ballistics. But there's something else I thought you ought to be informed about. It may be something and nothing. It could be only a clerical error.'

'Go on.'

'I was wanting to carry out some firing tests with 7.62 rounds similar to the rounds that were fired at you and Detective Horgan. They would have helped me to calculate the distance they were fired from, among other things, like whether telescopic sights were being used, and also given me a better idea what weapon the offender was using.'

Katie glanced at the clock on her desk. Detective O'Donovan was waiting for her in the car park and Denis spoke very slowly and methodically, as if he had to take each word out of his mouth and carefully examine it to make sure that it was the right one before he put it back into his mouth and actually spoke it.

'I was aware that there were two rifles in the armoury here that fitted the bill – a Russian Dragunov and a Yugoslavian Zastava M-70. They were both confiscated during drugs raids within the past six months and they were being kept here pending the corresponding trials of their owners.'

'Yes, I see,' said Katie. 'And what did you discover, from your firing tests?'

'I haven't carried them out yet.'

'Oh. So . . . what was it that you thought I ought to be informed about?'

'The Dragunov is missing,' said Denis. 'There's no record of anybody signing it out, but it's definitely gone.'

'But nobody can just take weapons out of the armoury without signing for them. And it's totally secure. At least, it's supposed to be. Nobody could even get in there, not unless—'

'Your guess is as good as mine, ma'am,' said Denis.

Katie thought for a moment and then she said, 'All right, Denis. Thank you for telling me. I'll make sure that one of my team looks into it.'

Denis left her office, and as soon as she had pushed her nickel-plated revolver into its holster and gathered up her black leather handbag she followed him. As she went down in the lift she stared at herself closely in the mirror, checking her eye make-up, and she thought that she looked surprisingly calm and collected and well groomed, considering the stress that she had suffered in the last eight hours.

She was very disturbed, though, by what Denis had told her about the missing Dragunov. If it hadn't gone astray as the result of a clerical error, then somebody must have taken it, and the only person who could have gained access to the armoury would have been somebody who had the necessary authority. Even so, how could they have removed it without the officer in charge of the armoury having noticed it? Or colluded in its removal?

She would have to have this investigated, and quickly, for the sake of her own safety if nothing else – especially if the Dragunov was the weapon that had killed Detective Horgan and was being used to take shots at her. But she would have to discuss it with Chief Superintendent MacCostagáin first, because it was more than just a missing rifle, it was a matter of station security and protocol, and it might mean that somebody's head would have to roll.

* * *

Mother O'Dwyer looked at Katie coldly and said, 'What are you accusing me of?'

'I'm not accusing you of anything,' Katie replied. 'I'm saying only that our first search of the convent may not have been sufficiently thorough. There are items that logically we would have expected to find, but haven't.'

'Your officers even went through my clothing and personal effects,' said Mother O'Dwyer. 'How could you not be satisfied with a search that included a photograph of my late mother and my . . . undergarments?'

'I'll be frank with you, Mother O'Dwyer,' said Katie. 'We've almost completed our excavation of the convent garden and so far we've found the remains of five hundred and thirty-seven children of varying ages.'

'I said to you before, Detective Superintendent, I have no further comment to make about anything that you might have discovered. You'll have to speak to our legal advisers.'

'But forget about who was responsible for these children's deaths and for dropping their bodies in a septic tank, rather than giving them a decent burial. I'm not looking for answers to those questions at the moment. What our searches have failed to find so far is any record of who all these children were, and how they died, and when.'

Mother O'Dwyer put on her glasses. 'All I can tell you is that there is no such record available.'

Detective Sergeant Ni Nuallán was standing by the window of Mother O'Dwyer's office with her back to them. She had been watching as the last few skeletons were carried out of the blue forensic tent in body bags and around to the front of the convent, where vans from the coroner's office were waiting to take them away.

Now, however, she turned around. 'Such a record could exist, though?' she asked Mother O'Dwyer.

Clever question, Kyna, thought Katie, *especially that word 'could'*.

Mother O'Dwyer hadn't actually denied the existence of such a record. She had said only that it wasn't 'available', whatever that meant. Now Detective Sergeant Ni Nuallán had put her in the position of having to tell the truth or tell an outright lie before God, and Saint Margaret of Cortona, too, in the picture on the wall behind her, with her arms spread out to heaven.

Mother O'Dwyer didn't answer, but tightly pursed her lips.

'*Is* there a record?' asked Katie.

'I'm – I'm answering no more questions!' snapped Mother O'Dwyer. 'Have I not made that crystal-clear to you? If you persist in harassing me, I shall be forced to lodge a formal complaint against you!'

'That doesn't bother me at all, Mother O'Dwyer,' said Katie. 'I've had more formal complaints lodged against me than you've said novenas. But if that's your attitude, I'm going to arrange for a comprehensive search of the convent, top to bottom, starting immediately.'

'You've done that once already!'

'Yes. But now we're going to do it again. And there's no point in complaining to your legal advisers. The warrant that's been issued by the district court allows us to go on searching until we're totally satisfied that we've found what we're looking for – or totally satisfied that it really doesn't exist.'

Mother O'Dwyer took off her glasses again, bending them backwards and forwards in anger and frustration.

'There is a choice, Mother O'Dwyer,' said Detective Sergeant Ni Nuallán, very gently.

'And what, precisely, is that, may I ask?'

'You could simply hand over the record of those children's deaths, and any other records that might not have been available the first time we searched.'

'Are you suggesting that we have been keeping some things hidden from you?'

'Yes,' said Detective Sergeant Ni Nuallán.

It was then that Mother O'Dwyer snapped her glasses in half.

* * *

As they drove back down Summerhill into the city, Katie said, 'How's it going with the nun-hunting?'

'It's still a dead end at the moment with Sister Virginia, but I was given a phone number for Sister Nessa by Cois Tine. I rang them on the off chance that Sister Nessa might have been using her experience in Malawi to help African women in Cork and it turns out that she had. She organized events for the African Women's Group – you know, like dancing and poetry and all that kind of stuff, as well as talks on health care and integration.

'I rang the number and the woman who answered told me that Sister Nessa was visiting her sister in England but would be back in Cork on Saturday. She didn't have a contact number for her, but I told her that Sister Nessa should call me the minute she arrived home. You know, like urgent, like.'

'That's good,' said Katie. 'At least we know she's safe. You have her address, don't you?'

'Of course, yes. She lives in Dunmore Gardens in Knocknaheeny, just opposite the sports ground. If she doesn't ring me on Saturday I'll go round there myself.'

They crossed over Brian Boru Bridge. A flock of seagulls was flapping and fighting over some black object that was floating in the middle of the river and just before they reached the other side Katie saw that it was a drowned dog.

'Apart from nuns,' she said. 'What about you?'

Detective Sergeant Ni Nuallán made a signal to turn into Anderson's Quay and waited for the approaching traffic to pass, but she didn't turn to look at Katie.

'I've put in my application,' she said. 'So far I've heard nothing, though.'

'You're still sure that you want to leave Cork?'

'I don't know what else I can do. It's affecting my concentration. It's making me depressed.'

Katie felt like reaching out and touching her shoulder, but she kept her hands firmly clasped together in her lap.

'We should talk about this, Kyna. There must be a way. You're one of the best detectives on my team and I don't want to lose you. I don't want to lose you as a friend, either. You're always there to give me moral support when I need it the most.'

'It just hurts too much,' said Detective Sergeant Ni Nuallán. 'There you are, every single day, and I'm not allowed to show you how I feel about you. I have to call you "ma'am" when all I really want to do is hold you in my arms and kiss you.'

Katie said, 'Kyna – I know it's difficult. I completely understand how frustrated you must feel. But even if you get a transfer to Dublin, what's going to happen there? What if you get a crush on another female officer? It happens all the time to people in uniform, but it's something we just have to live with.'

Detective Sergeant Ni Nuallán shook her head. She had tears in her eyes and her blonde hair was a mess, but Katie had to admit to herself that she had never seen her looking so pretty.

As they turned into the station car park, she laid her hand on Detective Sergeant Ni Nuallán's thigh and said, 'Come round to my house . . . maybe on Sunday. Let's spend some time together and talk it through. If you decide you still want to go, then so be it. But at least let's try and think of some alternatives.'

'What about your partner? What's he going to think?'

'John? John won't be any problem. He's left me.'

Detective Sergeant Ni Nuallán stared at Katie in shock. 'He's *left* you? I don't believe it! When did he leave you? Why?'

'Last night,' said Katie. She could feel a *tocht* in her throat and she had to swallow before she could say any more. 'I'll tell you all about it when you come around on Sunday. You *will* come around, won't you?'

The back door of the station opened, and two uniformed

gardaí came out laughing. Katie and Detective Sergeant Ni Nuallán stared into each other's eyes, but there was nothing else they could do to share the intensity of that moment. It was already rumoured in the canteen that Detective Sergeant Ni Nuallán was a carpet muncher.

'Yes,' said Detective Sergeant Ni Nuallán. 'I'll be there.'

Forty-six

Before she returned to her office Katie went to see Assistant Commissioner Jimmy O'Reilly. Tomorrow at noon the state funeral was being held at the Holy Trinity Church for Detective Horgan and the two officers who had been killed by the Spring Lane explosion, Garda Mullan and Garda Burns.

There would be a public parade along St Patrick's Street and Grand Parade to the church on Father Mathew Quay. During the funeral service a eulogy would be given by the Tánaiste, since the Taoiseach himself was indisposed with the flu. The Garda commissioner would read a lesson, Superintendent Pearse would talk about the ultimate sacrifice that Gardaí Mullan and Burns had made, and Katie had been asked to pay a personal tribute to Detective Horgan.

She knocked at Assistant Commissioner O'Reilly's door and he called out, 'Come on in, Barry!'

When she opened the door she was taken aback to see Bryan Molloy in there, sitting cross-legged in one of the leather armchairs by the window. Her first reaction was that he looked unwell. His face was as pale as suet and he had put on weight. His grey suit was far too tight for him and his neck bulged over his collar. His eyes bulged, too. It was plain that he was just as taken aback as she was, and so was Jimmy O'Reilly.

'Oh, it's you,' said Jimmy, turning around. 'I was expecting Barry Pearse.'

'Shall I go away, then?' asked Katie. 'It looks like you two have things to discuss.'

'No, no, Kathleen, come in, stay,' said Jimmy. 'You'll have to be a party to this sooner or later, so now you're here it may as well be sooner. Are you all right with that, Bryan?'

Bryan Molloy shrugged and sniffed, as if to say it was okay with him. He stared unblinkingly at Katie, though, with the same pit-bull expression that he had always given her when he was acting chief superintendent. Katie closed the door behind her, walked across the office and sat down facing him.

'Bryan came here today to see if we could come to some agreement about the Niall Duggan business,' said Jimmy.

'You mean his bribery of Donie Quaid to shoot Neill Duggan and supplying Donie with the weapon to do it? You mean *that* business?'

'I'm admitting to nothing,' Bryan retorted. 'However the feck he was killed, the death of Niall Duggan was the best thing that happened to Limerick since the Shannon Free Zone and you know that as well as I do.'

Jimmy said, 'Donie Quaid has gone to higher service so we can't arrest *him* for the shooting, and I have to agree with Bryan that Niall Duggan's departure did an awful lot to end the feuding between the crime gangs in Limerick. What I'm saying is, Kathleen, that even if you pursue your investigation to the bitter end, no earthly benefit will come of it and it's highly unlikely that the DPP will agree to a prosecution.'

'So where are you going with this, exactly?' Katie asked him. 'Are you ordering me to *drop* this case? Is that it?'

Jimmy pulled a grotesquely strained face, as if he were constipated. 'If I do that, Kathleen, listen, I could end up in a very compromising situation altogether, do you know what I mean? If one of those investimagational journalists from the *Examiner* happened to find out that I'd *ordered* you to pull the plug on it, against your own inclination, it could look like there was something that I didn't want to come out in public.'

'Well, don't you?' said Katie, although her heart was beating faster now because she knew how risky it was to challenge Jimmy so openly.

Bryan said, 'You don't understand, Katie, do you?' although his expression said *Jesus, why are women are so fecking thick?* 'I'm offering to drop the complaint I made against you to the GSOC.'

'So?' Katie replied. 'The GSOC have already confirmed for themselves that you supplied the gun that killed Niall Duggan. Well, they must have told you that by now. On the whole, I'd say that they're much more on my side than yours.'

Jimmy paced up and down a few times and then he said, 'Let's be practical, shall we, Kathleen? Let's draw a line under all of this unnecessary wrangling. It's only going to damage the reputation of An Garda Síochána and right now we need to appear honest, and efficient, and above all trustworthy.'

Counting them off on his fingers, he said, 'We have drug-trafficking to deal with, we have armed robbery to deal with, we have fraud to deal with, we have sex slavery to deal with, we have domestic violence to deal with. We need the public on our side and if you pursue this case against Bryan, that isn't going to help at all.'

'So what's this "agreement" you were talking about?' asked Katie.

'It's totally straightforward. On your part, you announce that you've decided to close the case against Bryan because of lack of evidence. And, let's face it, what evidence do you actually have apart from the word of some old Limerick brasser and a bunch of schoolboys? In return, Bryan will withdraw his complaint against you for harassment and conspiracy to undermine his authority.'

Katie looked across at Bryan, who was still staring at her as if he were gagging to be let off his lead. 'There must be more to it than that,' she said. 'What does Bryan get out of it, apart from a get-out-of-jail-free card?'

'First, he gets his service record officially recognized – and even *you* have to admit he has a very distinguished service record. Second, he has it acknowledged by An Garda Síochána that he was forced to resign for reasons of ill health and that he's entitled to his full pension and any sickness benefits that might be due to him.'

'And what about soliciting bribes from known criminals to have charges against them dropped? And what about the points that mysteriously vanished off the driving licences of the rich and famous?'

'That never happened,' said Bryan.

'Oh, no? Then why did the last commissioner have to resign?'

'You'd have to prove it, and you can't. Nobody can.'

There was another long silence. The tension between them made Katie's stomach muscles tighten and she desperately needed a wee. All the same, she thought she would rather wet herself in front of these two than agree to what they were suggesting. When he was in charge at Anglesea Street, Bryan Molloy had bullied her relentlessly, and just because she had outsmarted him that didn't mean that she was going to let him benefit from being a loser.

She could sense what was happening here. Hadn't Francis O'Rourke warned her how the the old-school, golf-playing Freemasons amongst the Garda's upper ranks felt about her? Bryan Molloy was one of them, and so was Jimmy O'Reilly, and they wanted a lid put on all of this, as tightly as possible.

She stood up.

'Well?' said Jimmy. 'It's a reasonable enough request, don't you think? And there'll be peace in our time.'

'I'll think it over,' she said. 'You need to be warned, though, that my immediate inclination is to have nothing at all to do with it.'

Bryan Molloy slapped both his hands on to the arms of his chair. 'Jesus!' he said. 'I always thought you were a fecking obnoxious self-opinionated bitch!'

'Bryan, for feck's sake, that won't do any good,' said Jimmy. 'I'm sorry, Kathleen, he's very stressed after everything that's happened. Please – think it over, like you say. But it won't do the force any good at all if we don't get this settled.'

'I'll get back to you,' said Katie. 'Us bosom-people are not so good at making snap decisions.'

It was only when she had returned to her own office and was sitting on the toilet that she realized that she and Jimmy had not discussed anything about tomorrow's state funeral.

* * *

Detective Dooley rang her. He sounded out of breath.

'Karosas has just turned up at the Ballycurreen Industrial Estate. I had a couple of guards posted there to keep an eye out for him. He's gone inside with a woman and some other fellow and they've switched on the lights and they're playing music, so it looks like they may be there some time.'

'You have the warrant to search his car, don't you?'

'I have, yes,' said Detective Dooley. 'I picked it up a couple of hours ago from Judge McNulty. I'm heading up to Ballycurreen right now with Tyrone from the Technical Bureau if you want to come along.'

'I'll be right with you,' said Katie. 'Are those two guards still there?'

'Yes, and I've asked them to stay there until we arrive.'

Katie hurriedly put on her coat and went down to the car park. Detective Dooley was already sitting in his car with the engine running and the passenger door wide open. She climbed in beside him and said, 'Okay. Let's go. Let's just hope this isn't a wild goose chase.'

Ballycurreen Industrial Estate was located off the main road that led up to the airport, only a short distance south of the Magic Roundabout. It was a dull collection of warehouses and storage units and offices, and by the time Katie and Detective Dooley arrived there it looked as if most of them had closed for the day.

Savitas Clothing Traders was housed at the very end of the estate, in a small white-painted unit with a concrete forecourt and double garage doors. A sign outside displayed a picture of a dapper pinstriped suit striding along on its own, with nobody in it, but carrying a cane tucked under its arm and a carnation pinned to its lapel. Katie could see the bronze unmarked police Honda parked across the road, half hidden by a giant blue trailer with *Irish Examiner* emblazoned on its side. Detective Dooley turned around and pulled in behind it, and almost immediately Tyrone from the Technical Bureau arrived in a dark-green van.

Katie and Detective Dooley climbed out of their car and the two gardaí and Tyrone came to join them. Both of the gardaí were male, and young, but they both looked quite fit.

'I'm not anticipating any trouble,' said Katie. 'All the same, Karosas has a bit of a reputation for cutting up rough. We think he may have picked up Roisin Begley from outside Havana Brown's on the night she was drowned and we have a warrant to search his car for any evidence of that.'

Katie and Detective Dooley crossed the road, with Tyrone and the two gardaí following close behind them. As they walked past Karosas's shiny black Lexus they ducked their heads down to have a quick look inside, but its windows were tinted too dark for them to be able to see anything but their own distorted reflections. Detective Dooley rang the doorbell outside Savitas Clothing Traders and then they waited.

'Fierce cold,' said Detective Dooley, clapping his hands together. 'They said on the TV that we might get some snow.'

'D'you think?' said one of the gardaí sceptically.

He was about to ring the bell again when the door opened and Davydos Karosas appeared, wearing a tan overcoat with a brown velvet collar and smoking a cigarette. From the top of the concrete stairs behind him, Katie could hear accordion music and laughter.

'What you want?' asked Karosas. He looked Detective Dooley up and down and then he saw Katie and said, '*You*! What you want?'

Detective Dooley held out the search warrant from the district court. 'We have a warrant to search your car, Mr Karosas.'

'My car? What for you want to search my car?'

'Your car was seen on Hanover Street on the night that Roisin Begley was drowned,' said Katie. 'We have reason to believe that you may have picked her up there.'

'Who? When was this? I don't know nobody that name. I never been near Hanover Street, never.'

'It's no good denying it, Mr Karosas. Your car was picked up on CCTV and you were driving it.'

'It's a mistake. I never pick nobody up. I don't know nobody that name.'

'If that's the case, you don't have anything to worry about, do you? Do you think we could have the keys, please?'

Karosas sucked hard at his cigarette and then blew smoke in Katie's direction. 'What I say no?'

'If you refuse to give us the keys to your vehicle, Mr Karosas, then we will have to gain access to it by force.'

'You make one scratch my car, you regret it for ever, I tell you that for free.'

'Then give me the keys.'

For nearly ten seconds Karosas said nothing. He didn't move, but smoke was still leaking out of his nostrils as he breathed. Katie said nothing, either, but held out her hand, making a beckoning gesture with her fingers.

'You know what you are, you pigs?' said Karosas at last. 'You are pigs.'

With that, he took his keys out of his coat pocket and dropped them into Katie's palm. Katie handed them to Detective Dooley, who passed them over to Tyrone. Tyrone pressed the remote button and the Lexus's amber lights flashed as the doors unlocked.

'You make one mark,' Karosas warned them.

'Please don't threaten us, Mr Karosas,' said Katie. 'We have a job to do, that's all.'

Tyrone set down his metal box of forensic equipment and opened up the car's passenger door. He leaned inside with his halogen flashlight, shining it this way and that. Although she could sense his extreme tension, Karosas remained in the open doorway, furiously smoking. Upstairs, the accordion music and laughter continued, although a woman's voice called out, '*Davydos! Davyd! Ką tu darai?*'

Karosas didn't answer but flicked his cigarette butt across the concrete forecourt and immediately took out another and lit it. He watched with barely contained rage as Tyrone slowly and methodically went over every inch of the interior of his Lexus with a large hand-held ultraviolet lamp – first the dashboard and the front seats and the footwells, then the back seats, and then the boot.

'Fuck, fuck, fuck, I don't believe this,' he kept on muttering. 'This is racist. You only do this to me because I am Lithuanian.'

'Of course it's racist,' said Katie. 'It has nothing at all to do with the fact that you have a record of violence and sex-trafficking and that you were caught on CCTV at a time when a vulnerable young girl went missing.'

'Dah, fuck you, you are pig!'

After about twenty minutes, Tyrone climbed out of the car and called Katie and Detective Dooley to come over and join him. He shone his ultraviolet lamp on to the headrest of the passenger seat and said, 'There . . . you see those fine bluey-white strands? Human hair, and it's blonde when you see it under natural light.'

'Karosas might have a blonde girlfriend,' said Detective Dooley.

'Of course, but I've taken samples and we'll be able to make a comparison with Roisin Begley's hair.'

Next he directed the lamp at the dashboard. 'Fingerprints, a whole fine mess of them, and this wasn't just from passengers opening and closing the glovebox. The newest prints are consistent with a passenger pushing hard against the dashboard with the heel of their left hand but also trying to grip it with both hands.'

'So they could have been struggling, is that what you're saying?' Katie asked him. 'Trying to stop somebody from pulling them out of the car?'

'That's a possibility, yes. Especially when you look at the seat.'

He pointed the lamp downwards and Katie could see that the leather had circular smears in the middle of it, as if it had been wiped with a cloth. Under natural light the smears were invisible, but in ultraviolet they showed up with an unearthly blue glow.

Tyrone said, 'Somebody was clearly making a hurried attempt to clean the seat, but they weren't nearly thorough enough. That's urine. At some point, whoever was sitting in this seat wet themselves.'

'And of course you've taken samples of that, too?' said Katie.

'Oh, yes. That could give us the most damning evidence of all. Well – that's always assuming that it matches Roisin Begley's DNA. If not, we'll just have to presume that Mr Karosas had a friend with him who couldn't wait until they got home.'

Katie wished that he would change the subject. The breeze that was blowing across the industrial estate was even chillier now and she was feeling that pressure on her bladder again. She was sure, too, that when they were driving here she had felt her baby stir.

'That's not all, though,' Tyrone added. 'This is the *pièce de* what's-its-name.'

'*Résistance,*' said Katie.

'Yes, that. In fact, there's several. I found these under the passenger seat. It looks like they dropped on to the floor, rolled backwards under the seat when the car accelerated, but then rolled forwards again when it slowed down and got caught underneath the floor mat. If somebody was trying to clean the car out in a hurry, which they probably were if these urine stains are anything to go by, they could easily have missed them.'

He opened up the breast pocket of his Tyvek suit and took out a small transparent evidence bag, laying down his ultraviolet lamp on the car seat and picking up his halogen flashlight instead so that Katie could clearly see what it contained.

Inside the bag were five or six sparkling opalescent beads, like flower petals, with crystals for stamens. They were identical to the beads that had made up Roisin Begley's bracelet – the bracelet that Abisola's selfie had shown her wearing at Havana Brown's only minutes before she went out to meet Davydos Karosas.

Katie walked back to the doorway. Karosas greeted her with a billowing cloud of cigarette smoke and said, 'Well? You satisfy?'

'Just answer me one question,' said Katie. 'Do you allow anybody else to drive your car?'

'*What*? You know what that cost, Lexus G3? I don't let nobody touch it. It make me sick in my stomach to see you pigs touch it. I have to have it valet now, get rid of your stink. I should send you bill.'

'So nobody has ever driven it, except you?'

'That's right,' said Karosas. 'You deaf or what?'

'In that case, I have to ask you to come with me to Anglesea Street Garda station for questioning.'

Karosas twitched his head as if he had Tourette's syndrome. '*What*? You crazy? What for? I don't come to your fucking Garda station. What for? Go and fuck yourself. Pig.'

'All right, if you won't come voluntarily, I am hereby arresting you for the abduction and murder of Roisin Begley,' Katie told him. 'You are not obliged to say anything unless you wish to do so, but whatever you say will be taken down in writing and may be given in evidence.'

Karosas twitched his head again and then he suddenly stepped back into the doorway and tried to slam the door shut. Before he could do so, Katie seized the sleeve of his coat and swung him against the wall, forcing the door open again with her shoulder. Then she hit him hard in the chest with her left elbow and punched him even harder on the cheekbone with her fist.

Karosas lost his balance and stumbled backwards towards the stairs. Katie stalked in after him, her fists raised, ready to kick him if he tried to resist her. Detective Dooley had now come in through the door after her and the two young gardaí were right behind him.

'It's okay, ma'am, we've got him!' said Detective Dooley.

Katie lowered her fists and was about to step back when Karosas pressed one hand against the wall to steady himself, swung his leg back, and kicked Katie in the stomach.

Katie toppled backwards and sideways into Detective Dooley's arms, stunned, unable to breathe, unable to speak. Detective Dooley laid her down gently on the floor, while one of the gardaí pushed his way past them and grabbed hold of Karosas's arms. His companion followed him and together they handcuffed Karosas and pushed him face-first up against the wall.

Katie lay on her side, holding her throbbing stomach with both hands and trying to drag air back into her lungs. The only sound that she could make was a thin, panicky squeak. Detective Dooley knelt beside her and laid one hand on her shoulder.

'Ma'am? How bad has he hurt you? Do you want me to call for the paramedics?'

She shook her head, but then she felt a sensation in her stomach like a washing-machine drum turning over, full of sodden, heavy washing. Her throat tightened and she vomited on to the floor, all of the sandwiches that she had eaten for lunch, and her coffee.

'I'm sorry, I'm going to call for a white van,' said Detective Dooley.

Katie shook her head again, but then she vomited a second time, mainly chewed-up pieces of apple and acidic yellow bile.

Detective Dooley stood up. He took out his phone and Katie could hear him asking for an ambulance. She tried to sit up, but her stomach muscles hurt so much and were clenched so relentlessly tight that she could only let out a whimper and ease herself down on to the floor again, so that her hair became stuck in her own wet sick.

She managed to raise her head a little and when she did so she saw Detective Dooley go up behind Karosas and shout, 'You bastard! You'd kick a woman like that, would you? You're nothing but a worthless lump of shite! What are you?'

Karosas tried to turn his head around. 'Fuck you,' he said. 'Fuck all you pig.'

Detective Dooley seized the curly black hair at the back of Karosas's head and slammed his face so hard against the wall that Katie heard his nose crack.

Upstairs, the accordion music stopped abruptly. Katie heard the woman call out, '*Davydos? Kas vyksta? Kas ten su jumis?*'

But then her stomach convulsed and the pain was so unbearable that she was blinded and deafened and she felt as if her whole world was contracting into nothing but a tiny speck. She was swallowed up by darkness, as if she had fallen down a well.

Forty-seven

She opened her eyes and there was a middle-aged nurse in a white top smiling at her.

She looked around and saw that she was lying in a hospital bed, in a private room. The blind was pulled down, but only a little more than halfway, so that she could see that it was dark outside.

She lifted up the blanket that was covering her. She was wearing a hospital gown with a pattern of small purple flowers on it.

Her stomach was throbbing, but mostly she felt numb.

'Where am I?' she asked. Her voice sounded muffled, as if she were wearing earplugs.

'You're at CUH,' said the nurse, still smiling. 'You were attacked, if you recall, and you suffered an injury. How are you feeling?'

'I don't know,' Katie told her. 'Strange. My stomach hurts. My back, too. Ouch. What time is it?'

'Three twenty.'

'Three twenty in the morning, you mean?'

'That's right. You've been under the anaesthetic.'

Katie tried to sit up, but her arms didn't seem to be strong enough to lift her. The nurse came over and helped her to lean forward while she tucked another large pillow behind her.

A succession of images was tumbling through Katie's mind. She remembered driving with Detective Dooley to Ballycurren Industrial Estate. She remembered talking to Davydos Karosas, and the stink of his cigarette smoke. Then wrestling with him in the doorway and punching him.

'I don't – I can't . . .' she began.

'That's all right, my dear,' said the nurse in a soothing voice. 'It's only the anaesthetic. It'll all come back to you.'

'I'm very thirsty,' Katie told her. 'Do you think I could have a drink of water?'

The nurse poured her a glass and held her head forward to make it easier for her to drink it. She was still swallowing when she suddenly had a flash of Karosas swinging his leg back and kicking her as hard as he could in the stomach. She spluttered and almost choked.

'There, there,' said the nurse, tugging out a Kleenex and dabbing her chin. 'We don't want to be drowning ourselves, do we?'

'My baby,' said Katie. She was panicking now. 'Is my baby all right?'

The nurse set the glass back down on the bedside locker and then sat down on the bed and took hold of Katie's hands. The look on her face was regretful and sympathetic, but in a professional way, as if she had to look regretful and sympathetic almost daily. Katie couldn't help noticing that one of her eyes was brown and the other was blue.

'You lost the baby, my dear, I'm sorry to tell you. That was a fierce hard blow you sustained, right to your abdomen. You've been badly bruised, although there was no other injury, thank God. He could easy have ruptured your spleen. The doctor tried his very best to save your child, but you had a placental abruption and it was too late by the time they got you here to the hospital.'

Katie reached down and felt her stomach. It still felt swollen, as it had for the past few weeks, although it felt very tender, too. She found it impossible to believe that there was no longer a baby inside her. How could it have gone? She was suddenly washed over by an overwhelming sense of loneliness. *It's just me now, all on my own. That little life inside me has left me for ever.*

'Was it a boy or a girl?' she asked, her voice still sounding muffled. 'Or was it too early to tell?'

'Too early to say with any certainty,' said the nurse. 'Whatever it was, though, a he or a she, the Lord will welcome it into His arms with the greatest of love.'

Katie nodded. She wasn't sobbing, but the tears were running down her cheeks and sliding down her neck into her hospital gown. The nurse said, 'You have somebody waiting for you downstairs. Do you want to see them now or shall I ask them to come back later?'

'Who is it?'

'A young lady. I think she works with you. She's been waiting ever since you were brought in.'

She handed Katie another Kleenex and Katie wiped her eyes. 'Yes . . . yes, all right, then. Thank you.'

After she had left Katie did her best to smarten herself up, dabbing at her eyes again to make sure that there was no blotchy mascara on them and tweaking at her hair. As she patted the left side of her head, however, she realized that her hair was stuck together with dried sick. She was still trying to pull it out when the door opened and Detective Sergeant Ni Nuallán came in.

'Kyna,' she said.

Without a word, Detective Sergeant Ni Nuallán leaned over the bed and kissed Katie on the forehead. Then she dragged over a plastic chair and sat down close to her. She looked very tired and her eyes were reddened as if she had been crying, too.

'You were *pregnant*,' she said. 'That was such a shock.'

'What? You didn't realize? I was absolutely sure that you'd guessed it.'

'Not at *all*! I just thought you were *blooming*, do you know what I mean, like? You seemed like you were so full of beans. But I thought that was because you were happy, that was all, because you had John back with you and you were getting on so well together. That was one of the reasons I wanted a transfer. If

387

you were as happy as all that, I thought there was absolutely no chance for me at all.'

She reached out and grasped Katie's hand. 'But I'm so sorry for you, losing the baby like that. It must be breaking your heart.'

'It wasn't John's,' said Katie.

'No? Oh. Serious?'

'That was why he left me. I had to tell him, and when I did he just walked out. I've tried ringing him since but he won't answer any of my calls. I haven't been back home yet to see, but I think he might have come back to collect all of his clothes.'

'Oh, Katie,' said Detective Sergeant Ni Nuallán. 'And now this. I'm so sorry.'

'Fate, I think,' said Katie, with her eyes filling up again with tears. 'One of those things that wasn't meant to be. One of those *children* who wasn't meant to be. They couldn't even tell if it was a boy or a girl.'

'We've formally charged Karosas and we have him in custody,' said Detective Sergeant Ni Nuallán. 'We're holding him for assaulting a police officer, as well as abduction and homicide. Tyrone should know by the end of the day if those hair and urine samples and fingerprints belonged to Roisin and he's testing those beads, too, for DNA.'

Katie nodded. 'That's grand. I should be able to get myself discharged later. I'm paying a tribute to Detective Horgan at the funeral.'

'You're doing nothing of the sort! I was talking to the doctor who treated you and he said that you have to stay here until tomorrow at the earliest. You need to rest and recover. Not only that, they want to keep you under observation to make sure you don't get blood clots or any other complications.'

'But it's a state funeral, Kyna. And Horgan was one of my team.'

Detective Sergeant Ni Nuallán emphatically shook her head. 'I've told Chief Superintendent McCostagaín what's happened to you. Well, not about losing the baby – he doesn't know about that. He sends you his very best wishes for a speedy recovery but Francis O'Rourke will stand in for you at the church.'

'Kyna—'

'No, Katie. You can't be responsible for every single person in the whole of Cork, twenty-four seven. One of those people in Cork is you and you need to take care of yourself. You don't want to end up having a breakdown like Liam Fennessy.'

'What about Barney? Barney needs to be fed and taken for his walk. He's all shut up in the kitchen and he must be wondering where I am.'

'Don't worry. We thought of that. Dooley phoned your father and told him what had happened. He's lent his spare key to one of his neighbours who's going to take care of Barney until you get back home.'

Katie lay back on her pillows. 'All right,' she said. 'But I'm going to get myself out of here as soon as I possibly can.'

'Get some sleep,' said Detective Sergeant Ni Nuallán. 'I'll be saying a prayer for you before I go to bed myself. Not just you, but the little one, too. My mum lost a baby once. Well, she probably lost more than one, but she never told us about all of them. After this one, though, I remember her saying that she was waiting for the clouds to clear away so that she could see a new star shining. She was going to call him Patrick.'

'I hadn't thought of any names yet,' said Katie. 'Now I don't have to, do I?'

* * *

At lunchtime she managed to finish half a bowl of tepid tomato soup and two cream crackers with cheese. Then she sat in the armchair by the window to watch the state funeral on television. A solemn parade marched along St Patrick's Street, with gardaí from every department in the country in full dress uniform, as well as firefighters and paramedics and TDs and local councillors. The pavements were crowded with hundreds of people and the men all took off their hats as the three hearses drove slowly past them, the coffins inside them heaped with lilies.

'Goodbye, Kenny,' said Katie under her breath as she saw his hearse turn the corner into Grand Parade. 'God bless you.'

* * *

Later that afternoon, Dr Mazdani came to examine her and ask how she was feeling. He was softly spoken and when he felt her stomach he did it with the utmost tenderness, as if he could actually feel Katie's pain through his fingertips.

'In one way, you were very lucky,' he told her. 'The kicking you received detached the placenta from the uterus and that starved your baby of oxygen. I am sorry to say that there was no way that it could have survived. However, you could have died yourself from loss of blood, so it was a good thing that they brought you here to the hospital so quickly.'

'When can I go home?' asked Katie.

'Unless there are any complications, you should be able to return home tomorrow. I must advise you, though, to rest for at least another week and to contact us immediately if you experience any unusual pains.'

He lowered her gown and then he said, 'I realize it might be premature of me to say this, but in case you are wondering, you should have no difficulty in conceiving again and bringing a child to full term.'

'Oh, you mean I can have a replacement?' said Katie, although she regretted saying it almost as soon as the words came out of her mouth.

Dr Mazdani sadly shook his head. 'No lost baby can ever be replaced, Mrs Maguire. One child is never a substitute for another. That is why I fight so hard to save the lives of unborn children. It is my calling, to be a protector of children.'

'Of course,' said Katie. 'I'm sorry. I think I'm feeling more than a little cynical at the moment.'

'No bother, Mrs Maguire. I understand perfectly.'

When Dr Mazdani had gone Katie pulled up her blanket and slept for another hour. When she woke up she didn't get out of bed but lay on her back with one hand resting on her stomach, staring at the ceiling tiles. Outside, the sky gradually began to darken again and one by one the hospital windows were lit up, and she could hear the squeaking of trolleys as the patients' evening meals were brought around.

She couldn't stop thinking of the words that Dr Mazdani had used. They reminded her of something that she had heard not too long ago, and the thought kept tapping at her brain again and again, as persistent as a wasp at a window. *A protector of children. A protector of children.*

Then she remembered. It had been Kyna, when she had reported back from her first visit to Mother O'Dwyer. She had been describing the picture of Saint Margaret of Cortona that hung on the wall in Mother O'Dwyer's office. 'I think that's how Mother O'Dwyer sees herself,' Kyna had told her. 'She may be a shrivelled old crow, but she thinks of herself as young and beautiful, like that picture of Saint Margaret, with her hands spread out to communicate with Jesus. She thinks she's just like Saint Margaret. I'd go even further than that – I think she thinks she *is* Saint Margaret, "a protector of children, both born and unborn, who still protects them, even today".'

Katie, of course, had sat in Mother O'Dwyer's office more than once and seen that picture of Saint Margaret for herself, and she had thought about Detective Sergeant Ni Nuallán's words while she did so. Did Mother O'Dwyer really believe she looked as radiant as that, and that she had truly protected the children in her care – regardless of the fact that hundreds of them had died and had ended up as skeletons?

Because none of the children had been baptised, and so couldn't be buried in consecrated ground, perhaps she had believed that their bodies were worthless in the eyes of God and could simply be thrown away like rubbish. Perhaps they had all died of natural causes and the sisters had simply been too poor to give each of them a proper funeral. But how could Mother O'Dwyer and Saint Margaret still be protecting them 'even today'? They were bones. What was there left to protect?

Again and again, she kept thinking of a large rambling house in Carrigaline that she had searched when she was a twenty-three-year-old garda, and how they had found nothing until her attention had been drawn to a large oil painting on the living-room wall of the owners' three cats.

She wondered if she was still suffering from shock. Maybe the opioids she had been given to dull the pain were affecting her thinking. But the wasp kept tapping away at the window. *A protector of children, even today.* Why '*even today*'? What did that actually mean? She knew from experience that offenders often gave away clues that led to their guilt being discovered, not because they were deliberately playing cat and mouse with their interrogators but simply because they couldn't get their offences off their minds. Sometimes, subconsciously, they wanted to be caught because they felt so guilty about what they had done. Even more frequently they had an irresistible urge to boast about it – even rapists and murderers and terrorists. *Especially* rapists and murderers and terrorists.

She turned over and picked up her iPhone from the bedside locker. She pressed Detective Sergeant Ni Nuallán's number and she answered almost at once.

'Yes, ma'am?'

'Where are you, Kyna?'

'I'm still at the station. I've a whole rake of things to clear up after the funeral.'

'How was it?' Katie asked her. 'I saw some of it on television but I wish I'd been there.'

'Very moving, actually. Everybody was bawling. The Tánaiste gave a lovely speech. She said that people who criticise the police should remember that when gardaí leave for work in the morning their wives and children have no guarantee that they're ever going to see them again.'

'Kyna – do you remember what Mother O'Dwyer said to you about that picture of Saint Margaret she has hanging on her wall?'

'What? Vaguely. Only that Saint Margaret had been a single mother herself once. Oh yes – and that she spoke to Jesus almost every day. The poor Saviour. He must have felt like hanging up on her sometimes. Why?'

'"A protector of children", wasn't that what you said? "A protector of children, even today."'

'That's right. That's almost exactly what she said, near enough.'

'I may be drugged up or suffering from post-traumatic stress disorder, but supposing Saint Margaret *is* protecting the children, even today?'

There was a long silence, and then Detective Sergeant Ni Nuallán said, 'To be honest with you, I don't really understand what you're driving at.'

'We've already agreed, haven't we, that the sisters must have kept *some* record of the children who died? But so far we've searched that convent top to bottom, even the attics and the cellars and under the floorboards, and we've found no record at all.'

'No, we haven't. But I still don't get what you're asking me.'

'Have you looked behind the picture of Saint Margaret?'

'No. Well, no, I shouldn't think so. No.'

'Well, could you go up there now, please, and take a quick sconce? If there's nothing behind it but a blank wall, then I'll know for sure that it's the codeine talking. In fact, I'm almost sure that it's the codeine talking. But I won't be able to sleep tonight until I know for certain.'

'All right, then,' said Detective Sergeant Ni Nuallán, although she sounded dubious. 'Do you want me to call you back?'

'Please, if you would. It's just that years ago I was searching a house in Carrigaline and we couldn't find anything until the owner started boasting about his cats being as good as guard dogs. "Better than guard dogs!" he said, and he was really strutting around as if he had got one over on us. But there was a painting of his cats in the living room and it occurred to me to look behind it and – would you believe it? – there was a wall-safe hidden there with over over fifty thousand punts in it and a bag of cocaine and half a dozen counterfeit passports.'

'All right,' said Detective Sergeant Ni Nuallan, still sounding dubious. 'I'm not sure we're going to find anything like that behind Saint Margaret. But I'll go up there and take a look and I'll get back to you so.'

Forty-eight

Less than five minutes later, Detective Inspector O'Rourke called her.

'How are you feeling, ma'am?' he asked her. 'Everybody at the station sends you their best.'

'A bit bruised, but better, thanks,' Katie told him.

'And, well, I'm sorry about your loss. That kind of surprised us, I have to admit.'

'You didn't know?' said Katie. 'I really thought you knew.'

'You never told us, ma'am. And none of us are mind-readers.'

'It's just that you were so – protective. Not only you, but Patrick O'Donovan, too. And one or two others.'

'Go away, I hope that we're always protective. Not of you, in particular, but of each and every one of us. That was what Joan Burton was saying in the church today, when she gave her address. It's a fierce pity you missed it.'

'I should be back at work tomorrow,' said Katie. 'Maybe not all day, but long enough to catch up. What about Karosas? Who's going to be interviewing him?'

'That's the second reason I'm ringing you, ma'am,' said Detective Inspector O'Rourke. 'Tyrone from the Technical Bureau has just fetched me the results of the tests he's been doing on the hair and the fingerprints and the urine sample from Karosas's car. We'll have to wait a little longer for the DNA results from the bracelet beads, but there's no question at all. Karosas took Roisin Begley into his car that night and all the circumstantial evidence suggests that he killed her. I'm going downstairs in a minute to interview him myself, along with Dooley.'

'Take it very easy with him, Francis,' said Katie. 'However you feel about him assaulting me, and my losing this child, don't show you're angry with him. He's very quick to come to the boil and that won't help us at all.'

'I'd be happy to give him a slap for you, I'll say that.'

'I know. I'd be more than happy to give him a slap myself. The doctor said he could have killed me. I'd love to be there to question him with you, but it's probably a good thing that I'm not. Don't let it become confrontational, that's all – that won't get you anywhere, not with Karosas. But he's a coward as well as a bully, and if you get him into a situation he thinks he can't get out of, you'll be surprised what he'll tell you to save his own skin.'

'You mean, like, who put him up to it?'

'You have it exactly.'

* * *

Davydos Karosas was leaning back in his chair with his hands in his pockets when Detective Inspector O'Rourke and Detective Dooley came into the interview room. His right eye was purple and swollen and almost completely closed, as if he had a plum instead of a monocle. As they sat down opposite him he showed them how bored he was by stretching his mouth wide open in a long and luxuriant yawn, so that they could see his yellow-furred tongue and all of his silver-filled teeth.

'We'd like to ask you a few questions, if you don't mind, Mr Karosas,' said Detective Inspector O'Rourke, with exaggerated courtesy, as he sat down at the table between them.

Karosas shrugged. 'Ask what you like. I no have to answer.'

'You're entitled to have legal representation, you do know that?'

'Of course I know that. You think I no do this before? Lawyer is waste of money.'

'You're sure? These are very serious charges against you and you can be represented at the state's expense.'

'I am sure. Because you can prove nothing.'

'You assaulted Detective Superintendent Maguire, causing her actual bodily harm. You kicked her and she had to be taken to the hospital. She might have died.'

Karosas stuck his finger into his right nostril and screwed it around. Then he took his finger out, frowned at it, and wiped it on his trousers.

'Mr Karosas, you assaulted her in front of three witnesses,' said Detective Inspector O'Rourke.

'So what?' said Karosas. 'It was self-defence. Those witness cannot deny that bitch hit me first. Look at my fucking eye. Fuck! You think if I hit that bitch first, she could do this to me? If I hit that bitch first, she would not be in hospital. She would be in cemetery. And good rid.'

Detective Inspector O'Rourke opened the blue plastic folder that he had brought in with him and held up a sheet of paper. 'Do you know what this is, Mr Karosas? A Garda technical expert examined your car – the car that you swore to Detective Superintendent Maguire nobody else has ever driven except for you. You saw the technical expert examine the car yourself, and this is his report. He found blonde hairs on the passenger seat, as well as traces of urine, both of which he matched to Roisin Begley, one hundred per cent. He also found Roisin Begley's fingerprints on the dashboard, in a pattern that suggested that she was forcibly removed from the car against her will.

'Not only that, he found beads on the floor of your car that belonged to the bracelet that Roisin Begley was seen to be wearing only minutes before she met you. You can say whatever you like, Mr Karosas, but all the evidence points to your abducting Roisin Begley and subsequently killing her.'

'You're stuffed, boy,' said Detective Dooley. 'Even you must appreciate that.'

Karosas looked around the interview room, first to the left, and then to the right, and then up at the ceiling, as if he couldn't quite understand what he was doing there. Detective Inspector O'Rourke and Detective Dooley waited patiently for him to answer, although Detective Dooley could see that Detective Inspector O'Rourke's fists were clenched so tight that his knuckles were spots of white.

'Okay, it was accident,' said Karosas at last.

'What was an accident?' asked Detective Dooley. 'Kicking Detective Superintendent Maguire or drowning Roisin Begley?'

'Drowning. I took her, yes, okay. But only to scare her, nothing else. He say not to hurt her or to leave mark. Only to scare, so she no speak in court.'

'Who said that?'

'Who you think?'

'You tell me,' said Detective Inspector O'Rourke.

'Of course Michael Gerrety. He say he pay me one thousand euro to scare her. Do whatever you like, he tell me, but not to leave mark on her body, so she can no prove nothing. Only scare.'

'So what happened, exactly?' asked Detective Dooley. 'You met her outside Havana Brown's and drove her away in your car. Why did she come with you?'

'I tell her I have money for her. Money for fucking with men but Michael Gerrety not pay her yet. Six thousand five hundred euros.'

'And she believed you?'

'Why not? She know me. I fuck her once myself and I pay her good.'

'So how did this "accident" happen?' asked Detective Inspector O'Rourke.

'We are driving. She is laughing. I think maybe she little bit drunk. I ask her if she can swim and she say yes, of course she can swim. I drive to marina, next to river, by slipway. I park there. I say how you like to swim now?'

'Then what?'

Karosas sat up straighter now and kept rubbing his hands on his thighs. 'She say no, she no swim in river. I say you no speak in court against Michael Gerrety. She say screw you, something like that. I pull her out of car and take her to edge of river, down on slipway. Now I say you promise you no speak in court against

Michael Gerrety, otherwise you swim. She try to fight me. She scream at me. Maybe I push her, I no remember. Then she fall in river. I think maybe she is okay, because she can swim. But river is very cold, and she is drunk, and she wears coat and tight skirt and shoes.'

Now he leaned so far forward that his chest was pressing against the edge of the table. 'She is gone. I look, but nothing. She no shout to me. She no wave. Nothing. She is gone.'

There was silence in the interview room for nearly half a minute. Detective Inspector O'Rourke scribbled down some notes, while Detective Dooley sat back with his arms folded. Karosas remained as he was, leaning forward, staring at the table top or nothing at all. Perhaps in his mind he was staring at the River Lee, at night, black and cold and polluted and slopping up against the slipway.

At length, Detective Inspector O'Rourke looked up from his notepad and said, 'So, Mr Karosas, to get this absolutely straight, Michael Gerrety offered to pay you a thousand euros to frighten Roisin Begley so that she wouldn't stand up in court and give evidence against him for having sexual relations with her when she was under the legal age of seventeen?'

'Yes,' said Karosas. 'But he no cheat me. When I tell him what happen, he give me the money anyway.'

'All of it?'

'Yes.'

'And you're prepared to testify to this under oath in the criminal court?'

'It was no murder. Absolutely no murder. Just accident. She fight me, she fall in river. Splash! That's all. Gone.'

Detective Inspector O'Rourke stood up. Detective Dooley could tell by the way that his mouth was puckered that he was tempted to say something blistering to Karosas, but he was holding it in.

'Thank you, Mr Karosas. I think that you're going to be needing a lawyer after all. More than that, though, I think you're probably going to be needing a bodyguard. Michael Gerrety never took kindly to anybody who dropped him in it, and that's for sure.'

'Chalk it down,' said Detective Dooley. He stood up and pushed in his chair. Usually, if he got a confession like this, he felt like punching the air and saying, *Yessss*! But all he could think of was Roisin Begley with her pretty heart-shaped face and her shiny blonde hair and her sparkling naivety – a naivety that had allowed scumbags like Gerrety and Karosas to groom her, and degrade her, and then to throw her in the river.

* * *

Detective Inspector O'Rourke rang Katie about half an hour later.

'We've wound up our preliminary interview with Karosas, ma'am. I'm not counting chickens, like, but I think we've cracked this one. He's confessed that Michael Gerrety offered him a thousand euros to intimidate Roisin Begley into keeping her mouth shut. He's trying to claim, though, that he never meant to drown her and that it was only an accident.'

'Well, he would, wouldn't he? But did Gerrety still pay him?'

'Yes, he did. He'd got the result that he wanted, after all, Roisin Begley's mouth shut, even if things went a bit further than he intended.'

'Thanks a million, Francis. You've given *me* the result that *I* wanted. As soon as I get in to the station tomorrow I'll read through Karosas's statement, and maybe question him myself. Then we can go and arrest Gerrety.'

'Glad I could give you one bit of good news, at least,' said Detective Inspector O'Rourke. 'As my old granny used to say, it takes only a single candle to show you the way back home, even on the darkest night.'

'I'm not too sure I understand what that means,' said Katie.

'Don't bother about it. I don't think she did, either.'

Forty-nine

When Detective Sergeant Ni Nuallán arrived at the Bon Sauveur Convent a fine rain had started falling. This time there were no floodlights shining in the gardens to make the rain sparkle. The search team had almost completed their excavations and would be clearing up tomorrow.

She rang the doorbell and after a long wait the door was opened by Sister Rose.

'Oh,' said Sister Rose. 'It's you.'

'You don't look very pleased to see me,' said Detective Sergeant Ni Nuallán, only half serious.

Sister Rose cast her eyes down at the floor. 'Of course you're welcome. All are welcome.'

'You're wishing you never showed me that jawbone you found.'

'It's – it's all been very disturbing. Perhaps those little children should have been left in peace.'

'In a septic tank? Is that where *you*'d like to be buried?'

'The body is not important,' said Sister Rose, still looking at the floor. 'It's the soul that goes to Jesus.'

'Oh, I see. Is that what Mother O'Dwyer told you? So why do we revere the bodies of our saints so much? Even dooshie little pieces of their bodies? The Vatican's been showing off the bones of Saint Peter, haven't they? And Saint Anthony of Padua, all that's left of him is his tongue but people still kneel and pray to it. And we still have Christ's foreskin, so I've been led to believe. I mean, for Christ's sake, Sister Rose. Of course the body's important.'

'I've made you angry,' said Sister Rose. 'I apologize.'

'No, no, it's my fault entirely,' said Detective Sergeant Ni Nuallán. 'I shouldn't be shouting at you. You brought those poor children some justice and that was very brave of you. Now, is Mother O'Dwyer available at the moment? There's something I need to take a quick sconce at.'

'We've just finished our supper, so she'll be in her office. I'll take you to her.'

When Sister Rose knocked at her half-open door, Mother O'Dwyer was bent over her desk, writing in her diary,

'Sorry to disturb you, Mother O'Dwyer, but Detective Sergeant Ni Nuallán would like a word with you.'

Mother O'Dwyer looked up. Her glasses were now joined together in the middle with Elastoplast. 'What is it now?' she said. 'Will you never leave us in peace?'

'I've been asked to take a look at something,' said Detective Sergeant Ni Nuallán. 'That picture on the wall there, as a matter of fact.'

Mother O'Dwyer turned around in her chair, took off her glasses and frowned at the picture of Saint Margaret. '*That* picture? Why? I don't understand. It's only a picture. A very sacred picture, but only a picture.'

'All the same, if you don't mind.'

'What difference would it make if I *did* mind? Very well, then, go ahead, but be careful with it, please. It's very old.'

Detective Sergeant Ni Nuallán went up to the picture and took hold of the sides of the frame. It was quite heavy, but not too heavy for her to lift up off the hook from which it was hanging and lower it down to the floor.

The wall behind it was nothing but a blank wall with the shadow of the picture frame on it. There was no wall-safe there as Katie had guessed there might be.

'Well?' asked Mother O'Dwyer impatiently. 'What exactly were you hoping to find?'

'I was just checking, that's all,' said Detective Sergeant Ni

Nuallán. She lifted up the picture and after three or four attempts managed to hang it back on its hook.

'I don't understand. Checking what?'

'It's because you said to me that Saint Margaret protects the children who were taken into care here, even today. We weren't sure what it was that you meant by "even today".'

'So you thought *what*? That there was something hidden behind that picture? A mural of Satan? Well, as you can see, there's nothing at all. You people, I don't know. I understand that it's your job to be suspicious but you're really clutching at straws now, aren't you?'

'I'm sorry if I've been a bother,' said Detective Sergeant Ni Nuallán.

'A very good night to you, Detective Sergeant,' said Mother O'Dwyer snippily, and picked up her pen. Lifting her left hand, she said, 'Go in peace.'

Sister Rose led Detective Sergeant Ni Nuallán back along the corridor to the convent's front door in silence, except for the clacking of her boot heels and a repetitive whipping noise. Detective Sergeant Ni Nuallán looked down and saw that one of her bootlaces was undone. She stopped beside the gleaming bronze statue of Saint Margaret and knelt down on one knee to tie it up again.

As she knelt there, almost like a supplicant in front of Saint Margaret, she noticed something that she never would have seen otherwise. The statue was standing on a mahogany plinth, about sixty centimetres high, with ebony beading around it. There was nothing remarkable about it except that there were four decorative bronze knobs, one at each corner, and the top right-hand knob had a tiny screw above it and faint semicircular scratches next to it.

'Excuse me, Sister Rose, would you stall there, please, for a moment?' Detective Sergeant Ni Nuallán called out. She crouched forward and examined the plinth more closely. When she touched the top right-hand knob with her fingertip she found that she could swing it to one side. It wasn't a knob at all, but an escutcheon, covering a keyhole.

How about that, she thought. *If the plinth has a keyhole, then it must have a door, and if it has a door, then it's not just a plinth, it's a cupboard.*

'What is it?' asked Sister Rose, coming back to stand beside her.

'Would you be kind enough to ask Mother O'Dwyer if she has the key to this cupboard here.'

Sister Rose looked baffled. 'That's a cupboard? I never realized that it was a cupboard.'

'Well, the way it's made, you're obviously not supposed to. But you can see that it's been opened up now and again, so somebody must have a key to it and I'm presuming that's Mother O'Dwyer.'

Sister Rose pressed her hand over mouth and her eyes widened.

'It's okay, you're grand,' said Detective Sergeant Ni Nuallán, seeing how frightened she was. 'I'll go and ask her myself.'

She walked back to Mother O'Dwyer's office and knocked at her door.

'Have you not left yet?' asked Mother O'Dwyer, taking off her glasses.

'Well, no, it doesn't look like it, does it? I've come back to ask you if you have a key for that cupboard underneath the statue of Saint Margaret.'

Detective Sergeant Ni Nuallán had seen suspects physically collapse when presented with irrefutable evidence against them, but Mother O'Dwyer appeared almost to crumble as if she were an Egyptian mummy that had suddenly been exposed to the air. Her jaw dropped and her face turned ashy white. She half stood up and then she sat down again.

'A key?' she said. 'To the cupboard?'

'That *is* a cupboard underneath the statue, isn't it?'

'Yes,' said Mother O'Dwyer. 'But the things inside it – they have to remain private. That's why they're in there.'

'Things like what?'

'I can't let you have the key. I'll have to call our legal advisers. I can't let you have it.'

'Reverend Mother, we already have a search warrant for the entire convent premises and surrounding grounds. Your legal advisers are aware of that. You can call them if you like but it won't make any difference and it will only delay matters. I'm asking you now for the key to that cupboard, since you obviously have one.'

Mother O'Dwyer's eyes were suddenly filled with tears. She crossed herself twice and when she spoke her voice quivered with emotion. 'I can't let you have it. I *can't*! The whole congregation will be devastated and brought to ruin. Oh, God in Heaven. Oh, Mary! Oh, what brought this on us? Oh, Jesus!'

'The key, please, Mother O'Dwyer,' said Detective Sergeant Ni Nuallán.

Mother O'Dwyer took a few deep breaths to compose herself and then she reached underneath her scapular with both hands. After a moment's fiddling she drew out a long fine chain with a small key fastened to the end of it.

'There,' she said. 'But may I plead with you that what you find inside that cupboard you treat with the utmost respect and consideration for those involved?'

'I have no idea what's in there yet,' said Detective Sergeant Ni Nuallán. 'I can't make you any promises until I find out what it is.'

She walked back to the statue of Saint Margaret, bent down and unlocked the door in the plinth. Inside, two shelves were stacked with hardback ledgers with maroon marbled covers, at least ten of them, as well as two expanding pocket files, fastened with thin green twine. Detective Sergeant Ni Nuallán tugged on her black latex gloves and then she lifted out the ledgers and the files and laid them on the floor. As she did so, she could see Mother O'Dwyer standing in the open doorway of her office watching her, a diminutive black figure, and whatever was recorded in these ledgers, she almost felt sorry for her.

Sister Rose helped her to carry the books into the room where she had been examining the convent's records with Sister Caoilainn. She set them out on the table and then picked them up one by one. They smelled of musty paper and incense. Each ledger had

405

a handwritten label stuck to the front that read *Saint Margaret's Refuge Deceased*, with the dates underneath. The earliest ledger was dated September 1932. The latest was dated was June 1973. Nearly forty-one years of dead children.

Detective Sergeant Ni Nuallán opened up the first ledger. The names of all the children who had died at Saint Margaret's Mother and Baby Home were written down here, in neat purple script. Their names, their mothers' names, the date of their birth and the date of their death, along with the cause of death. The Bon Sauveurs may have done everything possible to conceal the way these children had died, but at least they hadn't been so heartless as to leave their lives completely unrecorded.

Sarah Joan Donohue, born 17 October, 1931,
of Mary Fiona Donohue, of Margaret Place, Cork.
Died 11 September, 1932, of bronchitis.

William 'Billy' O'Keeffe, born 12 July, 1928,
of Ciara O'Keeffe, of Glasheen Road, Cork.
Died 21 September, 1932, of choking.

Detective Sergeant Ni Nuallán turned the page, and every page was the same. Hundreds of children who had died of respiratory problems, of measles, of chickenpox. One of the most common causes of death among the little ones was 'failure to thrive'. The ledger was even frank enough to record several deaths from 'malnutrition, as a result of persistent ill-discipline'. In other words, the children had misbehaved and had been punished by the nuns by not being fed.

In the later 1930s she noticed that an increasing number of deaths were attributed to 'vaccination against diphtheria'.

She closed the ledgers and opened up one of the expanding files. It was crammed with letters, still in their torn-open envelopes. She took out some of them and read them. Most of them were concerned with finding adoptive parents for Saint Margaret's children – or not, in some cases.

Aidan is slow in his cognition and finds simple tasks quite difficult. We are trying to find a place for him where he can be put to manual labour and given the constant admonishment he requires. Failing that we may have to him committed to St Kevin's lunatic asylum.

'Right,' Detective Sergeant Ni Nuallán to Sister Rose. 'I'm taking all of these away with me and I'll write you a receipt. If you can give me a hand to carry them out to my car.'

As she left the convent she noticed that Mother O'Dwyer's office door was now closed. It was still raining outside so she and Sister Rose had to hurry across the car park, like thieves hurrying away from a robbery.

* * *

Before she started up her engine, Detective Sergeant Ni Nuallán called Katie.

'You were wrong about the picture, but you were right about Saint Margaret.'

She told Katie about the ledgers and files that she had discovered under the statue.

Katie said, 'That's fantastic. Perhaps we can find out now who has such a grudge against the Bon Sauveurs. Mind you, from what you've said, that sounds like half of Cork.'

Fifty

The morning was sunny and clear as Josh Teagan trotted back into the stable yard with Saint Sparkle, but bitingly cold, so that the four-year-old bay was steaming.

'Ah, he's fit as a fiddle,' said the jockey after he had dismounted. 'He'll be passing the post before the rest of the field have even made their minds up which fecking race they're supposed to be running in.'

Riona patted Saint Sparkle's glossy flank and said, 'Fantastic. Take him in, Ryan, would you, and give him a good rub down.'

Her grey-haired stable lad lifted off Saint Sparkle's saddle and numnah and slung a large chequered cooling blanket over his back. Then he led him away, his hoof beats echoing like castanets against the surrounding buildings.

'Best fecking horse I've ridden in years,' said Josh, watching him go. 'You only have to get that feller up to speed and he just keeps on going. Fade? He don't know the meaning of the word. Mind you, he's a horse. He wouldn't know the meaning of any word, would he? Well, maybe "giddup!" and "whoa!".'

'I suppose you want paying,' Riona interrupted him, reaching into the pocket of her fake-fur jacket and taking out a thick folded bundle of euros.

'Always helps,' said Josh, wiping his red-tipped nose on his sleeve. He watched her counting out notes and then he said, 'Listen, I was talking to some of the lads, Thursday night.'

'Oh yes?'

'Well, it was Willie Sandford's wedding ceilidh, at the Mills Inn, you know, at Ballyvourney. The banter was savage like, but one or two them was telling me serious that I should be wide.'

'Really? And why's that?'

'After that O'Grady Steeplechase, there's some of the trainers saying that Weatherbys and Horse Racing Ireland should be looking into what you're up to, and even some of the bookies, too. There was a couple of managers there from Boyle's and Paddy Power's, like, and they was both sure that Sparkle would get the trip. Him being blown up like that – that was too fecking obvious by half.'

'Maybe they should mind their own business,' said Riona. 'They can say whatever they like but they'll have to prove it first.'

'Oh, come on,' said Josh. 'Sparkle's a stayer and everybody knows it.'

Riona handed him his money and then she said, 'Okay. Maybe you're right. But it hasn't been easy lately, the way things are. Too much competition and not enough cash flow. Too many breeders finding a way to finagle me out of their stud fees. I've had some unexpected expenses, too. People to pay off. Well – like *you*, for instance. It's not cheap keeping people's mouths shut.'

'I wouldn't rat on you, Riona, and you know that.'

'If you did, you'd never ride another race in your life, I can tell you. And not just because you were barred.'

'I'm only suggesting that you keep sketch for the race officials. Do you still have Sparkle the Second here or has he gone off to the knackery?'

'He's here still. I was going to keep him till April at least.'

'Tell me you won't be entering him for any more races. You'd be caught rapid for sure. If I was you, I'd be disposing of him as soon as I could.'

'You're not me, thank God, but I'll have a think about it,' said Riona. At that moment she had seen Andy Flanagan's Range Rover approaching along the avenue of lime trees, its transmission whining and its grimy windscreen glinting in the sunlight. 'Thanks for the heads-up, anyhow. I'll see you tomorrow so.'

'Thanks for the lids,' said Josh, holding up his money.

He walked off to Saint Sparkle's stable to collect his padded jacket and his motorcycle helmet. Meanwhile, Andy Flanagan circled his Range Rover around the stable yard with its exhaust rattling and pulled to a halt beside Riona. He climbed out, chafing his hands together.

'Good morning, Riona! Fine cold morning!'

'You're looking pleased with yourself.'

'I am, yes. I've found them for you. Sister Nessa and Sister Virginia, the two of them.'

'That's good news. Come inside and tell me about it.'

They went into the house and Riona took off her fur jacket and threw it across the back of the sofa.

'A nice hot cup of tea would crown me sure,' said Andy, still chafing his hands.

'Just tell me where they are,' Riona told him.

Andy took a dog-eared spring-bound notebook out of his coat pocket, licked his thumb, and turned over the first few pages.

'Sister Nessa was out in Africa for a while, so I guessed that if she'd come back to Cork she might have wanted to put her experience to good use. Well, you know these nuns, one or two of them like to do saintly works now and again. I talked to more balubas than you could shake a stick at, but I tracked her down in the end all right. She's fit and well and living in Dunmore Gardens in Knocka with some other auld wan.'

'And Sister Virginia? Sister Virginia is the one I really want, more than any of them.'

'It was a fierce pain in the arse finding *her*, I can tell you. I went to Carrigaline, which was her last-known residence, and asked in just about every fecking shop on Main Street. In the end I found that she had made friends with one of the women who used to serve behind the counter in Phelan's Pharmacy. This woman had moved down to work in the post office at Minane Bridge, and thank God when I went down there she was still there. A right heifer, so she was, too. But Sister Virginia had sent her a Christmas card and it had her address on it. Iona Park, in Mayfield. She's staying with one of her cousin's daughters.'

Andy tore the page out of his notebook and handed it over. Riona glanced at it quickly and then said, 'That'll be all, then, Andy. Thank you.'

'Do you want to settle up, like?' Andy asked her.

'I will as soon as I've made sure that both of these sisters are actually there, at these addresses, yes.'

'I've no reason to doubt that they're not. But fair play to you. I'll wait for you to ring me. And if you ever need any more detectivizing, you know where to come.'

He held out his hand but Riona didn't take it, so he shrugged and said, 'Oh, well. Good luck to you anyway,' and walked out of the living room into the hallway.

'Looks like you have another visitor,' he said as he opened the back door. A red Audi was parked next to his Range Rover, although there was nobody in it. Riona recognized it, though: it belonged to Saint Sparkle's owner, Gerry Brickley.

Andy drove off in a cloud of sour-smelling exhaust. Riona was about to cross the yard to Saint Sparkle's stable when Gerry came out of the stable next to it, closing the door behind him. He was wearing his usual Crombie coat and a pork-pie hat, and his face was as brick-red as ever.

'Riona!' he called out.

'Gerry! This is a surprise!' said Riona.

He came up to her, taking a leather cigar case out of his inside pocket and removing a cigar. 'Yes, well, I had an early meeting in Coachford with O'Donovan's Engineering so I thought I'd drop in to see how your new barn was coming along.'

He looked around and said, 'I thought you were building it right over there, where that old tractor shed was.'

'Things have been a bit delayed,' said Riona. 'I've been having a few problems with the planners.'

'You should have told me,' said Gerry. 'I know a couple of amenable fellows on the planning committee. Mind you, what are they objecting about? It's a horse barn, for Christ's sake, on a stud farm, up back of leap. I didn't know you hadn't even started construction. I needn't have rushed all of that helium up to you so urgent, and charged you for it.'

'Never mind,' said Riona. 'I should have it all sorted soon enough.'

Gerry looked back towards the stables and said, 'Don't you think that Sparkle's carrying too much condition? How's he been breezing lately?'

'That wasn't Sparkle you were looking at,' said Riona.

Gerry was about to light his cigar but now he snapped his lighter shut and said, 'What?'

'That's not Sparkle in there. That's another bay. O'Donoghue's Delight.'

'You're codding me, aren't you? I was sure that was Sparkle. He has the same red bruise on his right front hoof. I noticed it after he dropped out at Mallow.'

'No, Sparkle's in that stable right there, next but one. Come and take a look at him. I'll just fetch my jacket.'

Once she had put on her jacket, Riona took Gerry over to Saint Sparkle's stable. Inside, Ryan was rubbing down the horse's legs with liniment. Dermot was there, too, sitting on a bale of hay, drinking from a bottle of Murphy's and talking to him. He stood up when Riona and Gerry came in and looked around for somewhere to hide his bottle, but gave up in the end and set it down on the stable floor.

'What's the craic, Mr Brickley?' he said, giving him the thumbs up.

Gerry didn't answer him but walked slowly around Saint Sparkle, patting his sleek sides now and again, as if to affirm his ownership. *This beautiful thoroughbred, he's mine.*

'He's in grand condition, Mr Brickley,' said Ryan. 'I don't think we'll be having any trouble with him when he runs at Punchestown.'

Gerry bent down and examined Saint Sparkle's right front hoof. 'He had a bruise on the inside wall there, after that race at Mallow. It's gone.'

'Oh, come on, Gerry, horses often suffer bruises on their hooves,' said Riona.

'It's totally disappeared, though. Totally.'

'That's not unusual. Most of the time bruises are caused by the crimping of the lamina between the hoof wall and the coffin bone. It's not often that they're serious. On a fit horse like Sparkle, they can disappear almost overnight.'

'But that other horse – the one I just looked at, thinking he was Sparkle – *he* has a bruise in exactly the same place that Sparkle did – in the dish there, on the side of his hoof.'

'Coincidence,' said Riona. 'O'Donoghue's Delight suffers from a slight lack of balance. That can cause bruises, too.'

'Well, all right, I'll take your word for it,' said Gerry. 'I'm not a vet, I have to admit.' He stepped back and folded his arms and looked up at Saint Sparkle admiringly. 'I must say you've done a fantastic job with him, Riona. The Lord alone knows what happened at Mallow, but I think he's going to do us proud at the Boyle Sports Race Day.'

Dermot picked up his Murphy's bottle from the floor and held it up. '*Sláinte mhaith*!' he grinned. 'I'll drink to that!'

'I'll tell you what you *will* do, Dermot,' Riona told him. 'You'll go around to the back of the garage and you'll fix that leaking tap I asked you to fix two days ago.'

'Of course, yeah,' said Dermot. 'I'm on me way now.'

As he passed them, Gerry stared at Dermot narrowly. Then he saw that Riona was looking at him, so he smiled and said, 'I'd best be going, then. Lots to do. People to meet. Welding to oversee. Let me know if you're still having problems with that barn, Riona, and I'll see if I can pull a few strings for you.'

'Thanks, Gerry,' said Riona. 'Bye-bye.'

He had driven less than three miles towards Coachford when Gerry pulled into a farm gate by the side of the road and took out his iPhone. He was breathing heavily as he tapped out the number 1800 666 111.

'Garda Confidential,' said the operator. 'How can I help you?'

'Listen,' he said, 'they were appealing on the telly yesterday evening for information about a fellow with a finger missing on his left hand.'

'I see, sir. Do you think you might have seen him?'

'Only a few minutes ago. It's the same fellow for sure, because I recognized his face from the telly, too. He's kind of an odd-job worker at the Clontead Stud, north of Coachford. His name's Dermot. I don't know what his surname is, but you can't fail to recognize him. He's the bulb off his picture.'

'Thank you, sir. I'll pass this information on to the officers in charge of this investigation.'

'There's something else, too. I think there's some kind of a horse-racing racket going on at Clontead More.'

'A horse-racing racket? Can you tell me something more about it?'

'I don't know,' said Gerry. He was feeling panicky now and kept glancing into his rear-view mirror to make sure that nobody from the stud farm was coming after him. ' I don't have much in the way of proof, but I think that they might be running ringers. You know, substituting one horse for another so that they can fix the betting.'

'What makes you think that, sir?'

'I can't tell you now. I have to go.'

'If you can possibly call in at a Garda station, sir, and give them that information in person. They'll treat it as confidential, I can assure you of that.'

'All right, all right. Grand. I'll think about it. But now I have to go.'

He rang off and dropped his iPhone on to the seat beside him. Then he put his foot down and drove away from the farm gate in a slithering spray of mud and grass.

Fifty-one

Even before Gerry's car was out of sight, Riona hurried around to the back of the garage, where Dermot was crouching down and sorting through his bag of tools, searching for a spanner.

'Dermot! Quick! Andy's found them! Sister Nessa and Sister Virginia! I'm just going to change and then we're going after them!'

'What about this tap?' said Dermot.

'You've left it leaking for two days. You don't think another day is going to make any difference? Now hurry!'

'What's all the fecking rush?' Dermot asked her, closing up his tool bag and standing up.

'I've been waiting thirty years for this, that's the rush! I don't want to wait a minute longer!'

Dermot saw something in Riona's eyes that he had never seen before, even when they were slitting open Sister Mona's stomach or branding Sister Barbara's breasts with that red-hot monstrance, or cooking Sister Aibrean in the hog roaster. Her pupils had darkened until they appeared almost black, so that he could have believed that she was possessed. He had seen women in the Carraig Mor asylum who had looked like that – women who had screamed that Satan was inside them. Even the way she walked seemed to have changed – making her way back to the house with jerky arm and leg movements, as if she were being controlled by some demonic puppeteer.

While she went inside to change, Dermot opened the garage and started up his car. He had emptied most of the rubbish out of the back of it but there were still several tins of Ronseal in there which gave the interior a strong smell of fence varnish. He drove out into the stable yard and waited for Riona with his window open, smoking.

Ryan came out of Saint Sparkle's stable and said, 'You off, boy?'

Dermot handed him a cigarette and said, 'It's herself. She's gone skitzo again.'

'Well good fecking luck with that then.'

After about ten minutes Riona came out of the house with a long black coat slung over her shoulders. She was dressed in her full nun's vestments, complete with a cowl and a scarf and a large silver cross around her neck. Ryan put his hands together as if he were praying, which plainly didn't amuse her at all.

'Have you finished rubbing down Sparkle yet?' she snapped at him. 'Or are you just giving yourself another one of your undeserved breaks?'

'Sparkle's finished. He's grand. I've fed him his turbo flakes, too.'

'Right, well, I'll probably be away for at least two hours. You can take Mister Lintock out for a breeze, but go very easy. I think that bowed tendon has pretty much healed but I don't want it damaged again.'

'I have you. Don't worry. I'll ride him as if he was my own.'

'Yes. That's what I'm worried about.'

Riona climbed into the passenger seat of Dermot's car, tugging at her scapular and habit so that she was sitting comfortably, and they drove off.

'We'll go for Sister Nessa first, in Knocka,' she said.

'Poor Sister Nessa,' said Dermot. He had thrown away his cigarette but he was still breathing out smoke as he talked. 'She doesn't know what she's in for. By the way, what *is* she in for? We don't need anything special, like, do we? Not another hog roaster? That was a pig to clean, that fecking hog roaster. Hey – get it? Pig, hog! I'm a fecking comedian and I don't even know it!'

'Sister Nessa was a mean and nasty piece of work,' said Riona. 'She'd have you washing and ironing all the sheets and if you made

417

even the smallest brown mark on the sheets when you were pressing them, she'd pick them up and drop them on the floor and wipe her feet on them so you'd have to wash and iron them all over again. And if anybody gave a biscuit to Sorley, she'd snatch it away from him because she said that bastards didn't deserve treats.'

'She sounds like a saint all right,' said Dermot. They had reached Coachford now and he turned towards Dripsey and Cork. The sky was cloudless and frost was still sparkling in the hedgerows.

'Oh, she thought she was a saint,' said Riona. 'She modelled herself on Saint Agnes of Rome, the patron saint of virgins, so she believed that all of us girls at the home were the dirtiest of the dirty.'

'And what happened to Saint Agnes?' Dermot asked her. 'What I mean is, how did they top her, like?'

'She refused to burn incense to the Roman gods, because she said she was promised to Christ. She was only twelve years old and still a virgin, so by Roman law they couldn't execute her until she had lost her virginity.'

'That sounds sensible,' said Dermot. 'Chopping a girl's head off before she'd had it away, that would be a total waste of good pussy.'

Riona ignored that. 'The Roman priests sent her to a brothel to lose her virginity. They stripped her naked and dragged her through the streets behind a horse. The legend has it that her hair miraculously grew to cover her modesty, but I don't think that's going to happen with Sister Nessa.'

Dermot glanced over at her. 'Is that what you have in mind, then? Dragging her through the streets in the nip? Don't you think that somebody might notice?'

'We're not going to drag her down St Patrick's Street, for the love of God. A nice gritty country road, that's what I'm thinking. And we'll use this car instead of a horse.'

'That should send her on her way to join that saint of hers.'

'Well, I hope so. Although Saint Agnes survived it and they had to cut her head off in the end. She told the executioner to hurry up because a bride shouldn't keep her groom waiting. Meaning Jesus, of course.'

'Jesus,' said Dermot, as they joined the main R618 towards Cork. 'These fecking martyrs. Enough to make your hair stand on end. What about the other one? Sister Vinegar, or whatever her name is?'

'Sister Virginia. But you're right for once. She should have been called Sister Vinegar. I only have to remember the way she treated me and Sorley and it gives me the worst sour taste in my mouth. When Sorley wet the bed she made him sleep in it all night to teach him a lesson even though the sheets were soaking, and when he was potty training she wouldn't let him change his pants for the rest of the day if he accidentally shit himself, and the poor little boy was only eighteen months old.'

'And what do you have planned for her?' asked Dermot.

'Oh, something painful, I can assure you. She was devoted to Saint Perpetua, the patron saint of expectant mothers. Saint Perpetua was a married noblewoman in Carthage, which was part of the Roman Empire, and she was a nursing mother, too. She was martyred, though, because of her Christian faith. They stabbed her in between every bone in her body so that she would feel as much pain as possible before she died, and it was said that she was shrieking. She was in so much agony that she grabbed hold of the blade of the exectioner's sword and cut her own throat with it.'

'I don't know how you remember all that fecking stuff,' said Dermot.

'I remember it because I can't forget it, and those sisters made sure of that.'

'The only thing that I can remember from when I was younger is "The Bog Down in the Valley-O", said Dermot. He tapped the rings on his fingers on the steering wheel and sang, in a flat and wheezy voice, *The flea on the feather, and the feather on the bird, and the bird in the egg, and the egg in the nest, and the nest in the tree, and the tree in the bog, and the bog down in the valley-o!*'

'Mother of God,' said Riona. 'Apart from the fact that you missed out half of it, you've made my ears bleed.'

It took them just under an hour to reach Knocknaheeny, on the north-west side of the city. They turned off Kilmore Road into Dunmore Gardens, which was a row of neat but depressing bungalows facing a fenced-off sports ground.

'Sister Nessa's – that'll be further along,' said Riona. She pulled at her sleeves to straighten them and Dermot could tell that she was becoming agitated, the same as she had been when he dropped her off at the Greendale Rest Home to spirit Sister Barbara away.

He drove slowly, thinking about tying Sister Nessa to his tow bar, naked, and driving along the road with her dragging along behind him. He wondered how fast he could go before bits of her would start to fall off.

'*The tree in the bog,*' he murmured under his breath. '*And the bog down in the valley-o.*'

'Stop!' said Riona.

'Oh come on,' he said. 'I'm not that shite at singing.'

'No, stop the car, I mean! Turn around!'

'What? What's the problem?'

'Look up ahead of us, you blind eejit! Turn around!'

Further up the road, outside a small grey bungalow with a hedge around it, a Garda patrol car was parked and two uniformed gardaí were standing by the concrete pillars on either side of its driveway. Dermot jammed his foot on the brake and reversed, his Toyota whinnying like a horse. Then he wrestled with the steering wheel so that they could execute a three-point turn.

As he did so, Riona saw a blonde-haired woman in a dark-grey business suit walk up the driveway and speak to one of the guards.

'The shades!' Dermot panted, as they drove back down Dunmore Gardens towards the main road. 'What were the shades doing there?'

'I think they're on to us,' said Riona. 'That blonde woman – did you see her? I'll bet anything she's a detective. I think they've worked out what we're doing.'

'That's no fecking surprise. We haven't exactly been keeping a low profile, like, have we? I don't know why we haven't been advertising on the telly! We could have buried them in a bog somewhere and nobody would have been any the wiser!'

'But that's the whole *point*!' Riona retorted, clenching her teeth. 'I want them to be wiser!'

When they reached Kilmore Road, Dermot said, 'Now what? Do you want to go back to Clontead?'

'No. Let's go for Sister Virginia. Maybe the guards don't yet know that we're after her, too.'

'You mean *now*, like?'

'Yes, now! When did you think I meant? Next Thursday fortnight?'

'This is getting crazier than ever,' said Dermot. 'They're going to catch us, like. You know that.'

'Of course I know that. I don't care.'

'Well, me neither, so long as they put me in a proper prison and not that Carraig Mor shitehole with all them loonies. I'm allergic to loonies, I tell you.'

Riona unfolded the sheet of paper from Andy's notebook. 'Here it is. Sister Virginia lives in Iona Road, Mayfield. Do you know how to get there?'

'Do I know how to get there? We only used to fecking live there when I was younger. Two streets away from Roy Keane.'

'Good. Then let's go there.'

* * *

Iona Road was much smarter than Dunmore Gardens, although most of the houses were bungalows. These bungalows, however, were discreetly hidden from the road by well-trimmed hedges and white-painted walls, and there were new cars parked in the driveways.

They found the bungalow where Sister Virginia was living with her cousin's daughter and Dermot parked about three houses away, on the opposite side of the road. There was no sign of any Garda patrol cars here, or any unmarked car from which protection officers might have been keeping an eye out. The sun was still shining and there was only the faintest cold breeze blowing.

Riona crossed the road and went up to the porch. The front garden was covered with pebbles, with a concrete cherub holding up a bird bath, and the steps up to the porch were shiny red with Cardinal polish.

She rang the doorbell and she could hear chimes inside the house. She had been calm before, with the other four sisters, but now she could feel her heart palpitating. It was beginning to feel as if time was running out. The breeze made her shiver, as if somebody had stepped on her grave.

The door opened and a young woman in a red jumper appeared, holding a chubby baby boy. The boy had chocolate mousse around his mouth.

'Oh,' said the young woman. 'Can I help you?'

'I hope I haven't interrupted this little fellow's lunch,' said Riona. 'Is Sister Virginia in by any chance?'

'And you are?'

'Sister Margaret Rooney, from the Bon Sauveur Convent. I'm visiting all of the sisters who used to be part of our congregation to check on their welfare. It's part of our new outreach initiative, to make sure that none of our former sisters are neglected or abandoned, or need any kind of special care.'

'Oh,' said the young woman. 'That's strange.'

'Excuse me?'

'Well, my great-aunt isn't here. She's been very frightened about those sisters from your convent being murdered and she thought the same thing might happen to her. I told her she had nothing to worry about and that she was quite safe here with us, but yesterday she packed a bag and went back to the convent. She said she'd be safer there.'

'She's gone back to the convent?'

'That's right. Didn't you know? Tommy – not with your chocolatey fingers!'

'I – ah – no, I didn't know,' said Riona. 'But then I haven't been back to the convent myself since Friday. Ah, well, then, that's good. That's very good, saves me a bit of trouble. It'll be very good to see her again.'

'I'm sorry for your bother,' said the young woman with a smile and closed the door.

Riona stood in the front garden for a moment in her nun's vestments and stamped her foot and said, 'Shit!'

Almost immediately, the front door opened up again and the young woman was standing there, holding out a gilt medallion.

'She forgot this,' she said. 'You wouldn't be kind enough to give it to her, would you?'

Riona took the medallion and smiled. 'Of course,' she said. 'God bless you. And God bless your beautiful boy.'

I used to have a boy like that once, she thought. *But my boy was never allowed chocolate, and who was to blame for that? Your beloved great-aunt.*

She held up the medallion as she walked back across the road. It bore the image of a sorrowful-looking woman on it and was inscribed *S. Perpetua Mater Misericordiae* – Saint Perpetua Mother of Mercy. Just before she reached Dermot's car she dropped it down a grating.

'Where's Sister Vinegar?' asked Dermot as she climbed back in.

'Not there, Dermot. It turns out that Sister Virginia was so scared by all the news she's been hearing about nuns from the Bon Sauveur Convent being murdered that she's gone to seek refuge, guess where?'

Dermot waited for her to tell him, and when she didn't, he said, 'How the feck should I know? Jackie Lennox's Fish and Chip Shop?'

'The Bon Sauveur Convent, you fool. She's gone back to the Bon Sauveur Convent.'

'I just thought . . . you know . . . where else does vinegar end up?'

'Jesus, Dermot. I despair of you sometimes. They should have kept you in Carraig Mor for the rest of your life.'

'I'm only trying to look on the bright side,' said Dermot. 'If you can't have a laugh, like, what's the fecking point of anything? So, what do we do now?'

'We go to the convent and get her, that's what we do.'

'Ah, come on, you may be wearing the habit and all but they'll know you're only mock-ee-ah, won't they?'

'That's a risk I'll just have to take. If the guards are after us now, we won't have very much time before they realize that Sister Virginia's on our hit list, too. I *want* her, Dermot! I want to see you stab her and stab her and stab her between her bones until all she wants to do is cut her own throat.'

Dermot's mouth turned down. 'Okay, then. If that's the way you want it. You're paying the piper.'

He started up the engine, but as he did so Riona's iPhone rang. When she saw who was calling she touched his arm to tell him not to drive away yet.

'What is it?' she said. 'What's wrong?'

She listened and then she said, 'How?' Then she listened some more and said, 'Mother of God, you can't trust anyone these days. What a bastard! All right. Okay, Yes. Well, thanks a million. I owe you one. I'll fix it.'

Once she had ended the call she said to Dermot, 'Back to Clontead.'

'What? I thought you wanted to go to the convent.'

'Clontead, I said! And put your foot down!'

'I don't know,' Dermot grumbled as he pulled out into the road. 'It would help if you made your mind up now and again. With all due respect, like.'

'It's Gerry Brickley,' Riona told him. 'He's only told the guards that we've been fixing races. He showed up at the Garda station in the city about half an hour ago and said that he'd seen Sparkle the Second and he was sure we'd used him as a ringer.'

'The scummer! I can't believe it! We should go and fix him up before we fix up Sister Vinegar!'

'He's said worse than that, Dermot. He's identified you as one of the two men who dropped Sister Barbara into the fountain.'

Dermot said, 'I'll kill him! I'll fecking kill him! I'll cut his mebs off and shove them up his arse!'

'First of all, we need to get back to the stud, load up Sparkle the Second in a horsebox and get rid of him. Then they won't have any evidence that he was a ringer.'

'Lord Jay Suck, that's grand! That's absolutely grand! And where are we going to find a knackery that's going to take him without asking any questions? You don't even have a fake passport for him, do you? Fitzgerald's won't touch him!'

'We can get rid of him the same way Paddy Fearon got rid of all those other horses.'

'Are you pulling my chain?'

'Dermot,' said Riona, 'this is desperate. We're going to have to take desperate measures.'

'Oh, yes, to save *your* skin,' said Dermot. 'What about me? I'm going to be banged up back in the loony bin at this rate!' He paused for a moment to calm himself down, grinding his teeth. Then he nodded towards the iPhone in Riona's lap and said, 'Who was that ringing you anyway?'

'Just somebody who knows what's going on, that's all. Now make a bust, will you? The speed you're going, this is going to take us till Doomsday.'

'Never a truerer word spoken, Riona. Never a truerer word spoken.'

Fifty-two

Dr Mazdani wanted Katie to stay for another twenty-four hours at least, to make sure that she was suffering no complications, but after she had eaten a ham sandwich and a strawberry yogurt at lunchtime she told him that she was going to discharge herself.

'I think you are probably okay,' he told her. 'But, please, I beg you, take things very easy. Any bleeding, come back at once.'

An armed protection officer in a black windcheater had been posted in the corridor outside her room ever since she had been admitted. After she had dressed she asked him to bring his car round to the front of the hospital. While she was waiting she rang Detective Inspector O'Rourke.

'Francis? What's the story? I'm leaving the hospital in a minute and I should be home in half an hour.'

'How are you feeling?' he asked her.

'Like I've been through a mangle, to be honest with you. But surviving.'

'I was going to ring you anyway. It looks like we have a good lead on the nun case. A fellow called – hang on, I have his name here – a fellow called Gerry Brickley came into the station about eleven o'clock. He said he knew who that four-fingered hoodie was who tied that roasted nun up to the lamp post. He was sure that it was the same guy who helped to drop Sister Barbara into the Berwick Fountain.'

'So who is he, this four-fingered hoodie?'

'He's some gom who does odd jobs at a stud farm in Clontead, just north of Coachford. His first name's Dermot, but he doesn't know his surname. The stud's run by some woman called Riona Mulliken.'

'I've heard of her. There was some article in the *Examiner* about her not so long ago. One of Cork's most successful female breeders and trainers.'

'Well, she might be the most successful because she's been cheating,' said Detective Inspector O'Rourke. 'This Brickley fellow said he paid an unannounced visit to the stud this morning to look at the horse he's the owner of, and he only saw an identical horse. He reckons Riona Mulliken's been ringing. Brickley's horse was entered for the O'Grady Insurance Group Steeplechase at Mallow last Sunday but the horse that ran didn't even finish, and now Brickley's convinced that it wasn't his horse at all.'

'There's something else I read about Riona Mulliken, too,' said Katie. '*That's* why the name of Sister Bridget Healy rang a bell with me! Riona Mulliken tried to sue Sister Bridget Healy for the abuse that she had suffered while she was living at Saint Margaret's Mother and Baby Home and for having her child adopted without her permission. But Sister Bridget said she had signed away all her parental rights on the birth certificate and so the district court judge dismissed her action and awarded costs against her. I remember the story because Riona Mulliken said that Sister Bridget was a criminal in crow's clothing and that just stuck in my mind.'

'I like that,' said Detective Inspector O'Rourke. 'A criminal in crow's clothing. That would apply to most of the clergy I've ever known. That Father Jenkins, he was a terror. Rosary in one hand and you can guess where the other hand was.'

'Right,' said Katie. 'First of all we need to pick up this Dermot. Brennan will be the man for it. Do you want to send him out there with a couple of uniforms? Then we can make some more enquiries about Ms Mulliken and her race-fixing. If Dermot works for her he must know something about it. It may not be easy to prove it, though, and you know what the racing fraternity are like. Tighter than the stonecutters.'

'Wait just a moment,' said Detective Inspector O'Rourke. 'When he was at Mallow, Brickley saw Riona Mulliken having what looked like something of a heated argument with, guess who?'

'Francis, I'm not really in the mood for guessing games and there's a protection officer waiting downstairs to take me home.'

'Sorry. It was Paddy Fearon.'

Katie gave a wave to the nurse who had come to tell her that the protection officer was ready for her and mouthed '*Two minutes*!' Then she sat down on the side of the bed and said, 'Paddy Fearon? You're not serious.'

'It all fits together, ma'am. Some of the racehorses that were found on the beach had their coats dyed. We strongly suspect that it was Paddy Fearon who dumped them there. Riona Mulliken has been accused by this Brickley fellow of ringing. You don't need to take your shoes off to count to eleven.'

'All right, Francis. That's grand. I'll ring you as soon as I'm home. In the meantime can you find out as much as you can about Riona Mulliken? Horse Racing Ireland and Weatherbys should be able to give you most of what you need. And Ashley Iveson from the *Examiner*. Oh, and ask Dooley to have a word with his friend Michael O'Malley. He knows everybody in the racing game.'

'I will, of course,' said Detective Inspector O'Rourke. 'But there's just one more piece of jigsaw that might fit in. Gerry Brickley is the owner of Brickley's Welding and Construction in Castletownroche.'

'Is he now? I see. And?'

'When he visited the stud this morning he was expecting to see a new horse barn that Riona told him she would be building, but she hadn't even made a start on it. That surprised him because she'd bought several cylinders of helium from him, for the welding. Allegedly for the welding, anyway.'

Katie let out a breathy little whistle. 'Oh, yes, Francis, you're right. This definitely has that fitting-together feeling. But let's get as much background information on Riona Mulliken as we can before we take this any further. Just make sure that we collar this Dermot, asap.'

'I'll talk to you after,' said Detective Inspector O'Rourke. But then he said, 'Ma'am?'

'What is it, Francis?'

'You'll make sure that you take it easy, won't you? I'll keep you informed, but I can handle this, no bother at all. That was a fierce bad blow that Karosas gave you. It's going to take some getting over, in more ways than one.'

'Thanks, Francis. That's appreciated. I'll ring you later.'

* * *

As the protection officer drove her home to Cobh, Katie tried three times to call John but still he wouldn't pick up.

She found it hard to believe that he wouldn't even talk to her. Even if he had decided that her pregnancy meant an end to their relationship, didn't he even want to shout at her, or tell her she was a slut, or know who the baby's father was and where he was and why he wasn't around any more?

The protection officer helped her out of the car. He was only in his early forties but his hair was beginning to go grey at the sides already, his eyes looked like sun-faded agates, and he was very taciturn. He hadn't said a word to her all the way from CUH.

'I'll be keeping a watch outside, ma'am,' he told her. 'And you don't have to worry. I'll arrange for a relief to take over when it comes to the end of my shift.'

'I'll fetch you out some tea,' Katie told him. 'And you can come in and use the toilet if and when you need it. You don't have to pee in the bushes.'

The protection officer almost managed to lift the corner of his mouth into a smile. He accompanied her up to the front door and waited until she had let herself in. Barney came charging up to her with his tail thrashing and almost knocked her over.

'It's all, right, Barns. Don't jump up. I'm feeling a little sensitive, just at the moment.'

'You'll be okay, ma'am?' asked the protection officer. 'If there's anything you need, give me a shout.'

'Thank you,' said Katie. *I need a rest. I need somebody to hold me. I need a shoulder to cry on. I need my baby back, but my baby's gone for ever. I'm hurting, my stomach's hurting and I need to cry.*

Fifty-three

Dermot hooked up the single horse trailer to the back of his car while Riona waited impatiently, holding Sparkle the Second's bridle.

'You're not going to change your clothes?' Dermot asked her.

'No, because we're going to the convent first. It's not only Sparkle the Second we're going to get rid of today.'

Dermot shook his head. 'Listen, is this such a bright idea, like? There could be shades at the convent, too.'

'That's precisely why I'm not changing my clothes,' said Riona. 'What chance would I have of getting into a convent in my fur jacket and thigh-boots?'

'Oh well, fair play. But this is getting more and more cracked by the minute, there's no mistake about that. And I thought *I* was the one who was supposed to be rulya.'

'Go and fetch your shotgun,' said Riona.

'What?'

'I said go and fetch your shotgun. And a box of cartridges, too.'

'What have you got in mind, then? The Gunfight at the Fecking OK Corral?'

'Just fetch it, Dermot. You're wasting time.'

Dermot walked across to his lean-to shed at the side of the stables while Riona led Sparkle the Second up the ramp into the horse trailer and tied him up. Sparkle the Second let out a snort and she patted his nose.

'Sorry about this, Sparkle. This isn't your fault. There's a heaven for horses, don't you worry. All grass and sunshine and mares who feel like it.'

Dermot came back with the up-and-over shotgun that he used for killing rats around the stud farm and a box of Eley 28 gram cartridges. He tossed them on to the back seat and then he and Riona climbed into the car.

'Maybe we should say a prayer,' Dermot suggested.

'Good idea,' said Riona. 'Dear Lord save us from sadistic nuns and people who can't be trusted and incurable idiots. Now, let's go!'

* * *

It took them over an hour to reach Gardiner's Hill because they were towing the horsebox. Riona told Dermot to wait about fifty metres down the hill from the entrance to the Bon Sauveur Convent, in a cul-de-sac called Herbert Park.

'Turn around, though,' she said. 'You need to be ready to leave as soon as I get back.'

'You're still sure you want to go through with this?' Dermot asked her.

'Jesus. I don't know who's the worse nag, Sparkle the Second or you.'

'Okay, sorry. Just asking.'

Riona climbed out and slung her raincoat over her shoulders. Then she opened the back door, picked up the shotgun and broke it open.

'You're not taking *that* with you?'

'What does it look like?' said Riona. She took out two cartridges and loaded the shotgun, then she took out another four and pushed them into her raincoat pockets. Dermot was about to say something but decided against it. If he had learned anything about Riona, it was that once she had made up her mind that she wanted to do something she was unstoppable. Today she was making him feel totally helpless, as if he were being washed out to sea. He hadn't felt like this since he was first sent to Carraig Mor.

Riona shrugged her raincoat higher on her shoulders and hid the shotgun underneath it, holding it by the barrels. She gripped her lapels tightly together with her left hand to make sure that it didn't show.

'I don't know how long I'm going to be,' she said. 'It depends how quickly I can find Sister Virginia.'

'Take your time,' said Dermot, lighting a cigarette. 'It's not like I've got a doctor's appointment or nothing.'

'You were right before,' said Riona. 'You are a comedian.'

She walked off up the hill to the limestone pillars of the Bon Sauveur Convent. Two uniformed gardaí were standing outside, but as she approached they nodded and smiled and said, 'How's it going, Sister?' She smiled back, but said nothing.

She climbed the steeply sloping car park. A green van was being loaded with shovels and riddles and folded blue sheets of vinyl and some of the search team of Garda reservists were standing around, talking and smoking. Riona walked past them and up to the convent's front door.

She didn't have to ring the bell. The door opened as she was approaching it and an elderly nun came out, and smiled at her. 'Good afternoon, Sister,' she said and held the door open for her. Riona nodded, but still she said nothing.

Her footsteps echoed as she walked along the gloomy corridor past the gleaming statue of Saint Margaret of Cortona. The shotgun was beginning to feel heavy and awkward underneath her raincoat and inch by inch it was slipping down, so she stopped for a moment to adjust her grip on it.

As she did so, a young nun in white came out of a side room. She smiled at Riona at first, but then she frowned because she obviously didn't recognize her.

'Can I help you at all, Sister?' she asked her.

Riona said, 'Oh! Yes, maybe you can. I'm looking for Sister Virginia O'Cleary. I've been told that she's staying here for a while. She left her medallion of Saint Perpetua behind at her grand-niece's house and I've fetched it for her.'

'That's very kind of you,' said the young sister. 'I believe Sister Virginia's still sleeping at the moment because she hasn't been too well. If you give it to me, I can make sure she gets it when she wakes up.'

'I'd really prefer to put it in her hand myself, thank you. Can you show me where she is?'

'I don't think she's supposed to be disturbed. She's had some heart trouble.'

'I won't disturb her, I can promise you that. I'll be quiet as a mouse. I'll just tiptoe in and press it in her hand. It means so much to her.'

'Well . . . I suppose that would be all right. She's upstairs. Do you want to follow me? Shall I take your coat for you?'

'No, no, I'm grand altogether. It's fierce cold outside and I haven't warmed up yet.'

The young sister led Riona to the end of the corridor. Two flights of pale-oak stairs led up to a landing on the first floor, illuminated by a yellow stained-glass window. They climbed the stairs and went all the way along another corridor, with Riona's raincoat rustling as she walked. The shotgun was now feeling almost unbearably heavy and she was on the verge of dropping it.

'Here,' said the young novice. They had reached a door with a pewter crucifix on it and the number seven. She gently turned the handle and opened it up, turning around to Riona as she did so and pressing her fingertip to her lips.

Inside, in semi-darkness, Sister Virginia lay asleep. She was lying on a plain iron bed with brass knobs on it, covered by a fawn wool blanket. Apart from a walnut-veneered wardrobe and a framed print of Jesus holding up His hand in blessing, the room was completely bare. It smelled of antiseptic ointment and cloves.

Riona approached the bed. There, with her head resting on a flat skimpy pillow, was the woman who had made her Sorley sleep all night in cold urine-soaked sheets. Her eyes were closed and her toothless mouth was half open, and she was breathing in quick little gasps as if she were dreaming that she was running.

She was much older, of course, than Riona remembered her. Her cheeks were sunken and her hair was white, tied with a black velvet band. But Riona could never forget that hawk-like nose and the wart in the middle of her chin.

Riona turned around to the young novice, who was still standing in the open doorway. The novice didn't say anything but gave her an encouraging nod, as if to suggest that she should go ahead and place the medallion in Sister Virginia's hand, so that they could leave her to sleep in peace.

Instead, though, Riona turned back to the bed, opened up her raincoat and lifted out the shotgun. The young novice clearly didn't understand what she was doing, because she didn't move and didn't utter a sound. Riona took a step back and pushed the muzzle of the shotgun into Sister Virginia's mouth, right up against her gums.

Sister Virginia instantly opened her pale-grey eyes and half raised one hand. She stared at Riona for a split second as if she were saying, *Who are you, and what are you doing?* But then Riona pulled both triggers, one after the other. There was a deafening double bang and Sister Virginia's skull exploded, so that the pillow and the wall behind it were sprayed with blood and flesh and gelatinous lumps of brain and fragments of bone.

All that remained of her face was her lower jaw, with her long mauve tongue lolling over it. The bedroom was filled with pungent gunpowder smoke and the feathers from her pillow floated down on to the blackened, bloodied hole where her head had been resting.

Riona's ears were singing and she felt as if she had been kicked in the shoulder by a horse. She turned around and the young novice was staring at her in shock. She took a step back from Riona, and then another, and then she rushed off along the corridor. Riona stood quite still for a moment. She was sorry that she hadn't been able to inflict on Sister Virginia the prolonged agony she had intended for her. The best she could hope for was that she had realized in that final split second who Riona was, and why she was being shot.

Riona broke open the shotgun to eject the spent cartridges and took two more out of her raincoat pocket to reload it. Then she left the bedroom without looking again at Sister Virginia's body and walked back along the corridor. She walked briskly, but she didn't rush, and now she was carrying the shotgun openly.

Although she was still partially deafened by the shots she had fired, she could hear doors slamming and nuns calling out to each other and the pattering of feet. She started down the stairs, but she was only halfway down when a door on the right-hand side suddenly opened.

A nun came out, dressed all in black except for her white cowl, elderly and diminutive. She looked up at Riona and the lenses of her glasses gleamed yellow in the light from the stained-glass window.

'What have you done?' asked the nun in a thin, quivering voice.

Riona continued to descend the stairs until she was standing right in front of her. The nun barely came up to Riona's chest.

'What have I *done*?' she said. 'I've done what should have been done years ago. I've given Sister Virginia the punishment she deserved. I've shot her. She's dead.'

'You've *killed* her? In the holy name of Jesus, what did she ever do to deserve that? She was a pure and saintly woman. She did nothing but good all her life.'

'No, she didn't. She was a murderer. Just like Sister Bridget, and Sister Barbara, and Sister Mona, and Sister Aibrean.'

'Are you trying to tell me that you killed *them*, too?' said the nun in horror, and crossed herself.

'They were all murderers,' said Riona. 'How many children did they murder between them? How many lives did they crush? Now, step out of my way, will you? I've done what I came here to do.'

'No – you stay right there,' said the nun. 'I'm going to call the guards and have you arrested for murder.'

Riona lifted the shotgun and pointed it directly at the nun's heart. 'You will not, Sister. I would have no hesitation at all in killing you, too. Now, step out of my way.'

The nun took off her glasses and said, 'I am the mother superior of this convent and I am ordering you in the name of God to put down that gun and stay where you are.'

Riona stared at her. 'I *know* you,' she said.

'What are you talking about? Put down that gun! Sister Rose! Can you hear me, Sister Rose? Run outside and fetch those two guards! Warn them there's a woman here with a gun!'

Riona came closer to Mother O'Dwyer until the shotgun was almost touching the silver cross around her neck.

'I *know* you. You're Sister Hannah!'

'What? Who are you?'

'You're Sister Hannah! Horrible Hannah, I used to call you behind your back! You were just as mean to me as Sister Virginia! You were worse! You were always picking on me. You were always making me stay inside while the other girls went out. You were always sending me to bed without any supper. Don't you remember that time when I hadn't washed the dishes properly and you slapped me and slapped me as if you wanted me dead! You were *horrible* to me! You were always making me cry! And it was *you*, you bitch, it was you who told me that it was a good thing that my Sorley was taken away from me because I was nothing but a whore!'

She lifted the shotgun higher and curled her finger around the triggers. 'Oh . . . I could happily kill you here and now!'

'*Sorley?*' whispered Mother O'Dwyer. 'Your son was called *Sorley?*'

'Oh! So you *do* remember? Poor little Sorley who you treated almost as bad as me and then sent off to America to be adopted.'

'Riona?' said Mother O'Dwyer, still whispering. 'Riona Nolan?'

'You do have a good memory, Sister Hannah. Or *Mother* Hannah, or whatever you call yourself now. Now, for the last time, will you step out of my way because I am finding it very difficult to restrain myself from blowing an enormous great hole in you.'

'You can't,' said Mother O'Dwyer.

'What do you mean, I can't?'

'You can't kill me. I'm your mother.'

Riona frowned at her and said, '*What*? What in the name of God are you rambling about? You're not my mother! How could you be my mother? My mother was Shauna Nolan, God rest her soul!'

'Shauna Nolan was your adoptive mother. Your real mother is me.'

Riona gradually lowered the shotgun. 'I was *adopted*? Don't talk such shite! I was never adopted!'

'You were, Riona. It was all covered up. There were no adoption papers, not in the usual way.'

'I don't believe this, not a word of it! You're making this up so that I won't kill you!'

'No, Riona, it's true. I swear to you on the Holy Bible it's true.'

'So – if you're my real mother, why did you treat me so badly when I was taken in here? Why did you pick on me all the time? A real mother wouldn't treat her own daughter like that!'

'I'm sorry to say that I was ashamed of you. I was ashamed that you'd fallen, just as I fell. Every time I punished you, I suppose I was punishing myself. Let me say to you now that I deeply, deeply regret it. I regret it to the bottom of my heart.'

Riona looked around the hallway in disbelief. 'I can't take this in! You're lying! You were a *nun*, for Christ's sake! How could a nun be my mother?'

'I was very young, Riona, and very easily taken in. Canon O'Flynn used to pay regular visits to the convent from the Holy Family Church and sometimes hold Mass here. He was a very charismatic man, Riona, and I fell in love with him. That's all.'

'You're trying to tell me that Canon O'Flynn is my father and that you're my mother?'

'It's true, Riona. I swear it. If you kill me now, perhaps it's because the Lord thinks that I deserve to die for the sins that I've committed, but you will be committing an even greater sin by killing the woman who gave you life.'

There was a long pause. Riona stood with the shotgun half lifted, her ears still singing, and utterly stunned. Just then, though, the front door of the convent banged open and the two gardaí who had been standing beside the convent entrance came bursting in, wielding their batons.

'Lay down that weapon!' one of them shouted. 'Do you hear me? Lay it down now!'

Riona seized Mother O'Dwyer's scapular and pulled her roughly towards her. She held up the shotgun and called back, 'Stay where you are! If you come any closer I'll blow off her head! I mean it!'

'Lay down that weapon!' the garda repeated. 'There's an armed response unit on its way and you won't stand a fecking chance!'

Riona started to walk towards the front door, dragging Mother O'Dwyer along with her. Mother O'Dwyer kept saying, 'Don't, Riona! Don't! For the love of God, don't!'

Riona said nothing, but kept on walking. As she approached the two gardaí she raised the shotgun even higher. They both raised their hands and backed away.

'You're making a fierce bad mistake here, girl,' one of them said. 'This is only going to end in tears, I promise you.' Riona bared her teeth at him in a humourless grin and pushed Mother O'Dwyer out of the door.

Now she really hurried. Keeping a tight grip on Mother O'Dwayer's scapular, she stalked as quickly as she could down the sloping car park, out of the convent gates and down the hill. Mother O'Dwyer tripped once or twice, and lost her left shoe, but Riona pulled her to her feet again and kept on going. A reservist turned around and saw them and shouted out, 'Hey!' and started to go after them, but one of the gardaí came out of the front door and said, 'Don't! She's armed! We've already called for the ERU!'

Riona dragged Mother O'Dwyer down to Herbert Park. Two small girls in pink anoraks were playing hopscotch on the pavement and they stared at them in bewilderment. Dermot was sitting in his car smoking and listening to Cork 96 FM. As soon as he saw Riona and Mother O'Dwyer come stumbling around the corner he tossed his cigarette away and switched off the radio

'Jesus Christ, Riona! What the feck?'

Riona opened the back door of the car and pushed Mother O'Dwyer inside. Then she climbed in next to her so that she could keep the shotgun digging into her side.

'Please, Riona!' said Mother O'Dwyer. 'Please think twice about this! They're sending the armed guards after us! You'll be getting the both of us killed!'

'Just keep your mouth shut, Sister Hannah,' said Riona. 'Dermot, get us out of here, and quick!'

'We're pulling a fecking horsebox with a horse in it! I can't go that quick!'

'Sure, I know that, but quick as you can. We have a hostage, so it doesn't really matter too much. Nobody's going to give us any grief while we're holding the holy mother here.'

'Riona—' said Mother O'Dwyer, but Riona dug the shotgun muzzle even harder into her ribs and said, 'Don't! I don't want to hear it! I don't want to hear your prayers or your apologies or your excuses! My mother was Shauna Nolan and there's an end to it! Now shut your bake!'

'What's the story?' asked Dermot as they drove down Summerhill towards the city, the horse trailer bumping and jolting behind them.

'Sister Virginia's dancing with the devil, so that's another one of those witches accounted for.'

'I thought you were going to stab her, like.'

'I didn't have the time, Dermot. At least she saw my face before she went downstairs to meet Satan.'

Mother O'Dwyer clasped her hands together and closed her eyes and started to mutter a prayer. Riona jabbed her again and almost screamed at her, '*No praying*! *Do you hear me, you witch*? *No effing praying*!'

'By the way,' said Dermot, as they drove over the Brian Boru Bridge and the river filled the car with reflected sunlight, 'where are we heading off to, if you don't mind me asking?'

'Nohaval Cove, of course. We've a horse to dispose of.'

440

Katie took a long, warm shower, leaning her head back against the tiles and letting the water gush all over her face. Her stomach was still swollen and there was a huge charcoal-coloured bruise in the middle of it, tinged around the edges with crimson. All the same, it didn't throb as badly as it had done yesterday and she was beginning to feel less battered, although her back still hurt.

She stepped out of the shower, wrapped a towel around her head and put on her bathrobe. On the shelf over the bathroom basin there was only one toothbrush now, and John's razor and aftershave had gone. It was the same in the bedroom – all of his clothes had disappeared from the wardrobe. His sweaters, his shoes. In the hallway his coats and scarves were no longer hanging on the pegs.

He had taken his portfolio of paintings and drawings, too. All that he had left behind was the nude study of Katie, ripped in half.

Katie stood in the doorway for a moment and thought of all the people in her life who had left her, one way or another. Her mother. Seamus. Paul. And now John.

Under her breath she whispered the song that her father always used to sing at New Year. 'So fill to me the parting glass. Goodnight and joy be with you all.'

She went into the kitchen to make herself a cup of coffee. She thought it was strange that her tastes had changed so abruptly now that she was no longer pregnant, but she couldn't face the thought of green tea or chocolate ginger biscuits.

While she was waiting for the coffee to brew, Barney came and nudged at her leg with his nose. He looked up at her soulfully and she wondered if he had really had any empathy with how she was feeling, or if he was trying to tell her that he felt like a walk. *Dogs and men*, she thought. *There's no accounting for the way they treat you.*

She looked at her iPhone lying on the kitchen counter. She was tempted to give John one more try, but then she thought that would give him the impression that she was begging. If he didn't want her, if she disgusted him because she was shop-soiled, then that was his problem. She could find better men than him. Men who didn't run away from reality, like John had run away from Ireland when he was younger, and then run away from her. Twice.

'If that's the way you feel, boy,' she said as she poured out her coffee. At that moment, though, her phone rang and almost made her spill it.

It was Detective O'Donovan. 'I know you've only just made it back home, ma'am, but Detective Inspector O'Rourke asked me to ring you and let you know that Riona Mulliken appears to have shot dead one of the nuns at the Bon Sauveur Convent.'

'Tell me that's not true. Jesus.'

'Not only that, she's abducted the mother superior.'

'Are you serious? That old Mother O'Dwyer?'

'That's the one, Mother O'Dwyer, and Riona Mulliken's still armed with a shotgun as far as we know. She's heading south in a car that we believe is being driven by that Dermot fellow we were supposed to be arresting. A blue Toyota Avensis. The ERU have two cars tailing them and we've alerted Superintendent Barry at Carrigaline, too, because that's the direction they're taking.

'You're not going to believe this, though. They're towing a horse trailer, and it has a horse in it.'

'A *horse* trailer? With a *horse* in it?' said Katie. 'What murderer tries to make a getaway towing a horse trailer with a horse in it? What sort of a speed are they doing?'

'Only about 65 kph. We're right behind them but we don't want Riona Mulliken to panic, like, do you know what I mean? One of the sisters in the convent overheard her threatening to blow a hole in Mother O'Dwyer, and she blew the head off one of the nuns there when she was lying asleep, so I'd say she's serious.'

'Well – all we can do for now is follow her and see where she's going,' said Katie. 'She must realize that she can't get away. Are you following her yourself?'

'I am, yeah, and Dooley's with me. We're on the N28, just coming up to the Shannonpark roundabout. We don't know which way she's going yet . . . she may be heading for Ringaskiddy and the ferry terminal . . . no, she's taken the next turning . . . she's definitely making for Carrigaline.'

'I'm coming to join you,' said Katie, unwinding the towel from her head.

'There's no need for that at all, ma'am. Besides, you shouldn't be driving.'

'I have a protection officer right outside the house. He can drive me.'

'You're grand, though, really. Everything's under control. Detective Inspector O'Rourke says he's going to call for the Air Support Unit if he has to. The Eurocopter's only at the airport at the moment because it brought the commissioner down from Baldonnel this morning for a meeting with the county council. We could have it overhead in no time at all.'

'I'm still coming, Patrick. I'll call you when I'm leaving, so you can tell me where you are.'

'Ma'am—'

Katie ended the call, quickly swallowed a mouthful of scalding coffee, and then went through to her bedroom. She dried her hair roughly in front of the bathroom mirror and then dressed herself. Barney watched her hopefully as she put on a warm black roll-neck sweater and a speckled grey trouser suit.

'No walkies yet, Barns,' she told him, patting him on the head. 'Later, I promise you.'

Barney got the message, because he sat down for a few moments and then lay down, with his head on his paws, and looked up at her as sadly as a Christian martyr.

* * *

They had to take a circuitous, twenty-seven kilometre loop to reach Carrigaline, first driving north to join the main E30, then south on the N40 through the Jack Lynch Tunnel to join the N28.

Katie's protection officer drove hair-raisingly fast, however. Even though his BMW 5-Series was unmarked, it was fitted with blue response lights behind the front grille and a siren.

'You should have been a professional racing driver,' said Katie as they sped through Jack's Hole and then burst out into the sunshine again.

'I used to rally until I got myself involved in a bit of an accident,' said her protection officer. 'It wasn't my fault, but a young wain was badly injured and I gave up after that. Didn't exactly lose my nerve, like, but kept thinking what the consequences would be if something went wrong, and you can't rally in that frame of mind.'

'I don't know your name,' said Katie.

'Garrett. Stephen Garrett. Most of my friends call me Dusty.'

'Dusty? Why do they call you that?'

'I always kept myself to myself when I was a kid and nobody could ever find me. You know what people say when they can't find someone. They'll ask, "Where is he?" and somebody will say, 'up in Nelly's room behind the wallpaper," or something like that. That's what they used to say about me. "Oh, Stephen. He's up in the dusty garret."'

They were driving through the centre of Carrigaline now and they stopped talking because Garda Garrett had to concentrate on weaving his way through the early afternoon traffic. Katie glanced over at him, though, and couldn't help thinking what a good-looking, straightforward man he was. She realized now that he had stayed so silent when he was driving her home from the hospital because he had been shy – she, after all, was a detective superintendent.

Once they had left Carrigaline behind, Garda Garrett put his foot down again, even though the roads were becoming narrower and twistier and there were high hedges on either side. Katie clung onto the door handle as they slewed around corners and almost took off whenever the road dipped. After another ten minutes she saw a Volvo estate from the Regional Support Unit up ahead of them, and as the road straightened out she saw another Volvo estate ahead of that, and then an unmarked Ford Mondeo.

In front of all of them a khaki horse trailer was trundling along at no more than 40 kph. Its top door was open, although it was too far away and too dark inside for Katie to be able to see the horse that it was supposed to be carrying.

Garda Garrett slowed down and they fell in behind the patrol car. Katie called Detective O'Donovan to tell him that she had caught up with him.

'Does Riona Mulliken have a mobile number?' she asked.

'She does, yeah, and I've been ringing her constantly,' said Detective O'Donovan. 'It could be that she doesn't want to answer or maybe she doesn't have her phone with her. Either way I'm getting nothing.'

I know the feeling, thought Katie.

She looked out of the window and saw that they were passing through the little village of Nohoval – a single street of neat, freshly painted houses. There was a crossroads at the end the street, overlooked by Saint Patrick's Church. Standing in the garden in front of the church was a life-sized figure of the Virgin Mary, her pale-blue robes shining in the sunlight. When she saw it, Katie quickly crossed herself. She could see that the Toyota and its horse trailer were turning left, followed by the three Garda cars, and she had a dark, sick feeling that something really bad was going to happen.

'Where in the name of God are they heading?' asked Garda Garrett.

'Unless I'm mistaken, Nohaval Cove,' said Katie.

'That's where all those dead racehorses were discovered, isn't it?'

'That's right. That's where all those dead racehorses were discovered.'

The procession of vehicles drove slowly between the fields until they reached the clifftop at Nohaval Cove. The Toyota and its horse trailer jounced and jolted through the wind-blown grass until it was only ten metres from the edge, where it stopped. Katie called Detective O'Donovan and said, 'That's far enough, Patrick. Give them plenty of space.'

Detective O'Donovan halted his car on the track that ran alongside the very last field before the cliff top. The two Volvos pulled in behind him and seven armed gardaí in black windcheaters and bulletproof vests scrambled out, all of them carrying Heckler & Koch MP7 sub-machine guns. They hurriedly took up positions in a semicircle about sixty metres away from the Toyota and the horse trailer, some of them kneeling, some lying in the grass.

Katie climbed out of Garda Garrett's car and walked along the row of vehicles to Detectives Donovan and Dooley, who were both standing behind their Mondeo with their SIG Sauer pistols raised.

'You don't have to say anything,' said Katie, before either of them could speak. 'You didn't want me to come. But this one I have to see through to the end.'

The Garda sergeant from the armed response unit came up to them and said, 'Any luck yet making contact?'

'No,' said Detective O'Donovan. 'But you wouldn't call this a realistic attempt to escape, would you? It's not exactly the brainiest thing to do, making a getaway pulling a horsebox behind you and driving yourself to a total dead end. Like, how do they think they're going to get out of this situation, do you know what I mean?'

'They might ask that we allow them free passage to leave the country, like, you know, in exchange for the mother superior,' said Detective Dooley. 'Other than that, though, I can't see what their options are.'

'Free passage? They can whistle for that,' said the sergeant. 'You want me to see if I can raise them with the loudhailer?'

Katie thought for a moment. The wind was making a soft, sizzling sound in the grass and beyond the edge of the cliff the sea was glittering turquoise. She had a terrible sense of foreboding about this. Riona Mulliken had been seeking revenge on the sisters of the Bon Sauveur Convent. She had done it blatantly and openly, and with monstrous cruelty, but that was because she believed that the sisters had been monstrously cruel to her. What greater cruelty could you inflict on a mother than to take her child away from her? thought Katie. She herself had lost little Seamus, and yesterday it had happened again, and the emotional pain of that was indescribable. She realized that she could happily kill Davydos Karosas – maybe by having him kicked to death.

When she turned back to the sergeant she had tears in her eyes.

'Are you all right, ma'am?' he asked her.

'Of course, yes. Fierce cold wind this.' She wiped her eyes with the back of her hand and then she said, 'I'll talk to her. If you would fetch me the loudhailer.'

The Toyota and the horse trailer remained stationary and there was no sign of life except for the horse whuffling and impatiently stamping its hooves. When the sergeant returned with the loudhailer, he was also carrying a black bulletproof vest.

'Here,' he said, handing it to Katie. 'Don't want you full of holes. Bad enough the wind blowing around you, let alone blowing straight through you.'

Detective Donovan helped Katie to fasten the vest and then she picked up the loudhailer.

'Riona!' she called out. 'Riona Mulliken!'

She waited, but there was no response.

'Riona!' she called out again. 'This is Detective Superintendent Kathleen Maguire from Cork Garda station. I understand why you've taken Mother O'Dwyer! Can you hear me? I know what you've been through and why you've done what you've done!'

Still no response.

'I reckon we should shoot their tyres out,' said the armed unit sergeant. 'That'll make them realize they're not going anywhere.'

'Riona!' called Katie. 'Riona, all I want to do is talk to you! There *is* a way out of this!'

'Sure there is,' said the armed unit sergeant. 'Straight through the criminal court and into the women's wing at Limerick Prison.'

Katie turned to him and said, 'Will you keep your comments to yourself, sergeant?'

'Yes, ma'am. Sorry, ma'am. Just trying to ease the tension, like.'

Katie lifted the loudhailer again, but before she could call out anything the doors of the Toyota opened. Riona climbed out first. She was holding the shotgun in one hand and keeping it pointed into the rear of the car.

With a clattering sound, the armed gardaí all raised and cocked their sub-machine guns and pointed them at her, but the sergeant shouted, 'Hold fire! There's a hostage in there!'

Riona bent over and dragged Mother O'Dwyer out of the back seat. Mother O'Dwyer stood ashen-faced, with the wind whipping up her scapular so that it made a distinctive snapping sound. Riona stood beside her, pointing the shotgun at her head.

'Riona!' said Katie through the loudhailer. 'Please put your gun down! Please! No good is going to come of this! I know why you hate these sisters so much, but you've done enough now! You've shown us all how much you've suffered!'

Riona didn't answer but turned around and said something to Dermot, who now swung himself out from behind the steering wheel and stood up beside her. Riona handed him the shotgun and the armed gardaí all aimed their weapons at him, but again the sergeant shouted, 'Hold fire!'. He might have been flippant, thought Katie, but thank God he wasn't trigger-happy. She couldn't begin to imagine the repercussions if they allowed a mother superior to be shot dead right in front of them.

Katie didn't call out to Riona again. She could see that whatever Riona had decided to do, nothing was going to change her mind. She walked around to the back of the horse trailer, unfastened the catches, and let down the ramp. She went inside, untied Sparkle the Second, and then gently backed him down the ramp until he was standing in the grass.

'What the *hell* is she doing?' said Detective Dooley. 'She's not going to try and get away on that horse, is she?'

Detective O'Donovan glanced around at the fields behind them. 'It's crazy, but she might. We couldn't follow her, could we?'

'We could shoot the horse.'

'Oh, great, and have the ISPCA all over us.'

'The woman's killed five nuns, for the love of Jesus.'

'I know. But the fecking horse hasn't killed anybody.'

Stepping on to the trailer's mudguard to give herself a boost up, Riona swung her leg over Sparkle the Second and mounted him bareback. Then, gripping his mane to guide him, she eased him forward until he was standing beside Mother O'Dwyer and Dermot. All this time Dermot was keeping the shotgun pointed only centimetres away from Mother O'Dwyer's head.

'Holy Mother of God,' said Katie. 'I hope she's not thinking of doing what I think she's thinking of doing.'

Still keeping a firm hold on Sparkle the Second's mane, Riona leaned over and seized Mother O'Dwyer's right arm. Mother O'Dwyer tried to wrench herself free and drop to her knees so that Riona couldn't reach down to her, but Dermot shifted the shotgun into his left hand and thrust his right hand into the depths of her vestments, right between her legs, and heaved her upwards like a black sack of coal. Riona dragged her over Sparkle the Second's back and for the first time Mother O'Dwyer screamed.

'*God help me*! *Somebody help me*! *Jesus, save me*!'

The armed gardaí stood up and some of them began to walk forward, but Dermot prodded Mother O'Dwyer's buttocks with the shotgun and shouted out, 'Don't you even think about it, or I'll blow her fecking arse off!'

Sparkle the Second stepped forward a few paces. He was twitchy and kept shaking his head and snorting. It was clear that he could sense the hostility all around him. Riona was sitting on him bolt upright, as if she were entering a dressage competition, while Mother O'Dwyer was hanging over his back in front of her, face-down. She was kicking like a small child but Riona had a firm grasp on her belt to prevent her from sliding off.

Katie picked up the loudhailer again and called out, '*Riona*! *Don't*!'

But Riona turned Sparkle the Second around in a nervous 360-degree circle and then she abruptly dug her heels into his flanks. Sparkle the Second jerked forward and started cantering straight for the edge of the cliff.

'*Riona*!' Katie screamed out, although she knew it was far too late.

Sparkle the Second leaped off the cliff top as if he were trying to clear the highest hurdle that he had ever faced in his life – his head lifted, his front legs stretched out. For a second, he could have been Pegasus flying up into the air.

Then, however, he lost all of his momentum and dropped downwards, his hind legs frantically pedalling to feel some ground beneath his hooves. Mother O'Dwyer, screaming, slithered from his back. Riona somehow managed to stay astride him until his head pitched forward, and then they all disappeared from sight.

Katie heard a jarring crash as Sparkle the Second hit the rocks on the beach below, but the wind was too blustery for her to hear Mother O'Dwyer or Riona.

The armed gardaí now surrounded Dermot. He kept his shotgun raised but he continued to back away, grinning uneasily. Every now and then he quickly glanced behind him to see how close he was to the edge of the cliff.

'Come on, let's be laying that down now, shall we, feen?' said the sergeant. 'I'd say we've had enough dying for one day.'

Dermot hesitated. It was impossible to tell from his expression what was going on inside his mind. But then he suddenly tucked the shotgun stock into his shoulder and aimed it directly at the sergeant.

He didn't get the chance to pull the trigger. There was a staccato rattling of sub-machine gun fire and fragments of flesh flew off his body and into the air as if a flock of scarlet butterflies had been startled. He twisted around and around and then he fell back into the grass, his eyes still open, staring straight up at the sky.

Katie walked over and looked down at him. He was even uglier and more troll-like than Eithne O'Neill had depicted him.

'Not exactly an oil-painting, is he?' said Detective O'Donovan, right behind her.

'No,' she said, and thought for a moment of the painting that John had torn in half.

Next, she went right to the edge of the cliff. The tide was coming in and she could see Sparkle the Second in the surf. He was no longer Pegasus, the flying horse. His legs were sprawled apart and his belly had split open so that his intestines were rising and falling in the water. Not far away, Riona and Mother O'Dwyer were lying side by side on a tilted boulder that was almost like a rough limestone bed. They were facing each other and Mother O'Dwyer appeared to have her arms around Riona, as if she were consoling her.

Almost like a real mother, thought Katie.

Fifty-five

It was dark by the time Garda Sergeant Garrett drove Katie to Anglesea Street. She felt very tired, but they needed to hold a preliminary debriefing and she would have to make a statement to the media.

Almost as soon as she had switched on the lights in her office, Detective Inspector O'Rourke knocked at her door.

'How's it going?' he asked her.

'Oh, grand. That's if you like acting out Greek tragedies for a living.'

She sat down at her desk and he handed her a folder. 'That nun she shot, we've identified her as Sister Virginia O'Cleary.'

'One of the Sacred Seven,' said Katie. 'What was she doing at the convent?'

'It seems like she'd heard about all the other nuns being murdered and she was afraid for her life. She went to the convent for refuge.'

'Well, that didn't help her much, did it? Have they taken her to the mortuary yet?'

'Not yet. Probably later today.'

'Jesus. What a bloodbath. And there was me thinking that the Duggan twins were vicious.'

Detective Inspector O'Rourke pointed to the folder he had given her. 'There's a fair amount of background about Riona Mulliken in there already. She was ostracised by her parents when she got pregnant at the age of fifteen and sent to Saint Margaret's

452

Home. She stayed there for three years until her son was sent off to America for adoption. There's no record of what treatment she received there, but my guess is that she wasn't too happy about it.'

Katie opened the folder and glanced at the first two pages. 'How did she get into racing?' she asked. 'I read something in the paper about her trying to sue the Bon Sauveurs because they'd sent her son away for adoption without her consent. They said that she was one of Cork's most successful horse breeders, but that's about all I can remember.'

'That's right,' said Detective Inspector O'Rourke. 'After she left Saint Margaret's she found herself a job at a stud farm in Ballinhassig. Only a stable-girl, like, mucking out the horses. But she used to go to the races regular with the breeder who ran the place and that's how she caught Stephen Mulliken's eye – the fellow who owned the Clontead Stud. Stephen Mulliken had lost his wife to cancer a couple of years before and even though Riona was thirty years younger than him, he was lonely and wealthy and she was attractive and broke and one thing led to another and they got married.'

'Stephen Mulliken died in 1998 and Riona inherited the stud farm. I haven't had the time yet to talk to any of the racing lot, but it's common knowledge that things have been a struggle in the past few years for the smaller thoroughbred breeders. It's all profit for the big boys, like Darley and Coolmore, of course – but Darley and Coolmore own ten per cent of all the world's breeding stallions between them and they cover over forty per cent of the mares.

'I talked to a bookie friend of mine last week but he was very tight-lipped. Now that Riona's gone, though, he might be more inclined to talk about what she was up to.'

'Okay, Francis, thanks,' said Katie. 'I'll take this home tonight and read through it. What about the search at the convent? How's that going?'

'Just about wrapped up now. We've removed all of the remains and Bill Phinner and his team will be sorting through them over the next few weeks. It's going to take a devil of a long time, though.

At least we now have the records of who the poor kids were, even if we can't match their names to any specific skeletons. I have to say that was a class inspiration of yours, looking for the records behind that picture, even if that wasn't where Ni Nuallán actually found them.'

'No – all the credit for that goes to Kyna. She's still here, isn't she? She hasn't gone home yet?'

'She's still here, yes,' said Detective Inspector O'Rourke. 'She's been sorting through some of the other stuff she found under that statue. There's a heap of correspondence and adoption certificates and all kinds of stuff.'

'I'm still doubtful that we're going to be able to prosecute anybody,' Katie told him. 'Even those children who were starved or wilfully neglected . . . it's almost impossible to prove who did it. It was the same at Tuam. How can you arrest a whole conventful of nuns, especially when so many of the deaths are historic?'

'If the church just admitted it, and apologized, that would be something,' said Detective Inspector O'Rourke. 'The government said sorry for the Maggies.'

'Well, don't hold your breath,' said Katie. 'Now, what about Michael Gerrety, and Karosas?'

'Karosas has been formally charged and we're putting together the Book of Evidence, so that's all going ahead. I interviewed him again with a lawyer present and he's sticking to his story that Gerrety paid him to put the fear of God into Roisin Begley so that she wouldn't testify against him. He's still maintaining, too, that it was an accident and he didn't drown her on purpose.'

'And Gerrety?'

'It turns out that Gerrety's been taking a long weekend in Gran Canaria, but he'll be back Tuesday morning. I don't know how well you'll be recovered by then, but I thought you might like the pleasure of arresting him yourself, in person, like.'

'For that, Francis, I'd get up from my deathbed.'

Detective Inspector O'Rourke said, 'We still haven't located Fergal ó Floinn yet. For a fat, slow fellow he's proving very elusive.

Mind you, he's probably hiding from the Travellers as much as he's hiding from us. Paddy Fearon might not have been Mister Popular among the Pavees but they don't take kindly to people setting off bombs on their halting sites.'

'I'm convinced that Riona Mulliken paid Ó Floinn to plant that device,' said Katie. 'I'd just like to know how a woman like her managed to get in touch with a scummer like him.'

'Maybe that Dermot fellow knew him,' suggested Detective Inspector O'Rourke. 'Pity he's too dead to get any sensible answers out of him.'

Katie's phone rang. It was Detective Dooley, to tell her that the armed response officers had arrived, and Chief Superintendent MacCostagáin had returned to the station, and that everybody was gathering in the conference room for a first debriefing.

'Right,' she said, standing up. 'They're all ready for us.'

Before she could put on her jacket, however, Detective Sergeant Ni Nuallán came in. The sleeves of her pale-blue shirt were rolled up and her hair looked as if it needed a wash.

'Is it important?' Katie asked her. 'We're just about to go downstairs.'

'Oh, I think you'll want to see this first,' said Detective Sergeant Ni Nuallán. She handed Katie a transparent plastic folder.

Inside the folder were two sheets of paper, both of which had turned sepia with age. The first was a letter that had been written with a typewriter on headed paper. The heading was that of the *Very Reverend Canon Martin O'Flynn*, with his address in Montenotte.

Katie started to skim through it, but then she realized what the letter was about and read it more slowly, line by line.

'Holy Mary, Mother of God,' she said when she had finished.

'What is it?' asked Detective Inspector O'Rourke. 'We really should be getting down there.'

Katie held up the letter and said, 'It's an admission by Canon O'Flynn that he had an intimate relationship with Sister Hannah O'Dwyer at the Bon Sauveur Convent. He's telling the bishop that, regrettably, Sister Hannah is now with child. He's suggesting "in all humility" that Sister O'Dwyer's condition should be kept confidential and that when she gives birth her child should be immediately given up for adoption.'

'You're codding,' said Detective Inspector O'Rourke.

'The other letter,' said Detective Sergeant Ni Nuallán. 'Read it.'

The second letter was handwritten in mauve ink on lined notepaper. It was dated, but there was no address.

> *Dear Sister Bridget,*
>
> *I wish to express our deepest gratitude for the gift of our new daughter. She is a little angel sent from Heaven.*
>
> *She was baptised on Sunday and we have named her Riona Hannah, since my mother's name was Riona and you told us that Hannah is her mother's name, whoever she is.*
>
> *With all of our thanks again and may God be with you,*
>
> *Shauna Nolan.*

Detective Sergeant Ni Nuallán said, 'Riona Mulliken's maiden name was Nolan. Shauna Nolan was her adoptive mother. Her real mother was Sister Hannah O'Dwyer.'

'Do you think she *knew* that?' asked Katie. She couldn't stop herself picturing Riona and Mother O'Dwyer lying on the rocks at Nohaval Cove, arm in arm.

Detective Sergeant Ni Nuallán could only shrug.

Fifty-six

Katie slept badly that night. She kept having flashbacks of Sparkle the Second leaping off the edge of the cliff and Mother O'Dwyer sliding off his back like an oil slick, while Riona for a fraction of a second hung in the air, her arms spread wide like Saint Margaret of Cortona.

In the morning she took Barney for a walk, although she didn't go as far as the tennis club, as she usually did, because her stomach began to ache and the air was filled with drizzle.

'Nice soft day,' said one of the protection officers sitting in his car outside her house, reading his newspaper.

She went into the house and stood in the silent living room. So was this it? Was this how her life was always going to be? Alone, in utter silence?

She went through to the kitchen, but as she did so the doorbell chimed. When she went to open it there were two men standing in the porch. One of them was one of her protection officers, the other was a thin, scrawny-looking man with wet hair and a straggly beard and circular spectacles.

'This gentleman says you know him,' said the protection officer.

Katie stared at the scrawny-looking man in bewilderment. Suddenly, however, she realized who he was.

'Liam!' she said. 'For the love of God, where have you been? Look at the state of you!'

'So you *do* know him?' said the protection officer. Katie had noticed that all the time he had been standing there his hand had been resting on the butt of his SIG Sauer automatic.

'Of course, yes. It's Detective Inspector Liam Fennessy. Well – *Ex*-Detective Inspector Liam Fennessy. Liam – come on in! You're drenched!'

'Okay, then,' said the protection officer, and lifted his hand in salute.

Liam stepped into the hallway. He had always been thin but now he looked emaciated. His brown wool overcoat was sodden and his glasses were speckled with raindrops. He smelled of damp and body odour.

'I thought you were dead,' said Katie. 'I mean, after that letter you wrote me, what else was I supposed to think?'

Liam coughed and ran his hand through his hair. 'I'm sorry, ma'am. I was in a bad place, do you know what I mean? A really bad place.'

'Here, take this wet coat off and come into the living room and sit by the fire. You're shaking like a leaf, for goodness' sake!'

Katie helped him to struggle out of his overcoat. Underneath he was wearing a worn-out tweed jacket with holes in the elbows and droopy brown corduroy trousers. He went into the living room and slowly circled around as if he had just woken up from a dream.

'There, sit by the fire,' said Katie. 'How about a cup of tea? Or would you like coffee?'

'No, no, I'm fine, thanks,' said Liam. He sat down in the leather armchair next to the gas log fire. Barney had been lying in front of the hearth but he lifted his head and sniffed twice and then got up and trotted off into the kitchen.

Katie sat on the arm of the couch. 'I was sure that you were going to do away with yourself,' she told him. 'I'm just delighted to see you're still alive.'

Liam took off his glasses and rubbed them against the sleeve of his jacket. 'Like I say, ma'am, I was in a bad place. Totally broke, like. Totally lost my bearings. Breaking up with Caitlin, that knocked me sideways. I know I didn't treat her like I should have, but after she was gone it was like I went mad.'

'You should have come to me for help, Liam. And you don't have to call me "ma'am", not now. In your letter you called me Kathleen.'

Liam put his glasses back on and gave her a rueful grin. 'I was too proud, to be honest with you. Liam Fennessy, the great detective. And I felt so much better after snorting the coke. To begin with, any road.'

'So where have you been?' Katie asked him. 'Do you have somewhere to stay?'

'Oh yes. I have this room in Gurra. It's not much, and the whole place stinks of cabbage, but it's somewhere to sleep.'

'You do understand that we have a whole rake of charges against you, don't you?'

'Of course. Conspiracy in the murder of Garda Brenda McCracken. Conspiracy in the murder of Detective Garda Nessa Goold. Not to mention grievous bodily harm and kidnap and extortion.'

Katie said nothing for a long time. Liam stared at the fire and the flames danced in his glasses. His hands were dirty but she could still see the paler circle where his wedding ring had been. Pawned, more than likely, to pay off his drug-dealers.

'It might go easier on you if you give us some information on Bryan Molloy,' she told him. 'And after all, it wasn't you personally who planted the bomb that killed Garda McCracken, and you weren't even there when Detective Garda Goold was shot.'

'That doesn't make me any less guilty,' said Liam. 'And you can imagine what would happen to me if I ratted out Molloy. They'd find me hanging in my cell on day one, with a broomstick halfway up my rear end. Besides, I can't prove that he paid me. It was all cash money, passed under the table in pubs.'

'So what are you going to do? Now I know you're alive, we're going to be looking for you, and you can't stay on the run for ever.'

'I know that. But once you've taken the shilling, that's your destiny decided for ever, even if you can afford to pay it back, which I can't.'

Katie said, 'When was the last time you had anything to eat? Aren't you hungry?'

Liam shook his head. 'It's no good, ma'am. Kathleen, I mean. There's no way out of this.'

With that, he stood up. He unbuttoned his jacket and reached behind him, lifting up the grubby maroon sweater that he was wearing underneath it. He tugged a Kimber pocket automatic out of his belt and pointed it at her.

Katie stayed where she was, sitting on the arm of the couch.

'If you only knew how sorry I am,' said Liam, and she could tell by the way he was speaking that his mouth had gone completely dry. 'I never thought it was going to be like this, face to face, like.'

'It was you who shot Detective Horgan,' said Katie. 'It was you who tried to shoot me through the window. Right here, in this very room.'

'Not much of a shot, am I?' said Liam. 'I liked Horgan, too. I really did. He always made me laugh, even when I was feeling like shite warmed up.'

'So that's what you're going to do, kill me?' Katie asked him. 'You're going to stand there and shoot me while I'm still looking at you and talking to you and trying to think of a way to help you out?'

'You can't help me out. Nobody can help me out. Molloy wants you dead and that's the end of it. He's going to pay me five thousand euros for doing this. Where else am I going to get five thousand euros?'

'I can give you five thousand euros.'

Liam was panting now and his gun-hand was trembling. The Kimber automatic was only small, with a four-inch barrel, but it fired a .45 ACP round and it would kill Katie instantly.

'Oh, sure, you can give me five thousand euros, but what are you going to do then? You're still going to come after me, and

460

I'm still going to end up in Rathmore Road dangling by my neck from the ceiling!'

'You wouldn't kill somebody who was sitting down, would you?' asked Katie. She could hear how calm her voice was, but in reality she felt as if her insides had dissolved into ice-water. *I'm going to die now*, she thought. *This is actually where my life is going to end.*

Liam lifted the gun a little higher so that it was pointing directly at Katie's heart. As he did so, however, the front doorbell chimed again.

'Who's that?' he demanded.

'I have no idea. But whoever it is, the protection officer is going to be right outside, isn't he? And if *he* hears your gun going off—'

Liam bit his lip. Then he lowered his gun and said, 'Answer it.'

'What?'

'Answer it! Go on, for Christ's sake, answer it! But if you say one word—'

Katie went to the front door and opened it. There was no protection officer in the porch, only Detective Sergeant Ni Nuallán. She was wearing a navy-blue hooded raincoat, with her blonde fringe peeking out, and smiling.

'Kyna—'

Before she could say anything else, though, Kyna stepped into the hallway. '*Eugh*, what a *terrible* day! And the heating's on the blink in my flat! It's freezing! Oh, you have a fire lit, that's fantastic!'

Liam appeared in the living room doorway. His face was ghastly with strain.

'Who's this?' he croaked.

'Kyna Ni Nuallán. Surely you remember her.'

'My God,' said Kyna. 'Inspector Fennessy! I don't believe it!'

Liam stared at her. 'Oh,' he said, dully. 'Oh, it's you.'

'But what are *you* doing here?' asked Kyna, still talking cheerfully. 'I thought we'd seen the last of you! We *all* thought we'd seen the last of you!'

'Kyna—' said Katie, but she didn't have to say any more because Liam stepped back into the living room and raised his gun again.

'What's going on?' said Kyna. 'What's he pointing that gun at us for?'

'He came here to shoot me,' said Katie, trying to keep her voice steady. 'By order of Bryan Molloy.'

'What?' said Kyna, and then she turned to Liam and said, '*What*? You came here to *what*?'

'Shut up and put your hands up and shut the fuck up!' screamed Liam.

Kyna said, 'No, I'm having none of this! You put that gun down!'

'*Stay where you are*!' Liam's voice rose into a shriek.

'Kyna, *don't*!' Katie shouted at her, but Kyna threw herself at Liam and knocked him backwards. He stumbled over the coffee table and hit his head against the leg of the couch and Kyna fell on top of him. For a few moments they struggled together on the carpet, Kyna repeatedly lifting her arm to punch him.

Katie had already turned towards the nursery, where she kept her gun, when there was a very loud shot. She turned back to the living room doorway to see Liam rolling Kyna off him, onto her side. The white sweater she was wearing under her raincoat was stained with blood, which was already spreading fast. There was smoke in the room and the smell of burned propellant.

Liam was pulling himself up on to his feet and he was still holding his gun. Katie hurled herself towards the front door and opened it. She ran out on to the driveway and out through the gate on to the pavement into the drizzle.

'*Help me*!' she shouted, running towards the car where the two protection officers were still reading their newspapers.

Both of them immediately opened their doors and climbed out.

'He's armed! He has a gun!' Katie gasped as she reached them. 'He's just shot Kyna!'

Liam came running out of the gate and skidded to a stop like a character in a Charlie Chaplin film. He saw the two protection

462

officers and stayed where he was, although he didn't put up his hands.

'Get in the car, ma'am,' said one of the protection officers, opening the back door for her. 'Keep your head down.'

Katie got into the car and lay down sideways. She had a sudden twinge of agonizing pain in her stomach and she felt as if she might be bleeding, but all she could think of was Kyna lying on her living room floor with her bloodstained sweater.

For a long time she could hear nothing, only a passing car. Cautiously, she raised her head over the seat in front of her and saw the two protection officers standing about twenty metres away from Liam, both with their pistols drawn. It looked as if they were talking.

Then, quite deliberately, Liam raised his gun and pointed it into his right ear. Katie saw one of the protection officers bound towards him, but Liam fired before he was even halfway there. Liam's brains sprayed in a clutter into the beech hedge and he fell on to his side on the pavement.

Katie pulled herself out of the car at once and called out, 'Ambulance! Call for an ambulance!'

She ran past Liam's body without even glancing down at him, and into the house. Kyna was still lying on the carpet and Katie knelt down next to her.

Kyna's eyes were open, even though they looked unfocused, and she was still breathing. A thin runnel of blood was sliding out of the side of her mouth on to the carpet.

'Kyna, there's an ambulance coming,' said Katie. 'Please, stay with me, darling. You're going to be grand, I promise you. Please stay with me.'

'Cold,' whispered Kyna.

Katie wrestled off her jacket and covered Kyna with it. Then she leaned forward and stroked her hair and kissed her.

'Stay with me, darling. We're going to be so good together, you and me. Don't you dare think of dying on me. Don't you dare.'

'Cold,' said Kyna.

GRAHAM
MASTERTON

'One of our most exciting crime novelists.
If you have not read one, read them all now.' *DAILY MAIL*

BURIED

One

'Are you coming inside or not, you useless collop?' Declan demanded.

It was obvious, though, that Christy wasn't going to come any nearer. He stood on the front doorstep, his black and tan fur bedraggled by the rain, and Declan had never seen him look so apprehensive. His eyes were wide, and his nostrils were twitching, and every now and then he tilted his head sideways as if he were trying to peer inside the hallway and in through the living-room door, because he was sure that there was something frightening in there.

Colm called out, 'Declan, for feck's sake, will you stop discussing the weather with that mutt of yours and give me a hand with this fecking fireplace?'

'I'll tell you something, Christy, you're some jibber,' Declan told him. 'If you want to stay out there getting yourself soaked, that's your lookout. But if you die of pneumonia, don't come blaming me for it.'

He left Christy and went into the living room where Colm had knocked the brown-tiled fire surround loose from the wall and was now trying to lever it further away with a crowbar. The air in the tiny room was filled with dust and the floorboards were gritty underfoot so that the soles of his boots made a scrunching sound.

'Never known him act like that before,' said Declan, picking up a shovel and wedging it into the opposite side of the fireplace. 'It's almost like he's scared of something, do you know what I mean? Maybe there's a ghost in here, like.'

'That wouldn't fecking surprise me at all,' said Colm, violently wrenching the crowbar from side to side. 'The old feller who used to own this place, they discovered him dead down the bottom of the stairs, that's what that girl from Sherry Fitzgerald's told me. Tripped over his cat, so she reckoned. Broke his neck like a fecking stick of celery and they didn't find him for a month.'

Colm had reckoned that it would take them at least two weeks to renovate the whole house. It was a small two-bedroom property in Millstream Row, Blarney, in a terrace of eleven cottages that had been built sometime in the 1860s to house woollen workers from Mahony's mill.

Although the previous owners had lived in it since 1952, they had decorated it only once during the whole of their years there, with dingy brown floral wallpaper. In 1964 they had built a single-storey lean-to extension in the backyard to accommodate a bath and a twin-tub washing machine, but that had been their only concession to modernization.

Now that the widowed owner had died, the house had been sold to a young professional couple for 123,000 euros as their starter home.

Together, grunting like two prize hogs being prodded to market, Declan and Colm manhandled the fire surround out of the house and into the rain. Christy was still sitting there, soaking wet, and when he stepped back to allow them to shuffle out of the front door he shook himself furiously.

'You're a lunatic, do you know that?' said Declan, after he and Colm had heaved the fire surround, with a deafening crash, into the empty skip that was parked in the narrow road outside. 'Why don't you go in and get yourself dry?'

He bent down and took hold of Christy's collar, but when he tried to drag him into the house Christy stiffened his legs and growled. When Declan pulled harder he scrabbled his claws against the wet pavement and barked, refusing to step over the threshold.

'Sure look at him,' grinned Colm. 'I bet you're right about a ghost. How about it, Christy? Can you see a ghost in there, boy? Wooooooo!'

'Maybe there's just a smell he doesn't like, dead rat or something,' said Declan. 'Most people don't know it, but your Kerry beagle has an even more sensitive nose than a bloodhound.'

'Yeah, but come on, Dec. How much of him is Kerry beagle and how much is some stray mongrel that gave his mother the lad when her owner wasn't looking?'

'It's all very well you skittin', boy,' Declan retorted. 'This feller can smell if somebody's farted in Limerick, I swear to God. He can smell tripe boiling even before you've lit the gas.'

He yanked at Christy's collar one more time, but Christy snarled and bared his teeth, and Declan gave up. 'Okay, have it your way. You need a bath any road.'

Declan and Colm went back into the house. Now they needed to pull up all the floorboards in the living room because the new owners were going to replace them with hand-scraped Victorian oak.

Colm lit a Johnnie Blue and took three deep drags before pinching it out and tucking the butt behind his ear. Then he picked up his crowbar and used it to jemmy the skirting board away from the wall underneath the window. While he lifted the skirting board over his shoulder and toted it outside to the skip, Declan bent over and gripped the exposed end of the central floorboard, tugging at it again and again until he dislodged the nails out of the joists underneath. He tilted it up and dropped it to one side with a clatter.

Declan was used to finding builder's rubble underneath the floorboards of these old houses, as well as the skeletons of rats and mice. Once he had discovered a black tin box containing thirty-five pounds in Saorstát, the banknotes issued by the Irish Free State, a tarnished harmonica, and a Valentine's card for 'my own dearest Muirgheal'.

In this house, however, it looked as if several bundles of old clothing had been stuffed between the joists – a man's suit, a woman's maroon dress, a girl's yellow pinafore, and a baby's pink nightgown. They were all faded until they were almost colourless and covered thickly in fine grey dust, so it was anybody's guess how long they had been hidden there.

Declan pulled up another floorboard, and then another, the nails screeching in protest, and he was just about to start pulling up a third when he saw that a hand was protruding from the cuff of the man's green coat.

He stared at it for a long time, feeling as if his scalp was shrinking. The hand looked papery and dry, and it was almost completely flat, but he could tell that it was a real human hand all right. Some of the knuckle bones had broken through the desiccated skin and it still had all of its fingernails, even though they had turned amber with age.

He knelt down to examine it more closely, but he didn't have the nerve to touch it. Instead, he reached out and gently squeezed the sleeve from which it was protruding. There was no question about it: there were two stick-like arm bones inside it.

'Lord lantern of Jesus,' he whispered.

He was breathing hard through his nostrils now and his heart was thumping. He let go of the sleeve and cautiously patted the back of the coat, as if he were frisking it. Underneath the fabric he could feel the hard curved bones of a ribcage.

He sat back on his heels. Holy Mary, Mother of God, if there's a mummified feller inside of this coat, what's inside of the woman's dress? And the children's clothes, too?

Still kneeling, he shuffled himself sideways to the space between the next two joists where the woman's maroon dress was lying crumpled up, with buttons all down the back. He hesitated for a moment, because it didn't seem right to be touching a woman without her consent, even if she was long dead. Then he reached out and gently pressed against the bodice. Beneath the coarse dyed linen he could again feel ribs, although these ribs were looser, as if they had become detached from the spine.

These weren't bundles of old clothes at all, these were bodies.

Years and years ago somebody must have laid them face-down beneath the floor and then nailed the boards down over them. Declan still hadn't pulled up enough boards to be able to see their shoulders or their heads, but it looked to him as if a small family had been hidden there – father, mother, daughter and baby.

He stood up, wiping his hands on his black denim jacket. As he did so, Colm came back from outside, relighting his cigarette.

'Jesus, it's lashing,' he said, his head half hidden in smoke. Then he glanced down at the gap in the floorboards and frowned. 'What the feck's all them old clothes doing down there?'

'They're not just old clothes, boy, they're bodies,' said Declan. 'Man and a woman and their two wains, too, by the looks of it.'

'You're codding,' said Colm, but Declan pointed to the man's dried-out hand. Colm leaned forward and squinted at it short-sightedly, and then he said, 'Feck.'

'I'd say they was probably murdered,' said Declan.

Colm stepped over the gap and crouched down to see if he could make out what the bodies' heads looked like. 'You don't know that for certain,' he said. 'They could have died of the flu or something. People used to die like flies in them days, of all sorts. My old man's youngest sister died of the chickenpox when she was only three years old.'

He stood up straight again and nodded at the bodies. 'Maybe their relatives couldn't afford a funeral.'

'Oh go 'way. Even if you can't afford a funeral you don't bury your nearest and dearest face-downwards underneath the fecking floorboards.'

'I don't know. My Uncle Patrick was buried lying on his left side. That was the way he specified it in his will. Serious. He said that when my Auntie Saoirse was buried next to him he wanted to be looking at her.'

'What, he had X-ray vision did he?' asked Declan. 'He could see through coffins?'

'Don't be soft – he was dead, wasn't he?' said Colm. 'He was just being romantic, do you know what I mean, like?'

'Romantic? Stone-hatchet mad, more like. Anyway, give me a hand to take up the rest of these floorboards.'

Between them, Declan and Colm lifted up all of the floorboards in the living room and carried them outside to the skip. When they had finished they stood and looked in silence at the four bodies lying between the joists. It had stopped raining outside and a silvery sun had appeared behind the clouds, so that the living room was filled with colourless light like an over-exposed photograph.

The man was lying furthest away from the window, with his left arm by his side. His right arm was crooked up, with his forehead resting on it. His hair was thick with dust but it was still brown and curly. The woman had long black hair, very straight, fastened with a simple brown horn slide. The little girl had brown curly hair, too, tied with ribbons into bunches. The baby had a single dark tuft, like a leprechaun.

'Ah, the pity of it,' said Declan.

With a succession of hideous screeches, they prised up the last two floorboards. Underneath they discovered that the space between the joists was crammed with a tangle of thick grey hairs, which at first looked as if it could have been a coat or a shaggy blanket of some kind. Colm took his shovel and prodded at it, and then tried to pick it up. As he lifted it up, however, the blanket tore softly apart and one half of it dropped with a dull thump back into the floor space. Colm immediately dropped the other half, too, because now they could see that what they had uncovered was not a coat or a blanket but the dried-up bodies of two young Glen terriers.

'The family pets, I'll bet you,' said Declan. 'Whoever did this, Jesus, they didn't leave nothing alive, did they? Surprised there's no fecking goldfish down here.'

Because the adults' hair was so thick and so dusty it was not immediately obvious what had happened to them, but Declan and Colm could tell from the baby and the little girl how this family had died. They had all been shot once in the back of the head, including the puppies.

Declan crossed himself. 'You'd best ring the guards,' he told Colm.

Colm nodded and took his mobile phone out of his shirt pocket. Both of them had been deeply sobered by what they had discovered. They could have been sleeping, this dust-covered family, like characters in a fairy tale. Declan was surprised that he wasn't frightened or horrified by them, only saddened. He almost felt as if he had known them, despite the probability that they had been nailed down under the floorboards long before he was born. They didn't smell – not as far as he could tell, anyway – although Christy must have picked up the scent of human decay, even if it was decades old, and that was why he had refused to come inside. Either that, or he was psychic and Colm had been right about a ghost. Or ghosts, plural.

HOW TO GET YOUR FREE EBOOK

THE KATIE MAGUIRE THRILLERS

FREE EBOOK

TO CLAIM YOUR FREE EBOOK OF WHITE BONES

1. FIND THE CODE
This is the first word on page 114 of this book, preceded by HOZ-, for example HOZ-code

2. GO TO HEADOFZEUS.COM/FREEBOOK
Enter your code when prompted

3. FOLLOW THE INSTRUCTIONS
Enjoy your free eBook of WHITE BONES